Captive

Christina Phillips

Heat | New York

THE BERKLEY PUBLISHING GROUP
Published by the Penguin Group
Penguin Group (USA) Inc.
375 Hudson Street, New York, New York 10014, USA
Penguin Group (Canada), 90 Eglinton Avenue East, Suite 700, Toronto, Ontario M4P 2Y3, Canada
(a division of Pearson Penguin Canada Inc.)
Penguin Books Ltd., 80 Strand, London WC2R 0RL, England
Penguin Group Ireland, 25 St. Stephen's Green, Dublin 2, Ireland (a division of Penguin Books Ltd.)
Penguin Group (Australia), 250 Camberwell Road, Camberwell, Victoria 3124, Australia
(a division of Pearson Australia Group Pty. Ltd.)
Penguin Books India Pvt. Ltd., 11 Community Centre, Panchsheel Park, New Delhi—110 017, India
Penguin Group (NZ), 67 Apollo Drive, Rosedale, North Shore 0632, New Zealand
(a division of Pearson New Zealand Ltd.)
Penguin Books (South Africa) (Pty.) Ltd., 24 Sturdee Avenue, Rosebank, Johannesburg 2196,
South Africa

Penguin Books Ltd., Registered Offices: 80 Strand, London WC2R 0RL, England

This book is an original publication of The Berkley Publishing Group.

Copyright © 2011 by Christina Phillips.
Cover design by George Long.
Text design by Kristin del Rosario.

PRINTING HISTORY
Heat trade paperback edition / February 2011

Library of Congress Cataloging-in-Publication Data

Phillips, Christina, (date)
    Captive / Christina Phillips. — Heat trade paperback ed.
        p. cm.
    ISBN 978-0-425-23882-0
    1. Druids and Druidism—Fiction.   I. Title.
    PS3616.H45455C37 2011
    813'.6—dc22
                                                    2010036295

PRINTED IN THE UNITED STATES OF AMERICA

10 9 8 7 6 5 4 3 2 1

Captive

For Mark,
Victoria, Charlotte and Oliver.
Believe in your dreams.

Acknowledgments

Huge thanks once again to my awesome critique partners Sara Hantz and Amanda Ashby—aka, for some obscure reason, the Tiara Mafia—for cracking the whip and dangling chocolate at appropriate moments. Between you and my faithful Chap Stick, I made it through.

To my wonderful agent, Emmanuelle Morgen, who wanted to know Morwyn's story and encouraged me every step of the way—thank you! I'm thrilled you love Bren as much as I do.

Thank you to my amazing editor, Kate Seaver, for your advice and the brainstorming sessions, to Katherine Pelz for all your help, and to Elizabeth Tobin and the Berkley marketing team for all your support.

To the incredible Tony Mauro and the Berkley art department, thank you all so very much for creating such a fabulous cover!

To Nige Redwood, Cath Baughen and Peggy Phillips—thank you for always being there when I needed you.

And to Mark, Victoria, Charlotte and Oliver—thanks for all the late-night takeaways and lattes!

Preface

In AD 50, seven years after invading Britain, the Romans advance into Cymru, the western peninsula, to mine her rich mineral deposits of gold, copper and lead.

The local tribes do not take kindly to this invasion.

Led by their priestly class, the Druids, the people of Cymru rebel against the might of the Eagle.

The Roman Emperor, Claudius, perceives Druids as a dangerous menace to the expansion of the Empire.

Resistance will not be tolerated.

He orders their extermination.

The Druids flee to their sacred Isle of Mon to gather their strength to fight anew. But in the summer of AD 51, Morwyn, a Druid priestess, leaves the Isle to join the rebels in Cymru.

Bren, a Gaul auxiliary stationed in Cymru, has spent the last three years undercover in the Roman Legions. His loyalty to his Briton king is absolute. But his time is running out . . .

Chapter One

The forest was quiet. Too quiet. Her horse shifted in clear unease and Morwyn glanced at her three companions.

"What do you see?" Einion's voice was hushed.

Morwyn clamped her teeth together to prevent the harsh response from tumbling into the unnatural silence. What did she see? Did they think her a seer, a tool of their cursed goddess, the Morrigan?

She half expected an unearthly fire to consume her for her treacherous thoughts, but none did. She loosened her grip on the reins and took a deep breath.

Her companions believed in her powers. It was the reason they'd left the Isle of Mon and ventured with her back into the occupied territories of their beloved Cymru.

If she was successful in her quest to discover the heart of the rebellion, they would return to the Druid sanctuary and tell the others. She wasn't the only one who longed to fight for freedom rather than hide in sacred groves dedicated to cowardly gods. And then a great army of Druids would join the displaced Briton king Caratacus, who was causing such disruption to the despised Roman Legions.

"Caratacus is close." She knew that, and it had nothing to do with visions from the gods. She no longer had visions. No matter what her fellow Druids might think. Her knowledge was based on information gleaned from those who had arrived on Mon over the last few moons, and her resolve to join the insurgents had strengthened when Gawain left the Isle to stand by the Catuvellauni king, Caratacus.

A sharp pain sliced through her breast, raw and savage, jagged with guilt, as she recalled Gawain. The man who had loved her. The man she had tried so hard to love in return, but never had.

Because her heart had belonged to another.

Her grip tightened on the reins. She would avenge Gawain's death with the last breath in her lungs, the last drop of blood in her veins. He had loved her, and he deserved nothing less from her.

She would never succumb as a slave of Rome. She'd rather a glorious death in the midst of battle, securing the freedom of her people.

"How close?" Drustan, another young Druid and, like both Einion and Morcant, not yet fully trained, glanced around the edge of the glade as if expecting the Briton to miraculously appear before them.

They expected her to proclaim a sign. She was the most senior Druid here, and yet even she hadn't finished her training before the bloodied invasion had devastated their existence. But no older Druid from Mon had wanted to take the chance of returning to Cymru without solid, irrefutable proof of where, precisely, the Briton king commanded his rebels.

No light summer breeze rustled the leaves on the looming trees. The air hung heavy and still as if waiting for the wheel of life to turn, to irrevocably alter her course forever.

An eerie shiver inched along her spine and chills scuttled over her arms, raising the fine hairs. Instinctively she curled her fingers around the jewel-encrusted dagger secured at her waist. She no longer believed in her gods and no longer received their signs, and the only thing that was about to change was that Rome would discover her mistake in enslaving Cymru.

Wind rushed, barely a handbreadth from her face, and Einion lurched from his horse, an arrow embedded in his throat. For one agonizing moment Morwyn froze as she watched him slide to the tangled undergrowth, shock glazing his dying eyes, before her warrior training and self-preservation kicked hard in her gut.

She swung her horse around, rejecting her dagger in favor of her spear, as a handful of riders emerged from the concealing trees. *This wasn't the way Romans fought.* But she had no time to curse their tactics nor berate her lack of foresight as the forest erupted with Druid war cries, barbarian yells and the frenzied snorts and thundering of attacking horses.

Sweat and blood and the stench of fear from animal and man drenched the air. They were outnumbered. But not outmatched. Morwyn drove her spear upward at an angle, pierced through the shapeless mail shirt worn by the enemy, and scarlet pumped over his scale armor, staining man and beast and trampled forest floor.

Savage satisfaction pounded through her veins as he opened his mouth in a silent scream. They would teach these Romans to ambush them, to take them by surprise, to—

Her breath punched from her lungs as something slammed into her back, pushing her forward, pushing her dangerously close to impaling her breast on the blunt end of her spear. And then she was falling, with the loathsome weight on top of her, and she hit the ground with bone-splintering force.

"Fucking barbarian bitch," he hissed in Latin, his mouth by her ear as she tried not to suffocate on the churned and bloodied earth that pressed against her cheek and nose and mouth. "Teach you to respect your masters."

Muscles tensed as he ripped her gown from her neck, exposing

her back to the elements and the accompanying jeers of the remainder of the enemy. Where were Drustan and Morcant? Had they
perished? Was she the only one left?

Nausea rolled through her stomach, clogged her throat. She
was willing to die for her people, but she'd envisaged a great and
glorious battle, not an insignificant skirmish. Not degradation
and rape. She blocked out the obscenities being thrown her way
and stealthily reached for her dagger.

Brennus rode through the forest, taking unseen paths and hidden tracks so there was no possibility of the Legion's auxiliary
exploratores discovering an unwary passage to the stronghold of
the mighty Caratacus.

If the Legion discovered who Bren truly was, even crucifixion
would be considered too easy a death. But he had no intention of
letting the Roman bastards discover his true identity, not until it
was too late for them to do anything about it.

Not until their Roman blood drenched the earth and the conquered lands were free once again.

Within moments of leaving the hidden enclave he heard the
unmistakable sounds of battle ahead and pulled up short. He
couldn't be seen. By now, he should already be across the bor-
der on his way to the Roman headquarters at Camulodunon—
Camulodunum—in Britain, one hundred and sixty miles to the
east, to deliver a military dispatch. The dispatch he'd just smuggled
to his king.

Something drew him closer. Trees thinned, and he caught sight
of the very exploratores he served with. The battle—such as it had
been—was over. From the coarse comments it was clear a woman
had been taken captive and they weren't wasting any time before
enjoying their spoils.

His gut tightened with distaste. To preserve his deception he
had, in the past, fought in the line of duty to Rome, even slaughtered

compatriots. Sacrifice a few to ensure the freedom of many. War was a bitch and casualties a fact of life. Warriors knew the odds—defeat or victory.

Today, that small band of Celtic warriors had paid the ultimate price.

He jerked his horse around, prepared to head deeper into the forest. But fetid memories clawed through his soul and phantom screams of agony pierced his brain, shredded his heart. *Mercy begged for and denied.* Compassion trampled underfoot and the sour stench of spilled blood scorched his throat.

Futile rage seared his veins, momentarily blinded his vision as the foul recollections scalded his reason. Within a moment he regained control, regained his senses, and against every logical, tactical instinct he urged his mount toward the others.

The woman might be a warrior trained for battle, but he still couldn't stomach the thought of her being brutalized before butchered.

So engrossed in humiliating their victim, not one of the scouts turned at his approach. A cursory glance disproved his earlier supposition, and a fresh wave of disgust roiled through his blood.

These Celts were no warriors. They were traders.

Dead traders.

Bren dismounted, shoved the nearest man from his path.

"Dunmacos," the man said, using the hated name Bren had appropriated three torturous years ago. "Just in time for a turn with the Cambrian whore."

"After me," Trogus grunted, as he hunched over the partially naked woman. "Turn over, bitch, or I'll fuck your arse instead."

She wasn't crying in fear, or begging for mercy. She was so silent for a moment Bren thought her already dead. Until he saw her fingers curl around the handle of her dagger.

He thrust Trogus aside, dropped to his knees and gripped her wrist in a bone-crushing vise. Instantly her face lifted from the dirt, and infuriated, dark eyes flashed at him.

Something hard punched through his chest, as if he'd just ridden full pelt into a stone turret. Even covered in filth and blood the woman's strong Celtic beauty glowed through, condemning him for daring to touch her. For denying her the satisfaction of using her dagger.

"Get out the fucking way, Dunmacos." Trogus gave the woman's thigh a brutal kick, and she winced but still didn't make a sound. Her eyes never left Bren's. "You can go next, if I leave anything worth having."

He didn't loosen his grip on her wrist. She didn't loosen her hold on her dagger.

"No." He didn't bother looking up at Trogus. "I claim this one. And in return I won't advise the praefectus you attacked and murdered a group of traders." Only then did he glance up and catch the furious gleam in Trogus's lust-glazed eyes. "I never came across you."

Trogus hissed between clenched teeth, but there was nothing to discuss. Bren outranked him. Outranked all of the exploratores here. And that wasn't all. The praefectus of their auxiliary unit trusted him implicitly.

As much as any Roman would trust a foreigner.

"Take her, then." Trogus spat on the ground and looked as if he'd like to kick her again. Instead he flung Bren a smoldering glare as if something had just occurred to him. "What are you doing here?"

"Dispatches. I'll take the woman to warm my bed at nights."

"She'll butcher you in your sleep." The sneer Trogus arrowed his way suggested he'd very much like to witness such an occurrence. "We'll take the goods as compensation. Unless you have any objection, Dunmacos?" It was a covert threat. Any other time Bren would have risen to the challenge but right now another challenge glared at him from the ground.

Not that he'd let Trogus get away with such insolence entirely. "Take all but the woman's personal items. I don't want to have to purchase another gown for her."

As the scouting party rifled through the traders' packs, Bren leaned toward the woman and spoke in the local dialect.

"Drop your dagger."

Beneath his fingers he felt her grip tighten, although he knew the pressure he exerted around her wrist was close to shattering bones. But she made no other movement, as if realizing that, for the moment, her best chance of unmolested survival was by lying low and remaining still.

Within moments, the exploratores had claimed their spoils and were leading the riderless horses away, back to the garrison. With little effort he rolled the woman onto her back, holding her wrists above her head. It would be easy to break a bone, give her no choice but to abandon her dagger. How much more satisfying, though, should she decide to discard it of her own free will . . .

"Drop your weapon, and I give you my word you'll remain unharmed."

Her lips parted. Full, luscious. Inviting. Without warning, his cock pulsed, a sharp reminder of how long it had been since he'd taken a woman, how long it had been since he'd even enjoyed solitary relief.

"Roman coward." Her voice was breathless, her Latin accented but clearly educated. Enticing tendrils of luxuriant black hair escaped her braid and framed her dirt- and blood-smeared face. "Your word means nothing to me."

"I'm no Roman." He answered her in the same language and kneed her thighs apart, bracing his weight on forearms and knees, trying yet failing to smother his unwelcome arousal. Gods, he wanted her. The contemptible need pounded through his arteries, vibrated against his temples. "I'm from Gaul."

Her lips curled back, exposing white, unbroken teeth. "Then you're worse. A spineless mercenary for their gutless Emperor."

For a moment Morwyn thought she'd pushed him too far. His eyes, an extraordinary shade that reminded her of new leaves unfurling, glinted with danger and his fingers tightened around her tender wrists.

But she wanted to push him too far. Wanted him to lose control, just for an instant, so she could plunge her dagger into his heart and escape this ignoble fate.

Instead, his odious erection brushed against her and she tensed, waiting for the inevitable attack, waiting for a scalding surge of revulsion to flood her captured flesh. But he made no further move to mortify her, his gaze roaming over her face as if he were memorizing every tiny detail.

Liquid heat bloomed deep within, so shocking, so unwanted, the pleasure mutated into pain. A dark, dangerous pain that speared through her womb and trembled through her damp channel. She clenched her teeth, clenched her muscles, but still, tremors of despicable desire vibrated with tempting promise through her long-abandoned clit. How could her body be capable of such brutal a betrayal?

This was her sworn enemy. A man intent on rape and humiliation.

And she wanted him.

"Be wary." His breath singed her lips but it wasn't foul, wasn't repulsive. "Such careless words can be mistaken for treason."

Once again his rigid cock brushed against her womanhood and she wanted to spread her thighs, pull him into her. Feel the hardness of male strength thrust deep inside as he took her violently, mindlessly, so she could forget, for a few fleeting moments, everything but exquisite physical pleasure.

His green eyes scorched her. His muscular body pinned her helplessly against the undergrowth of the forest floor. How easy it would be to succumb to the lust blazing through her blood, the lust reflected in every hard, unyielding angle of her captor's face.

But she had sworn never to take another man again. Never again worship the goddess who had manipulated her loyalty, betrayed her trust and scorned her love.

The Morrigan could suffer her abstinence. Morwyn would honor her vow of celibacy, the vow she'd made the night her entire world had shattered.

"I would never betray my people. Your Emperor doesn't have my loyalty."

He closed the small distance between them, broad chest flattening her sensitive breasts and aching nipples, his chain mail serving only to accentuate every ragged breath he took.

"Who are you, Celt?" There was command in the question, despite the desire, and through the heavy thud of arousal a spark of warning pierced her lust-drenched brain.

She would succumb to no man. Would never bow before the invaders of her land. But if this Gallic bastard, a mercenary for Rome, didn't mean to kill her outright, there was chance for escape.

A chance that would vanish instantly should he discover her true origins.

The Emperor hated Druids, afraid of the spiritual power they held over their people. Since that night, a full turn of the wheel ago, when the great goddess, the Morrigan and Arawn, lord of the Otherworld—*when all their gods*—had deserted them and they had fled to the Isle of Mon, his hatred had grown. Fractured reports had reached them of the merciless slayings. That was why when she and the others left Mon they hid their Druidry, disguised themselves as traders.

Such subterfuge hadn't saved the lives of Einion, Drustan or Morcant. But it might possibly extend hers.

"You know what I am." It was hard to keep her voice level, hard to hide the erratic flutter of her treacherous heart. So cursed hard to keep her thighs utterly still when they ached to wrap around this barbarian's hips and crush him into her hungering embrace.

Silence, as if he contemplated her words. "Traders." He paused, raked his eyes over her face, and she held her breath, willing her pulses to slow, but if anything, they hammered more rapidly than before. Then he glanced above her head, at the exquisitely crafted gold bracelets that adorned her wrists. She hoped he had no idea of their true value. No trader could afford to wear such riches. *Why had she insisted on wearing them?* "From where?"

She flexed numb fingers around her dagger, then gripped it more securely when she felt his hold upon her wrist momentarily lighten. Her limbs were deadening but if he gave her the slenderest of opportunities, she wouldn't hesitate to slash open his throat.

"Why? So you can send your band of Gallic mercenaries to slaughter more innocents?"

"No. So I can verify your words."

If she directed him to a nearby village, would he truly spend time discovering if she spoke the truth or not? She doubted it. He was delivering dispatches for the military. He'd told the filthy dogs who'd ambushed her he intended to use her to warm his bed during the journey.

And he was alone. No, he wouldn't waste time verifying her word when her word was of no account, when all he saw when he looked at her was a woman he could use for sexual satisfaction.

"Two days' ride west. I'll tell you no more than that."

His eyes narrowed as if he didn't believe her. "And where were you heading?"

Her gaze didn't waver. "To the new Roman fortification. The civilian settlement is always hungry for our goods."

From somewhere deeper in the forest a wood warbler's shivering song shattered the taut silence. Before she realized his intention his forearm pinned hers securely to the ground, bringing the length of his body against hers. Heavy, masculine. How long had it been since she'd been crushed beneath a man, since she'd been held, touched, *wanted*?

The grip around her wrist increased beyond endurance but still she held on, despite the stabbing pains, despite the way her vision flickered. He'd have to kill her before she relinquished the only weapon she possessed.

With his free hand he prized her deadened fingers from the hilt of her dagger and she could do nothing to stop him. His body enslaved her from ankles to thighs, hips to breasts, and now that he gripped her dagger, he released her throbbing wrist.

She panted into his dark, foreign face. A face that wasn't Roman, but beneath his helmet he had the hated Roman military hair. Short, stark. Nothing to grip in lust or fury.

"What are you waiting for?" She flung the words at him in her own language. "Fuck me and have done with it."

And she wouldn't embrace him. Wouldn't wrap her legs around him. Wouldn't succumb to the despicable need spiraling through her blood; the need to have a man in her arms, a man inside her body.

Rape was abhorrent to her people. To their gods. And especially to the Morrigan. She'd endure his assault because there was nothing else she could do, but it would mean nothing. It wouldn't touch her. Wouldn't break her.

And by the sacred blood of all her ancestors, she'd find a way to slaughter him afterward.

For a long moment their eyes clashed. His cock seared her, hard and solid and demanding despite the barrier of his tunic and her ruined gown. Heat ignited; muscles clenched; her flesh trembled for satisfaction.

He raised himself onto his hands, his groin still melded with hers. Tempting her with the savage delight he could offer.

No. Sex with the enemy could never be a delight. She tried to fist her fingers but they were still numb, still uncoordinated. She glared at him instead, daring him to comment on the way her body softened beneath his in blatant invitation.

A smile twisted his lips. As if he knew exactly what was going through her mind. Curse her despised gods, but how she would relish plunging her dagger into him, castrating him before ending his miserable, misbegotten existence.

He rolled off her, kneeled beside her and contemplated her as if she were his own personal property. She refused to smooth down her crumpled gown or wipe her hair and the filth from her face. Let him look long and hard at how his compatriots had mistreated her.

"I've no intention of taking you in the open forest, Celt, where anyone could stumble upon us." He raked his glance over her and she gritted her teeth, refusing to acknowledge the foul ripple of disappointment that shuddered low in her gut at his words. "I'll wait until you beg me."

Chapter Two

Ignoring the bone-deep ache in her wrist, she pushed herself upright. Beg him? She would sooner tear out her tongue than ever admit such a treacherous desire.

"Since you have no use for me"—and the way his cock had burned her tender lips proved how much of a lie *that* was—"then let me go."

He stood up. She had to crane her neck to maintain eye contact but it was all she could do for the moment. She didn't yet trust her legs to support her. She'd rather remain seated on the ground than stumble to her knees before him.

"Let you go?" He appeared to contemplate her words. "Alone, in occupied territory? I don't think so."

Air hissed between her teeth. "I can take care of myself."

He didn't reply. He didn't have to. The disbelieving glance said enough.

She flexed her fingers, blocking the pain of her abused wrist. She was so close to the heart of Caratacus's resistance. She could feel the call of freedom vibrating in the air, enticing her, if only she could find the right path.

And this Gaul intended to drag her with him to—wherever his cursed duty took him.

Without warning he hunkered before her and she glowered into his face, ignoring without success the harsh line of his jaw and high, aristocratic cheekbones. In another lifetime, before the Romans had invaded Cymru, she might have looked twice at this warrior. Might have invited him into her bed, enjoyed his charms and battle-hardened body.

But now he was a creature of Rome. And no matter how her deprived clit ached for fulfillment she would never lower herself so irredeemably as to slake her need with one such as this.

Because she had no intention of ever slaking such need again.

Breath gusted. Of course she hadn't. She had made a vow; she would honor that vow. It was no hardship. She was simply disorientated by the attack and this Gaul's unexpected denial of his base urges.

His arrogance.

Yes, his arrogance. To assume she would ever beg for his touch. Crave his possession.

"I don't have time to return you to your village." His voice punched her back to the present. "Or escort you to the garrison. And I won't leave you here at the mercy of any passing legionary."

"It wasn't a legionary who murdered my fellow Dru—traders."

Heat flared through her at her error but he appeared unaware she had almost given herself away.

"No. But on your own and in your current state, you're fair game for any man wanting a rut."

She staggered to her feet, ropes of fire searing her thigh where the other filthy auxiliary had kicked her. "And you don't want to *rut*?"

He stood also and deliberately examined her dagger, as if it held great interest to him, before sheathing it beneath his chain mail. "I'm not that desperate."

Not that desperate? Pride snaked through her, stiffening her spine, momentarily obliterating the burning pain in her thigh, the throbbing ache of her ribs.

"Then you have no reason to encumber yourself with my presence. I'll return to my village and relay the bloody murder of my countrymen."

He shrugged as if he no longer wished to discuss the matter. "You're coming with me whatever your personal thoughts on the matter. You have no horse, you can barely stand and, in case it's escaped your notice, you no longer have any weapons."

No horse? She glanced wildly around, but the only mount nearby was the cursed Gaul's.

Her heart thudded against her bruised ribs, every beat an agony of pain and indecision. He was right. She could barely stand. There was no chance she could walk for any distance, certainly not back to Mon.

But she couldn't go with him. It was tantamount to accepting his authority, to accepting she'd been enslaved.

His calloused fingers grazed her naked shoulder, where her gown had been torn from her, and she jerked back. She didn't want his touch. Couldn't take his touch. Not when a part of her wanted *nothing more* than his cursed touch.

The Gaul's jaw tightened as if he took offence at her response. "Get changed." His voice was harsh. "Your things are there." He jerked his head to her pack, which had been ripped open and the contents strewn across the forest floor.

Next to the broken body of Drustan.

Stomach twisted, regret speared through her heart. It was her fault he was dead. Her fault they were all dead. If she hadn't been so determined to seek out Caratacus and avenge Gawain, they would all still be safe on the Isle of Mon.

Safe. Hiding from the enemy once again. The way they had hidden from the enemy before.

The way she'd vowed she would never hide again.

Swallowing the bitter taste of defeat, she hobbled toward the scattered items. She hoped they'd left her medicine bag intact. If she was going to escape, she needed to deaden the agony in her leg and the multitude of other aches and pains flaring across every particle of her body.

And slip something into the Gaul's waterskin. Something to incapacitate him so she could take his horse, equip herself with weapons and find the rebels.

With a smothered groan she sank to her knees and began to gather her things. She heard the Gaul mutter an oath and stamp toward her. "Here." He thrust one of her gowns into her arms. "You'll have to forgo tending your wounds until we stop for the night."

Instantly she became aware of her exposed back, and heat rushed through her at the way she'd allowed him unfettered access to gloat over her battered flesh. She slung him a resentful glare but he missed it because he was snatching up her possessions from the ground as if they were a personal affront to his existence.

For a fleeting moment an odd warmth wormed through her sore heart at his apparent thoughtfulness. And then reality returned.

He wanted to hurry her along. So he could start his journey.

She shuffled around so her back faced him and gingerly tugged the ruined gown from her shoulders before pulling the new one over her head. Curse the gods, her limbs were stiffening at an alarming rate. She'd have to poison him quickly, before they even left this forest, so she could find safety to rest before fatigue overwhelmed her.

As she tossed her bloodied gown against a nearby tree, he once again hunkered before her, her pack clasped loosely in one large hand.

"Are you ready? We have a long ride ahead before the first inn."

His words might have extended sympathy, if his voice wasn't so hard and his expression so impassive. But she didn't want his sympathy. Only a modicum of trust so she could overpower him with her herbal magic.

"Yes." She glanced toward her fallen Druids. "But aren't we going to prepare them for their journey onward?" She may have lost faith but her companions deserved their rightful ceremonies. And while she was preparing the sacred ritual, she'd find a way to contaminate the Gaul's supplies.

"No." His response was as uncompromising as it was unexpected. She stared at him in disbelief. He might be a Gaul, but he was still of Celtic blood, and unless prevented by battle they never left their dead kin to the mercy of carrion crows.

"No?" Had she misunderstood?

He gave an impatient sigh. "I've no time for this. Their gods will grant them safe passage for so honorable a death."

"Honorable?" She snatched her pack from him and rifled through it, searching for her supplies of herbs and roots. "They hid behind trees. That's not the Roman way."

"No, it's the Gaul way." He held an intricately embroidered bag in front of her nose. "I'll take care of this. I don't trust you not to attempt to poison me as soon as my back's turned."

She refused to give him the satisfaction of responding. And since her options were severely limited, she'd pretend subservience, wait until he lowered his guard and then revert to her original plan.

"Where are you going?" Her voice sounded haughty even to her own ears. But she'd never been a slave. Never deferred to any but senior Druids. If she wanted to fool this Gaul, she'd have to try harder than that.

But she still couldn't help glaring. He'd have to be a village simpleton not to guess her true feelings toward him.

He eyed her, as if weighing whether she deserved an answer or not.

"Camulodunon. It's three days' hard ride from here, and I can't afford a slower pace to accommodate you."

Camulodunon. Her seething resentment against her captor vaporized as prickles of shocked excitement skittered through her blood.

Reports had reached them on Mon that their beloved princess, Morwyn's dearest friend, had escaped the Emperor's wrath and migrated to the prosperous Roman town.

She'd never thought to see Carys again. Had accepted their lives had splintered and their paths were no longer destined to cross.

Anticipation bubbled deep in the pit of her stomach. This could well be her only chance of traveling to Camulodunon. Once there, surely she could hunt down her friend, discover how she was. Perhaps even persuade her to return to Cymru and fight beside the Briton king?

Half-formed plans of escaping the Gaul fragmented. She'd use him to give her safe passage to Camulodunon. Once there, she could lose him, find Carys and heal her own injuries. She might even uncover information useful to the rebellion.

If she still believed in such things, it was almost as if the gods were conspiring to bring them together again. But she didn't believe in her gods. When her people had needed their protection the most, they deserted them. And in their vindictiveness they turned on the very ones they were meant to defend, leaving them vulnerable to the encroaching Roman Legions who now swarmed across her beloved land.

An odd sensation of loss whispered through her soul, sending chills across her arms and an accompanying ache deep in her breast. She needed to speak to someone who understood her lack of faith. And who better than Carys, who'd turned her back on the Morrigan before Morwyn even conceived of the goddess's fallibility?

"Whatever you're planning," the Gaul said, "you can forget it. Can you stand?"

She ignored his outstretched hand and pushed herself upright. Flames ate through her thigh, clawed into her hip. She dug her teeth into her lower lip and hunched her shoulders in an effort to contain the hiss of pain that threatened to escape. Nothing was broken. Her muscles were only badly bruised. In a day or so her leg would once again support her full weight.

She'd be fully mobile by the time they reached the town. She'd make sure of it.

And then something occurred to her that twisted all her plans inside out. "Do you intend to take me all the way to Camulodu-non?" Or murder her on the way, after she'd served her purpose?

"Yes." His response was uncompromising, as if he expected her to argue the fact. He took her pack from her and secured it to his horse. "And if you don't cause me too much grief, I'll bring you back again. Allow you to find your people."

"Noble of you." The words were out before she could prevent them and she ignored the dark look he slung her way. She grit-ted her teeth as she limped toward his mount. She didn't want to antagonize him now, not when he was taking her where she wanted to go. But if he insisted on displaying such arrogance, who could blame her for responding?

"On the other hand I may decide to keep you indefinitely." His smile was anything but friendly. "What's your name?"

She sucked in a deep breath. She needed him so she had a chance of finding Carys. No matter what he said to her, all she had to remember was as soon as they reached Camulodunon she was free. If telling him her name lulled him into a false sense of believing she was willing to obey his every command, it was a very small thing to offer.

"Morwyn."

He maneuvered the horse so it stood next to a fallen log, giving her easier access. At least it would have been easier, had she been able to risk putting all her weight on her injured leg. She hovered for a moment, unwilling to ask for his help and yet knowing she had to.

"You can call me—"

"Yes, I know. Dunmacos." She spat the name at him. Curse the gods, could she not learn to hold her tongue? Before he had the chance to respond, and judging by his icy glare he certainly intended to respond, she temporarily smothered her wounded pride. "I fear I require assistance."

Without a word he mounted his horse and then hauled her onto the padded leather seat as if she weighed nothing. She suppressed the flicker of awe at his strength, because it was nothing to admire.

It meant he was in prime condition. Less likely to give up searching for her when she escaped, if such escape angered him sufficiently.

His hard, muscled arms snaked around her, resting against the tops of her thighs, and she stiffened as arrows of primal pleasure seared her flesh. She tried to keep her gaze straight ahead but couldn't help glancing with depraved fascination at the deep scars on his forearms and battle-worn fingers as they loosely held the leather reins.

"Get comfortable." His chain mail grazed her back and she jerked forward, straightening her spine even farther in an attempt to keep some distance between them. It was bad enough his slightest touch caused forbidden lust to rage through her blood. Hard enough to accept she found every part of his body irritatingly intriguing. She certainly didn't want to risk leaning against his chest. Her body would likely puddle with frustrated longing.

She was under no illusion that once they stopped for the night, once she was no longer covered in filth and blood, he'd take her. What galled her was that the knowledge didn't fill her with disgust or terror or even utter disinterest.

But what did it matter how she felt? Until they reached Camulodunon, she was his captive. She could fight the inevitable or she could use it to her advantage. Pretend to succumb, to enjoy his touch. Allay his suspicions that she wanted only to run her spear through his foul heart.

She'd taken an oath to never enjoy another lover. Partly because she'd been so devastated over the discovery that Aeron, the only man she'd ever loved, was a traitor to their people and partly out of a sense of obscure respect for Gawain's memory.

But mostly she'd taken the vow as vengeance against the Morrigan. The goddess who demanded her children should never deny the exquisite gift of sexual pleasures she had bestowed upon them.

As the Gaul urged the horse forward, blood heated her face, spread across her breast, pooled between her thighs. She could delude herself as much as she liked but the truth was plain. She wanted the Gaul. There was no doubt he would claim her that night.

He was an enemy of her people. To enjoy his touch was paramount to treason. The Morrigan would rage at the indignity. Curse
at the corruption of her decree.

Her temples pounded and she gripped the wooden-framed saddle to keep her balance as the perfect solution unfolded in her mind
like dark, loathsome petals. She could enjoy the Gaul and still keep
her vow. Because to willingly embrace the oppressor of Cymru
would infuriate Aeron's evil soul, not touch Gawain's uneasy rest
and most of all incense the Morrigan beyond endurance.

Chapter Three

━━◆◆◆◆━━

Trogus was still battling a black rage and an unrelenting erection as he and the other four exploratores entered the garrison, leading the traders' horses. He wasn't due any leave for days, so visiting a local whore was out. And unless he managed to drag a passing slave girl into a dark corner and slake his lust, all he had to look forward to was self-gratification.

Again.

Fucking Dunmacos. Shoving his nose where it wasn't wanted. Trogus couldn't even report him, since that would result in the bastard informing the praefectus that they'd attacked a group of traders.

Fucking stupid law. Who gave a shit if a few more Cambrians perished? As far as he was concerned they were all fair game. Being posted to this barbaric province after the exotic splendors of the East was intolerable. Why shouldn't they avail themselves of a few luxuries when opportunity arose?

The horses they'd have to give up to the Legion, but the enameled bridles, jewel-encrusted daggers and other various goods would fetch a good price on the black market.

But he'd coveted the dark-haired woman. The bitch who'd murdered his fellow tribesman. If Dunmacos didn't kill or sell her before returning, then by the gods Trogus would find a way to have her.

And make her pay.

So intent on the many and varied ways he intended to make the Cambrian whore pay for depriving him of both quenching his lust and the company of a man he'd considered a friend, he scarcely acknowledged the greeting of an approaching auxiliary.

Until the other man stopped in front of him and gripped hold of the metal bridle, blocking his path.

"Trogus. You serve with Dunmacos, don't you?"

Trogus shifted on the saddle, trying to ease the frustration pounding through his cock. "What of it?"

The auxiliary jerked his head toward his silent companion. "Gervas is blood kin. He arrived with the new contingent from Carthage this morn."

Trogus hid his disgust. Dunmacos was bad enough, but another of his kin in the same garrison was pushing sanity.

"Dunmacos is on dispatches." He wondered if that was common knowledge. "I believe."

Gervas stepped forward. Despite the advantage of still being mounted, a chill slithered along Trogus's spine. Bastard looked even meaner than Dunmacos.

"It'll be good to see my cousin again." Gervas's pale blue eyes bored into Trogus's and he resisted the urge to look away, despite the understated aura of menace that radiated from the other man. "I weary of following his progress through reputation alone."

Trogus grunted in grudging assent. Dunmacos's reputation was certainly admirable and the reason why Trogus took his shit. He had no desire to be facing the wrong end of the other Gaul's sword.

"If my sources are true and he's on dispatches, you'll see him again before the week ends."

Gervas's fingers idly stroked the handle of his sword. "I look forward to it."

Chapter Four

Although he wasn't holding shield or sword, through sheer habit Bren used leg control to guide his horse along the wide Roman highway. It had nothing to do with being unwilling to move his hands from Morwyn's firm thighs.

He glanced down at her head. Her hair was tousled, matted with dried earth and crushed grasses, and he resisted the impulse to unbraid her plait and use his fingers to unsnarl her tangles.

Gods. Briefly he closed his eyes. What had he been thinking to drag her with him? But what else could he have done—left her there, alone and defenseless?

If Trogus had returned, her life would be forfeit. And even if she'd escaped the other auxiliary's wrath, the forests and mountains were swarming with legionaries far from home who wouldn't think twice about using a lone Cambrian woman for their own barbaric pleasure.

Wasn't that what he intended?

He'd done many unpalatable things in his life. Taking a woman by force, even if that woman happened to be an enemy, wasn't one of them.

And Morwyn wasn't his enemy, no matter what she thought. Although he doubted she'd put up much resistance if he demanded her compliance. Not after the way her lush body had molded against his as he'd pinned her to the forest floor.

He let out a measured breath, forced the memory aside. Now wasn't the time to start with the erotic fantasies. He was behind schedule, his progress inevitably hampered by his unexpected traveling companion, and needed to make up the miles before they could rest this night.

Much as it galled him to admit, the graveled highway certainly improved the speed of travel. Unfortunately it also made troop movement easier from one side of Britain to the other.

But the rebels had no intention of fighting the Romans in the open countryside. Their strength lay in their knowledge of the land, the ability to melt into the forests and mountains. They'd weary the Legions with incessant attacks, demoralize their ranks, insidiously spread the rot from within.

Gaul, the homeland of his father's ancestors, had finally succumbed to Roman dominance during his great-grandfather's lifetime.

Eight years ago the first Legion contaminated Briton soil, the birthplace of his mother's lineage. But it had been another three years before he'd taken heed of her kin's call for rebellion.

Two years later he'd buried his old life. But when they triumphed over their enemies, as they would, what then? He'd no longer be Dunmacos. Would no longer need to pretend an allegiance that turned his gut with disgust.

He'd be free to return to his previous existence. Except there was nothing left for him to return to.

At the first post house he pulled over to change horses.

"Need any help?" He wondered if the woman was exaggerating the extent of her injuries, in an attempt to lower his guard. It wouldn't work.

She pressed her lips together and swung her leg over. "No, thank you." She took her time reaching the ground and then swayed as if momentarily disorientated. "Are we stopping to eat?"

He unhitched the saddle packs as a young boy ran from the stables to assist.

"No." When was the last time she'd eaten? He turned to the boy. "We'll take bread and dates with us." He had military rations but why use those when fresh food was available?

Morwyn heaved a sigh and he glanced at her. She was looking at the timber-built post house with its flint courtyard as if she'd never seen anything like it before. She probably hadn't. It had been constructed for use by the Emperor's Imperial Post, and the only reason they could travel this way was because he'd been granted a special permit from the garrison's commander.

"Do you make this journey often?" She limped toward him and he glared at the way her eye had swollen shut since they'd left the forest. It looked as if she'd been punched in the face.

"Rarely." But he knew Camulodunon well. In his youth he'd spent a great deal of time in the ancient Briton town, before the Romans had invaded.

It was different now. No longer the place that resided in his memories. But beneath the gaudy Roman veneer it was still the birthplace of his maternal blood kin.

He jerked his head toward the building in silent command, and with a dark, sideways glance she obeyed.

"The Romans must think highly of you if they trust you with their secrets." The way she said it left no doubt that she wasn't offering him a compliment.

"They do." Not enough to ordinarily trust him with such a mission. These top-level dispatches were usually entrusted only to Roman officers of the cavalry, not foreign auxiliaries, no matter how impressive their equine skills.

It had not been without risk of discovery, but his persistent contamination of the food chain had finally borne fruit, and dozens of legionaries were convinced Charon waited in the shadows to

ferry them across their cursed Styx. Added to the usual numbers
of injured and sick, the Legion was severely undermanned. And so
he, because of Dunmacos's reputation from the past and his own
actions in the present, had been given the honor.

He swiftly dealt with the formalities of changing horses and
didn't miss the furtive glances the post house master shot Morwyn's way. It was obvious he thought Bren responsible for the
woman's battered state.

Another outrage to add to Dunmacos's foul reputation. Gods,
he loathed the man, even though the man had been dead these last
three years. The identity he'd assumed clung to him like a cloud of
putrid flies. Sometimes he doubted he'd ever be able to scrub the
residue from his soul.

When the fresh horse was ready he once again mounted first and
hauled Morwyn up in front, her fingers strong as they gripped his
arm, her luscious lips compressed in uncompromising disapproval.

And once again she held herself rigid and proud, as if his slightest touch repelled her.

He dumped the bundle of bread and dates between her thighs
and she stiffened further, as if he'd attempted to grope her. Irritation, edged with raw lust, knifed low in his gut. He'd told her he
wouldn't touch her unless she wanted him to. But then, why should
she believe him, when she thought him a traitor to his own people?

His irritation magnified, steamed through his blood, melded
with the molten lust sizzling through his veins. If they'd met under
different circumstances, would she still repulse his proximity? Still
shoot him such disdainful glances? Or would she embrace the heat
that flared between them and welcome him into her arms?

"Eat." It was a harsh command. "There'll be nothing else until
we stop for the night."

Morwyn gripped the saddle with both hands and gritted her teeth.
How much longer did this barbarian intend them to travel? The
sun was sinking on the horizon and she was in sore need to relieve

herself. But she'd rather bite off her tongue than confess to such weakness.

Twice they'd changed horses since leaving the forest. He'd scarcely uttered two words to her. Not that she wanted to converse with him. But curse the gods, she would do almost anything to abandon riding and rest her head for the night.

Except before she could rest, she would have to submit to his bestial cravings. Anticipation shivered through her womb, tightened the muscles in her thighs, dampened her sensitive core. Her fingers dug more securely into the timber-framed saddle and she glared at the handful of circular wattle-and-daub huts in a village some distance from the newly constructed Roman road.

She would enjoy multiple orgasms this night with the enemy of her people. And each one would be a spear through the heart of the Morrigan. Each one would mock the twisted soul of Aeron.

Gawain would never know.

Heat, heavy and languorous, bathed her tight channel, licked her sensitive clit. She tensed the muscles in her legs, fought the overpowering urge to squirm, to relieve at least one pressure, because soon she wouldn't have to ignore her body's demands anymore. Soon, this Gaul bastard would take her and she could slake her pent-up lust without guilt or shame.

The Briton village receded and up ahead she saw Roman-built dwellings, and relief washed through her as she felt the horse slow. Her spine was fit to splinter. How often during this interminable journey had she battled against the desire to relax her muscles and sink back against the Gaul's unyielding chest?

As he pulled up outside the largest building she slashed her treacherous thoughts. She would have him. But she would never show him the slightest weakness. An enemy used vulnerability for his own gain.

Limbs stiff to the point of inflexibility, she allowed him to help her dismount. His hands were surprisingly gentle, as if he guessed her fatigue. Instantly she straightened, ignoring the way her bones burned in protest, and shot him a sharp glance.

For a moment she imagined she saw an oddly brooding expression in his green eyes, as if he regretted making her ride so hard without first tending her injuries. But then he turned away, barked orders at a terrified-looking boy, and marched into the building.

After a brief hesitation she followed him. There wasn't anyplace else she could go. But still that odd look haunted her, burying inside her brain as if trying to show her something of infinite importance.

Whispers drifted through her mind but they made no sense. Impatiently she knocked them aside, dismissed them.

Yet still they lingered. Insistent and intruding. An intriguing, if impossible, supposition.

She was the Gaul's vulnerability.

The inside of this Roman dwelling was, like the previous two they'd stopped at, constructed from timber and stone, and the walls were straight like their roads, not curved like the Briton roundhouses. But it was larger, different, and she was reminded of the taverns and brothels that had sprung up around the Roman fortifications in her beloved Cymru.

The Gaul—she couldn't bring herself to use his name, even inside her own mind, as if that would somehow diminish the extent of his enmity—was talking to the innkeeper. Morwyn walked as regally as she could manage across the stone floor toward them. She was no slave to remain in the background. No meek Roman matron who hovered behind her master. Only when she reached the Gaul's side did she remember her plan to show subservience in order to make him lower his guard around her.

Too late now. Not that he appeared to notice her. He was too busy issuing commands of the innkeeper, who, after one swift glance at her, riveted his attention on the Gaul.

"And make sure the water's hot," he said in Latin, by way of dismissal, and the innkeeper all but bowed in his anxiety to assure him the water would most certainly be hot.

Morwyn clutched her gown and fisted her fingers in the soft fabric. She couldn't think of water. Anything but water. And she could no longer deny her need. She'd have to ask.

"This way." The Gaul barely glanced at her. "The inn has private latrines."

She hobbled after him, no longer able to keep up her haughty pretense, but since he wasn't looking at her that didn't matter. They bypassed the tavern where drunken men groped half-clad, dull-eyed girls, and went toward the back of the building where he led her into a side room.

She pulled up short and stared at the long bench, with its six openings cut into the timber seat. Affront bubbled deep in her gut, which served only to aggravate her pressing need further.

"I don't use Roman *conveniences*." She emphasized the word so he would be in no doubt as to her opinion of such foreign intrusions.

He shrugged and finally looked at her. His face was all hard lines and uncompromising angles and again his eyes fascinated her, in a way nothing about him should fascinate her.

"Suit yourself." He planted himself down. "It's here or nowhere. You're not going outside."

She glared at him, then flung a withering look at the nearest opening. It looked . . . disgusting.

"I refuse to sit on something countless others have placed their naked arses upon." She curled her toes, couldn't prevent swaying. "It's unclean."

"Then squat."

Bastard. She hiked up her gown and angled herself over the loathsome hole.

"I suppose you prefer this barbaric method, do you?" She tossed him a resentful glance and struggled to keep her balance with her protesting muscles. *Ah*. The relief shimmered through like countless minuscule orgasms. *Bliss*.

"In truth? Yes. I find it preferable to digging my own hole."

Curse the gods, was he laughing at her? Or was she imagining that annoying quirk to his lips? As if he found her predicament amusing?

"I, on the other hand," she said with more hauteur than her current position warranted, "prefer the sanctified rituals of my ancestors."

She almost lost her precarious balance when his lips jerked into a definite grin. It vanished within an instant, as if it had crept upon him unawares, but gods. What a difference it made to his harsh features. For one oddly lingering moment she wished she could extend that lightening of his countenance; wipe the ingrained lines from his brow and the grim set to his mouth.

Before she had the chance to digest such treacherous thoughts, a man stumbled into the room, obviously a Briton by his hair and clothing. His lecherous leer floundered when she turned toward him, and then the Gaul was on his feet, in front of her, shielding her from the other's eyesight.

Unsure what to make of that, she shot a scandalized glance at the sponge on a stick, which was clearly designed as some kind of cleaning device, and shuddered in horror.

"I'm finished." She stepped forward and he instantly moved out of her way as if physical contact with her was the last thing he wanted. Probably because she was still covered in the residue of her earlier battle. Well, if he allowed her outside, she could find a stream, couldn't she, and cleanse herself? Because did he really imagine she *enjoyed* being covered in dried blood and gore from her enemies?

The Briton muttered something under his breath, the only words she caught being *whore* and *fucking Gauls*.

"You," the Gaul said in a strangely quiet voice, "shut your fucking mouth." And then he smashed his fist into the Briton's face, sending him sprawling across the latrines.

Chapter Five

It was the cold ferocity of the Gaul that stunned Morwyn into silence. She was used to violence, men fought over the most trivial of slights. It wasn't his reaction to the slur aimed his way that shocked her.

If he'd lost his temper, continued with his attack on the bleeding Briton, she could have understood his initial, bone-crunching punch. But he simply turned toward her, placed his hand between her shoulder blades and propelled her from the room as if nothing had happened.

She let out a shaky breath. His fingers scorched her flesh through her gown, even though his touch was so light as to be nonexistent.

The hand he'd used on the Briton just moments ago.

"Do you attack every man who makes a passing insult on your heritage?" If so, he'd spend most of his time fighting. Maybe he enjoyed it, even if it didn't show on his face or in his eyes.

"No." His fingers slid along her spine, causing heated shivers to plague her flesh, before he finally severed contact. "That wasn't the reason I hit him."

Gods, what did he mean by that? That he attacked without provocation, without reason? Would he have floored the Briton even if the man had been a mute?

The knowledge should concern her. Such unprovoked flashes of violence could erupt at any moment, without any forewarning. If he broke a stranger's nose without blinking, he could just as easily snap her neck without a second thought.

Yet, bizarrely, she wasn't afraid of him. And it made no sense because he was her enemy, she was his captive, and an unfounded certainty that he wouldn't use his fists on her couldn't be trusted.

Despite his outward facade of calm, he was unstable. If she wanted to remain alive, she'd do well to remember that.

And yet she'd done nothing but insult him since the moment he'd flung the other Gaul bastard from her. Not once had he even raised his voice, let alone his hand. Not once had she felt her life was threatened or safety endangered.

For a moment her convictions wavered and his words once again hummed in her mind. *That wasn't the reason I hit him.* But why else would he have attacked? The Briton had said nothing else of import. Done nothing else, save give her a lustful glance.

Possibilities shimmered, outrageous half-formed thoughts, and then the coldly obvious answer slammed through her brain, freezing all other fleeting suppositions.

He'd lied to her. Why hadn't she instantly reached that conclusion? It was obvious. The Briton had insulted him and the Gaul had retaliated and the only thing she couldn't understand was why he hadn't simply admitted it.

An older woman came up to them, shot her a glance she couldn't fathom. Why should a stranger look at her with sympathy? She straightened her already rigid spine and smothered the scowl that threatened to surface. It was easy to pretend she didn't mind being the Gaul's captive during the endless ride as she devised ways of ensnaring his trust. In reality she discovered it clawed her guts to think anyone should imagine she truly inhabited such lowly status.

"This way," the woman said in accented Latin, and led them

in the opposite direction to the latrines, along a stone-floored passage. She paused and opened a plain timber door. "The water will be ready shortly."

Bren dismissed her with a curt nod and waited until Morwyn entered the room. She glanced around, a disapproving frown on her face, as if she didn't think much of the plain Roman bed that consisted of a wool-stuffed mattress laid on a support built up from the floor. He'd deliberately ridden past the *mansio* situated in the last town, the inn and administration station that provided for official travelers. With his permit he was entitled to rest there but preferred the Romanized inns run by Britons.

Usually.

Although he doubted Morwyn would have been impressed by the more luxurious surroundings of accommodation constructed by the Emperor's command.

He kicked the door shut and opened his pack that had been left on the bed. Her embroidered bag lay on top of his spare clothing. He'd briefly inspected its contents back in the forest and been intrigued by the vast array of ingredients, many of which he didn't recognize. For a trader, she appeared to possess an impressive knowledge of the healing arts.

She leaned against the end of the bed, her arms folded. Although she'd not uttered one word of complaint throughout their long journey, he knew she was exhausted by the tautness of her body, the shadows beneath her eyes. A flicker of guilt tugged deep in his chest at the way he'd not allowed her to clean up earlier. He smothered it. Now that they had stopped for the night she could bathe, tend her injuries and rest.

For a moment visions of them sharing the bed invaded his mind. Tangled sheets, tangled limbs. He continued to hold her accusing gaze, not allowing his thoughts to heat his expression because if she wanted to act on the pull between them, she could come to him.

But he knew her pride was such she would never admit to such an attraction. Tonight was going to kill him.

He dropped her bag on the bed, out of her reach. Frustrated desire may kill him, but he had no intention of allowing this woman free reign to achieve the same end.

She let out an impatient breath, as if she'd been waiting for him to make some remark and had finally given up. "I need to wash."

He grunted in assent. Her deepening frown told him she didn't appreciate his response.

"Is there a nearby river?" Her tone was haughty. As if she was used to giving orders, to having her needs accommodated. A trader? In truth?

"Yes." Of course there was a river nearby. Romans never built anything if they could help it without close proximity to running water, to service their admittedly impressive sanitation and heating requirements.

She bared her teeth in a poor approximation of a smile. "Then will you allow me to visit this river to tend to my needs?" Clearly the request caused her great pain.

Only then did he realize he'd been staring at her, fascinated by the way her dark eyes glittered in the glow from the pottery lamps, at the way her black hair tangled about her face.

His gut tightened at the livid bruises that mottled the left side of her face, marring her otherwise clear, fresh complexion. At least, what he could make out of it beneath the grime and dried blood.

Fucking Trogus. Bren would find a way to dispose of that piece of shit before the time came for him to leave the Roman garrison and join his disposed king. The man had irritated him from the moment he'd arrived from the East, with his complaints about the remoteness of the province, the unreliable weather and the barbarous inhabitants.

She was still waiting for his answer. With more difficulty than was acceptable he tore his gaze from her. "No."

"No?" Her voice was sharp. She'd abandoned all pretense of humility and he preferred that. It was honest. She'd drive her dagger through his heart if he gave her the slightest chance and he'd be wise not to forget that.

Morwyn was no fragile girl who needed his undivided protection. She was a strong Celtic woman. But he couldn't dislodge the uncomfortable certainty she still needed his protection.

"*No?*" she said again, limping around the end of the bed and coming to stand directly by his side. He gritted his teeth and refused to give her the satisfaction of looking at her. Although it took a vast amount of willpower to continue checking the contents of his pack and not give in to the urge to glance at her again. To touch her again.

"Do you intend for me to stay in this disgusting state all night?" She all but spat the words at him. "Does the filth of battle heat your blood? Does my degradation inflame you?"

Finally he abandoned his pack. Not that he could recall what he'd been searching for anyway.

"Your degradation repels me." Let her make what she wished of that statement. When she stiffened in clear affront and heat blushed her cheeks, he was under no illusion exactly how she'd taken his words.

It didn't matter. It made no difference that she so misjudged him. It wouldn't change his mind about taking her with him.

There was a hard thump on the door before it slammed open to admit two boys hauling a large wooden tub. Morwyn shot them a withering look and he thought she was about to reprimand them for their unbidden entrance. But instead she pressed her lips together and surreptitiously leaned against the bed once again, as if she were perilously close to collapsing.

"Over here." He indicated where he wished them to leave the tub. Next to the bed. After a wary glance at Morwyn they scuttled out, although whether they were intimidated by her bruised and bloodied face or the scathing glare she arrowed their way, he couldn't be sure.

"This," she said, eyeing the tub as if it were a manifestation of the Emperor himself, "had better not be what I think it is."

Since the tub could have only one purpose, he failed to see the point in responding. His silence appeared to further irritate

Morwyn as she folded her arms and sat on the edge of the bed, her dark eyes spitting venom at him.

It appeared there was no pleasing her. He folded his own arms, straightened to his full not-inconsiderable height and glared back.

The boys returned with large timber buckets and tipped steaming water into the tub. Morwyn didn't deign to glance at them throughout their many repetitions and he didn't break eye contact with her. Finally, when his peripheral vision showed him the tub was two-thirds full, the boys left once again but this time pulled the door shut behind them.

"If you truly believe I'm going to wash your filthy body, Gaul, you've lost your senses."

Perceptions shifted as her words hit him. Gods. She thought he wanted her to scrub his body? His cock hardened, hot and heavy with denied lust and endless nights of solitary frustration. Despite his best intentions to ignore the demands of his body, he shifted his weight in an attempt to ease the pressure between his thighs. But it didn't work because erotic visions of her hands sluicing water over his chest, massaging his knotted shoulders and encircling his engorged erection drenched his heated mind.

Such a pleasurable activity hadn't occurred to him. But now that she'd thrown the image in his face he could barely think of anything else.

He needed a bath. But her need was greater. With reluctance he abandoned the fantasy, a fantasy that would never materialize because Morwyn would never willingly give him such self-indulgent delight.

And if she didn't give it willingly, where was the delight?

But he had no intention of allowing her to think she could rule him with her acidic tongue.

"If cleansing me had been my intention this night, then that's what you would do, Morwyn."

Her breasts heaved in outrage beneath the square cut of her gown, momentarily distracting him. Renewed waves of desire speared low in his gut, splintered through his pounding arteries.

Did he really think he could share a bed with this woman and not be tempted to ignore her disdain, overcome her protests?

Beneath her haughty manner and icy glares passion simmered. He'd felt it in the forest, felt it every time they brushed against each other. If she didn't open her arms to him tonight, could he overcome his pride and open his?

"Would I?" It was a blatant challenge to his authority. He didn't bother replying to her. Instead, with great deliberation, he removed his mail shirt and placed it on top of the timber chest along the wall next to the bed.

"Yes." He waited while she ground her teeth, and when it appeared that was all she had to say about the matter, he returned to her side and struggled against the overpowering need to plunge his fingers through her hair, to force her to look at him. "The bath is for you."

Her head jerked up without any physical assistance from him. Her eyes, even her injured one, were wide with shock, lips slightly apart. Even her aggressive posture sagged, arms falling to her lap.

Again he waited, this time until she recovered sufficiently to regain the use of her tongue.

"I don't . . ." She floundered for a moment. "I don't sit in tubs of stagnant water."

"The water's fresh." He picked up her bag and opened it, but still couldn't work out what half the contents were. "Do you need cleansing oil? Or do you have something in here you use?"

She pushed herself to her feet and glowered into the tub. "Does it amuse you to torture me with Roman barbarism? What's wrong with the local river?" Her nose wrinkled. "At least that wouldn't be *hot*."

"Then imagine this is a warm spring." Strange. He hadn't realized he'd got out of the habit of using rivers and streams. But for the last three years while he'd been with the Legion he'd used their baths and grown accustomed to their lengthy, decadent rituals.

Obscurely, he'd assumed Morwyn would appreciate a hot bath in which she could soak away the aches in her limbs. Did she have to make every moment of their enforced time together deliberately difficult?

And then an oddly defeated sigh puffed from her and she turned toward him. Exhaustion etched her face, clouded her eyes. He didn't move a muscle.

"Please, let me go to the river. I promise I'll come back." She glanced at the tub. "You have this instead."

"I'll use the public baths later." There was an annex next to the inn with a small but adequate bathing complex. He hadn't taken Morwyn there. He'd thought she'd prefer privacy.

Maybe he'd been wrong about that. But that wasn't the only reason he'd arranged for the tub. In the public baths, with the rules for segregating the sexes, he wouldn't be able to keep an eye on her, and he didn't intend to lose her. Not yet.

He wasn't sure why.

Silence sizzled as she glared at him yet again. "And I suppose you have no intention of leaving the room while I use *this*?" She jabbed her finger at the tub.

The tension twisting his muscles relaxed by the merest degree. "None."

Her fingers clenched. "I need my bag. For my personal requirements."

"Tell me what you need."

Her hands twitched, in clear frustration. "Don't you trust me?"

"As much as you trust me." He offered her a cynical smile, but it was touched with regret. Because the ironic truth was she could trust him. He would never betray her or their people.

And because of that very pledge she was destined to remain in ignorance of their mutual loathing of the Roman invaders.

He could confide in no one, for his own safety and for theirs.

She sucked in a deep breath. "Very well." She appeared to prefer honesty as much as he did. "I'll show you what I need and you can hand it to me."

The small clay pot she pointed out appeared to be a harmless lotion, so he gave it to her and she balanced it on the edge of the tub. He reclined on the bed, bracing his weight on his arm, watching her through half-lidded eyes.

"Aren't you even going to turn your back while I undress?"

"Allow me some pleasure this night. It's been a hard day." Gods, was that the truth. It was going to be a hard night also if she didn't choose to spread her thighs for him.

He knew she wouldn't. And yet still his cock throbbed with masochistic anticipation.

Instead of flinging caustic words—or even her pot of lotion— at his head, an odd expression flickered over her face. As if the thought of him enjoying her nakedness hadn't occurred to her.

How could it not have occurred to her? She knew he wanted her. Not just from the forest. Every time he looked at her she had to see the lust in his eyes, the lust he tried to smother but knew he failed.

She had to feel the smoky attraction between them, no matter how she might want to deny it.

Slowly she pulled her plait over her shoulder and tugged the leather tie from the end. Just as slowly she began to unbraid her hair, tress by tress, her eyes never leaving his.

Her hair was beautiful. Thick, black and glossy. Fascinated, he broke eye contact and watched her fingers comb through her shimmering curls, watched her tip her head to one side so her hair cascaded to her thighs. He imagined his fingers spearing through that midnight mass, imagined her spread across his pillows, imagined sinking into the silken heat of her body.

As if she guessed his thoughts a small smile touched the corners of her lips. Then she tugged at the ties of her bodice, loosening her gown, sliding it from her shoulders in a maddeningly sensual caress. Only then did he realize his free hand had slid beneath his tunic, was grasped around his cock. Only then did he realize the reason for her smile.

He didn't care. He smiled back and massaged the length of his shaft. A pleasurable torture. He wouldn't allow himself to come in front of her. But perhaps, later, if she continued with this seductive enticement, he'd come inside *her*.

The thought heated his mind, hammered against his temples, and as she stepped out of her gown the glow of the lamps cast mystical shadows across her lush body. Full breasts taunted him, her dark nipples as tempting as juicy berries. His starved gaze devoured the curve of her hips, the tautness of her belly. The dark tangle of curls at the juncture of her thighs.

And there his gaze lingered, hypnotized, ensnared. And his self-control shuddered with agonized demand on the precipice.

Chapter Six

Morwyn saw the lust flare in the Gaul's eyes, and corresponding tugs of forbidden desire tightened low in her belly. Why had she thought this barbaric bathing ritual a bad idea? It was the perfect means of inflaming him beyond his limits of control. He would become so aroused he'd take her, despite his insulting words of rebuff earlier, and then she could scorn the Morrigan in the basest manner possible.

She braced one hand on the edge of the tub, shot him a smoldering glance over her shoulder and allowed her hair to slide provocatively across her back. It wasn't she who repelled him. It was the remnants of the battle that clung to her.

His gaze scorched her naked flesh and the knowledge he so desired her pleased her more than it should, but what did it matter? No one would know how much she wanted him. No one but the Morrigan. And that cursed goddess was the only one who needed to know.

Tentatively she dipped one finger into the water. It was hot. Much hotter than the warm springs of Cymru. The thought of immersing her body into such contained, wet heat was oddly enticing.

"Do you need more cold water?" His voice rasped, as if his self-control were in imminent danger of disintegrating.

She slid her hand and wrist into the tub. It was more than bearable. "No." Gripping the side of the tub more securely, she gingerly stepped inside, allowing her arms to take the bulk of her weight.

Slowly she sank down and a startled wheeze gusted from her lungs as the wet heat engulfed her legs, thighs and belly and lapped against the undersides of her breasts. The water was hot but shockingly delicious as it bathed her grazed skin and sore muscles.

Her fingers still gripped the edge of the tub as if it were her lifeline, and with effort she forced them to relax and sank against the back of the tub. Although she was still irritated he hadn't allowed her to bathe in the nearby river, she had to admit this method had merit.

"How do you like it?" His smoky voice weaved into her mind, as hot as the water and infinitely more sensuous.

She considered telling him she hated it. But somehow she couldn't muster up the energy to project an emotion she was far from feeling. And besides, it was too late in the day to deliberately antagonize him. They were moments from fucking. She could be magnanimous when victory was within her grasp.

"More than I should." She slid a little farther into the water, feet braced against the end of the tub, hair floating around her submerged shoulders. "This is pure Roman decadence."

"They have their uses."

She cracked open one eye, realizing only as she did so that she'd been perilously close to sliding into tranquil oblivion. He still reclined on the bed, still grasped his cock beneath his tunic—*if only he were naked so she could watch*—and his gaze was still fixed on her.

For a moment she pondered on his comment. It had sounded very un-Roman. As if he didn't think much of them. But that couldn't be so. He worked for them. Why would he pledge them his loyalty unless he believed in their ways? Believed in their arrogant determination to conquer and subdue the civilized world?

The thought slithered from her mind. It wasn't important. But staying awake was. Languidly she pulled the stopper from her pot and massaged the lotion into her wet hair and scalp. The essence of spring flowers in hidden glades steamed from the water, permeated the air, far more aromatic than whenever she cleansed in rivers or streams.

Taking a deep breath, she plunged beneath the scented heat to rinse her hair, and the side of her face throbbed in jagged protest. She shot upward, coughed out water, cupped her tender cheekbone. How badly injured was it?

The Gaul instantly ceased his self-gratification. "Does your face hurt? Do you have anything you can take for it?"

Of course she did. She possessed a vast variety of pain inhibitors, but she wasn't going to tell him that, because depending on quantities and combinations they could also be used as potent poisons.

Not that she still intended to poison him. At least, not yet.

With difficulty she forced her hand from her cheek. She would show no weakness before him. "It doesn't hurt." It simply throbbed and stung as if tiny fires blazed across her flesh. She could deal with it.

He didn't look convinced, but he didn't argue the point. Nor did he resume his previous pastime. After a moment's thought she decided that was for the best. She wanted him hot and hard and desperate. Not partially sated by his own hand.

She lifted one leg from the tub and rested her foot on the edge. She would give him something worth watching, and save the best till last when he could no longer contain himself. A smile of anticipation tugged at the corners of her lips as she washed away the dirt from battle and travel. She flexed her muscles, allowed him to view the shapely form of calf and glimpse of thigh. And then she administered the same dedication to her injured leg, slow, sensuous, and the heated essence of springtime and undercurrent of blistering desire thudded in the air around them.

Beneath the water she slid her hand over her mound, across her sensitized pussy. Without conscious thought her fingers eased her swollen lips apart, felt wetness intrude, imagined it was the Gaul exploring her sheath, tantalizing her pulsing clit.

Breath gusted; her head fell back. And then she caught sight of him staring at her, eyes blazing, body taut. And recalled it wasn't the Gaul touching her. She was touching herself, arousing herself, and if she continued, she would come over her fingers, come in this bath, come before her watching enemy.

Lust pounded through her mind, flooded through her veins. Shivers danced through her at the pleasure she'd take in watching his face as she brought herself to climax. But that was a fantasy she could never indulge. Because by doing so, she would please the Morrigan. And she would never again willingly please that goddess.

But still her finger teased and pressure thundered, overwhelming, demanding to be sated. She pressed down on her swollen flesh, imagined it was the Gaul's cock causing such exquisite friction, and a moan of frustration escaped before she clamped her teeth together and dragged her reluctant hand across her belly.

She hadn't denied the goddess satisfaction for so many torturous moons only to surrender now, when victory was so close. Only a few more moments and she would no longer need to fight her body's primal urges. Would no longer need the mild sedatives she'd began taking at night to calm the molten desire for completion that raged in her blood.

The sedatives that kept the dreams at bay.

Dreams so visceral she'd feared them visions. Feared what the visions tried to foretell. And so she'd convinced herself they were merely bad dreams from her memory and not glimpses of a terrifying future from a vindictive goddess.

Shivers skittered over her arms and she pushed the thoughts aside. Tonight, even without recourse to her magic potions, she need have no fear of either simmering desire or spine-chilling dreams keeping her awake.

She cupped her aching breasts, skin slippery with lotion, and brushed her thumbs over erect nipples. She had to stop. But need coiled deep within, a ravenous beast she'd denied for too long, need that corroded her senses and screamed through her blood for blessed release.

Through the scented haze that steamed from the water she watched the Gaul leave the bed and come toward her. He knelt by the side of the tub, and in the exotic glow of the lamps his mesmeric green eyes ensnared.

Slowly he dipped his hands into the water, his intense gaze never leaving hers. Despite her best intentions her fingers slipped upward to allow better access to her sensitized nipples. She squeezed hard, relishing the stab of painful pleasure that ricocheted straight to her womb, despite the echo of warning that pounded in her burning mind.

He was the one who had to pleasure *her*. But still she couldn't drag her hands from her body. Because the way he looked at her as she touched herself aroused her more than she had imagined possible.

Finally he finished cleansing and the tips of his battle-scarred fingers trailed up her rib cage. Ribbons of fire ignited countless tiny flames under her flesh, inside her veins, and she relinquished her breasts, arching her back, inviting his touch.

But he didn't immediately cradle her breasts in his hands or lower his head and suckle her willing nipples. Instead he began to loosen the tangles teasing her hair, infinitely gentle, astonishingly patient. She curled her fingers over the sides of the tub to keep her balance, to keep herself from rubbing her engorged clit, but most of all to keep herself from winding her arms around his shoulders and melding her naked body against his.

"Your hair is beautiful." His husky voice invaded her blood, stoking the flames licking through her veins. "Like silk from the East."

"I know nothing of silk from the East." It wasn't quite true.

She had heard the exotic East produced breath-stealing luxuries, but hadn't seen any herself. Until this moment such foreign decadence had never interested her. But now, obscurely, she wanted to know more. "What's it like?"

It had *nothing* to do with wanting to hear the Gaul speak again in that bone-tingling smoky whisper.

His fingers tugged through an obstinate tangle and she sighed as corresponding tugs shivered over her skull and along her neck and spiraled through her painfully erect nipples. She was his enemy, his captive, and yet he took the time to arouse her as if they were besotted new lovers.

Her eyelashes fluttered. Despite his tender touch she must never forget he had abducted her by force. That his compatriots had murdered her fellow Druids. That this Gaul deserved nothing more than to feel the thrust of her blade through his corrupt heart.

Yet the thoughts were distant in her mind, as physical sensation drenched her weary senses.

"Soft." His fingers had reached her scalp. Jagged darts of pleasure tumbled through her brain and she tightened her grip on the edges of the tub before her bones melted and she slipped beneath the water in mindless delight. "Imagine strands of water sliding over your flesh without splintering into droplets."

A disbelieving smile tugged at the corners of her lips. Who would have thought this tough Gallic bastard could evoke such a tangible notion? "Beware your men never hear you utter such poetic beauty."

He gave a grunt that sounded like a suppressed laugh and raked her tangle-free hair back from her face, then twisted it into a single wet rope to snake over the edge of the tub. The tips of his fingers trailed from the nape of her neck across her naked shoulders, leaving chills of fire in his wake.

"What else do you want to know?"

She wanted to know when he was going to take her. When she could finally give in to the urge to hold him in her arms, explore his warrior-hard body, feel his cock thrust inside so she could come. So she could throw the final insult in the Morrigan's face.

Recalling the Morrigan, recalling the *real* reason Morwyn was allowing herself to enjoy this captivity, caused an icy chill to permeate her heated thoughts. For a moment she held her breath as confused fragments of desire and need and revenge tumbled through her mind.

Fucking the Gaul made sense. But wanting to prolong this conversation, wanting to hear the husky note in his voice as he caressed her wet skin, didn't make sense. They didn't need to talk. Talking wouldn't enrage her goddess.

And yet she couldn't find the strength to twist around. To shatter this strange, ethereal sensation of intimacy.

It was an illusion. She knew that. But it was peaceful to enjoy this fleeting moment out of time, to push to the back of her mind the death and devastation she'd witnessed since the cursed Roman Legions had invaded her land.

What else did she want to know?

"Have you served in the East?"

His fingers momentarily stilled, as if he hadn't expected her to ask such a thing. She had no need to ask such a thing. Yet she wanted to know. Even if knowing made no difference to how this fragile alliance would end.

Besides, she needed to earn his trust. That way he'd allow her more freedom when they reached Camulodunon. And pretending an interest in his life, encouraging him to talk, was one way of ensuing he lowered his innate suspicion.

Even if her pretense was false.

Without warning he began to massage her shoulders, thumbs and fingers kneading her knotted muscles, and waves of delicious pleasure radiated from wherever he touched. Again her eyelids flickered as bliss enveloped her battered body. If he continued so, she wouldn't need his cock to finish. Gods, how good it felt to have a man's hands on her once again, and her toes curled against the side of the tub as her neck dropped forward, allowing him the most vulnerable access.

"I served in the East for a short time." His warm breath grazed her shoulder. Deep in her mind a warning stirred at how unguarded she was. He could snap her neck with one swift movement and she'd be unable to defend herself. But why would he murder her now, when it was clear she would offer no resistance to his demands? And if brutality was his specialty, he would have raped her back in the forest.

She was as safe here as she would be anywhere with him.

"How long have you served your Roman masters?"

His thumbs dug into a sore muscle and she groaned in response, unsure whether the unexpected pressure caused pleasure or pain. He wound her hair around one hand but didn't jerk her head up as she expected. Instead he appeared satisfied to know she was utterly in his power.

For now. But later, when he writhed in ecstasy as she rode him into oblivion, the power would be all hers.

"A long time." There was an edge to his voice, as if he no longer found her questions entertaining.

"Yet you speak of them with contempt." Again her eyelids flickered. Gods, it was hard to keep awake as the scented heat of the water and magical ministrations of the Gaul's fingers relaxed her to such a degree she could scarcely summon the energy to think, never mind converse.

This time he did pull her head up by her hair, but it wasn't vicious. Just inexorable, letting her know he could. Letting her know she had no choice.

A groan escaped as he forced her neck over the rim of the tub. His face was close to hers and she blinked, disoriented by his upside-down visage, and his other hand slid around her vulnerable throat, strong fingers closing over her erratic pulse, applying pressure, a heartbeat away from severing her thread to this life.

Her lips parted, breath gasped. The flickering glow from the lamps cast enticing shadows across his roughened jaw and she had the overwhelming urge to reach up, drag her nails across his face, pull him to her, feel the abrasive texture of his day-old beard flay her tender flesh.

"And you, Celt, speak without first weighing your words." His thumb trailed slowly along the line of her jaw, back and forth, a lazy, seductive motion that sent tremors skittering along her taut skin without relaxing his death grip on her throat. "Haven't you yet learned to hold your tongue when in the presence of your enemy?"

"I've never before been captured by my enemy." Her voice was breathless, her lungs depleted. Her throat ached and the tub dug into the back of her neck. But that all faded against the way his thumb continued to stroke her, almost as if he didn't realize what he was doing, yet the careless caress stoked the dark eroticism bubbling deep in her blood.

She would put up with a great deal more discomfort for the pleasure his touch evoked.

And his thumb stilled. She sank her teeth into her bottom lip to stop herself from begging. She would never beg for his touch. But gods, how she wanted it, and how despicable that she craved him so.

His gaze roved over her face before locking with hers. Even upside down his eyes enchanted. How easy it would be, looking into those mystical green depths, to forget who and what he was.

"We could negotiate a truce." His words sank into her, as dark and rich and forbidden as the most decadent of unknown Roman luxury imported from the exotic East. And then his meaning permeated her lust-dazed mind. Victory stabbed through the swirling flames of desire, melding and intensifying, and unbearable heat ignited low in her womb, fiery tendrils flickering around her sensitized core.

Already he had grown to trust her enough to offer a truce. If she didn't wish to travel to Camulodunon for her own reasons, how easy it would be to incapacitate him after they'd fucked, and make good her escape.

"What do you have in mind?" It was a blatant invitation but she didn't care. Every muscle, every nerve, every particle of her skin screamed for release. If he didn't drag her from this water soon, if he didn't toss her onto the bed, immobilize her with his hard body and take her with savage, frenzied thrusts, she'd have no choice but to crucify her pride and reverse the scenario.

Chapter Seven

Her skin was warm, wet and silky soft beneath his rough fingers. She didn't trust him, and yet she offered the vulnerable column of her throat without resistance. For a fleeting moment he tightened his clasp on her, felt her pulse accelerate in anticipation or alarm, but there was no fear in her dark eyes as she gazed up at him. Only lust, desire and a clawing want that mirrored his own.

Still gripping her hair so she couldn't move should such a thought occur to her, he slowly slid his other hand from her throat across the enticing swell of her breast. She drew in a ragged breath but didn't push him away. Water lapped over his hand, over her nipples, and he had the sudden vision of joining her in the tub, pulling her onto his lap, plunging his shaft deep into her welcoming cleft.

Air hissed between his teeth. The tub was too small. He lowered his head so their breath mingled and slid his hand beneath her breast, cupping its slippery weight, pinching her erect nipple between thumb and forefinger, never taking his eyes from hers.

If only he could trust her not to slit his throat while he slept, or poison him as they ate. But too much pride glittered in her eyes for her to ever truly embrace her perceived enemy. He'd have to settle for a more superficial truce.

"When we stop for the night, we agree to forget our warring heritage."

Her lips parted, breath shortened, and she subtly angled her body so her luscious breast pressed more securely into the palm of his hand.

"Can you make me forget?" Her arm emerged from the water and languid fingers trailed over his jaw. A featherlight touch yet edged with danger as her nails dug into his throat and dragged down to the neck of his tunic.

He could make her forget. And maybe, for a few fleeting moments, she could make him forget, too.

But it wasn't his heritage he wanted or needed to suppress. Mindless oblivion beckoned, and as much as the promise of sexual satisfaction enticed, the tempting notion of deadening his memories, no matter how temporarily, mocked him with contemptuous impossibility.

"Yes."

She didn't answer, but the tip of her tongue teased her upper lip in a deliberately seductive gesture, as if daring him to take what she refused to verbally offer. He lowered his head. She wouldn't resist. No matter how she despised him, she still craved their joining.

He slid his hand from her wet globe, trailed over her ribs, across her taut stomach. Her long eyelashes flickered, her breath gusted. Silken skin tantalized his palm, fired his blood, thundered through his heart.

Soon, his self-imposed celibacy would incinerate beneath the desire that scorched between them. A celibacy he'd never willingly embraced yet one that had become part of his existence, as integral as the nightmares that plagued his sleep, the visions that haunted his waking hours.

A discordant thud against the door jarred his brain, shuddered through his bones, disconnecting the intoxicating moment.

Morwyn opened her lust-glazed eyes and stared up at him in unfocused bemusement.

His hand fisted in her hair and then slowly he relaxed his fingers and allowed her luxuriant tresses to slide free over the outside of the tub. With equal reluctance he dragged his hand from the water, over her slick body, the curve of her breast, the hard nub of her nipple. For a moment he gripped the edge of the tub, grasping at his fractured concentration, before sucking in a pained breath and snatching the length of cloth that lay on the floor.

"Cover yourself." His voice was harsh. He had no intention of allowing any other to see her naked. "Stand up." But gods, he had every intention of seeing her so himself.

Her eyes narrowed, as if she contemplated disobeying. "Why should I?"

Contemplation be cursed. She would never obey him voluntarily. Once again he leaned over her, offered her a mirthless smile as frustration seared his arteries and fried his reflexes.

"Because I doubt you want those louse-ridden boys to see you as a mortal Venus."

Her frown intensified. "Heathen Roman goddess. You insult me." But she curled her fingers around the edge of the tub and heaved herself up, as if the procedure pained, as if her muscles protested at such unwelcome exertion.

She wasn't anything like the deity the Romans worshipped. With her delectable rounded arse, sculpted waist and finely toned arms, she was nothing less than the visage of the Maiden Morrigan, the great goddess he had worshipped in his youth.

Slowly she turned to face him and his mouth dried. Water slid from her shoulders, traced over her breasts, dripped from the dark tips of her nipples. But she made no move toward him, no sign she was vexed by this untimely interruption.

Perhaps she wasn't.

The notion scraped across raw nerves and he thrust the cloth at her before he abandoned the last shredded remnants of control and fucked her regardless. And lost, forever, the remaining fragment of the man he truly was.

He marched to the door, legs as stiff as his cock and, with a glance to ensure Morwyn had covered herself, jerked it open.

The innkeeper's wife, laden with platters, avoided his glare and he stepped aside so she could enter. The two boys followed her, their hot eyes fixed upon Morwyn with blatant relish. Bren clenched his fists. They scarcely reached his shoulder and yet the way they looked at her enraged him as if they were grown men leering at a helpless girl.

Standing in the center of the tub, Morwyn looked nothing like a helpless girl and every cursed Roman inch a confident Celtic woman, comfortable with the undoubted effect she had on impressionable young males.

Only with difficulty did Bren refrain from slamming the door so it shattered in its frame. Instead he watched the woman and boys deposit their offerings on top of the chest before making their way back to him.

Except one of the boys hovered, clearly besotted by the wet vision before him.

"Do you need any help, mistress?"

"Daric! Get over here." Horror laced the woman's tone, as if she expected Bren to behead the boy for such audacity.

"No, thank you." Morwyn sounded like a queen addressing one of her loyal subjects and the smile she bestowed on the lad knotted Bren's guts, although he wasn't sure why. "The Gaul can attend to my needs."

She made him sound like her slave. An odd thread of amusement slithered through him at the thought and again he wondered who she truly was. Somehow he couldn't envisage her as a trader, someone who haggled and compromised and knew when to hold her tongue or smother her pride.

His illogical irritation against the boys evaporated. They weren't attacking and Morwyn was in no danger. He strode back to her and shoved the boy toward the door. "You can empty this tub now."

As the three of them scuttled from the room he turned to her. She was staring at him, a frown creasing her brow, as if she was trying to work something out.

"Does everyone cower before you in terror?"

Her question shouldn't matter. And yet a dull ache punched through his chest, instantly gone, but the echo remained.

Not a flicker of such emotion touched his face. "I've yet to see you cower before me, Morwyn."

She arched her eyebrows. "And you never will, Gaul." She glanced at his outstretched hand, as if contemplating whether or not to accept his assistance. And then he recalled her injured leg.

"Do you wish me to lift you out?"

Her eyes glittered in the flickering glow from the lamps. For a moment he thought she was going to accept his offer. But then she glanced at the open door and appeared to reconsider.

"I can manage." She tucked the cloth securely around her breasts, gripped the edge of the tub and gingerly lifted her injured leg. Even in this muted light he could see the ugly bruises marring her lower thigh.

Trogus would pay. With interest.

With a smothered sigh she sat on the edge of the bed and began to dry her legs with the second cloth. Her movements were graceful, sensuous, but she appeared unaware of her seduction. There were no sideways glances, no fluttering of eyelashes. She appeared on the verge of exhaustion.

Bren shifted his weight from one foot to the other but it did nothing to relieve the arousal thudding along the length of his shaft. Why had he arranged for food to be delivered to their room? Without such interruption they could now be slaking their desire.

But no. He'd not wanted others to see Morwyn's battered face when they ate in the tavern. Hadn't wanted to tolerate the inevitable muffled whispers, be the recipient of more distrustful looks, have his character assassinated yet again for actions he'd not committed.

The boys returned, began to empty the tub with their buckets. He dragged his gaze from the hypnotic sweep of Morwyn's hands along her legs and strode to the chest.

"I trust you're hungry."

"So long as it's not filthy Roman imports." She dried her arms, seemingly unaware or unconcerned by the furtive glances thrown her way by the boys as they entered and left the room.

He sniffed the guinea fowl. "Imported, yes. But not filthy."

Her sigh was audible. He looked over at her as she dried her hair with the cloth, and she caught his gaze. "I'm so famished I'll eat their heathen food. My pride doesn't extend to starving myself over such a minor point."

His lip twitched but through sheer force of habit he suppressed the smile that threatened to escape. Gods. He'd met her only a few hours ago yet she'd tempted him to laughter more often this day than he could recall during the last half-dozen years.

"I'm glad your survival instincts are so strong."

She gave the ends of her hair one final squeeze before tossing the saturated cloth onto the floor by the now-emptied tub. "My survival instincts are intact." She pushed herself from the bed and came beside him to frown at the food. The top of her head didn't even reach his jaw. "I doubt it will kill me to eat such barbarous offerings on occasion."

Her fresh scent invaded his senses, clean and pure. But she appeared utterly focused on the food, as if their earlier interaction had never occurred.

As the boys dragged the tub from the room and finally shut the door, Bren handed her a plate. "You may find you like it."

She wrinkled her nose as she scooped up some carrots. "There's nothing wrong with our own food. These people are Britons. Why do they serve Roman muck?"

He tore the guinea fowl into portions and dropped a quarter

onto her plate. She stared at it as if he'd just offered her a severed hand.

"Not everything foreign is inherently inferior."

Morwyn wiped a finger across the poultry and then licked the flavor with her tongue. Her frown didn't waver. "It is when the foreigners concerned are Romans."

Mostly, he agreed. But he'd lived the Roman way for too many years now not to have seen advantages to their systems. Their military system in particular. They hadn't conquered the civilized world through luck alone, no matter how his people might wish that was so.

"Sometimes survival calls for compromise." As he'd compromised for the last few years, inveigling himself with the enemy to learn their weaknesses, exploit their arrogant pride.

"No." Morwyn's tone was firm as she settled herself against the pillows on the bed, her plate piled surprisingly high considering her opinion of the feast. "I'd never go against my principles, simply to survive under the yoke of Rome."

"And yet you have no compunction in eating their imported food." He poured the wine and sat beside her, and shot her a sardonic glance as she ate the guinea fowl with apparent relish. Would she enjoy the Roman wine as much? He hadn't thought to ask if she'd prefer the locally brewed ale.

She wiped her chin with the back of her hand. "Nothing else is available." Then her brow creased as if she realized she'd just inadvertently agreed with him. "This is different. It's not what I meant at all."

"It's still a compromise." He shoveled in a mouthful of vegetables so she wouldn't see the grin threatening to crack his lips. He didn't know why he found contradicting her enjoyable. Gods, he couldn't recall the last time he'd enjoyed a conversation to this degree.

Except he could. *More than six years ago.* For a moment the memories seared through his brain, recollections of laughter and

love and careless words that could be uttered without first analyzing their possible intent.

And tonight, with Morwyn, he once again spoke without
thought of how his words might be interpreted. With a woman
who believed him her worst enemy, a woman who would betray
him given the slightest opportunity.

"I don't agree." There was an edge in her voice, as if she didn't
appreciate having her remarks twisted. "In fact, what could be
better than nourishing myself on the enemy's food in order to—"
She snapped her jaw together as if she belatedly recalled to whom
she was speaking, before once again biting into the enemy's food.

"Stab him in the back?" It was ironically amusing they both
believed in that. Because that was exactly the plan he'd been following for the last three years.

She swallowed the guinea fowl and looked as if she were about
to choke, but after a moment she composed herself. "Not literally."
She didn't meet his eyes. This conversation might be stimulating
but it also served as a reminder. He couldn't trust her. No matter
how he wished otherwise.

"What, then?"

An oddly vulnerable look flashed across her face, as if she were
recalling painful memories. Of whom did she think? Her lover?
Had he died at the hands of the enemy? Was that the reason Morwyn was so vocal in her condemnation?

If so, they had another bond in common. Another he could
never share with her.

"I'd never betray my people." Her voice was scarcely above a
whisper, as if once again she forgot whom she was talking to. As
if the words came from her soul, and weren't uttered with the pri-
mary objective of insulting his honor. "Not for the enemy. And not
for the gods."

The gods? That, he hadn't expected. Under what circumstances
did she imagine their gods would want them to betray their people?

He might not think that much of the gods anymore. Couldn't

remember the last time he'd worshipped them or offered them sacrifice. But no matter how he despised them for ignoring his agonized entreaties so many years ago, deep in his heart he knew they'd never willingly submit to the Roman invaders.

Slowly she turned to look at him, her dark eyes unfocused as if she were no longer in this room with him, but reliving her past. Silently he offered her a goblet and she blinked, as if emerging from a trance, and took the wine without protest.

She gulped down the golden liquid as if it were water, despite the way her nose crinkled as if the taste didn't best please her. But he wasn't about to risk drinking the water provided by the innkeeper. Even now, he preferred to fill his waterskins from the source, where it gushed unpolluted from the earth.

Silence stretched between them, yet it wasn't a silence of animosity nor did it crackle with resentment or fear. If circumstances were different, he'd think it companionable.

Her head dropped against his shoulder and need blazed through his groin, igniting the embers, reawakening his lust. He looked down at her, expecting a sultry smile or at least eyes reflecting the extent of their mutual desire.

Only the top of her head was visible as she slumped against him, and he snatched her goblet before it tumbled from her slack fingers.

She'd fallen asleep. It had nothing to do with how much she trusted him, because he knew she didn't trust him at all, and yet still an odd pain split through his chest at how vulnerable sleep had rendered her.

Without shifting the arm upon which Morwyn rested, he piled their plates and goblets onto the timber chest. He was sweaty and filthy from their ride and now, while she slept, was the perfect moment to visit the bathhouse.

Stealthily he slid from her unconscious embrace and lowered her head to the pillows. She curled into a ball, hair spread around her like black flame, oblivious to how the damp cloth barely covered her enticing breasts or luscious buttocks.

It would be so easy to leave her as she was. But if she awoke, she'd take instant advantage to escape. And it wasn't safe outside for a woman alone, no matter how skilled with a dagger she might be.

But even as the thought slithered through his mind, even as he made sure she'd be unable to leave him without his consent, the harsh truth bubbled like acid through his lies.

He didn't want her to disappear in the night because her quick tongue and tempting body relieved the stark reality of his existence.

Chapter Eight

From the depths of slumber, Morwyn stirred. Various points of her body throbbed and disjointed memories tumbled through her mind.

She was with the Gaul. She didn't recall falling asleep and stealthily peered through her lashes but he wasn't lying by her side. Surely it wasn't morn already and he'd risen?

Before irritation could flood her at the possibility he'd slept by her side *all night* without touching her, she realized the light was all wrong. The lamps were still burning. The remains of their meal still cluttered the top of the chest.

Perhaps he'd merely gone to the bathhouse.

Heat flickered low in her womb and a smile tugged at her lips. Gaining his trust had been easier than she'd thought. If she wasn't so desperate to see Carys, there would be nothing to stop her from escaping her captor while he luxuriated in his Roman masters' bath.

But even though she had no intention of escaping, she most certainly needed her medicine bag. It had been many moons since she'd bothered with the contraceptive teas. Not since the Druids had fled Cymru and Carys had chosen her Roman lover above her people. There had been no need. From that night she'd no longer welcomed Gawain into her arms and there had been no other man since.

The heat speared from her womb, tingled through her already damp pussy. It would be easy enough to persuade the Gaul to procure her hot water. Even if he did now work for the enemy, he was still Celt-born. Would know how a woman needed to protect herself against unwanted pregnancy. But in case he'd been tainted by the foul Roman view of femininity, she'd tell him the infusions were for some other womanly complaint.

She smiled again, well satisfied by her plan, and ignoring the protests of her abused muscles stretched languorously, arms above her head, flexing cramped legs.

Unaccustomed weight dragged the ankle of her uninjured leg and she froze, momentarily stunned into stupidity, unable to comprehend the obvious reason for such constraint.

He wouldn't dare. She wouldn't believe it. But still she remained prone on the bed, unwilling to see the evidence with her own eyes as rage thundered through her blood and pounded against her temples.

Finally she jerked upright and glared at the ugly shackle enclosing her ankle that attached to an equally ugly iron chain that trailed over the end of the bed.

He'd put her in chains.

An inarticulate hiss spilled from her lips, and her fingers clawed uselessly against her thighs. So much for imagining she'd gained his trust. The bastard had tethered her like an animal, as if she were his property, as if she were—

The door cracked open, as if whoever entered wanted to do so without waking her. She clamped her teeth together and glowered as the Gaul caught her eye, and he kicked the door shut behind him, obviously no longer concerned with stealth.

He approached, as if nothing were wrong. She wouldn't lower herself to speak to him. Wouldn't demean herself by engaging in a confrontation. She'd lie down, turn her back and show him just how little she cared that he'd *put her in chains*.

"I didn't think you'd be awake yet." He sat at the foot of the bed but the Roman scents and spices or whatever he'd used in the barbaric bathing ritual saturated the air, weaved into her senses, distorted her mind.

Her fingernails dug into her palms. She didn't care that he no longer stank of horse or travel. It made no difference that his hair was damp, his jaw freshly shaved, or that he smelled like something that had walked out of her most erotic dreams.

He glanced as her imprisoned ankle. She resisted the urge to curl her toes because then he'd know his scrutiny bothered her. Enraged her. Gods, if he got any closer, she'd gouge out his eyes and force them down his bastard Gallic throat.

Unbelievably he reached out toward her enchained leg, and her resolve snapped.

"Don't you dare touch me." She jerked her legs across the bed, the shackle a loathsome weight around her. When he turned back to her, as if he was about to justify his act, she leaned forward so he wouldn't be under any illusion as to how she felt. "How dare you chain me like a *slave*?"

His jaw tensed, as if he didn't appreciate her accusation. "That wasn't my intention."

Injustice bubbled deep in her gut that he should treat her so basely. And although she tried to ignore it, she also knew her pride seethed at the knowledge she'd been unable to gain his trust, been unable to hoodwink him as easily as she'd so smugly imagined.

"How could you have intended anything else?" She kicked her leg, making the chain clank, a hideous sound that reinforced how helpless she was. If he kept her chained the entire time they were in Camulodunon, she'd never have a chance to escape.

"I *intended* to release you upon my return." He sounded as if he was having second thoughts about following through, but it didn't matter what he intended. He'd already shown her, more clearly than any lying words, what he thought of her.

"You had no right to tether me in the first place." Her breath shortened and she gripped the cloth over her breasts before it slithered to her waist. She wanted to hate him, and she did. She wanted to despise him, and she most *certainly* did.

But she didn't want to still desire him. Didn't want this ravening lust thundering through her veins or pounding between her thighs. And yet she did still desire him and her body craved his as much as it ever had.

"Are you going to argue the matter all night?" No hint of apology or shame at his actions colored his words. If anything, he sounded as if he believed her in the wrong to question him.

As if he truly did consider her nothing more than his slave.

She straightened her rigid spine. "I wouldn't demean myself to argue with such as *you*."

"Then go to sleep." His voice was harsh and he rose from the bed and strode to where he'd left his pack against the far wall. She caught sight of an iron key dangling from his fingers. "Enjoy your self-righteous indignation."

Her fingers twitched with useless rage. Had he really intended to unlock her shackles when he returned, even if she'd still been asleep? But he'd seen she was awake and still he'd approached with the key.

Her breath escaped in a noisy hiss. Had she held her tongue, or at the very least not insulted him, she'd be free already.

But at least now she knew how little he truly thought of her. She wouldn't underestimate him again. Wouldn't assume a friendly word or disarming smile equaled trust.

Pride demanded she sling one final condemning insult in his face before grandly turning her back on him and feigning sleep. And if she did that, she risked him never removing the chains of degradation. The image of her hobbling behind him, in view of countless others, haunted her, and a shudder crawled through her soul.

What did he want from her? A groveling apology for speaking her mind? A promise to never cross him again? A pledge that she'd obey him in every word he deigned to utter?

Her throat closed, choking on the mere thought of subjugating herself so. Instead she clamped her teeth together, an effective barrier against an inadvertent remark escaping. Rigid with affront, she lay down on the bed, jerked the cover up to her chin and, after a moment's hesitation, rolled onto her side facing him.

Never turn your back on the enemy.

In the fathomless black of the abyss, the entire world slipped sideways. Morwyn groaned, burrowed back into the endless silence, but still the world rocked, centering on her shoulder, insistent and relentless.

"Morwyn." The voice penetrated the darkness bathing her mind and the blissful obscurity of slumber shredded like wisps of summer clouds in a warm breeze. "Wake up. We have to leave."

The heat of his fingers sank into her blood as he clasped her naked shoulder and shook her in a very unlustful manner. She scowled into the pillow, her eyes still tightly screwed shut, and surreptitiously pressed her thighs together in an attempt to relieve the unwelcome throb of arousal.

And realized she was no longer chained like an enslaved chattel.

"If you don't hurry, you won't have time to eat." He sounded impatient. Good. Why should she care if she made him late? She stretched as well as her painful muscles allowed and smothered another groan at the thought of a second full day in the saddle. By the time they reached Camulodunon, she'd scarcely be able to walk straight.

She rolled onto her back and squinted up at him. He was dressed in tunic and mail shirt and the grim expression on his face suggested he wasn't impressed by her continued disobedience.

For a moment she contemplated remaining in bed. It would serve him right if he had to physically drag her from the room. Except her pride wouldn't allow it. It was humiliating enough knowing the innkeeper's wife pitied her for being in the Gaul's power, without drawing any more attention to the fact.

And at least he'd removed the shackles. He didn't intend she look like a slave in public, even if he treated her as one in private.

She sat up and discovered the cloth had disappeared during the night. And the Gaul, who had slept beside her, still hadn't taken advantage. If she didn't know better from the way his cock had dug into her when they were in the forest or how he'd looked at her and touched her while she bathed last night, she'd assume he preferred boys.

Scowling, and unable to help it, she climbed from the bed and snatched up her gown from the floor. Had he fucked another woman while in the bathhouse last night? It was the only reason she could imagine as to why he hadn't taken her upon his return. Surely it had nothing to do with how she'd insulted him?

And even if it had, why hadn't he slaked his lust at some point during the night? She was no longer covered in dried mud or crusted blood. He'd ensured there was no way she could have procured and hidden a dagger with which to gut him.

As she tied her bodice with savage precision, she hoped it had been a singularly unsatisfactory coupling. And judging by the dark glare on his face and the waves of tension that crackled in the air around them, it certainly hadn't done much to relieve his frustration.

In frigid silence they walked to the latrines and attended to their needs. She hoped he didn't bother opening his mouth to her again until they reached Camulodunon. Filthy, lying Gaul.

Despite her best intentions she shot him a surreptitious glance from beneath her lashes. Already his jaw was rough with an overnight beard, but the faintest scent still lingered from his sojourn in the bathhouse.

And he hadn't lied to her. No matter how she tried to twist his words or misinterpret his actions. How much better she'd feel if he had. Then she could justify her wounded feelings instead of knowing she had nobody but herself to blame for her misguided illusion of having gained a foothold in securing his trust.

She picked up her pack and followed him outside. It was early, the sun still low in the pale blue sky, and the air was fresh as it gusted through her loose hair. With an impatient sigh she pulled open her pack, aware the Gaul watched her. As if even now, after he'd gone through every item before allowing her to touch her own things, he still didn't trust her not to find a lethal weapon hidden among her possessions.

Her fingers curled around a leather thong and she pulled it free, unable to resist slinging him a scornful glance as she began to braid her tangled hair.

Apparently satisfied she had no intention of garroting him with her strip of leather, he turned to issue instructions to a young stable lad. Obviously he had no intention of allowing her to break her fast, although she was sure *he* had.

And if he imagined she was going to complain or beg him for food, he was delusional. She'd sooner chew on grass.

The innkeeper's wife emerged, looking exhausted as if she'd been up half the night, and handed the Gaul a package. The aroma of fresh bread tantalized and, despite gritting her teeth, Morwyn's mouth watered and her stomach growled.

She knotted the end of her braid and glared as the Gaul turned toward her. Let him stuff his face. She hoped he choked. And then she'd take the horse and make her own way to Camulodunon. How hard could it be?

He shoved half the package at her without a word, his green eyes scorching her, before turning around and taking possession of the horse from the stable boy. Part of her wanted to sling the bread at his head. She didn't need his food. She could fend for herself. And yet she couldn't because she was his captive. Beholden to his whims. If he decided to starve her, there wasn't much she could do about it.

Except he wasn't starving her. He was feeding her. And that annoyed her as much as if he'd stood in front of her and eaten the entire loaf without offering her a single crumb.

Feeling obscurely this was a contest of strength and she'd failed at the first hurdle, she transferred her glare from his back to the bread and, finally, with self-righteous resentment, began to eat.

The sun was sinking on the far horizon as they clattered to a halt outside another Romanized inn. Morwyn loosened her grip on the timber-ridged saddle, her fingers molded into claws from their extended inertia, her head throbbing from the relentless travel without comfort of shade.

She had never believed it possible to travel so far in one day. The countryside and villages merged into a continual blur as the Gaul had urged them ever onward, allowing her only the briefest respite whenever they changed horses. And still Camulodunon wasn't in sight.

As always, he assisted her in dismounting, as if conscious of her injured leg. But the moment she was on the ground he released her, as if the contact repelled. She slung him a dark look as he hauled their packs from the horse. Not one word had passed between them since he'd woken her this morning. Sometimes she got the impression he was waiting for her to apologize.

In which case they were destined to travel in eternal silence. She wouldn't lower herself to speak to him, never mind beg his forgiveness for an imagined slight to his honor. He possessed no honor and therefore such slight was impossible to give.

She tramped after him, her spine threatening to crumple after the punishing regime of the day. Gods, her back ached. How many times had she almost slipped into slumber, how many times had she caught herself slumping against the Gaul's rigid chest?

And how often had she wished to simply remain lying against him, cradled within his unyielding arms, and allow her weary body to rest for a few precious moments?

Too often. It was humiliating. She caught up with him at the door and reassured herself, not for the first time, that the only reason such treacherous thoughts had crossed her mind was because of her exhausted state.

The entrance was small, nothing more than a space with which to conduct brief business. He accomplished that within moments, securing them a room for the night and a fresh horse for the morning. As with every other place they'd stopped, she was the recipient of fleeting sideways glances, expressions ranging from pity to complete disinterest, as if she were of no account.

She wasn't sure which response was more insulting. Her bloodline was noble and her previous existence as an acolyte of the cursed Morrigan had always assured her of deference whenever she was among her people.

But of course, these weren't her people. These were only Britons, and Romanized Britons at that. *Her* people would never surrender so easily to the enemy.

The Gaul shot her a glance over his shoulder, almost as if he could hear her thoughts. But he didn't say anything, merely waited for her to reach his side before they entered the noisy tavern that led directly from the inn's entrance. With a jerk of his head he indicated a table in the corner of the room, shoved up against the wall, and again waited until she moved in that direction. As if he didn't trust her not to run off the moment he turned his back on her.

They sat facing each other. Raucous laughter and drunken voices vibrated through the air but silence screamed between Morwyn and the Gaul across the ale-stained timber table.

It didn't matter. He didn't need to speak to her. And she certainly didn't need to speak to him.

"So we're not eating in our room this eve?" Just because she didn't *need* to speak to him didn't mean she should suffer the rest of this interminable journey as a mute. Conversation would make the time pass more swiftly, and since she had no intention of pandering to his wounded pride, she wasn't breaking her promise to herself. It *certainly* had nothing to do with wanting to hear his voice again, because if all she wanted was to hear a male voice, there were plenty in this heathen Briton tavern.

If he was surprised by her breaking the deadlock, he didn't show it.

"Would you rather have?" He didn't sound as if he cared one way or the other. But his intense gaze never left her face.

A warm tingle danced in the pit of her belly. She ignored it as best she could because it was obvious the Gaul had no intention of following up on the lust that had once simmered between them.

And she no longer wanted him to. Not after last night. And just because she still retained a modicum of desire for him was irrelevant.

"I have no opinion on the matter." She accompanied her words by flicking an uninterested glance around the darkened interior at the rowdy inhabitants, but it was impossible to ignore the only person in the room who snared her interest. Sooner than she'd intended, her focus once again arrowed in his direction. There was the faintest trace of a smile on his lips, as if he found her remark amusing.

"I find that . . ." He paused. Deliberately. "Difficult to believe."

Why did he smile at her? It made it hard to remember how vital it was to remain on her guard. Made it easy to forget that in his eyes she was nothing more than a spoil of war.

The reminder galled. "Why should you? You've made it clear you find my opinions worthless."

"When?"

Morwyn blinked, unsure she'd heard him correctly. "What?"

"When have I made it clear your opinion is worthless?"

Was he serious? He didn't look as if he were jesting. She expelled a disbelieving breath and rolled her eyes for emphasis. "You abducted me against my will. Or had you forgotten?"

"For your own safety."

Arrogant Gaul. "You can believe that if you wish, but you know it's nothing but a lie."

He leaned back in his chair and his feet nudged against hers as he stretched out his long legs beneath the table. She refused to move to accommodate him, and refused to acknowledge the way her heart thundered in her breast at so slight a contact.

"Do I?" The quiet words were a challenge. She stared at him, unwilling to examine his accusation because, curse the foul gods, he wasn't entirely wrong.

"If I hadn't been injured, I would have been more than capable of continuing my journey alone."

"But injured and horseless?"

She rapped her fingernails on the table as she clawed through her mind for a suitable response. And couldn't find one. She decided to move on.

"You disregarded my wish to bathe in a river."

"With good reason."

"Ah." She pounced on his words, rested her forearms on the table and leaned toward him. "So you don't deny my opinion on *that* was of no consequence to you?"

"It was dark outside."

She made a sound of disgust.

"The river backed onto a Roman settlement."

That, she hadn't known, but she wasn't going to back down for the second time. "You could have stood guard over me."

Again his lips twitched as if laughter threatened, and she stared at him in reluctant fascination, wondering why he found her amusing and, since he so obviously did, why he so studiously fought to hide it.

"I chose comfort over conflict."

The memory of the bath slid into her mind, heating her blood. She would never admit it to this Gaul but she had enjoyed the experience of luxuriating in that hot tub.

Only as a novelty. Given the choice she'd certainly never forsake the familiarity of her rivers and springs for decadent Roman bathing rituals.

The food arrived and with strange unwillingness she drew back from the table to allow the serving wench access. The girl's breasts spilled from her untied bodice and Morwyn shot the Gaul a sharp glance, but oddly his gaze was still fixed on her, as if the sight of the wench's nakedness enticed him not in the slightest.

Why did she even care whether he looked? It shouldn't make any difference to how she felt, and yet it did. And the words hovering on her tongue—words condemning him for enslaving her last night as she slept—withered.

If she continued this conversation, she would win, for there was nothing he could say in his defense that would change her mind or the facts. So what was she waiting for? Why did she hesitate?

Was it because, despite everything, she enjoyed conversing with this Gaul? If she threw last night in his face, she knew, without question, their current fragile harmony would shatter.

Was she considering compromising her integrity for the sake of flirting with a man whose compatriots were directly responsible for the deaths of her fellow Druids?

Chapter Nine

Bren watched as subtle nuances of emotion flickered over Morwyn's face. Suspicion, confusion and, finally, inexplicably, guilt. She didn't have to open her mouth for him to know the direction of her thoughts. She'd be mortified if she realized how easily he could read her.

As the serving girl left their table, he waited for Morwyn's next accusation. She may have broken their silence but she wouldn't ignore the reason for it. He stifled a sigh. It had seemed a good idea at the time. A way to ensure she couldn't escape should she wake while he was gone.

For some reason he hadn't anticipated how vitriolic her response would be if he hadn't released her before she stirred. But what had really pissed him off was the knowledge she was entitled to her anger. That he had no right to chain her like a slave. That no matter how many excuses he gave himself for his actions, not one justified treating her as a conquered spoil of war.

Her dark eyes narrowed and he waited for her condemnation.

She'd obviously been waiting for this moment all day. If luck was with him, she'd tell him what she thought of him and then be prepared to move on.

But since he and luck had only the most fleeting of acquaintance, he wasn't holding his breath.

"And what," she said in a regal voice, never taking her gaze from his, "do the Romans call *these*?" She jabbed her finger at the various vegetables that had been served up with the more traditional British stew.

He stared at her. She wanted to know about the food on her plate? Why wasn't she spitting venom at him for last night? It had darkened her features. Glittered in her eyes. Since when had Morwyn ever held her tongue for fear of angering him?

Something foul twisted through his guts. Was that the answer? That she now feared him? That she would join the others who cowed in terror before him? Had he ensured her continued company only to taint it irretrievably?

She leaned across the table. Her attitude wasn't one of servility. What the fuck was going on?

"Should I call the serving wench back?" Her tone was deceptively innocent. "Perhaps she can list the ingredients for us."

"Possibly." His tone was guarded. It was rare he found himself in a situation where he wasn't in absolute command. But in this moment he floundered. He had no idea what Morwyn was talking about.

She pursed her lips as if his answer didn't please. "I shouldn't be surprised if she'd be willing to show you all her ingredients personally."

And now she'd lost him completely. He hoped his confusion didn't show. Until now he'd taken for granted his ability to accurately read a situation. Gods, it was the reason he was still alive. The reason why he'd escaped being murdered a dozen times during the last three years.

Even though he enjoyed the conversations with Morwyn he

knew how much she resented him, how she considered him her enemy. How she would sooner drive a dagger through his heart than offer him a modicum of trust.

That was why he didn't allow her to keep her embroidered bag. He had adequate knowledge of healing herbs and potions, as any warrior worth his salt did, but Morwyn's supplies surpassed the norm. He was under no illusion she would poison him within an instant were she given the opportunity.

And now she should be condemning him for chaining her. It was the logical continuation of their previous conversation. He'd known its inevitability as they bartered words on why he'd rescued her from Trogus, why he'd not allowed her to bathe in the river.

Yet she spoke of food. Of the serving wench. And for the life of him he couldn't make any connection.

"I've no desire to examine her"—he hesitated for a moment—"ingredients." He had the distinct impression Morwyn was referring to the serving girl's half-naked breasts. Why? Was she attempting to divert his interest from her to another? Did she still think he'd force her against her will, despite how last night he'd ensured not so much as his foot intruded on her privacy?

Despite how he'd lain awake for hours battling an agonizing erection and sweat-drenched fantasies?

"Not to your taste?" She raised her eyebrows and began to eat the stew.

At least that was a straightforward question. "No."

She chewed and swallowed, lips together, every action screaming of her high birth. Who was she, really?

"I suppose you prefer a demure little mouse who trembles at the thought of crossing her master."

An odd notion occurred to him. Was she *flirting*? It had been so long since he'd bothered to notice such interplay between the sexes it was hard to recall the rules of engagement. But once, long ago, he'd enjoyed the pastime.

In another life.

"A mouse wouldn't last long with me." His voice was gruff and he scowled at his stew, unable to believe she really was flirting with him, the man she so blatantly despised. But if not, then what?

"Not a mouse, then." She sniffed the wine and took a minute sip. "But clearly your preference is for a woman who defers to you in every matter. One who craves your protection and swoons if you so much as raise your voice to her."

A dull ache wrapped around his heart. Squeezed like a vise. Bled him dry and tossed the useless husk aside.

Eryn, his first love, tiny and fragile, had looked to him in every matter. But she had been no timid mouse. And he would have carved out his heart before hurting her with word or deed.

Eryn. Her name whispered through his mind, tangled in his memories. As a boy he adored her; as a youth he desired her. And as a man he'd failed her.

"In that case I'll find myself a Roman woman."

Morwyn shot him a sharp glance but he was concentrating on devouring his food, as if he hadn't eaten in days. She frowned, took another mouthful and tried to work out why he'd suddenly retreated.

She'd enjoyed baiting him. To see him at a loss for words was highly entertaining. Especially when it was obvious he struggled to comprehend whether she was being serious or jesting. Had he never flirted? Or was he simply incapable of it?

They ate in silence for a few moments but tension skittered through her blood, scraped along her nerves. How could he just sit there, ignoring her? He'd taken her from Cymru for his own purposes and then not bothered to follow through.

And now he wasn't even talking to her. She shifted on the hard seat and flung him another glance. He wasn't even *looking* at her. So why did he insist she accompany him to Camulodunon?

She drained the wine, and the noise from the tavern echoed through her mind. It wasn't wholly unpleasant but she had no intention of passing out as she had last night. What she needed was fresh water to clear her head, but it appeared such a basic need was lacking.

Irritation mounted. When he'd disarmed her in the forest his arousal had been evident. He'd even told that filthy dog who'd been intent on rape that he was taking her to warm his bed at nights. And when she bathed before him, he'd been riveted.

So why did he ignore her? Why didn't he take her last night?

Since the age of fourteen, almost half her lifetime ago, only one male had ever spurned her. But Aeron, the High Druid and ultimate betrayer of their people, had never shown any interest in her sexually.

On the other hand this infuriating Gaul had. And now that she was in his power he chose to slight her.

She speared a foreign vegetable and chewed it viciously, as equally savage thoughts pounded through her mind. A distasteful certainty coalesced and no matter how she tried to dismiss the notion it gained momentum and flooded her injured psyche.

He wanted her. And resented the fact. Because she was nothing like the women he usually lusted after. Meek, subservient.

Roman.

The thought of being compared with a Roman woman and *found wanting* was more than she could stomach. She pushed her plate aside, pride seething. If that was the type of female he preferred, then she had no use for him, in or out of bed.

For a moment the thought hovered, jangling her nerves. And then she realized the incongruity of her thought and heat scalded her cheeks.

She had no use for him out of bed. The only reason she willingly stayed with him was because he gave her safe passage to Carys. And fucking him was only a pleasant side benefit. A way to get back at the Morrigan.

Except they had yet to fuck.

Her toes curled, fingers clawed. Curse the gods, why did she care so much? She had been without sex for many moons. To insult her goddess by embracing her enemy would be enjoyable but if it didn't happen, it made no difference.

Against her better judgment she flicked him another dark glance. He was watching her, his face expressionless, as if anticipating her making a bid for freedom.

Oh, she would make a bid for freedom. When the time was right. And if he continued to treat her as an undesirable encumbrance, she'd slash his throat before she left too.

She ignored the fact she had no dagger. Ignored the real possibility he would leave her chained the entire time they were in Camulodunon. She'd find a way to get back at him because how dared he fight his desire for her? How dared he despise the fact he lusted after her?

How dared he deny her satisfaction?

Morwyn turned her back on him in bed, her body rigid with affront at his continued distance. He hadn't even bothered procuring her a bath. Instead they had washed in a bucket of lukewarm water, and even if he had allowed her to go first, she still felt ill-cleansed.

As he extinguished the last lamp and the room plunged into darkness she allowed her muscles to slowly relax. But even that was an effort because every nerve stretched in awareness at his close proximity. The heat emanating from his body.

The chill of the space between them.

No shackle imprisoned her ankle.

She clenched her hands. Forced her breath between her teeth. This journey was testing her sanity to its outer limits. While on Mon, she'd been approached on several occasions by men wanting more than friendship. But, despite her body's need, she'd never been tempted to take them up on their offers.

Her need to scorn the Morrigan had been greater.

But now, lying in bed in the dark, all she could think of was the Gaul. How he would feel. How he would taste. And the

most despicable thing of all was she knew, deep inside, that wanting him had nothing to do with wanting to abuse her goddess's
divine gifts.

She was back in the Morrigan's sacred grove on the Isle of Mon.
The grass was sharp green, the sky vivid blue, every color so vibrant
her eyes ached. Somewhere in the back of her mind, beyond the
reach of consciousness, she knew this wasn't real. Knew it was just
another dream. But when Gawain came to her and took her hands,
relief, woven through with remorse, sliced her heart.

"I'll find the Briton king, Morwyn. And fight for our freedom
the way we should have fought, before Aeron created his cursed
spiral. Before he concealed us from the Romans." The last words
vibrated with fury. With loathing at how the Druids had been prevented from protecting their people.

No dream. This was a memory. The last time she'd seen Gawain
alive before he'd left the Isle to seek out Caratacus.

"Let me come with you." The words spilled from her lips even
though she knew his answer, as if this memory demanded to be
replayed over and over, an endless loop, despite her knowledge of
how it would all end.

His fingers tightened around hers. She could feel their strength
as if he truly stood before her and held her hands, but still ethereal wisps of precognition fluttered in her mind. Distorting the
moment. Confusing her ability to distinguish between reality and
reminiscence.

"No." He released her and stood looking down at her, as if
committing her to memory. "I need to go alone." He hesitated for
a moment as if debating his next words. "I need to get away from
you."

She watched him turn and walk away, proud and alone, and
her heart ached. No matter how she longed to leave this Isle and
join the rebels, she couldn't go with Gawain. He deserved, at least,
the right to leave on his own terms.

The sky darkened; the air chilled. Shivers raced over her arms as shadows lengthened and the trees thickened, becoming dense and impenetrable. Unformed terror gripped her, twisted her guts, sent her stumbling backward.

Run. Desperately she tried to turn, to flee, but her limbs were paralyzed, rooting her to the spot. She could do nothing but watch as the clouds rolled across the threatening sky, as thunder rumbled ominously in the distance and as a formidable mountain rose from the blackened trees.

Her heart hammered against her ribs, panicked and painful. A terrible foreboding snaked through her blood, formless yet tangible. Unknown yet terrifyingly familiar. As if she had witnessed what was to occur countless times in the past, and would continue to witness forever into eternity.

Water splashed her feet and she leaped back, breaking the paralysis, and looked down. A raging river slashed across the land, dividing her from the mountain; a river of murderous intent, tainted with scarlet.

Lungs contracted, throat closed. She jerked her gaze up and stared at the massive stone ramparts on the far mountain. Had she been here before? Was this real, or a dream? A memory her waking self had forgotten?

Or a vision of what was to come?

War cries slithered into her consciousness and her perspective instantly altered. Now she was on the mountain, behind the ramparts, looking down as the hated enemy forded the deadly river. Arrows arched across the sky, an endless torrent, but it meant nothing. Would get them nowhere. She didn't know how or why the certainty gripped her in a remorseless vise. Only that it did. Only that she needed to escape, that she needed to find someone. That she needed to *warn the others.*

She pushed her way through faceless warriors as panic mounted and sweat drenched her clammy skin. Up ahead a familiar figure came into view and relief swamped her, momentarily deadening her limbs and causing her mind to spin.

"Gawain."

He didn't hear her, continued issuing orders to another. She stumbled over fallen bodies—where had all the dead come from?—pushed others from her path. She had to reach Gawain. Had to warn him.

But no matter how fast she ran, she could get no closer to him. Always he was beyond her grasp, beyond her vocal range. She watched him briefly embrace another man before turning his back, a show of utmost trust, and fathomless fear coiled around her throat.

The faceless warrior drew his dagger and it glinted like sunlight caught in a waterfall, before he raised his arm and plunged the deadly blade into Gawain's back.

Chapter Ten

Strong arms enfolded her, held her securely against an unyielding expanse of masculine chest. Her heart thundered against her ribs, crushed her lungs, caused air to gasp from parted lips.

A dream. Just a dream. Her panicked mind repeated the mantra as Gawain fell to his knees, as his blood pooled on the ground, as his assailant vanished into the roaring throng of disoriented warriors.

And yet, as always, conviction seared her soul that this was more than a figment of her imagination. More than a random, repetitive dream. Gawain was dead, murdered by one he trusted. Murdered by one of their own, even as the enemy advanced.

A dry sob scraped her throat, and instinctively she clutched at the muscled arm that encircled her waist. "Gawain." The whisper rasped into the silence of the retreating nightmare, the darkness of the endless night. But the solid body shielding her back didn't dissolve into the fevered recesses of her mind.

Heated breath fanned across her nape, causing shivers to race over her vulnerable flesh.

"You're safe." The low voice rumbled against her ear, deep and decadent. "I've got you, Morwyn."

The lingering terror faded as awareness trickled through her brain. The Gaul held her in an intimate embrace, his hard body meshed to hers, his erection pressed securely against the small of her back.

Her breath stumbled, heart tripped and then thudded with painful intensity. Without conscious thought her fingers fanned across his forearm, and tremors of delight rippled through her blood at the abrasive texture of his skin and hair against her palm.

Firm lips drifted across the hollow where neck curved into shoulder. "You're safe," he repeated, voice husky. His arm tightened almost imperceptibly around her. "Don't be afraid."

Skin tingled beneath his questing lips. But he explored no further, for her gown obstructed his progress and he made no move to rip it from her body, to allow him unfettered access.

But still he held her. Hard against soft. Coils of desire knotted low in her belly, twisted through her womb, sent glowing tendrils spiking through her trembling sheath. Even through his tunic and her gown his cock burned her flesh, tantalizing her with promises of how thoroughly he could satisfy the clawing frustration shredding her reason.

Under pretext of stretching, she stealthily molded her bottom more firmly against his thigh, trapping his cock more securely, threading her fingers through his. Hot breath gusted across her shoulder, teeth grazed her sensitized flesh, but still he didn't act on the lust pounding between them.

His face was still buried against her shoulder and she rolled her head back, nestled her cheek against his cropped hair. It prickled, extraordinary, erotic, like nothing she had ever experienced before, and another involuntary shudder ripped through her body.

Fingers entwined, she dragged his hand up from her waist, over her belly. When she paused he continued the momentum and cradled her breast, scorching her flesh as if no fabric separated their contact.

With a harsh gasp her hand convulsed around his. She needed more than a gentle touch, more than a fleeting caress. Liquid fire scalded her veins, pooled between her thighs, arrowed through her womb. Heart thundered in her chest and echoed in her ears and she rolled over, facing him.

The room was pitch-black and she could see nothing. He held her in one arm, firm and unyielding, his hot breath fanned her face, and the hard length of his hair-roughened legs trapped hers.

Words tumbled in her mind, incoherent, bereft of pride. She clamped her lips together, bit down on her tongue. She wanted him. Needed him. But gods, she wouldn't beg him.

Instead she speared her fingers through his hair and darts of shocked pleasure radiated from her fingertips and along her arm, splintered across her shoulder. There was no length to grasp, and, far from disappointing, it was exotic. Intoxicating. As arousing as the uncompromisingly male scent of woods and foreign soap and faintest hint of horse that emanated from his heated flesh.

She dug her nails into his scalp, scraped them along his skull and across the nape of his neck. He arched into her, cock rigid and demanding against her belly, and with a rough movement pulled her gown up to her waist.

The bedcovers lay twisted around her feet and shivers burned her exposed thighs and naked bottom. She wanted to strip him, have him rip her gown from her, but she couldn't wait, couldn't articulate her demands. Instead she gripped his tunic and jerked it up. She needed him now and there was no need for words, no need for endless fore-play. No need to analyze how or why she felt this way, because it was night and it was right and if she didn't come, she would die.

Roughened fingers traced over the curve of her hip and she flung her leg over his thigh to allow him unrestricted access. He followed her soundless cue, his hand delving between her legs, dis-covering her tender lips.

She closed her eyes, breath gusted, and curled her hand around his scorching shaft. He groaned, or perhaps it was her, because never had she felt anything that promised so much.

"You're wet." His voice rasped from the dark, disembodied. Erotic. She squirmed against his probing fingers, the pressure of his thumb against her swollen clit verging on the unbearable.

Somehow she found her voice. "And you're hard." She accompanied her words by rolling her palm over his shaft, massaging his head, and thrills chased from her womb to her nipples at the moisture gathered there already.

His mouth claimed hers, unerring despite the lack of light. Internal shudders ricocheted at the ferocity, the plunder, the sheer bestial dominance as his tongue invaded, demanding her utter surrender beneath his onslaught.

Thudding pressure gained momentum low in her belly, echoing through her sensitized pussy. He was hot, unrelenting, his mouth devouring, and she returned every thrust of tongue, every graze of teeth.

And still it wasn't enough.

A growl purred in the back of her throat and she slung her leg more securely over his thigh. He dragged his hand from her wet core, gripped her rounded buttock. She wound her free arm around his back, forcing him up from the mattress where he lay on his side.

Her teeth sank into his bottom lip and he stilled. She bent her injured leg, ignoring the discomfort, and maneuvered until he raised his body sufficiently for her to slide her leg beneath him.

She smiled against his trapped lip and then flicked her tongue over the abused flesh. Finally she relinquished her hold on his erection and wrapped both arms around him, gripping his firm arse, reveling in the sensation of having him between her spread thighs.

His cock nudged her wet entrance and sparks of fire pulsed through her core. Her palms molded his tight buttocks, explored his rigid muscles. Uninhibited shivers of delight raced through her as he kneed her thighs farther apart and she dug her nails into his flesh, savage and wild, needing him to crush her, to hold her, to *claim her.*

Would she need to beg? *Could she beg?* Her lips parted, words hovered, and then he surged into her. Hot, hard and so shockingly large the air vaporized from her lungs in a startled gasp as long-unused muscles stretched to accommodate.

A strangled groan tore from his throat, echoed through the darkness. Blindly she stared up at him, wanting to see his eyes, watch his face, but all she could see was a black silhouette against the pitch of night.

For an endless moment he didn't move. Jagged breath hissed through her teeth as she forced her tense muscles to relax. He filled her so utterly, as if any sudden movement might shatter her irretrievably. But gods, it felt so good. So right. To once again feel the hardness of a man embrace her. To relish the sensation of his cock inside her, groin to groin, her thighs cradling his, her fingers clawing the taut flesh of his lower back.

He braced his weight on his elbows and pushed himself up. His hands entrapped her face, fingers splayed through her tangled hair, and the sensation of possessiveness was so erotic shivers chased over her skull, skittered along her sensitized nape.

Only the sound of erratic breath and frenzied heartbeat filled the air. He could be anyone, anyone she chose, but it had been moons since she'd wanted Gawain, and her fantasies involving Aeron had long since withered.

This was the Gaul who held her. The Gaul whose hand roughly molded the curves of her body before gripping her bottom. The Gaul whose rasping breath scorched her lips as he angled her to his complete satisfaction.

His throbbing erection dragged with torturous delight across her clit, back and forth. Slowly. Deliberately. A mindless scream of pent-up passion boiled through her mind, sizzled through her blood. *Back and forth.* She clenched her internal muscles, squeezed him tight, gasped in satisfaction at the primal growl that rumbled through his body.

Their clothes impeded her. She wanted him naked, to feel his flesh against hers, to have him suck her nipples, cradle her breasts, scrape his fingers across her belly and hips and thighs.

But all she could do was claw at his cursed tunic. Gouge his back through the rough material. And wrap her legs around his waist and suck him deep inside where time and place and tribal pride vaporized into primitive need.

Harsh pants of approaching climax filled the impenetrable black. *He could be anyone.* But he was the Gaul. And the knowledge inflamed, as much as his increased thrusts, as much as the way he grasped her hair in one hand and her arse in the other.

As much as the friction pounding between her thighs, riding her quivering pussy, teasing her swollen core to unreachable heights.

He rammed into her, pain and pleasure indeterminable, and the breath rushed from her lungs at the force of his possession. Teeth sank into the damp curve where throat met shoulder, mouth hot and wet, a knife-edge of unbearable sensation stabbing straight through the heart of her being. Liquid fire raced through her clit, speared her womb and splintered deep in her gut as his guttural roar seared the air.

He pumped into her, hot and endless, and she could scarcely move beneath his violent onslaught. Heart thundered; blood scalded; sanity quavered on the fiery precipice. And still he fucked her, as if he would never stop, and gods, she didn't want him to stop, didn't want this midnight magic to ever end.

Molten spirals coiled deep in her womb, tightening muscles, skimming across skin. She tried to hold the moment, to savor it, prolong it, but it spilled from her unbidden.

Echoes of her hoarse scream vibrated in her ears but she didn't care what he thought, didn't care that he'd know how desperately she craved this joining. Didn't care about the past or the future or the fact he was her enemy. Because everything was in this moment and in this moment they were one.

Chapter Eleven

﹡❖❖❖﹡

He collapsed on her, his face buried against her neck. His body was hard and heavy and immovable. Crushing her bones, smothering her lungs.

Strength gushed from her limbs and her legs slid from his back, falling to the bed, feeling oddly light and disconnected as if they didn't belong to her. Only by twisting her fingers into the fabric of his tunic did she prevent her arms from following. Because it felt too good, too cursed satisfying, to hold him close and feel every erratic pant of breath, every rapid thud of his heart.

A smile tugged at the corners of her mouth. His short hair tickled the side of her face, and his day-old beard scraped the tender skin of her shoulder. He felt unlike any man she had ever known before.

There had been no tender words. No artful seduction. Just rough, unpolished sex.

Languid tremors flickered through her sated channel, still filled by his impressive length. She still couldn't move her head, as his fingers were embedded in her hair, tangled around his fingers, and the sensation verged on pain.

Pleasurable pain. Another languid ripple teased her sensitized flesh. *If only they were naked.*

But she was too exhausted, too wondrously sated to voice her request. Time enough to see his body later. When dawn broke, before they needed to rise for another torturous day in the saddle.

He rose, severing their contact, and a mewl of protest escaped before she could prevent it. He cupped her face in an oddly tender gesture, fingers trailing the length of her cheek before he rolled onto his back, fingers tugging her hair as he disengaged.

She panted into the heated black. Sweat slicked her skin and her gown was unbearable but she couldn't find the strength to strip. The musky scent of sex wafted in the air and his hot seed trickled between her spread thighs.

Her eyelashes flickered as liquid satisfaction drifted through her veins. It had been a quick fuck, but she could find no fault with the outcome. Doubtless that was because it had been so long since she'd found release, but gods, the deprivation had been worth it for such savage pleasure.

Again the smile tugged at her lips and slumber beckoned. Next time the Gaul would learn that when it came to such matters, *she* liked to take charge. And there would be a next time. They wouldn't reach Camulodunon for another day or two at least, and then surely they would stay a night in the town. Plenty of time for plenty of pleasuring.

A soft sigh escaped and she slipped further along the path to oblivion. And only then did the discordant thought whisper through her mind.

She had only enjoyed this as a means of debasing the Morrigan.

Bren stirred as the first fingers of dawn eased into the room, and for a moment confusion bathed his mind. When was the last time he'd felt so relaxed, so well rested? So uncharacteristically *tranquil*?

Dark fragments of memory tumbled into place and he cracked

open one eye. Morwyn was asleep beside him, tangled hair framing her face, kiss-swollen lips slightly parted.

Desire tugged deep in his groin, hardening his already burgeoning erection. Stealthily, so as not to awaken her and have to face harsh reality, he rose onto his elbow.

She looked so peaceful when asleep. No one would guess she possessed a tongue incapable of remaining silent. Were he truly her enemy, he would have ripped the offending flesh from her mouth for voicing nothing but treason from the moment they'd met.

An odd sensation stabbed through his chest. She had to learn caution. Learn how to hide the fire in her eyes, the hate in her heart. Know that sometimes the truth could get you killed.

His gaze drifted over her disheveled hair, her rumpled gown. Lingered on the mark of possession he'd branded her with during the night, and the desire clawed deeper into his gut.

In the heated black, she'd welcomed him. But only because she had been half-asleep and half-petrified from her nightmare. And only because, in that disconnected moment of time, she'd imagined he was Gawain.

Gawain. The name scraped along his nerve endings. It was a commonplace name. It didn't mean the Gawain he'd once encountered was the same man Morwyn dreamed of. The man she'd imagined she was loving during the night.

He was under no illusions that once she was fully conscious, she'd spit in his eye rather than allow him to enjoy her again. Slowly he peeled the sheet from her legs. Her gown was twisted around her waist, revealing naked thighs. His gaze snagged on the luscious curls of her pussy, at the glimpse of plump lips, the suggestion of fresh dampness.

Chest tightened, lungs constricted. He could have her one more time before facing her fury. Lose himself in her sweet heat, hear her throaty moans of pleasure as he filled her. And maybe, once again, he'd momentarily forget the evil soaking his soul.

He trailed his fingers over the smooth flesh of her inner thighs.

She stirred, legs parting farther as if in silent invitation, and he took advantage of her vulnerability.

Sliding into her tangled curls, the scent of primal sex and sated lust drifted in the air. She was wet already, her arousal evident, and he drew in a deep breath, savoring her erotic essence.

Gently he caressed the hood of her clitoris, using her juices as lubrication, fascinated by how readily her body responded to his touch. Again she stirred, angling her hips toward him, her breath noticeably ragged. Somehow he tore his gaze from her glistening pussy to look at her face. She was still asleep, lips still parted. Dreaming, doubtless, of her absent lover.

The notion jarred. Rising, he moved between her thighs and used his knees to spread her farther for his visual delight. Pink flesh tantalized and he swallowed a groan, unwilling to wake her until he was inside her, until she was so mindless with lust she'd willingly accept their mutual completion.

He pulled at the loosened ties of her bodice with fingers that shook. Thank the gods she *was* still asleep and couldn't observe such weakness. It was only because it had been so long since he'd lain with a woman . . . discounting last night.

But last night had been swathed in velvet blackness, where they could be anyone. Now, when she opened her eyes, she would see the face of the man that caused her body to orgasm with abandoned delirium. And it wasn't Gawain.

Breath hissed between his teeth as he eased open her gown. The tightness of her bodice prevented complete exposure, but somehow it was infinitely erotic being able to allow only one full, creamy globe to escape its confines.

Her luscious nipple beckoned, proud and erect, and he sucked the rosy berry into his mouth as he increased the pressure against her blossoming core.

Languid fingers trailed through his hair. She was close to waking, close to realizing who aroused her while she slept. He cupped her mound, slid a finger into her wet cleft, knew he couldn't hold on much longer.

Releasing her succulent nipple, he angled his weight on one arm so he could watch her face. Her cheeks were flushed, lips parted, and he knew at any moment her eyes would open and desire would mutate into derision.

But not yet. He nudged her entrance with the head of his cock. So hot. So wet. Blood thundered in his veins, pounded against his temples, and, gritting his teeth against the primal groan that threatened to escape, he surged into her welcoming channel.

She contracted around him, strong and sure, ripples of pleasure that radiated along her sheath and across his straining shaft. Her body was so tight around him, an embrace so intimate the sensation of stretching her delicate flesh streaked along his invading cock and splintered his mind.

Her eyelashes flickered and her unfocused gaze meshed with his, eyes darkening with rising desire. Slowly he dragged his hand from between her thighs, over her hip, then pinched her nipple between thumb and finger. She sucked in a shocked gasp and her eyes glittered, but before she could give voice to the scalding words tumbling on her lips, he claimed her in an openmouthed kiss.

Swallowing her words of condemnation. Exploring the heat of her mouth, challenging her tongue for dominance, overriding her loathing with lust.

Her heels smashed into his arse, jerking him farther into her body, and a strangled groan filled his mind, rumbled along his throat. Her teeth sank into his tongue and pain throbbed, harshly arousing. She clawed the back of his neck, gouged his flesh, before releasing his tongue and tearing into the skin of his inner lip.

The metallic taste of blood swept through his senses, tensing his muscles. Intoxicating. Like nothing he'd experienced before. Yet like everything he'd wanted before.

He ripped his bloodied mouth from her, panted into her flushed face. She didn't look away. Didn't condemn him. Without breaking eye contact the tip of her tongue licked a drop of his blood from her lip. And then she swallowed.

It was blatantly provocative. As potent as any of his most

lascivious fantasies. Need pounded along his cock, wrapped merciless fingers around his iron-hard balls. Breath gusted and he clung grimly to the edge of sanity. He would prolong this moment. Stoke their passion. Fuck her until all thought of vengeance incinerated within her mind. Until no man existed but him.

"Stop thinking, Gaul." Her voice rasped in the sex-drenched air, and she followed her words by wrapping her legs around his waist in a brutal vise.

But he was beyond thinking. Couldn't even form the words to respond to her taunt, because she clenched her muscles around him in a grip so tight stars exploded behind his eyes.

"Fuck." The tortured word fell from his lips as he struggled to maintain control. But control slipped from his grasp because the only grasp his mind could comprehend was the one Morwyn controlled around his throbbing cock.

"Yes." She dug her fingers into his scalp. "That's right, Gaul."

Involuntarily he rammed into her, unable to stop the primal imperative scorching his blood, erasing his reason. There was only this woman beneath him. This woman's heat engulfing him. *Consuming him.*

He braced his weight on both hands, to give better leverage. She gasped as he changed the angle of his penetration and her hands slipped from his head, slid over his back and gripped his backside. Gods, he couldn't hold on. He couldn't—

Her finger delved into his crevice and even the most basic of thought processes shattered. Sensation flooded through his body, radiating from his tight balls, thundering along his rigid shaft, hammering her to the mattress with every mindless, ecstatic thrust.

Dimly, beyond the pounding beat of his heart and blood, beyond the exquisite release pumping from his cock, he heard Morwyn's choked gasps. Felt her nails score his backside, her legs clamp even more firmly around him.

Felt her climax splinter through her as if it were his own, an indescribable melding of scorching heat and tangled limbs.

Completion.

This time he didn't collapse onto her. This time he panted into her face as delicious spasms, the uninhibited aftereffects of her orgasm, claimed her.

Claimed him.

And in that moment a rare certainty formed in his mind. This was more than a simple, fleeting fuck. More than a casual slaking of lust. Languid heat slid through his veins, bathed his thoughts, cradled his battered soul.

She looked up at him, eyes regaining focus. Instinctively he tensed, and the illusory moment of peace, of somehow *belonging*, shattered. Wrenching his barriers back in place, he waited for her venom. Her denials.

"And a good morn to you too, Gaul." Her voice was ragged. Her words unexpectedly civil. His eyes narrowed, waiting for the punch. Waiting for her to realize who it was invading her body. Who had brought her such abandoned pleasure.

Instead her fingers trailed a languid path down his thighs, and against his better inclinations his cock appreciated the gesture. Morwyn smiled, as if his reaction was entirely satisfactory.

"You don't say much, do you?"

Did she require an answer? After a moment when she continued to stare at him as if she did, indeed, require a response, he managed to locate his voice.

"What would you have me say?"

Amusement flashed over her face and shock speared through his chest. He had to be mistaken. Why would Morwyn be amused by this situation? He had expected anger that he'd taken advantage of her. Or perhaps denial that she'd enjoyed their coupling.

Acidic words, maybe even her knuckles embedded into his face.

Anything, in truth, but the extraordinary way she was currently behaving.

"Oh, I don't know." Her nails dug into the corded muscle of his lower thighs. "Perhaps how I was the best fuck you've had this moon? That would do for a start."

Since she was the first woman he'd had in countless months,

that went without saying. Somehow he knew that answer wouldn't suffice.

"Why? Would you believe me?" And was he really conducting a conversation while still impaled within her welcoming body?

It was surreal. Took him back to a time when life was for living, not merely surviving.

A familiar ache wound its way through his guts, but for the first time tempered by—by what? He couldn't fathom. Knew only that the ache was not as all-consuming. That he didn't feel unclean and despicable the way he usually did after laying with a woman.

"That," Morwyn said, pulling him abruptly back to the present, "would depend upon how sincerely you said the words."

He shifted his weight and her legs slid from his back to thump onto the mattress. But still they remained joined.

There was no time for this interlude. They had to get back in the saddle. Yet he couldn't bring himself to sever this strange, tenuous connection. He'd enjoy this tranquil moment for a little longer, at least.

"Morwyn." Bracing his weight on one arm, he cradled her face with his free hand. Wasn't sure why. It just felt right. "You're the best fuck I've had for a long time."

The faintest trace of a smile lifted her lips. "Passably sincere. You're forgiven."

"And what of me?" Why had he asked her that? *Gawain* thudded through his mind. Bren had no desire to be compared—and unfavorably—with her absent lover.

Gods, let the Gawain of Morwyn's dreams not be the man Bren had so violently crossed paths with.

"You?" Morwyn's eyebrows rose as if the question astonished her almost as much as it did him. Then her dark eyes glittered, as if with suppressed mirth. *But that couldn't be so* . . . "Let me think." She glanced at the ceiling as if contemplating the matter, and a thread of disbelief coiled in his belly as he finally understood.

She was flirting with him. *Again.* And again, it had taken him too long to recognize. Was he really so disconnected from normalcy?

Once again she dug her nails into his flesh, as if aware his attention had momentarily scattered. "Your performance," she said,
as if addressing a slave who had been ordered to entertain her,
"was . . . passably adequate."

Their eyes clashed, and an unfamiliar congestion curdled deep
within his chest. It took a moment to realize the sensation was that
of suppressed laughter.

His lips twitched, but the laughter remained buried within the
cavern of his withered soul. "Merely adequate?"

"Doubtless you'll improve with practice."

The laugh caught him unawares, echoed around the room. A
strange, unfamiliar sound. Morwyn smirked up at him, clearly
well satisfied by his response.

He twisted her hair around his fingers and gently tugged. Just
enough to make her wince.

"And do I need plenty of practice?" An inane question that
meant nothing. He was wasting time, was further delaying his
arrival in Camulodunon. But still he waited for her reply.

The tip of her tongue teased the seam of her lips in a slow, sensual caress. The need to remain in bed with her, to forget about his
duty to king and country, thudded in his brain with treacherous
insistence.

"Yes." Her husky voice curled around his senses. "And next
time you can start by stripping for my pleasure."

He kissed her, harsh and swift, before pushing himself upright
and out of her. Before he succumbed to his desires and took her
again, and risked Roman investigation into the details of his
delayed arrival when he finally reached Camulodunon.

"Next time," he said as he watched the annoyed frown flicker
over her face, "you will strip for *my* pleasure, Morwyn." Because
there was no way he'd ever strip naked before her. Not unless they
were both blinded by the night, and perhaps . . . not even then.

Chapter Twelve

Morwyn stifled a groan as the Gaul once again hauled her up onto the saddle. While her bruised muscles from the brief and humiliating battle in the forest were now healing, other muscles twinged in protest.

She smothered a smile as she attempted to find a more comfortable position. She'd been so long without a man her body was as sore and her pussy as tender as if this morn had been her first time.

"Are you ready?" There was a thread of concern in his voice, despite the gruff tone. She wondered if he even realized such emotion had shown through.

"I'd much rather spend the day in more leisurely pursuits." She tossed him a glance over her shoulder. And caught an odd expression on his face before it was instantly masked by his usual implacability. Truly, this Gaul was an enigma. "But since you've made it very clear that isn't an option, I'm not sure why you asked the question."

His incredible green eyes flickered as if he was unable to completely conceal his emotions from her after all. It was also

obvious he had no idea of such vulnerability in his tough mercenary shell.

She waited while he processed her comment. While he struggled to ascertain whether she was being serious or, yet again, was
merely playing with him.

Why she kept succumbing to the urge to flirt with him was
something she couldn't quite understand. But since it passed the
time, why shouldn't she?

It didn't mean she was beginning to like him. But his inad-
equate social skills intrigued her. It was . . . *amusing* to watch him
attempt to decipher the meaning behind her remarks.

"It's not an option because I have time constraints." His jaw
tensed for a moment as if unsure whether to continue. "I meant—
are you all right?"

Her nipple still tingled from where he'd suckled her earlier. Her
thighs ached and her pussy was deliciously sensitive. She felt thoroughly fucked and thoroughly satisfied, and the longer she gazed
into his hypnotic eyes, the more she wanted to drag him behind a
convenient bush and pin him to the ground.

"I'd prefer to have bathed this morning." And while she hoped
he thought she referred to a river or spring, in truth she wouldn't
have complained if he'd procured her another Roman tub. Instead,
it had been another bucket. Scarcely satisfactory.

In more ways than the obvious. Since once again, the Gaul hadn't
removed his tunic. Tonight, she intended that would be rectified.

"Tonight." He urged the horse forward onto the Roman road
and she gripped the padded edge of the saddle in readiness. But
he didn't dig his spurs in right away. "You can experience the full
Roman bathing ritual."

An illicit spark of excitement flared deep in her chest. She
hoped it hadn't shown on her face because she'd rather tear out her
tongue than admit such foreign decadence appealed.

"If you insist on inflicting such torture, then I have no choice."

"And if I believed such ritual would be so torturous, I wouldn't
inflict it upon you."

She gave a disdainful sniff and cursed their awkward position. Her neck had started to ache. She'd have to break eye contact soon.

"You have no problem inflicting any number of tortures upon me." She refrained from rubbing the straining tendons in her neck. She didn't want any movement to distract him from this conversation.

His lip twitched in a way that was becoming familiar. Fascinated at how his hard face softened, she stared at him, wondering why he found it so difficult to laugh. As if he considered it a weakness. "How many days until we reach Camulodunon?" *How many nights did they have before she left him in Camulodunon?*

The relaxing of his features might have been a fantasy, so instantly did the usual harsh, uncompromising visage return.

"We arrive in Camulodunon later this day." And then he dug his spurs in.

Morwyn stared straight ahead, unseeing, blood heating her cheeks. He hadn't noticed her disappointment. Of that she was convinced.

But why was she disappointed? Her objective had always been to reach Camulodunon and find Carys. She wanted to see Carys again. Wanted to leave the Gaul. To show him she was no slave to be hauled around the country at his slightest whim.

Except she hadn't expected the opportunity to leave him would be quite so *soon*.

But what difference would another day make? She'd achieved her goal of multiple orgasms with the enemy. The Morrigan would surely be screeching at her sacred crossroad, cursing Morwyn for her blasphemy. She didn't need any more time with the Gaul.

And yet the sordid truth echoed in her mind. She wanted to have him again.

The sun was directly overhead when they finally reached Camulodunon. It was clearly a popular destination for merchants and traders, with travelers on foot and horseback both entering and leaving the shockingly large settlement. An arch proclaimed entrance to the Roman town but from this distance Morwyn couldn't see the point of it. After all, there were no ramparts protecting the inhabitants from attack necessitating such purpose-built entry.

As they approached the massive two portal arches, she realized it had obviously been constructed to commemorate the Roman conquest, and the Gaul slowed to a sedate walk.

Despite not wanting to be affected by anything that declared victory so blatantly, she couldn't help the thread of awe that snaked through her. It was craftsmanship such as she'd never seen before. Certainly there was nothing to compare in Cymru, where the Romans had ravished her land in order to construct their hated fortifications.

"Impressed?" The Gaul's breath brushed against her ear. He didn't sound either impressed or repelled. To her disbelief arousal shivered through her at the sound of his voice. It was the first time he'd spoken since they'd left this morn.

But then, she hadn't attempted to engage him in conversation. She'd been too distracted by her own tangled thoughts to risk talking. In case she said something that inadvertently gave away how much she still *wanted* him.

She concentrated on the freestanding arch before them. It was flanked by narrow foot passages, and the whole was set between projecting quadrant-shaped guard chambers. They, at least, were familiar. As were the foreign brick-and-mortar buildings beyond it.

A fortification. And yet, somehow, quite different from those she'd seen in Cymru.

Impressed? Certainly, if she had to be brutally honest, the architecture itself was impressive. But *that* was entirely different.

"By coarse Roman arrogance?" She sniffed and frowned as she caught sight of an extensive Latin inscription carved onto the stone arch. Only the last few words penetrated her outraged mind.

"... *brought the barbarian peoples across the Ocean under the authority of the Roman people.*"

The Romans had the nerve to call *them* barbarians?

Perhaps, in the past, she'd been guilty of considering the Britons as borderline barbarians. But compared to their common enemy, such distinctions were nothing. While they remained under the yoke of Rome, she was prepared to consider Britain an extension of Cymru.

And the only barbarians in the land were those who willingly served the depraved Roman Emperor.

Such as the Gaul, whose thighs cradled hers and whose arms grazed her waist. The man who had rescued her from his despicable countrymen in the forest, who took her insults without physical retaliation. The man who both fascinated and infuriated her in ways she'd never before imagined.

Because she had never before been a captive of the enemy. Or been victim to such unquenchable lust whenever she so much as thought of a man.

She loathed all Romans on principle and their spineless mercenaries by extension. Yet the longer she remained in this Gaul's company, the harder it was to remember all the reasons why she couldn't allow her defenses to crumble.

Irritated, she deliberately looked over her shoulder at the receding triumphal arch. *That* was the reason. If she forgot, for even one moment, who he was, she risked losing her identity and pride. As Britain had lost hers.

"Is this a fortification or settlement?" She shot the Gaul a dark glance, blaming him entirely for her ignorance. The buildings were regimented, nothing like the sprawling hill forts she was used to, but something was oddly amiss.

He didn't return her accusatory glare. "They didn't need a military base here. They needed a colonia." For a moment she imagined she saw contempt gleam in his mesmeric green eyes, but surely that was only a projection of her own affront?

"A colonia?" She'd heard Camulodunon had been secured by the Romans and turned into a prosperous town, but her notion of what exactly comprised a Roman town was hazy. Somehow she'd imagined a larger version of the settlements that sprung up around the fortifications in Cymru.

But this town wasn't a ramshackle combination of tents and huts and timber. It had been built with purpose in the famed Roman design.

He dismounted and helped her to the ground. His hand lingered longer than necessary at her waist before he released her. "The barracks were converted into houses for veterans. They call this their capital city of Britannia."

Morwyn narrowed her eyes as she surveyed the bustling market with its noisy livestock, gaudy trinkets and strange exotic imports. Britons and Romans mingled freely, and the scents of animals, sweat and indecipherable spices invaded her senses.

Camulodunon. Ancient tribal settlement of the disposed Caratacus who now defied the might of the Eagle in the far west, among the mountains and forests of her beloved Cymru.

She followed him without comment as they skirted the market and piles of steaming dung and headed down a side road. No dusty trails for the Romans. Even in their towns they couldn't abandon their love of road-building.

They came to an inn, and as the Gaul negotiated room and horse hire, Morwyn glanced at the other buildings. They appeared to sell everything from food to sex.

Wherever Carys was, it wasn't here. Her Roman would have installed her in far statelier surroundings, as befit her status. But with such a large town to search, where was she to begin?

"The innkeeper will show you to our room." The Gaul was staring at her and she blinked back her focus, hoping he hadn't guessed the direction of her thoughts. "You can eat in there, away from prying eyes."

She didn't care about prying eyes. Although, curse the gods, did her insides have to tighten with anticipation at the thought of being alone with the Gaul again so soon?

"Very well." Why deny she was hungry, and not just for food? But she certainly wasn't going to let him know that, not yet. Not until they shut the door on the rest of the world.

After all, there was plenty of time to find Carys. Afterward.

She stepped toward the innkeeper. The Gaul didn't move.

"I'll meet you back here later."

She froze and turned to look at him. "You're not coming with me?"

"I've business to conduct." His gaze scalded her. A wordless promise of what that night would bring.

Except she wouldn't be there that night.

Her heart thudded against her ribs, an oddly slow, echoing beat, as if it were disconnected from the rest of her body. She knew she had to tear her eyes from him, knew she had to make a careless response. Knew she had to alleviate any lingering suspicion he might harbor that she would escape as soon as he turned his back.

But she couldn't. Because a despicable, treacherous slither of her soul didn't want to escape. Not yet. She wanted another night with him. Just one more night. That was all. And then she could walk out of his life without a backward glance, without a second's hesitation.

Without a breath of regret.

"Can't it wait until the morn?" Curse her tongue, had she truly said that aloud? In an effort to appear nonchalant she shrugged and pretended not to notice the dagger-sharp interest that flared in his eyes. "You need to eat too, after all."

"I'll return as soon as I can." He paused, as if debating whether to continue. "We leave for Cymru at daybreak."

Subconsciously she acknowledged his use of the term *Cymru* rather than the Roman *Cambria*. But mainly she acknowledged that if she didn't take this chance to escape, she wouldn't receive a second. His military business was obviously fleeting, and would be completed this day.

She had no choice. It was now. Or never.

"Good." Her smile felt brittle, unconvincing, and so she looked away from him toward the inn. "This heathen town sickens me."

Despite her best intentions she glanced back at him and caught the familiar tug of his lips, as if he fought against a smile. Why would he smile at her deliberate insult?

He closed the distance between them and the breath tightened in her chest, constricting and exhilarating. Gods, it was as well they would spend no more time together if every time he drew near, her body betrayed her so blatantly.

"Here." His voice was husky and for one insane moment she thought he was going to kiss her. Here, in public. And she wanted him to because then, in her mind, she could pretend it was a farewell.

Instead he pulled her medicine bag from his pack and handed it to her. For a moment she stated at it, uncomprehending. He'd taken it from her because he didn't trust her not to poison him. Did this gesture mean that now he *did* trust her?

He let out an impatient breath as if her non-reaction irritated. "You need this, Morwyn. For your womanly requirements."

She dragged her gaze from the bag to stare into his face. He was frowning and looked harsh, uncompromising, as if the slightest wrong word from her would cause him to cut her throat.

Slowly she held out her hand and he dropped the embroidered loop over her palm. He considered her his captive. Had tethered her like a slave. And yet he was returning fundamental power to her, by giving her the means to control her own body and destiny.

Slaves had no such rights. And she knew, from observation and rumor, that Roman men had long ago stripped their women of all primal feminine knowledge—if, indeed, they had ever possessed it.

Her Gaul worked for the enemy. But he hadn't embraced all of their twisted culture. An uncomfortable obstruction closed her throat, as if ancient grief choked her and she couldn't think why his gesture touched her so profoundly.

After all, she didn't need the contents of her bag. Carys could give her what she required in order to cleanse her womb of her Gaul's seed.

"Thank you." Her voice was as husky as his. His green eyes entranced, as they had the first time she'd seen him. Somehow she knew that, no matter how many summers or winters she saw, she would never forget the hypnotic shade of his eyes.

His stone-carved expression softened by an almost infinitesimal degree. So slight she wondered if anyone else could even notice.

"This doesn't mean I trust you not to attempt to poison my food." His voice was low, for her ears only, and again the corner of his mouth quirked as if attempting to smile.

She forced her lips to curve. It was far harder than it should have been. "Oh, there's no fear of that, Gaul. We're still days from Cymru. I've no desire to be stranded so far from home."

This time, for one brief breath-stealing moment, he flashed her a true smile, and again she was staggered by how much younger, how much less battle weary, he looked.

She doubted he was any older than her. And somehow, inexplicably, that realization caused the dull knot in the pit of her stomach to tighten.

"Then I'm safe for another few days." He turned to leave, then suddenly faced her once again and cradled her jaw in a fleeting, tender gesture before swinging on his heel.

A ragged gasp tore from her lips and she hugged her waist as she watched her Gaul disappear around the corner.

The thought lingered, probed deep into her mind, worried around the edges of her consciousness.

Her Gaul.

A shiver trickled along her spine, caused the hairs on her arms to rise in disbelief. Since when had she started to think of him as *her* Gaul?

Chapter Thirteen

Morwyn opened the door of the bedroom and glanced along the deserted hallway. She'd half wondered whether the innkeeper had been instructed to lock her up, but obviously not. Perhaps, then, he'd been ordered not to allow her to leave the inn on her own?

She would soon find out.

Heart thudding, although she wasn't sure whether through anticipation at the prospect of escape or regret at betraying the Gaul's trust, she slung her medicine bag over one shoulder and pack over the other and left the inn without being accosted.

And how absurd to feel she was betraying his trust. He had abducted her. He had no right to keep her against her will, and she had every right to walk out on him at the first opportunity.

Her fingers strayed to her bag. Somehow, the simple fact he'd given it back to her . . . changed things. She couldn't quite work out why, just that she no longer felt entirely justified at deserting him.

She smothered a groan at her jumbled thoughts and glanced over her shoulder. She wasn't deserting him. The sooner she found

Carys and they formulated plans to return to Cymru and join the
rebellion, the sooner this uncomfortable sensation of *loss* would
pass.

But she couldn't entirely ignore the realization that she would
have felt so much better if the Gaul had told the innkeeper to keep
her a prisoner. If, instead of simply walking out of the inn, she'd
needed to use subterfuge and cunning.

With a deep breath she straightened her shoulders, tilted her
jaw and marched toward the market. She'd take a quick look
around the town first, take stock of the populace, before deciding
whom to approach with her inquiry.

Carys was a distinctive-looking woman. Morwyn didn't have
any doubt she'd soon find someone who could direct her to her
friend's whereabouts.

Morwyn stared up at the monstrous temple that dominated this
entire sector of the town. It sat on a podium, twenty sweeping
steps above where she stood, a heathen display of columns and
arches and vulgar statuary.

She expelled a shaky breath and wiped her hand across her
sweaty brow. She'd been wandering around the town for too long
already, and was no closer to deciding whom she could approach
for information.

Her idea of asking a Celtic elder had come to nothing, since she
hadn't found any. Were they all in hiding from the conquerors? Or
had they been slaughtered?

A group of Roman men, dressed in long white togas, strolled
past. Would they know of Carys? Her lover had been a centurion,
but rumor insisted he'd been promoted to the senatorial ranks.

She didn't fully understand the complexities of the Roman military, but did know her friend's lover possessed power. It was very
likely these men would know his name. But even if she could bring
herself to speak to them, she was under no illusion as to how she'd
be treated.

Gods. Why had she imagined it would be a simple task to track Carys down? In the forest she'd thought Camulodunon would be just a slightly larger version of the settlements she was used to. A place where, with her connections, anyone could be found. But she was no longer in Cymru where her status ensured her questions would be answered with respect.

And this was getting her nowhere. She'd go back to the second, far larger, marketplace she'd found, the one next to this offensive temple, and make discreet inquiries of the stallholders. She hadn't spoken to any of them before because they were all dressed as Romans, but now that she thought about it, how likely was it that they were?

Perhaps they merely dressed that way, in order not to draw attention to themselves. And she supposed she could understand that. Since leaving the tavern she'd been subject to countless sideway glances. Even a few lecherous gropes from lewd-mouthed bastards that she'd swiftly taken care of.

A pity she didn't still have her dagger. What would her Gaul do with her dagger now she had left him? Sell it? Or would he keep it as a memento of their fleeting night together?

"Mistress Morwyn?"

The breathy whisper penetrated her mind, the words so utterly unexpected that for a moment she remained frozen to the spot. Who would address her in such a manner so far from home?

"Is—is that you, mistress?" Now the voice quavered, as if afraid it had made a fatal error.

Slowly she turned. A dark-haired Celtic girl, perhaps sixteen or seventeen summers, gazed at her with a tentative smile. A smile that inexplicably wavered, only to be replaced by clear horror.

Morwyn ignored the urge to step back, because despite the girl's strange behavior there was something vaguely familiar about her. "Yes, I'm Morwyn." She smiled in an attempt to alleviate the girl's distress. "You know me?"

The girl swallowed and visibly attempted to collect her scattered senses. "Yes, mistress. From Cymru. You're the chosen acolyte of the Morrigan herself."

Morwyn's smile began to ache. "Yes." But no longer. "What's your name? What are you doing here?" And more important, did she know of Carys's whereabouts?

"I'm Branwen." She blinked a couple of times, as if trying to refocus. Gods, what was the matter with the girl? "I live here with my grandfather and the Lady Carys."

"Carys?" Morwyn gripped Branwen's shoulders, excitement pumping through her blood. "You must take me to her instantly, Branwen. Can you do that?"

Branwen gave her an odd look, as if she couldn't understand her urgency. "But of course, mistress. That's why I spoke to you. Carys is just back there—in the forum."

Bren waited with mounting impatience in the antechamber of the basilica. The building, constructed under the pretext of allowing the local tribal aristocracies to be responsible for their own administration and decision-making, in reality was little more than a base for the military stronghold.

He ignored the Celtic civilians who drifted through the chamber. The traitors who embraced the enemy way of life and coveted both prestige and social advancement through Roman bureaucracy. While the people they allegedly served choked on the yoke of enslavement.

When freedom swept the land, their collusion would not go unpunished.

A minor official strutted across the mosaic floor and looked at Bren as if he were a cockroach. "The Tribunus Laticlavius will see you now." He jerked his head to indicate where Bren should go.

Without deigning to respond, Bren approached the half-opened door. Tribunus Laticlavius. A derisory laugh rattled inside his brain. The Romans set such stock by their victories and triumphs and yet they thought nothing of appointing a raw boy, who knew nothing of the bloody reality of war, into a position of such potential power.

Based solely on his family connections and blood.

The Roman, dressed in a white tunic with a wide purple stripe to denote his senatorial rank, had his back to Bren. Hands braced on the edge of his desk, he was apparently studying detailed cartographies.

"Sir." It wasn't said from respect. Only to inform the Roman he was no longer alone in the room. The Tribunus straightened, rolled up his maps and turned.

Bren scarcely managed to keep his expression blank as shock punched him in the gut. This was no green boy, but a full-grown man. Warrior hard, horrifically battle scarred, and with piercing blue eyes that caused eerie shivers of recognition to scuttle along his spine.

Taut silence screeched between them, as if the Roman recognized him too.

But how? From where? Bren couldn't place him. Didn't even recognize the face, and those injuries weren't the kind a man would forget, no matter how much he wanted to.

"Dunmacos," the Roman said.

And in that moment, he knew.

Three years ago, within weeks of assuming this cursed identity, Bren had been assigned to a Legion in Gaul. Still reeling from the orgy of slaughter and the quagmire of blood that he'd so recently escaped, it had been a bitter release to use Dunmacos's chilling reputation as an outlet for his rage. For months he'd reacted with crippling ferocity to the slightest insult, the merest hint of disrespect among the other auxiliaries. Until there wasn't the faintest doubt in even the most suspicious mind that he was who he claimed to be.

And this Roman, Tiberius Valerius Maximus, had been a centurion.

But his face hadn't been disfigured back then. And these scars weren't recent. They looked ancient, weathered. Similar to burns, but not. It looked as if the man had been roasted alive and yet somehow survived.

What the fuck had happened?

Bren gave a sharp nod and handed over the dispatch. The Roman continued to stare at him as he broke the seal Caratacus's aged scholar had painstakingly repaired, as if he recalled every violent incident Bren had instigated during the brief months they'd shared the same garrison.

Let him recall. Officially Bren had never bloodied so much as a Roman nose during that tour of duty. And the ones he'd killed were untraceable. Combined with Dunmacos's past, Bren's conduct at that time had ensured him of the utmost respect and trust any Roman aristocrat would bestow upon a foreigner.

Finally the Tribunus lowered his eyes to the dispatch. His expression remained carved in stone as he read how more troops were required by the Legion in the West. How the ambushes and mobile tactics of the displaced Briton king were far more than a mere irritation; how they now ate into the moral fiber of the legionaries on the front line.

This was all the proof the insurgents needed to know their strategies were working. They could defeat the enemy and emerge victorious, no matter how overwhelming the odds appeared.

The Roman looked at him. Bren kept his expression as unreadable as his enemy's.

"My response will be ready later this day. Remain within sight of the basilica."

It was a dismissal. "Sir." And that was perfunctory. A meaningless word to end their confrontation, and Bren turned and marched out of the Tribunus's presence.

Once outside he sucked in a deep breath and glanced toward the forum that separated the basilica from the gaudy temple erected in honor of the Emperor Claudius. If time permitted, he'd bring Morwyn there after receiving the dispatch. It was nothing like the markets she would be used to from Cymru.

Thinking of Morwyn caused a spear of heat deep in his gut. Lust he recognized, heightening his senses and stirring his cock.

Yet there was something else, something less easy to explain. Something that lingered like a candle's flame in the belly of a cave; unexpected and unwanted.

Sex was all he and Morwyn shared. As soon as they returned to her homeland she would make a bid for freedom. And unless he intended to shackle her like a slave, he'd have no choice but to let her go.

She wasn't the type to suffer slavery, even if he was inclined to inflict such upon her. She wouldn't stay with him voluntarily. And he would never ask such of her anyway.

Irritated by the trail of his thoughts, he caught sight of the public baths opposite the basilica. He could do with a thorough cleanse. And there was no better place in which to glean unofficial information than from careless gossip and unwary confidences exchanged while the noble citizens of this Roman colonia relaxed their pampered bodies.

Morwyn's heart thudded high in her chest as she followed Branwen into the forum.

"Did Carys send you after me?" But why hadn't her friend followed herself? Alarm streaked through her. Had Carys's precious Roman incapacitated her in some way?

"No." Branwen glanced at her, then looked hastily away. "She didn't see you. I didn't say anything to her in case I was mistaken."

"So she's well?" Visions of Carys immobilized by fractured legs or fettered by irons faded.

Again Branwen glanced at her, but this time a smile transfigured her face. "Oh yes, mistress. She's very well. Glowing."

For some reason the knowledge that Carys was *glowing*—what a strange choice of word—didn't entirely please her. Of course she wanted her friend to be happy. But it sounded as if she was utterly contented, and how could that be when she was isolated from her people, so far from everyone who loved her?

And then Morwyn caught sight of her, sitting on a stone bench in the shade of a forlorn-looking tree, and her thoughts scattered as emotion choked her throat.

Carys, the girl she'd grown up with, loved as dearly as a younger sister. The one Cerridwen, the goddess of wisdom, had chosen at the hour of her birth. The woman whose friendship she'd missed so acutely from the day they had parted.

"Carys," Branwen said as they approached the bench, and Morwyn fleetingly wondered at her lack of respect. Carys was their princess, as well as a powerful Druid—even if she hadn't completed all her training before their world had shattered. Why would a peasant girl address her so intimately?

And then, between one heartbeat and the next, in the moment as Carys turned to look at them, Morwyn registered the long white gown she wore.

Disbelief curdled her belly, shivered through her blood. Carys was dressed as a Roman matron.

"Morwyn?" Carys rose from the bench, wonderment etched on her beloved features.

The Morrigan preserve them. The prayer slipped through her shocked mind before she could prevent it, but she lacked the strength to recant. Because Carys was *pregnant.*

Words lodged in Morwyn's throat; confusion paralyzed her brain. Carys flung her arms around her, held her close. As close as her distended womb would allow. And still she couldn't unlock her tongue.

"I can't believe you're here." Carys sniffed against her throat, as if she was perilously close to tears. Of their own volition Morwyn's arms wrapped around Carys, seeking as much as giving comfort, and as if in response, the babe kicked hard against Morwyn's belly.

Carys laughed, a watery sound, and pulled back, still clinging to Morwyn's arms. And then her smile faded.

"Sweet Cerridwen." Tenderly she ran a finger along Morwyn's face. "How did this happen? Where else are you injured?"

Her face. She had almost forgotten. "There was a minor skirmish, nothing to concern yourself with." She glanced at Branwen and finally understood the reason for the girl's scandalized expression. "Rest assured I spilled the guts of at least one of the murderous dogs."

Carys shook her head and took Morwyn's hands. "It's so good to see you, Morwyn. But how did you get here? Is Gawain with you?"

Familiar pain sliced through her heart at the mention of his name. "No." She couldn't tell Carys about Gawain. Not yet. Her gaze slipped to Carys's belly and dull rage thudded through her mind. Already the Roman was using her as his broodmare. How could Carys bear to stay with a man who so callously disregarded her rights?

Only her long golden hair remained the same as it had always been. Braided, and threaded through with tiny, glittering jewels.

Carys tugged her down to the bench and continued to hold her hands, as if she would never let go. "You came alone?" A frown creased her brow. "Through occupied Britain? But how—"

Morwyn squeezed Carys's fingers and shot a glance at Branwen, who had retreated to give them sufficient privacy. "I'm here, Carys. That's all that matters. It's you I'm worried about."

Carys smiled, clearly confused. "You've no cause to worry. I've been teaching Branwen the sacred knowledge of Cerridwen. She's a fast learner, Morwyn. But now you're here I have no fear of the birth at all."

Morwyn stared into Carys's bicolored eyes, shock rendering her momentarily mute. Had she understood correctly? Surely she was mistaken.

"You're teaching Branwen—*what*?"

Carys flicked her a haughty glance, one she knew so well. And despite the circumstances relief rolled through her. No matter what the Roman had done to her since that night Aeron had attempted to obliterate their people, he hadn't managed to crush her fierce pride.

"I'm teaching her all I know." Yet there was a thread of defiance in the regal tone, as if Carys wasn't entirely sure of the propriety of her actions. "What would you have me do, Morwyn? Keep my knowledge to myself? What good is that?"

"But she isn't a Druid." Their ways were sacrosanct. Their knowledge couldn't be shared with just anyone. It was passed down from Druid to acolyte, a training that began in childhood and continued for twenty summers.

"No." There was a trace of bitterness in Carys's voice now. "As far as I'm aware, I'm the only Druid in Camulodunon. And even I was only halfway through my training. Should I allow all I know to die with me, Morwyn?"

Involuntarily Morwyn glanced at Carys's swollen belly. "You aren't going to die, Carys."

Carys tugged on her hands in an impatient gesture. "Of course I'm not going to die during childbirth, Morwyn. I plan on having many children and yes, I intend to teach them all I know. But that's not enough. Don't you see? That just won't be *enough*."

The rage resurfaced, obliterating even the shocking revelation that Carys was sharing her sacred secrets with an outsider. "Many children? Is that all you are to him? A convenience to produce numerous heirs for *Rome*?"

Silence vibrated between them and for one fleeting moment Morwyn was reminded of the last time she'd insulted the Roman. The look on Carys's face was identical to that time in the sacred mound, when Morwyn had drawn her dagger to plunge through the Roman's heart.

But this time Carys didn't smash her fist into her jaw. This time she took a deep breath and exhaled slowly between her lips.

"You know Maximus isn't like that."

Curse the gods. "He's a Roman, Carys. All they care about is producing sons for their corrupt Empire."

Carys took Morwyn's hand and pressed it against her belly, and she felt the babe move, as if distressed by the tone of their voices. A painful lump lodged in her throat. A babe was still a babe, no matter its parentage. And with Carys as his mother, at least he would learn there were two sides to every bloodied conquest.

"Maximus already loves our daughter." Carys's voice was soft. "And it's I who want a dozen children, not him. He'd be happy enough with one, Morwyn. With this one. *Our daughter.*"

She wanted to refute the words. Tell Carys she was wrong. But deep in her heart, she knew Carys was right.

Maximus, the Roman who had stolen her beloved's friend's heart, wasn't like other Romans. Morwyn had witnessed his devotion to Carys as Aeron had tortured him and attempted to subjugate them all to his twisted will. And she had seen the love in his eyes as they had said their farewells.

He would defend Carys's rights to the death.

She snatched her hands free, wound her arms around her waist. "If he respects you as you deserve, then why make you dress like a weak-minded Roman woman?"

Pain flickered across Carys's face. "He doesn't. This is my choice."

Her fingernails dug into the palms of her hands but it did nothing to calm her simmering temper. "Why? Because you're ashamed of your Druidic heritage?"

She braced herself for Carys's response. But instead of vitriol, she sighed and slumped against the trunk of the tree as if exhausted.

"You're still angry with me for leaving."

Morwyn rounded on her, infuriated she would twist her words and change the focus of their discussion. "Of course I'm not. This has nothing to do with you leaving." And as the words fell from her lips, she knew she lied.

She had never forgiven Carys for falling in love with the enemy. For choosing him above her people.

Had never forgiven her for leaving.

"Maximus has never asked me to adopt any of his ways." Carys flicked her a sideways glance. "But he's a Tribunus. I made the decision to dress as a Roman in public purely to reduce speculation and gossip that might harm his career. It doesn't *mean* anything."

"So you subjugate yourself for the sake of your husband's *career*." Morwyn could scarcely speak for the repugnance clogging her chest.

"No." Carys sounded oddly wistful. "It's a compromise, Morwyn. The less attention I draw in public, the more I can accomplish in private."

Unable to remain still, Morwyn leaped to her feet and paced the length of the stone bench, every step refueling her sense of injustice.

"You shouldn't have to compromise."

"We all live with compromise now." Carys suddenly sounded very old and very wise, and shivers crawled over Morwyn's arms. In that moment, Carys reminded her of their ancient queen, Druantia, whom Aeron had murdered.

She stopped her agitated pacing and stared down at her fellow Druid.

"I'd never compromise my integrity for a man."

Carys's right hand caressed her belly, as if she were comforting her unborn child.

"Nor I." Then she looked straight in Morwyn's eyes, as if daring her to doubt her word. "But I'd do anything to protect Maximus and our babe."

Chapter Fourteen

❖

Bren sat in the corner of the hot room as steam hissed up from the floor and obscured the other inhabitants. During exercising he'd overheard some interesting, if ultimately unbelievable, speculation regarding the Tribunus's wife. And while abandoning his dignity in the cold room he'd been privy to disgruntled Roman landowners complaining about the ingratitude of the Britons they'd displaced.

They showed no interest in the upheavals in the West. They were, for the most part, veterans, who desired nothing more than to live out the rest of their days in comfort, secure in the arrogant assumption the local populace would never dare rise up against them.

Eyes half-closed, he gave the impression of uninterest and boredom, while his brain processed and filed every snippet of conversation. There was no telling when an apparent insignificant word could prove vital upon reflection.

Everything could be used against the enemy.

Seated on the bench, Morwyn steeped her special herbs and roots in the hot water Branwen had procured. It wasn't ideal but would suffice for her purposes. She glanced up at Carys, who was watching her with a serene expression on her face. An expression she'd seen countless times on the faces of those carrying the child of the man they loved.

She'd not expected to see it on Carys. Before the invasion, neither of them had craved motherhood. Carys because she hadn't been interested in taking a lover, and Morwyn because the thought of choosing a man for such honor didn't appeal.

Carys sighed faintly and shifted position on the stone bench, as if uncomfortable. "How is my mother? Is she still on Mon?"

"Yes. And she's very well, although misses you greatly." She was also one of the senior Druids who waited for irrefutable proof of Caratacus's position before leaving the Isle. A chill shivered through her soul. Should she tell Carys? Or would she betray such confidence to her husband?

"I dearly wish she was here with me." Carys caressed her belly as if unaware of her action. "There's always darkness in my mind whenever I think of Mon. I'm so happy you're here now, Morwyn."

A trickle of unease shivered over Morwyn's arms. Yes, she was here. But she didn't intend to stay. And she had never intended to return to Cymru without Carys.

But that was before she'd discovered Carys's pregnancy. Before she'd been reminded, so forcefully, of the depth of the love Carys possessed for her Roman husband.

"Why?" Her voice was sharper than she intended. "Is life so peaceful here? Does the call for freedom no longer touch Camulodunum?" She deliberately used the Roman name for the ancient Briton settlement, but experienced no sense of victory when Carys's eyes filled with pain.

"Peaceful?" Despite the vulnerability in her eyes, Carys's voice was scathing. "When the Romans drove the Britons off their land,

and then used them as slaves to build their heathen temples?" She waved her hand in the direction of the temple adjacent to the forum. "Don't be naive. We may never see peace in our lifetime."

Morwyn stared at her, shock punching through her gut. This sounded like the Carys she knew, the Carys who had loathed the invaders and wanted nothing more than to drive them from her beloved land.

She leaned close, brushed her lips against the other woman's ear. "Whose side are you on?"

Carys's breath gusted against Morwyn's cheek. "I never betrayed our people. I never will." She pulled back and caught Morwyn's eyes in an unflinching gaze. "I'll never betray my husband, either."

Frustration clawed through her chest. "How can you not betray one or the other? When you decry Rome, you betray your husband. When you put his culture above ours, you betray your heritage."

Carys gave an odd smile, as if she understood Morwyn's accusation but at the same time pitied her for having uttered it. "Maximus knows my feelings and opinions. There're no secrets between us, Morwyn. He respects my heritage and, although I hate how his people conquered our lands, I've grown to respect certain aspects of his."

Blasphemy. The word thundered through her mind. There was nothing to respect in the Roman way.

"So you tell your husband everything?" Just as well Morwyn hadn't revealed her plans for joining Caratacus, or that Carys's own mother planned on joining the rebels.

Carys's smile wavered and she finally broke eye contact. "Yes." But she was staring at her fingers as they twisted the fabric of her foreign gown.

"You never were a good liar."

Carys shook her head and looked up. "I know what you're thinking and you're wrong. The only secret I keep from Maximus is the knowledge that could send him to his death should he ever learn of it."

That, she hadn't expected. "What do you mean?"

Carys sighed and spread her fingers across her thighs. "Do you remember the vision I told you of? Before Aeron lost his mind and murdered Druantia?"

"Yes." She remembered, because she'd been horrified at the thought of Carys taking the sacred root and entering the gods' domain without human anchor in the mortal realm.

"I saw . . . many things." Carys hesitated, as if reconsidering her decision to confide. "This isn't over yet, Morwyn. Britain will burn, and I'll do everything in my power to ensure Maximus is in Rome before that happens."

"And if you told him, he would insist on fighting." It wasn't a question. She knew, in some measure, how Carys's mind worked. "When is this great burning? Soon?" Had Carys foreseen Caratacus's victory? But if so, why hadn't she ensured her husband was already at sea?

Carys clenched her fists. "I don't know. But I trust Cerridwen will give me enough warning to save my kin."

Did Carys still worship Cerridwen?

"You'd run, rather than fight?" Condemnation dripped from every word and Carys shot her a piercing look before she straightened her relaxed posture.

"Maximus would never run, and that's why I will never tell him. If we die in a bloody battle here, who will carry the flame of knowledge into the future, Morwyn?" Carys leaned forward, her eyes glittering with iron purpose. "Cerridwen can't be allowed to fade into the mists of time. She must survive."

Shivers scuttled over her arms at the intensity of Carys's declaration. "I thought you'd turned your back on the gods." The words tumbled from her lips, unbidden, immediately regretted, because of course Carys hadn't turned her back on Cerridwen. She would never turn her back on the goddess who had chosen her at the moment of her birth.

Carys frowned and confusion flickered over her face, as if that was the last thing she'd expected Morwyn to say.

"The Morrigan is the only goddess who ever turned from me." And then her face lit up and she clasped Morwyn's hand. "That's why you're here, isn't it? Because of the Morrigan."

Blood heated Morwyn's face and she attempted to free her hand without success. She'd been so sure Carys had abandoned their gods. Been secretly craving the chance to discuss how confused she was by her lack of faith. But it had been nothing more than wishful thinking on her part.

"No. It's nothing to do with the Morrigan."

Carys let out a clearly contented sigh. "The Morrigan saw the light, didn't she? She realized Cerridwen's way is the only way to continue onward."

When all the Morrigan demanded was her children hide on the Isle of Mon? Huddle in sacred groves and give sacrifice that they were still alive? While their people remained enslaved to the invaders?

"No, Carys." Her voice was harsh. "I no longer believe in our gods. Do you understand? I despise them for allowing Aeron to control them so—so *utterly.*"

Silence shivered in the air between them. Even the incessant noise from the market faded. For a moment she wondered if her lifelong friend would turn from her for her sacrilege, but then Carys took her hand as if she imagined comfort was required.

"He didn't control them." Her voice was gentle, as if she somehow understood, but how could she understand? She had left Cymru that night. She hadn't fled to the Isle of Mon and continued to hide from the enemy behind sacrifice and prayer. Carys had gone with her lover and faced the world to live among their enemies.

How could she possibly understand?

"Morwyn." Carys gave her hand a shake to drag her back to the present. "Aeron manipulated the gods, just as he manipulated all of us."

"True gods would never allow themselves to be so manipulated." She snatched her hand from Carys and clenched her fists against her thighs. "*True* gods would never have spewed their wrath on their people the way they did that night." She glared at Carys, but in her mind all she saw was that dark night in the forest, the unholy wind that had ripped trees from their roots, and the eerie fires that had sprung up as the earth herself had howled in fury.

"They were angry at being deceived." But now Carys didn't sound so sure, as if deep in her heart she acknowledged Morwyn was right.

Morwyn gave a bitter laugh. "They were angry at the innocent. And all the Morrigan cared about was ensuring her faithful Druids escaped to the sacred Isle. So we continue to worship her, far from the putrid stench of the Roman invasion."

"Maybe the Morrigan needed time to—to assess what had happened." Carys sounded as if she was trying to convince herself as much as Morwyn. "And she came to realize the only way to survive is to continue to teach our people everything we know."

"Hidden on an Isle where only Druids are welcomed?"

"No." Carys frowned, as if trying to work something out. "Why would you have left Mon, unless the Morrigan wanted you to?"

Because she had intended to join the rebels. She couldn't tell Carys that.

"I no longer worship her." She sucked in a deep breath, couldn't maintain eye contact. "I've turned from her, Carys. She's not my goddess. I pushed her away and closed my soul to her." She risked shooting the other woman a glance, but Carys appeared thunderstruck. "It's been many moons since she came to me. She no longer exists in my heart."

"But you're here." Carys sounded as if that explained everything. "Why would you be here, unless the Morrigan had guided you?"

Morwyn let out an exasperated breath and glared at Carys. "Because I wanted to avenge Gawain's murder, that's why! It has nothing to do with the *Morrigan*."

Carys's eyes widened and she grabbed Morwyn's arm, fingers digging into her flesh. "Gawain's dead? Sweet Cerridwen, no. He can't be dead. How? What happened?"

Morwyn didn't want to talk about his murder. Didn't want to relive that paralyzing sense of helplessness as his lifeblood pumped from his body.

But the overwhelming need to share the horror was too great.

"He was betrayed. Stabbed in the back by one of our own." A shudder raked through her bones. "As we fought the enemy."

Carys wrapped her arms around her, hugged her tight. "I'm so sorry. Morwyn. I loved Gawain as a brother. This is—I can't— who was it? Who killed him?"

"I don't know. I couldn't see his face. Couldn't get to him, Carys. I can never *get* to him."

Slowly Carys pulled back. "You can never get to him?"

The nightmare pounded through her mind, as vivid as if she watched events unfold before her eyes. "He never hears my warning. And the dead keep on piling up around my feet."

Carys slid her hands down Morwyn's arms and held her chilled fingers in a firm grip.

"Where did this happen?"

Frustration ripped through her. "I don't *know*."

"But you were there?"

"Yes. I'm always there, but too far away to save him."

All she could hear was her heart pounding in her ears. All she could see was Gawain falling to the bloodied ground. And all she could smell was the acrid stink of battle.

"Morwyn." Carys's voice was gentle, but unrelenting. "Gawain could still be alive."

Too late she realized where Carys was leading with her questions. "No. He's dead. I can feel it, here in my heart."

"You weren't there. You didn't watch him die. The Morrigan hasn't abandoned you, Morwyn."

For the third time Morwyn snatched her hands from Carys, and this time leaped to her feet in order to glare down at her friend. "This isn't a vision. I don't have visions anymore." *They were nightmares.* And the certainty Gawain had died came from the bond they had once shared. *Nothing else.* "Do you hear me? Gawain is dead." And it was all her fault. He may never have left Mon if she hadn't severed their relationship.

And yet even as the thought tortured her, she knew it was untrue. Gawain had wanted to leave Mon from the moment they had arrived.

Carys stood, and, despite her foreign gown and pregnancy, she had never looked more like a proud Druid princess. "I believe you're wrong. You have to embrace the Morrigan again, Morwyn. You have to find out what she's trying to tell you."

Why couldn't Carys accept the truth? She drew in a sharp breath, tried to channel her thoughts, but then Carys looked beyond her, a smile illuminating her face, and with a stab of regret Morwyn knew they would never again have the chance to speak so freely with each other.

"Carys." Maximus held his wife's hand and brushed his lips across her knuckles. Morwyn glanced away, an odd pain slicing through her chest at the tender note in his voice.

"Maximus, look." Carys threaded her fingers through his and turned to her. "Morwyn's arrived. She's going to stay with us."

Of course she was. Where else could she go? And yet for some reason the assumption irked.

"Morwyn." Maximus smiled in greeting, and for the first time Morwyn noticed the scars marring his face. Scars inflicted by Aeron's evil magic. "Welcome. It's good to see you again."

She doubted that, but offered him a tight smile in return. No longer was he dressed in the Roman centurion uniform. Instead he wore the white toga and purple stripe of the cursed aristocracy.

He stepped toward her, fingers still linked with Carys's. "I've wanted to thank you for saving my life that night, Morwyn. I know how hard that must have been for you."

She didn't want to have this conversation with anyone, least of all Maximus.

"It was nothing." She waved her hand in a dismissive gesture and hoped he would leave it at that. She had acted out of pure instinct that night, but even now couldn't think of it without her guts twisting into knots of confusion.

"What are you doing here?" Maximus said, as if this was a perfectly normal greeting of old friends, instead of the most excruciating moment of her life. "Did you travel alone?" He sounded vaguely shocked by the possibility.

She shrugged, as if the matter was of little account. "I accompanied the Gaul. I wanted to see Carys in any case."

"The Gaul?" Both Carys and Maximus pounced on her words as if it were some extraordinary confession.

For a reason she couldn't fathom, heat rose in her cheeks. "Yes. He had business in Camulodunon so I—I came too." Why was she protecting him? It didn't make sense. Especially since she had no intention of ever seeing him again. And besides, what did it matter if Carys and Maximus knew she'd initially been abducted? She was free *now*.

"A Gaul?" Carys sounded fascinated. "Do I know him? What's his name?"

Gods, why hadn't Morwyn kept her mouth shut? "No, you wouldn't know of him. He's an auxiliary in one of the cursed Legions." She shot Maximus a glance, but he appeared unmoved by her insult. "His name is Dunmacos."

"Dunmacos?" Maximus sounded as if she'd just uttered an obscenity. "By Mars. You didn't travel willingly to Camulodunum if you accompanied that scum."

Her spine stiffened in affront. Who was this Roman to call her Gaul scum?

"Maximus?" Alarm threaded through Carys's voice. "Do you know of this Dunmacos?"

He turned to her. "Remember I told you of the Gallic butcher? *That* was Dunmacos."

Carys visibly blanched. "Goddess. Why didn't you tell me how you truly received your injuries, Morwyn?" She reached out to gently trail her fingers along Morwyn's face. "How did you escape him?"

Morwyn jerked back. Resentment curdled deep in her belly at the assumptions Carys and her husband were making.

"I told you." Except she hadn't told her everything. "I was with three fellow Druids when we were ambushed. They were killed, and I—You can imagine what they had in store for me. Dunmacos"— she said his name with a touch of defiance—"was the one who saved me from such indignity."

"So he could rape you himself." Carys's eyes flashed with fury. "Maximus, you have to hunt down this barbarian and ensure justice is served."

"I'm perfectly capable of serving justice, Carys," Morwyn said. "And while I expected nothing less from him, he did *not* rape me."

"Then who chewed on your neck like a rabid animal?"

Morwyn resisted the instinct to press her fingers against the tender flesh of her throat. Bizarrely, she recalled a similar situation when she'd been infuriated on Carys's behalf, thinking she had been raped by the enemy.

Carys had been defensive. Morwyn had never understood why. Until now.

And it didn't make sense. Carys had loved her Roman. *Morwyn* felt nothing for the Gaul. So why did Carys's insistence of his guilt irritate?

"My last lover." She knew she should leave it at that, but somehow couldn't help herself. "And he is neither rabid nor an animal."

Carys let out a ragged breath and pressed her hand against her belly. "Then you traveled with this Dunmacos of your own free will? He truly hasn't abused you?"

She thought back to the forest. He might have abducted her, but much as it irked to admit, she understood his reasoning.

Of course, she still hadn't—and never would—forgive him for shackling her like a common slave. But since she knew how Carys would react to that piece of information, she decided to keep it to herself.

Again, *why*? Why did she care if Carys and her husband ripped the Gaul's character to shreds? They could say nothing about him she hadn't already thought herself.

"When I discovered he was traveling to Camulodunon, I decided to accompany him." It was, if she conveniently closed her eyes to a few details, the absolute truth. "For an auxiliary attached to the Roman Legions I found him—honorable."

The sane section of her mind curled up on itself in despair but she ignored it. He *had* shown her honor and she had no compunction ensuring Carys and her husband were aware of that.

Carys looked wary; Maximus completely unconvinced. "As honorable as any man can be who was responsible for the devastation of his entire village." His voice was grim, but before she could take issue with his outrageous claim he turned to Carys. "Take care, my Druid princess." His words were soft, as if for his wife's ears only, before he tilted her chin with one finger and claimed her lips.

The he turned back to Morwyn. "Take my advice. Now that you're free of him, never think of returning. Our home is yours for as long as you wish."

Chapter Fifteen

After Maximus left them, Carys took Morwyn's hands. "Come. We have a town house not far from here. Although we won't be there for much longer. We're having a villa built in the countryside, for more privacy."

An odd reluctance snaked through her limbs, and instead of allowing the other woman to lead her from the forum, Morwyn resisted the gentle tug.

"Carys." It wasn't fair to let Carys think she intended to remain in Camulodunon indefinitely. "The reason I came here was to ask you to return with me to Cymru."

Carys continued smiling but it was a brittle smile, a smile that threatened to shatter at any moment. "You want me to leave Camulodunon?"

Yes. But she knew Carys never would. Not without Maximus.

Weariness bit deep into her soul, a bone-aching sadness at the knowledge that, no matter how enduring their friendship was and ever would be, they were now ultimately on opposing sides. Carys

CAPTIVE 133

might believe in freedom for her kin, but she would never willingly
take up arms against her husband's people.

Morwyn jerked her head in denial. "No. I wouldn't ask you.
Not now." Her glance slid to Carys's womb. "You have other pri-
orities now."

"But you will stay until after the babe is born, won't you?"
There was a vulnerable note in Carys's voice. "She's due to arrive
when day and night are equal. I think that's a good time for her
birth, don't you? A day of perfect balance."

It was also in three moons.

Three moons without seeing her Gaul.

The thought slid into her mind, unwanted and treacherous.
Heat flooded through her veins, twisted deep in her belly. *Where
had that come from?* She had already made her decision not to
see him again earlier this day, when they had parted at the inn.
Whether she stayed with Carys for three moons or six, the outcome was the same.

Yet the thought sank into her mind like poisoned hooks, and as
impossible to dislodge without ripping flesh.

When she returned to Cymru she would join with the rebels.
She had no intention of seeking out a Gallic *auxiliary*. Was she
insane? Why had this notion even entered her head?

"Yes." Her voice was hoarse. "It's the perfect day for her birth."
The perfect day for a child with parents who should inherently
be enemies. Druid princess and Roman aristocrat. But what true
balance could such a child ever attain when she was raised in the
Roman way? When her matrilineal heritage was being eaten away
by her father's power-hungry Emperor?

"You can do so much here, Morwyn. You were almost fully
trained before Druantia was murdered. Imagine how much you
can teach our people."

In an occupied town? For one chilling moment clarity flashed
through her mind. She could stay here with Carys. Help raise her
daughter.

And slowly her status would erode.

How could it not when she'd have to rely on her friend for so much? She would have to hide her Druidic ancestry, hide her true loyalties. Worship foreign gods she believed in even less than her own.

And never see her Gaul again.

"I can't do it, Carys." As the words fell from her lips, she didn't know if she meant she couldn't stay as a dependent or give up the chance of spending a few more days with her Gaul.

It had nothing to do with the auxiliary. She needed to return to Cymru, find the rebels and fight for freedom. But buried deep inside the darkest recess of her mind, she knew the sordid truth.

She just wanted to hold her Gaul until the raw pain eating her heart subsided.

Carys let out a shaky breath. "You're leaving." It wasn't a question. "You're going to fight, aren't you?" She didn't wait for a reply. "Don't you see, you can't help anyone if you die. You have to live, the same as I have to live, so the Flame of Knowledge burns forever into the future."

"Cerridwen's Flame of Knowledge. She needs only you for that. Not me." Because *Morwyn* was an acolyte of the Morrigan. And she no longer believed in the great goddess.

"There are so few of us left. We're all needed, Morwyn."

And that was why she had to fight. *Because there were so few of them left.*

After collecting the dispatch from the Tribunus, Bren went to the forum. It was a spontaneous decision, acted upon between one breath and the next, and even as he examined the brightly colored goods on the market stalls, he couldn't quite comprehend what he was doing there.

Except he could.

He wanted to give Morwyn something frivolous and pretty. Something that wasn't necessary for survival but created purely for pleasure.

Something to compensate for the way his countrymen had ripped her gown and bloodied her body.

And murdered her companions.

He ignored the last thought. There was nothing he could do about that. But there was something he could do about the rest.

Silken ribbons, tied to a pole and fluttering in the warm summer breeze, caught his attention. Reminded him of the feel of her hair, soft and wet, as he'd washed it the other night.

The smile had already twisted his lips before he even realized, and he allowed it to linger for a moment before reverting to his more usual countenance.

The ribbons were a luxurious indulgence. He purchased half a dozen.

As he made his way through the noisy throng of stallholders shouting their wares and buyers haggling for a bargain, an odd sense of peace settled deep in his gut. Instantly alert, he stiffened, glanced around, but could find no reason for the irrational sensation.

Besides, if someone were following him, *peace* was the last thing he'd be feeling. He took a few more steps, gingerly probed the unnatural emotion. And an image of Morwyn drifted across his consciousness.

Scarcely aware of his action, his fingers slid over the handle of her dagger, which he'd attached to his belt. There was something about it that nagged at the edges of his mind, as if the answers to unformed questions were buried in its gleaming blade.

When they reached Cymru he'd return it to her. But for now, despite her assertion he was safe from retribution, he'd hold on to it. Not only because he wouldn't have to worry about being stabbed through the heart as he lay on their bed, but also because Morwyn was unlikely to attempt an escape without her weapon for protection.

Not that she'd try to escape in Camulodunon. Why would she? The Romans infested the town like rats. She'd be in as much danger from molestation here on her own as she would in the occupied forests of Cymru.

His cock stirred at the knowledge she was back in the inn, waiting for him. It was a strange notion, to know a woman waited for him. Logically he knew it meant nothing, because Morwyn had no choice but to remain at the inn.

Yet still anticipation of seeing her, of taking her once again, tightened his groin and constricted his breathing. Without conscious thought he quickened his pace, impatient to see her face when he gave her the ribbons. Would she pretend uninterest or show genuine delight? He could imagine both scenarios, and had not the faintest clue which way she would react.

And then he saw her, on the other side of the square, and his heart kicked against his ribs in shocked denial.

It couldn't be her. But there was no mistaking her long black hair in its untidy braid, or the vibrant sky blue gown she wore. Or the proud way she held herself, as if she were a queen among peasants.

Others collided into him, but their curses meant nothing as he remained immobile. As he watched, she embraced the woman she'd been talking with. A Roman noblewoman. How did Morwyn know a Roman noblewoman? This was no chance encounter. The two knew each other, and by the way the Roman clung to Morwyn, they were far more than casual acquaintances.

A dull rage knotted deep in his gut. He'd been so sure she would remain at the inn. But given the first opportunity, she'd escaped.

Only now did he recall her interest in Camulodunon. Only now could he see she'd gone along with his demands because it suited her to. She had never intended to return to Cymru. She'd allowed him to see what he'd wanted to see, and not what should have been obvious to a half-wit.

He'd been blinded by lust. And she'd used that against him.

His fingers curled around the hilt of her jewel-encrusted dagger. He had no rights over her. The Roman had clearly given Morwyn her protection. All he had left was the memory of their night together and her dagger.

The memory would drive him insane if he let it, and the dagger would fetch a good price at market. Except he knew, even as the savage thought crossed his mind, he would never sell the cursed dagger. He'd keep it, to remind himself how futile it was to ever imagine he deserved a reprieve from his cursed existence.

Morwyn turned from the Roman and headed out of the forum. For a moment Bren remained paralyzed, following her progress with an uncompromising glare, until realization hit.

She was leaving the sanctity of the forum. Abandoning her Roman. Once out on the streets it would be much easier to capture her again. To escort her back to the inn.

To fuck her until she forgot why she wanted to leave him and remembered only that he was the one who wrenched mind-splintering orgasms from her convulsing body.

Keeping a good distance, he followed her. Where was she going? To meet with another Roman?

A chill iced his blood. Was she a spy for the Romans? Was her vocal loathing for the invaders nothing more than a cover?

Could he kill her as coldly as he'd kill any other Celt he discovered to be engaged in such betrayal?

He had in the past. But they hadn't been Morwyn.

Sweat slicked the palms of his hands. A physical weakness he hadn't experienced since boyhood. Still she continued, as if she knew exactly where she was going, and still he hung back, unwilling to hold a dagger to her throat. Unwilling to ask her the questions to prove her a traitor.

The streets became less crowded. At any moment she might turn and see him. He couldn't put it off any longer. He could either allow her to walk away, or abduct her now.

Let her go. He couldn't believe she was a traitor to her people. All she had wanted was her freedom.

His chest constricted, as if his lungs had trouble accessing air. It made sense to let her go. She was an encumbrance. She slowed him down. And despite it all, his pace quickened and he crossed the road, decreasing the distance between them. Intending to grab her and keep her until they returned to her homeland.

He couldn't think further than that.

She came to a sudden halt, turned toward a building and vanished inside.

With a jolt of disbelief, he realized they were back at the inn. She had returned to him of her own free will.

Chapter Sixteen

He remained on the road, expecting her to emerge at any moment. But she'd had her pack with her. Why would she return to the place she was escaping from? For all she knew, he had already discovered her absence and would be waiting for her, dagger drawn.

Grimy beggars rummaged in the rotting rubbish discarded by the side of the inn, and a couple of gaudily painted women from the adjacent brothel propositioned him. And still Morwyn didn't reappear.

Finally he entered the inn, was given directions to his room, and stood outside the door. His heart thundered against his ribs, as if he were about to go into battle. Yet he was ice-cold when he faced a battle, his mind clear and body under absolute control.

Rattled by the knowledge she could so easily shatter the calm he'd taken years to perfect, he thrust open the door. She was standing by the window, arms folded, looking in his direction as if she'd been waiting for him.

As if she had never left.

Lust raged, but he remained by the door. She might have

returned only to plunge a newly acquired dagger through his heart. He wanted her, but not at the expense of his life.

He'd strip her of all weapons first. Then interrogate her. And then fuck her until this insane craving eating his reason was vanquished.

"There's no need," Morwyn said as her arms dropped to her sides and she closed the distance between them, "to look so happy to see me."

"Should I be?" Instinctively his fingers curled around his dagger. Only to realize it was the bejeweled hilt of Morwyn's dagger he grasped.

Her glance dropped to his hand and he caught the fleeting surprise that flashed across her face, as if his action made no sense to her. As if she hadn't the slightest idea he knew she'd had ample opportunity to arm herself.

"I take it your business didn't go well." She looked up at him, no hint of fear or trepidation in her tone or expression. Despite the fact he gripped a dagger as if she were his mortal enemy.

With more effort than should have been necessary, he unhooked his fingers from the handle. Even if she lunged at him with a dagger in both hands, what kind of man was he if he couldn't disarm her without resorting to a weapon?

"What makes you think that?" Was she fishing for information? To pass on to her Roman friend?

Why would a Roman noblewoman be interested in such matters? Gods, his brain was fogged. If Morwyn were a man, she would already be on the floor, a heartbeat away from having her throat cut. He didn't do supposition or ponder on possibilities. If threatened, he retaliated. Instantly and without compunction.

And here he was, standing before Morwyn and making excuses for her behavior instead of demanding to hear the truth.

"Perhaps," Morwyn said, stepping directly in front of him and tilting her jaw so she could maintain eye contact. Her arms remained at her sides. "Because you look as if you've just been thrust into one of those barbarous gladiatorial arenas without warning."

He didn't wonder how she knew of such arenas when there was none in Cymru. Morwyn appeared to know many things, not least the Latin of the aristocracy. Had the Roman noblewoman taught her?

"My business is completed." Why did she stand so close? The musky scent of aroused woman—of Morwyn—invaded his senses, as potent as any exotic aphrodisiac from the East. His fists clenched against his thighs. He would not be seduced by her wiles. Not until she'd answered his questions.

Except he couldn't remember his questions.

She edged even closer. Her breathing was ragged, her dark eyes dilated.

"You smell of Roman spices."

"You don't sound repelled."

For answer she shoved him against the door, and it slammed shut behind him. And despite his mistrust, despite his resolve to remain in control, a treacherous smile tugged at his lips.

No woman had ever shoved him so unceremoniously. His beloved Eryn had been too gentle to engage in such rough play and the few women he'd taken since were faceless and fleeting and afraid of offending him.

"Ah." Morwyn dragged her nails up the back of his neck and across his scalp. Shivers of lightning stabbed through his brain. "You find me amusing, do you? A pleasant diversion from your taxing auxiliary duties?"

"Yes." His voice was smoky with arousal, and with one swift maneuver he spanned her waist and spun her around, so she was the one pinned against the door.

His captive.

She dug her nails into his head, dragged him toward her. "Is that all?" Her warm breath smelled of aromatic berries and sharp woodland spices. Scarcely aware of what he was doing, he pulled up her gown. No concealed weapons were strapped to her thighs. "Just *yes*? Amusing and diverting?"

"No." His lips brushed hers. "You're also infuriating and unpredictable." His hands cupped her rounded bottom, the flesh taut and smooth against his fingers. "Intolerable."

She smiled, and he felt her teeth against his lips. "That's better, Gaul. You are a fast learner, after all."

He laughed, the sound shocking him, but not enough to cut the laugh short. "Do you always talk so much during sex?" It was a novelty. For the last six years sex had been merely a physical release. There'd been no need for idle talk. But now, inexplicably, he enjoyed the breathless exchanges.

"Not always." Briefly, shockingly, she nipped his lip. "Sometimes I scream."

Her words were as potent as if she'd sunk to her knees and taken him into her mouth. His fingers gripped her flesh, jerking her roughly against his erection.

"You'll scream for me."

She angled herself against him, and despite the barrier of his clothes between them, he could still feel the damp heat of her tempting him.

"Make me." It was a dare. A challenge.

His grip tightened and as he slammed her more securely against the door, he hefted her upward. With a smile of feminine triumph she wound her legs around his waist, and he felt her cross her ankles in the small of his back, and her grip was lethal.

He bared his teeth as frustration pounded through him. He needed to free himself, but couldn't risk Morwyn sliding from his grasp. As if she could read his mind, she gave a breathless laugh and ruthlessly dragged the bottom of his tunic up to his belly, heedless of how the material tangled around his cock.

An involuntary hiss scraped between his teeth. And then her fingers curled around him, guiding him, taking control.

She rubbed his sensitive glans across her clitoris in a sensual, circular motion, her juices sliding over him in delicious, minute waves. Her lips parted, her eyes glazed, but she never took her gaze from him.

Angling her more securely against the door, he braced her weight on his forearms. Her muscles were rigid around him, a viselike grip that merged pain and desire until he couldn't fathom whether the sensation was pleasure or agony. It didn't matter. It speared through his body, lancing his cock and tightening his balls. Catapulted through his arteries, scorching his blood and sending fiery tendrils of unimaginable lust through his groin and gut and chest.

He needed to touch her. Feel her softness, her heat. His fingers slid over the curve of her buttock, seeking her core with unaccustomed urgency. The damp curls of her pussy welcomed him, drew him onward and sucked him into her hot sheath with exhilarating prowess.

Gasping into her flushed face, he inserted a second finger, pressing against her slick walls, stretching the tender flesh for his exploration. Her strong muscles contracted, squeezing his fingers together, and he resisted the pressure, forcing her open. Her eyes lost focus and her hands involuntarily gripped his cock and the back of his neck in a punishing duet.

The groan scalded his throat and stars exploded behind his eyes as she squeezed him in an unbearable embrace. Tremors danced through her tight cleft, rippled over his fingers, and her swollen clitoris burned the head of his engorged shaft.

"Morwyn." Her name fell from his lips, wild and raw, and he slipped one finger from her to tease her sensitive bud.

For answer she hitched herself up a minute degree and jerked his erection under her without care for his comfort. But he didn't care for comfort, not when the entrance to her wet channel teased his throbbing head. Not when his fingers caressed her exposed pussy and his probing cock, when she slowly, too slowly, lowered herself onto him.

He dragged his fingers, drenched with her fragrant juices, along the length of his shaft as he invaded her welcome depths.

She enveloped him in a snug embrace, sinking onto his rigid flesh, and his fingertips caressed her passion-swollen lips as she sucked him into her delectable body.

Jagged gasps of impending climax gusted from her luscious mouth. She gripped his arse with her hands, jerking him upward and into her, and counterbalancing each thrust with a violent one of her own.

Gods, but he wanted her naked, wanted to feel her succulent breasts against his chest, feel her hard nipples stroke his flesh, see his cock pound into her with every frenzied beat. And then it didn't matter as her head dropped back and inarticulate moans fell from her tongue, so excruciatingly erotic his testicles hardened in instant reaction.

Her fingernails gouged his arse; her legs threatened to crush his ribs. And her convulsing sheath shattered the last remnant of control as he hammered into her, coming with savage abandonment and primal roar.

⊰⊱⊱O⊰⊰

Morwyn clung to him, limbs trembling with delicious fatigue, as he rammed her against the door. She could feel his hot seed pumping into her with every frenzied thrust, flooding her channel and filling her womb, and an odd sense of contentment bathed her soul.

For long moments they remained melded together, harsh pants rending the air, erratic heartbeats echoing through her mind. He made no move to disengage, and despite the hardness of the timber digging into her back, and the first twinges of cramp that threatened her calves, she had no inclination to push him away.

Instead she indulged her secret desire and lost herself in the mesmeric green of his eyes. Eyes that no longer glinted with distrust but smoldered with embers of uninhibited lust.

She had turned her back on Carys for this.

The thought drifted through her mind. For a moment it felt perfectly right. And then, with sluggish realization, she recalled the rebellion back in Cymru.

That was the reason she had left Carys. To join with Caratacus. How had she forgotten, for even a moment?

Her Gaul's beautiful eyes captured her attention once again. How extraordinary she should think them beautiful, but they were. A startling counterpoint to the harsh, unsmiling visage he presented to the world.

Except when he smiled. When he smiled, she could see the man he might have been, if he hadn't turned his back on his people and joined the enemy forces.

But the thought was distant, almost inconsequential. Because despite the feeble attempt at self-delusion, she knew exactly why she had returned to him.

Because of him. Returning to join with the rebels was only a secondary consideration and something she didn't want to think about. Not now, when he was still inside her, when he still held her and looked at her as if she meant something more than a quick fuck.

The thought glinted, an uneasy prickle through her mind. What else was he, what else could he ever be, but a quick fuck? So why did she want, for even a fleeting moment, to be more than that to him?

"What are you thinking about?" His voice was hoarse but his gaze was steady. And his grip on her as secure as ever, as if her weight didn't tire him at all.

She pushed all thoughts of the disposed Briton king aside. Plenty of time to think of such things later. When she left her Gaul.

"I'm thinking you satisfy me quite admirably, for my enemy."

His lip twitched, but a stab of disappointment sliced through her when he didn't allow himself a full smile.

"And yet you didn't scream."

She'd scarcely had enough breath to stay conscious, never mind anything else. And her heart had thundered so violently it was a miracle it hadn't burst from her body.

Words of explanation almost tumbled from her lips but something stilled her tongue. It was easy to flirt. But she'd never lost her voice during sex before and couldn't quite believe she had just now. After all, she had screamed most adequately last night.

But she had to say something in response.

"Then next time, you'll simply have to try harder."

A silent laugh shook his body, as if he knew full well how deeply he'd satisfied her. Fascinated by his reaction, she stared at him. She always enjoyed flirting and only once in her life had she been involved with a man who had taken exception to her particular brand of humor. They had barely lasted one night together.

But never before had she made so many potentially disrespectful comments. Then again, she'd never before been abducted, and as far as she was concerned he deserved every word she'd slung at him.

Yet that initial animosity had passed, and now that she considered the matter she realized there was something about pushing this Gaul's limits she found irresistible. When else had she insulted a lover's performance while they were still joined as one?

Any man would feel justified at taking offense. If she believed the outrageous claims of Carys's husband, then Dunmacos wasn't the sort of man to allow a woman to utter such slurs without savage retribution.

Yet all he did was smother a laugh. Because he knew she didn't mean it. Knew she'd been so consumed with mind-shattering orgasms she'd all but passed out.

It was unnerving, to consider he knew such things about her. Because until this moment she hadn't even known them herself.

"I will, if you will." His husky whisper, threaded with amusement, nonplussed her for a moment, until she realized what he meant.

Gods, he was flirting in the same manner. Why was that so arousing?

"That depends." With stiffening fingers, she tugged the hem of his tunic. "I'm tired of fighting your cursed clothes. Next time I want naked flesh." His name thudded in her brain, and incomprehensibly her heart hammered in sudden nerves.

Say his name. How hard could it be? She sucked in a sharp breath and forced the name between her lips before she could change her mind. *"Dunmacos."*

His half smile froze, and his eyes became chips of wintry ice. Bemused by such a swift change in his manner, she stared at him, uncomprehending.

"Don't." His voice was harsh, bitter, as if she had just accused him of—She couldn't imagine. She'd insulted his heritage, his loyalties and his sexual prowess and he hadn't so much as tossed a genuine frown her way. What had she said now?

A glimmer flashed through her mind, but it didn't make sense. Why would he not want her to say his name? That couldn't be the reason. There was something else.

"Don't what?"

He eased out of her, leaving her chilled and exposed and oddly rejected. But that was insane, because every copulation ended with withdrawal and never before had such a natural action invoked such a feeling within her.

"Don't call me that." Now his voice was as cold as his expression, but not nearly as cold as the hard knot that lodged midway between her stomach and throat.

"Then I won't." Hating him more than she thought possible to hate anyone without plunging a dagger into his neck, she gingerly unhooked her ankles and slithered ungracefully down his legs. At least he didn't let go of her backside until her feet were firmly on the floor.

She remained leaning against the door for support and glowered at him. She had left Carys to be treated like this? As if she truly were his slave and unworthy to utter his name to his face?

An odd spasm twisted his features, as if her glare pained him. Once her blood was properly flowing and she could feel her legs again, she would certainly give him pain. A swift knee between his thighs should suffice.

"Only my enemies and acquaintances who wish me dead call me by that name."

She stared at him in disbelief, thoughts tumbling in disarray. He sounded as if he'd never said such a thing before, and never would again.

He sighed heavily and, as if he didn't realize what he was doing, gently brushed a damp curl from her cheek. His finger lingered on her flushed skin as if he couldn't help himself.

She didn't knock his hand aside. Even though her pride insisted.

"Do you still want me dead, Morwyn?" There was no hint of vulnerability in the question. He sounded exactly what he was. A tough auxiliary who worked for the Romans.

Except for the fleeting glimmer in his eyes. The glimmer that said so much more than his words ever would.

Something twisted inside her chest, a burning pain that coiled on itself, burying deep inside. Oddly it felt as if it was her heart, but that was absurd. All she felt for this Gaul was physical lust. That didn't—couldn't—touch her heart.

And yet, she didn't want him dead. She didn't even have to consider his question because the thought of him lying at her feet, bleeding, dying, was enough to churn her stomach.

Her enemy. The enemy of her people. But she no longer wanted him dead.

"No." The word was low, dragged from her soul, betraying everything she had ever fought for. "I don't want you dead, Gaul."

His calloused finger traced the outline of her face. Gentle and erotic and, bizarrely, somehow comforting. He looked as if he was about to say more, as if he struggled with an internal battle, and finally he exhaled a sigh as if in defeat.

"I believe you."

But that wasn't what he had wanted to say. She knew it, as surely as if he'd told her himself. And yet conversely she also knew he *did* believe her. So what had he wanted to say to her before his cursed military training had curbed his tongue?

"So I'll continue to call you the Gaul, shall I?" The stinging hurt scalding her breast had subsided, almost vanished. And, strangely, she preferred calling him *the Gaul* to his given name.

Dunmacos was a stranger whom Maximus knew. A man she had never encountered and never wanted to.

But the Gaul—her Gaul—he was the man standing in front of her. The man cradling her jaw in the palm of his hand, as if she were something precious and fragile.

Unnerved by the errant direction of her thoughts, she tried to recall the cold look on his face from a moment ago. The ice in his eyes.

And failed.

Chapter Seventeen

"You can call me anything," he said, "except for that hated name."

She let out a breath, unaware she'd even been holding it. "A bold statement. You might wish to rethink your stand on that."

For answer, he wound his arm around her shoulders and maneuvered her from the door. It was such an intimate gesture, yet lacking all sexual intent, as if he knew her legs were still shaky and she needed, but would never request, assistance.

She sat on the edge of the bed and he brought over a bowl of water, so she could wash her hands. With manners that befit the highest in her hierarchy, he waited until she'd finished before cleansing himself.

He was no lowly peasant. But she'd always known that. Would she ever discover who he truly was?

As he returned the bowl to the table, he glanced at the food she hadn't touched.

"You didn't eat much."

She almost told him she hadn't been hungry. But why lie?

Now she was starving, and what did it matter if he knew she had
explored the town?

"I didn't have time. I went out after you left."

He shot her a look of undisguised astonishment, although he concealed his expression almost instantly. It was as if she'd confessed to a
grievous crime, one he could scarcely wrap his mind around.

Or perhaps he was simply amazed she had dared to leave the
inn without his express permission.

The thought quirked her lips. Hadn't he told her he found her
unpredictable?

"Why?" His tone was guarded. As if he couldn't imagine any
reason for her doing such a thing.

She shrugged and stretched her legs, rotating her ankles and
curling her toes. "I wanted to see my friend again."

The look on his face was worth the twinges of cramps attacking her calves, and she hid the smile that threatened to surface.
Clearly he believed she had lost her mind.

"Your friend lives in Camulodunon?"

"Yes. I hadn't seen her in . . . a while."

He appeared to be digesting her revelation, and finding it
extraordinarily hard to swallow. "She was a good friend of yours?"
He sounded as if he found that beyond belief, as if he had assumed
she possessed no friends at all, never mind lifelong ones.

Oddly, she realized she wasn't offended by his assumption.
Probably because he still looked confused by her casual remarks.

"She's like a sister to me. We grew up together." And they had
always believed they would grow old together too. Along with the
men they chose and any children they might have decided to birth
in the future.

But that had been another future. For another time.

Doubt clouded his eyes, as if what she said made no sense. He
appeared to be weighing up her words, and she had the distinct
suspicion he no longer believed her. But why would he think that?
What did she have to gain by lying about such a thing?

"That's why you speak the Latin of the patricians."

Of everything she thought he might have said, that wasn't one of them. Had she imagined that look of skepticism on his face? Once again he wore his mask of implacability.

And how intriguing he had leaped to such a conclusion. How had he linked her lifelong friend with her ability to speak the language of the invaders?

"We shared a tutor. My Latin isn't perfect because I was older when I began lessons."

He glanced at the food as if her conversation no longer interested him, and began to pile cold meat onto a platter. "A Roman tutor?" His voice was casual but she caught the underlying tautness, as if far from uninterest he was, in reality, acutely interested in her words.

Baffled by such odd behavior, she stood and began to pile fruit and strange-looking vegetables on a second platter.

"No, of course not. He was Gallic." She shot him a glance but he continued to examine the food. Carys's elderly tutor might have originated from Gaul, and he might have been a Druid. But he had also possessed a Roman-bred mother.

She decided not to mention either of those last two facts.

"You must have been young when you began your lessons." He turned and gave her a probing look before settling himself on the bed to eat.

She sat beside him, closer than necessary, although she wasn't sure why.

"I was almost seven when my friend was born." She couldn't tell him Carys's name. He knew Maximus. He might well know the name of Maximus's wife. And for some reason she couldn't quite fathom, she didn't want him to make the connection.

Again he shot her a glance, and this time there was the faintest trace of sympathy softening his hard features. As if the fact she had been taught Latin by a native of Gaul was somehow . . . tragic.

But that was insane. Why would he think such a thing? It was a massive advantage to understand everything the enemy said. He knew that. He spoke fluent Latin too.

Since he was now intent on eating and there wasn't the slightest trace of sympathy on his face, she half wondered if she had imagined it.

"Didn't she expect you to stay in Camulodunon for a time?"

Morwyn licked her sticky fingers and glanced at him. He caught her look and held it, but it wasn't challenging. More as if he was genuinely interested.

"Yes, of course she wanted me to stay." The words were out before she could think through the implications. But then, what implication could he draw from such a statement?

"Why didn't you?"

Because she'd wanted to see him again. Blood heated her face, an infuriating reaction, but she couldn't help it. And worse, her brain couldn't conjure up another reason as to why she'd turned down Carys's invitation. It was as if her only and entire motive for leaving Camulodunon was centered on this Gaul.

And it wasn't. She had to leave Camulodunon because . . .

The *real* reason drifted with an odd undercurrent of reluctance across her paralyzed mind and she almost sagged in relief.

"Because I have to return home." And find where the rebels were hiding. How had she forgotten that? It was her overriding goal. But her gaze dropped from his and she concentrated on her food, because she would die if he somehow guessed by a flicker of her eyes or expression that she wasn't completely convinced by her own reply.

The Gaul sprawled on the other end of the bed, watching her comb the tangles from her hair. After they'd finished eating she'd cleansed her other gown as well as she could and left it to dry over the table. At least it no longer stank of sweat, although there was nothing she could do about the clinging odor of horse or travel until she returned to civilization.

Gods, she needed to bathe. The image of a Roman tub floated through her mind, and instead of immediately dismissing it, she savored the notion for a few brief moments.

Perhaps she'd suggest such a thing to him. But this time they could indulge together.

She smothered a sigh. Clearly, she had not yet had enough of him. She could only hope that, by the time they reached Cymru, her desire for him would cool.

Otherwise her nights would be plagued not merely by frustrated, lust-driven dreams, but a face and a body instead of an anonymous fantasy lover.

He opened a pouch that hung from his belt. Idly she watched him. How odd it was, to be sitting at the foot of the bed as if it was the most natural thing for them to share a quiet, domestic moment together.

She had never lived with a man when such a situation might have arisen. And she certainly wasn't living with her Gaul, and yet she couldn't shake the feeling, no matter how incongruous.

"Here." He pushed himself upright and deposited something onto her lap, scattering her errant thoughts. Bemused, she stared at the riot of vibrant colors splashed across her gown.

"What is it?" Gingerly she picked up the end of a sunshine golden length of material and gasped. It was cool, soft like the most luxuriant of fur, yet also as smooth as a babe's skin.

Enthralled, she traced the tip of her finger across a length of forest green ribbon that reminded her of the Gaul's eyes. Entranced, she picked up a strip of scarlet and then of summer-sky blue.

"Silk," she said, looking at him as he once again reclined at the other end of the bed. He looked uncomfortable, as if he was unused to giving gifts, and offered her a one-shouldered shrug in reply.

A painful tug knotted the top of her stomach, as if a fist gripped her and twisted her insides without mercy. While she had been contemplating leaving him, he had been purchasing silken ribbons for her.

"They're beautiful." She threaded the green one through her fingers, delighting in the silky sensation against her skin. "Thank you." And then she couldn't help herself. "Why?"

His discomfort was palpable. Even though they weren't touching, she could feel the way his muscles tensed, as if the last thing he had anticipated or wanted to do was explain his reasoning for giving her such an unexpected gift.

"Because." It was a growl.

She rolled onto her knees and, holding her treasures in one hand, crawled up the bed beside him. He eyed her with evident suspicion, as if anticipating more unanswerable questions.

"Because?" She sat back on her heels, resisting the urge to wrap her arms around his neck and show him just how much his gesture meant to her.

Because it shouldn't mean that much to her. He had likely bought them only because he felt guilty for abducting her in the first place. And yet even knowing that didn't change the way she felt.

She still wanted to wrap herself around him. And, most worrying, never let go.

He let out a disgruntled breath, as if she were a great annoyance. Anyone catching sight of the scowl on his face would be forgiven for running in terror. Yet she had no fear because no matter how he grimaced or glared, he could never quite hide the truth of his feelings from his eyes.

Was she the only one who could see that?

Maximus was mistaken in his opinion. This Gaul with the astonishing chink of vulnerability in his eyes could never be responsible for the crimes leveled against him.

"*Because.*" The word was loaded with intense irritation. "Your gown was ruined in the forest."

But not by him. Once again she stared at the ribbons, fascinated by how the colors shimmered as she twisted the silk between her fingers.

He hadn't got them for her to apologize for abducting her, or

chaining her like a slave. He'd bought them because his foul countrymen had attacked her.

Her brain knew such distinction meant nothing. Either way he
had given them to her as a wordless apology for wrongs inflicted
upon her.

Yet another, irrational, part of her—her mind, perhaps?—
insisted that the distinction meant everything.

Bren watched Morwyn enter the public baths as if it were something she did on a daily basis. He leaned his shoulder against one
of the fluted stone columns that graced the entrance, checked the
military dispatch was still safely secured, and folded his arms.

Morwyn would be a while. When he'd suggested she visit the
baths, she'd looked thrilled and hadn't even tried too hard to hide
her reaction. As if she no longer cared whether he knew the thought
of such indulgence fascinated her.

But while her face told him she had no reservations about trying out the Roman baths, her tongue launched into a scathing dia-
tribe of the invaders' decadence. He hadn't bothered arguing with
her, and after a moment she'd stopped midsentence and started to
laugh.

Unexpected and contrary. Her convictions were as rock, yet she
laughed at herself when the irony of her comments became absurd.
If he thought she would say one thing, she said another. And while
he'd imagined she would deny having left the inn if asked, she'd
instead told him without any prompting. As if she considered it her
right to come and go as she pleased and it had never crossed her
mind he might think otherwise.

Her pleasure at the ribbons had been gratifying, although he'd
been taken aback both by the extent of her evident delight and by
his own private satisfaction of her response. They were only ribbons. He was glad she liked them but it was scarcely cause to ignite
an odd warmth deep in the pit of his soul.

He sucked in a deep breath and narrowed his eyes at the

still-bustling forum on the opposite corner of this most prestigious square in Camulodunon. Something wasn't right. He didn't expect Morwyn to confide in him, but the things she had let slip didn't add up.

If she'd been a companion—or, more likely, a slave—to a patrician child, then she would have been in another province, as Britain had only been occupied for eight years. Maybe Gaul—she had admitted as much when she'd mentioned the tutor.

Yet she acted as if Cymru was not only her homeland, but the only place she had ever been before traveling to Camulodunon. Why did she insist she had never experienced the Roman ways before when she'd spent most, if not all, of her childhood in a Roman household?

More to the point, why was he so interested? It didn't affect his plans one way or another. And yet still he wanted to know how old she had been when she'd left Cymru. How long she'd been back. Why her Roman mistress had allowed her to leave, when the bond between them was so obvious.

Maybe she just wanted to wipe the experience from her mind. He could understand that. If she'd been abducted from her family while still a child, no wonder she'd reacted so furiously when he'd chained her like a slave.

And he couldn't even ask her. Because then he'd have to admit he'd seen her in the forum, embracing the Roman, and hadn't mentioned it before.

It was only later, as Morwyn emerged from the bathhouse glowing and pampered and wearing the green silk ribbon in her hair, that it occurred to him he'd just missed the perfect opportunity to read the military dispatch.

Chapter Eighteen

Instead of returning to the inn, the Gaul took her into a tavern in the forum. They sat near the door, for both light and fresh air, and Morwyn breathed deep, savoring the strange, foreign aromas that scented her hair and body.

"What's your verdict on the Roman bathing experience?" His eyes glinted at her, as if daring her to say how much she had loathed the procedure.

"Extraordinary." She'd forgotten how utterly wonderful it was to be massaged so thoroughly. She hadn't been so pampered since the Romans had invaded and she and her fellow Druids had fled to the magical enclave Aeron created. An enclave prohibited to all others, including their slaves and servants who had been left to fend for themselves.

He made a noncommittal noise that sounded rather like a grunt. As if he didn't believe her.

She rolled her shoulders, felt deliciously aroused. "Of course, I've been massaged in the past." Now why had she told him that? She didn't want him guessing she wasn't really from the trading class. But too late to worry about that now. Besides, he didn't look as if he'd jumped to the conclusion she was of noble blood. And certainly she'd said nothing that could point to her Druid ancestry.

"Have you?" His voice was completely neutral, as if he found nothing either strange or commonplace about her comment.

"Oh yes." She flicked her hand in a dismissive gesture. "But never before have I been so thoroughly *exfoliated*." She stretched out the word for emphasis, and exquisite shivers danced low in her belly at the memory.

At least that caught his attention. He looked at her as if unsure he'd heard her correctly, and then transferred his attention to the amphora of wine on the table as if it fascinated him.

She propped her elbow on the table and rested her chin on the backs of her fingers. He was pouring water for her from his personal waterskin and wine for himself, which was a little odd but she wasn't about to complain. Wine befuddled her mind and she'd never much cared for the sour taste of ale.

"My legs," she said, as he raised the goblet to his lips, "feel as soft as my silken ribbons."

His eyes darkened. "I'll examine your claim later." His voice was low, vibrated with desire. Satisfied with such reaction, she leaned a little farther over the table.

"And my pussy is near naked."

He choked, wine splaying from his mouth, and shot her a look of utter disbelief. A smug smile tilted her lips and she waited for his response. He appeared unable to articulate one.

"Well?" she prompted. "Do you intend to examine *that* claim later also?"

"Intimately." His voice was hoarse, and he took a hasty gulp of wine as if that might ease his throat.

"And this night," she said, "I intend to examine *you* as intimately."

For a fleeting moment she thought a grim disgust flashed across his face. But it vanished so swiftly perhaps it hadn't been there at all. Because now he looked at her in a way that made her damp and tight and deliciously uncomfortable between her thighs.

Gods. How could she want him so savagely so soon after slaking her lust? Was it because her skin still tingled from the thorough cleansing ritual she'd enjoyed?

Or was it simply because the Gaul was . . . *her Gaul*?

They arrived back at the inn just as dusk fell. He hadn't touched her on the journey but she'd been achingly aware of him next to her, and on the few occasions his arm had brushed hers, lightning skittered along her nerves.

By the time he opened the door to their room she was so aroused she wanted to throw him to the floor and ravish him.

She sucked in a shaky breath. She'd done that once already this day. Although the door had substituted for the floor and he'd craftily switched their positions so he'd been in control.

This time he wouldn't wrest power from her so easily. This time she would—

Her thoughts shattered as he gripped her shoulders and jerked her toward him, his mouth on hers. Hard and hot and merciless as he invaded and plundered her parted lips.

A moan slid along her throat, echoed through her mouth, and she thrust her own tongue against his, seeking and finding. He tasted of wine and spices and primitive aroused male.

She buried her fingers in his hair, so short, so foreign and yet so surprisingly erotic. His hands slid from her shoulders and without breaking their ravaging kiss he tugged open the ties at her bodice.

Her fingers dropped to his chest and feverishly she attempted to locate his elusive fastenings. He broke contact, panting in her face, his eyes dark in the flickering light from the lamps.

"Take off your gown." His rough command sent tremors through her wet sheath but she wasn't about to let him get away with issuing orders.

"No." She flashed him a smile and tried to drag his chain mail from his chest.

He captured her fingers with one hard hand. "Remove your gown." He pressed her hands against her breast and released her. "Or by the gods I'll rip it from you."

A spear of primal lust lanced through her womb, cascaded through her blood. Her breath shortened and she stared up at him. "You wouldn't dare."

His fingers slid into her bodice and his knuckles grazed her sensitized flesh. She arched against him, felt his hands fist, and then he ripped her bodice to her waist as if it were made of nothing more substantial than spring leaves.

Astonishment and disbelief tumbled through her, but before she could even take a breath, violent desire incinerated all other emotions.

"Never," he growled against her flushed cheek, "dare me, Morwyn."

"Gallic barbarian." She kicked off her leather footwear and pulled her ruined gown from her shoulders, allowed it to puddle around her feet. His gaze remained melded with hers. "Now you strip for me."

He tore off his chain mail and dropped it onto the floor. Her breath lodged in her throat and her glance slid from his to rivet on his chest. But he made no move to remove the tunic, and with an impatient gasp she reached for him, to finish the job herself.

Swiftly he gripped her wrists in one large hand before she made contact and jerked her arms above her head, her bracelets tumbling down her forearms. Before her startled mind could fathom what he thought he was doing, he marched her backward and she had no choice but to comply or be dragged.

"Unhand me." It sounded more like a plea to continue than a demand to acquiesce. The half smile he offered her suggested he thought so too.

A strange tenderness threaded through the sharp lust spearing low in her belly. She craved his smile. How insane to find such a natural expression so captivating.

Except on her Gaul it wasn't natural. He rarely smiled. And

when he did she had the incomprehensible urge to savor it, as if it were a gift from benevolent gods.

The backs of her legs hit the edge of the bed. "Sit."

From sheer habit she opened her mouth to disagree, because nobody gave her orders. But instead she merely expelled a noisy breath and sat as gracefully as she could manage with her arms still extended above her head.

He kneed her thighs open and stood between her parted legs. Yet still his gaze remained locked on hers. As if her face was the most arousing and fascinating part of her body, despite the way she was open for his most intimate of inspection.

And, inexplicably, that knowledge sent tremors skittering across the skin of her lower belly and the sensitized flesh of her breasts.

"Now will you strip for me?" Her voice was husky and she twisted her wrists but his grip didn't relax. She trailed her feet up his rock-hard calves, balancing precariously as she explored his rigid thighs, bracing her weight on her captured hands.

Slowly he leaned forward and she could do nothing but go with the momentum. Flat on her back, legs hooked around him, she glared up at him. His smile was pure decadence, wiping years from his face, and she struggled to recall why she was angry with him.

What did it matter if he refused to relinquish control, when he smiled like that? Entranced despite herself, she stared at him, his face so close to hers. Towering over her like a conquering warlord, pinning her to the bed as if she were his captive spoil of battle.

"Have you forgotten?" His smoky voice curled deep within her womb as potent as any Druidic aphrodisiac. "I need to examine the veracity of your claims."

She squirmed helplessly, digging her heels into the tops of his thighs, but he refused to lower himself onto her, to alleviate the pressure between her legs.

"Then make haste." Her fingers flexed and clawed but still she couldn't escape. "You torture me with your tongue."

His lips all but brushed hers. "Not yet. But I will."

The promise in his words lanced through her heated blood, tightening muscles and shortening breath, and erratic gasps fanned his face. Again he smiled, as if her reaction pleased, and slowly he loosened the grip on her wrists.

"Don't try to escape." His fingers trailed the length of her arms, caressed her shoulders. She remained prone, unable to move a muscle, as if his words hypnotized.

She had not the slightest inclination to escape. She even forgave him for not stripping first, because that could come later. After he had fulfilled the promise glinting in his mesmeric eyes.

As if her silence satisfied, the tips of his roughened fingers continued to trail over her heated skin to the curve of her waist, the flare of her hips. Slow and maddening and unbelievably erotic. A featherlight touch she could feel all the way in the deepest recesses of her soul, as if flesh and psyche melded beneath his exploration.

"Back up." There was the faintest undercurrent of a tremble in his command, as if his control wasn't as absolute as he would have her believe. And because of that she obeyed, bracing her feet against his hips and pushing back onto the bed, until she sprawled across the mattress, legs spread in helpless abandon.

The palms of his hands glided over her thighs, her knees, her calves. Air hissed between her teeth and she dug her fingers into the mattress. Still his eyes never left hers. As if he wanted to watch every tiny reaction his touch evoked. As if that was of more import to him than examining her blatantly exposed pussy.

"Your legs," he said, as his palms once again skimmed her shins, "are as silken as your ribbons."

She knew that. It wasn't her legs she wanted him to examine. Even if every touch caused shivers of desire to spill across her skin in ever-increasing spirals of anticipation.

"Some Roman implements have their uses." Not that she would admit such to anyone else. But the Gaul wasn't anyone else. He was the one admiring her smooth skin, and what did it matter if she confessed to enjoying the unexpected session of indulgence in the baths?

He would never repeat her words to those who would despise her for such weakness. And it wasn't as if she would ever have the chance to experience that foreign pampering again.

His fingers splayed against the inside of her thighs, but still he maintained eye contact. How did he exert such self-control? Were their positions reversed, she would be all but devouring his cock with her eyes and mouth.

The fantasy was so real in her mind she squirmed again and wrapped her hands around his wrists. He didn't move, except for his lips, and his smile scorched what little air remained in her lungs.

"Patience," he said, "is not one of your virtues, Morwyn."

"I never claimed it was." She sounded parched, as if she were dying of thirst. And she was dying, but of hunger. Hunger for his touch.

His hands slid farther up her thighs and she gasped frantically for breath. But still he didn't touch her where she needed him. Still he didn't look at her where she wanted him to look at her.

"Patience," he said again, but this time there was a raw undercurrent in his tone, "is overrated." His intense gaze slid over her trembling body, lingering on her breasts, before focusing between her thighs.

She saw his jaw lock, felt his fingers tense, and wet desire thudded through her aching sheath. Slowly he knelt on the floor, never taking his eyes from her, and she braced her weight on her elbows so she could watch his face.

Breath hissed between his lips. "I've never seen anything so tempting."

She flexed her internal muscles in an effort to contain the rapidly escalating lust. It didn't work. "My near-naked pussy arouses you?" The strangeness, when she'd examined herself in the bathhouse, had excited her in a way she'd never before imagined. The realization her Gaul had never taken a woman with such a severely groomed pussy not only heightened her own desire but thrilled her in a way that, in a dark corner of her mind, shivered with unspoken danger.

He widened her thighs, opening her farther for his pleasure. The air chilled her damp inner lips, but only momentarily. His scorching gaze warmed her as rapidly as if he were a forest fire.

"Your pouting lips entrance me." He grazed his thumb across her shaved flesh and she jerked, shocked not only by his intimate touch but by his smoky words. "Your musky scent intoxicates." Both thumbs slid into her, but only by the merest degree, before he gently spread her for his further visual exploration.

Gods, no man had ever examined her so thoroughly. Her heart thundered against her ribs, the air evaporated from her chest and it hurt, an unbearable pain she couldn't explain and didn't want to ever end.

The tips of his thumbs caressed her. Up and down the length of her, just inside her, tantalizing. Maddening. *Incredible.*

"Your clitoris"—his lust-drenched voice spilled through her mind, igniting tremors of fire in her blood—"begs to be sucked."

A ragged groan echoed in her ears, vibrated along her throat. "Stop," she gasped, struggling to find the words she needed, "talking."

He lowered his head between her legs and looked up at her over the length of her body. "I thought you wanted me to talk more." Despite the raw need in his voice, there was dark amusement too. "Changed your mind?"

Unable to remain upright any longer, she collapsed onto the bed. Disbelief pounded through her mind. "Your timing," she panted, glaring up at the ceiling, "could be better."

Breath gusted against her exposed flesh, as if he silently laughed. And then his tongue stroked over the swollen bud of her clit and exquisite streaks of agonizing pleasure convulsed her sensitive nerves.

"You taste of the springs of Cymru."

Somewhere insubstantial, where reason still lurked, she knew it couldn't be so. She had bathed in Roman essence, been sprinkled with Roman scents. But his words caused her clit to throb, her internal muscles to tremble and her juices to spill, and another incomprehensible groan fell from her lips.

His tongue slid inside her and she could *feel* him tasting her, as if she were an exotic fruit he had never before encountered. Her eyes closed and fists clenched and she tried to wind her legs around his head to keep him close and tight against her. But his elbows were across her lower thighs pinning her in place, and so she forced her languid arms from the bed and dug her fingers into his scalp.

"You like this." Was he asking her a question or stating a fact? She didn't know and didn't care. All she wanted was for him to never stop. His tongue stroked inside her wet channel, flicked her sensitive lips and swirled around her swollen clit. And his hand splayed across her lower belly, applying additional sensual pressure, and gods, if he *didn't* stop soon, she was going to come inside his mouth.

With a strangled gasp she dug her nails into his head. "Stop." It wasn't what she meant but she didn't have the breath to explain. And so she attempted to drag him up but he refused to be dragged. Instead he sucked her clit between his lips, a kiss so intensely arousing starlight streaked across the indigo of her mind, shattering the remnants of her control.

Her hips bucked and he cupped one rounded buttock, holding her while he continued to lick and suck and kiss as if he intended to murder her by eroticism. Her body pulsed and her sheath convulsed as he thrust his fingers deep inside her while his tongue cradled her trembling clit.

Wheezing gasps rattled her chest but before she could drag her scattered senses together he was on top of her, bracing his weight on one hand while the other clawed through her hair. His eyes were wild as he stared down at her, and as his cock nudged her wet entrance she lifted her heavy legs and wrapped them around his waist.

He rammed into her, thick and long and right. *So right*. As if this joining with this man was something she had been searching for all her life, without even knowing for what she had searched.

The thought was insane but still it lingered, like a flickering

candle in the darkness of her mind. And when he came, hammering her into the mattress with every glorious, brutal thrust, the
feeling didn't dissolve but bloomed, like a deadly pestilence.

Somewhere in the back of her mind she knew it was wrong.
But it made no difference. Because being with her Gaul felt so
unequivocally *right*.

Morwyn stirred from the depths of a blissful, dreamless sleep. The
room was silent, but beyond her closed eyelids red light tinged, as
if a lamp still burned.

She cracked open one eye, expecting to see her Gaul asleep next
to her. The bed was empty. Without knowing why, a frisson of
alarm snaked along her spine, as if his absence was a portent of
unknowable disaster.

Stealthily, although she still couldn't fathom her cautiousness,
she opened both eyes and blinked to bring focus. On the other side
of the room by the single lamp sat her Gaul with a rolled parch-
ment. As she watched, he carefully removed, with apparent expertise, the wax seal and proceeded to read the contents as if he had
every right in the world to do so.

Chapter Nineteen

The sun was sinking onto the western horizon, and Morwyn knew all she should feel was elation that soon she'd once again be in Cymru.

But the overwhelming emotion thudding through her veins wasn't relief. It was a confusing maelstrom of dread and loss. *Grief.*

Because once they were back in the land of her birth, she would have to leave her Gaul and find Caratacus.

"Not long now." The Gaul's familiar smoky voice drifted by her ear as she leaned back against his chest. How different the journey home had been from the one to Camulodunon. Had it truly been scarcely six days since they had met?

Sometimes, as they galloped across the British countryside or lay sated and entwined in the black heat of night, she had trouble recalling how her life had been before that encounter.

A ragged sigh tore through her lips. Once she joined the rebellion, she would forget him soon enough. Yet a hard knot deep in her gut ridiculed her conviction.

The Gaul would not so easily be wiped from her memory.

"Morwyn." One arm was around her waist, holding her close, as if he could exert perfect control over the horse by using only his legs. "I promised to see you safely back to your kinsfolk."

Had he? She couldn't recall. "There's no need. I can find my own way." Except that wasn't true. She didn't know the way, and what made her assume she would have better luck on her own when even with her fellow Druids the Briton king's hideout had remained elusive?

His arm tightened. It was a blatantly possessive gesture but strangely she wasn't offended. Perhaps because before this day ended—or, at most, first thing in the morn—she would leave him forever. And never again experience the sensation of being held so securely in his arms.

"I would see you safely home." There was a dangerous thread in his voice, as if he would accept no dissent. She threaded her fingers through his, trying to ignore the sharp pain that sliced through her chest.

His sense of honor would never allow her to leave by herself in territory he considered hostile. He left her no option but to steal away when he least expected it. Unable to even exchange a fitting good-bye.

"If you insist." She injected a touch of impatience in her tone so he wouldn't become suspicious. But the words were like stale blood in her mouth, foul with the knowledge she lied.

His breath gusted against her cheek, as if he was debating whether or not to continue. "I'll be unable to escort you until my next leave of absence. Only a few days. Not long to wait."

She smothered the foolish hope that leaped in her breast. It made no difference whether his intent was to accompany her home in the morn or another moon. There was no village and she certainly would never allow him to escort her to Mon.

Besides, her destination was unknown even to her. Unless . . .

A thought stirred. He was taking her to the settlement that surrounded the Roman fortification in Cymru to which he was attached. If she stayed a day or so, she might pick up gossip to assist in her search for Caratacus. Perhaps—although she knew it highly unlikely—even discover another Druid.

"You expect me to live in a barbaric Roman barracks?" She shot him a mock-disgusted glance over her shoulder and knew instantly it was a mistake. Because he smiled at her, the smile that lightened his face and caused his eyes to crinkle. The smile she'd grown used to over the last few days, but now it caused an ache to unfurl deep within the region of her heart.

"No." He sounded amused. And no longer attempted to hide it as he had when they had first met. "I'll find you lodgings in the town."

Despite the entrancing sight of his smile and intriguing knowledge of how much more relaxed he appeared, irritation spiked at his easy assumption that she would have no qualms about accepting his protection.

"I'm more than capable of securing my own lodgings, Gaul." She could barter one of her bracelets. They were of excellent craftsmanship and would fetch a good price, and it wasn't as if she required accommodation for more than a night or two.

His smile faded and his expression hardened. A silent sigh echoed through her mind at the transformation. Once again he reminded her of the day they had met in the forest.

"I know that." A thread of irritation heated his words, as if he'd taken offense at her remark. "But the old ways are changing, Morwyn. No matter how you wish otherwise, the Roman ways are infiltrating. It's not safe for a woman alone to secure lodgings. But if they know you're with me, no one will dare touch you."

An angry buzzing filled her head, as if a swarm of bees sought escape. Beyond the waves of fury pounding against her skull, she knew he had intended no insult. Had merely been telling her the way things now were.

But it didn't seem to make any difference to her tongue.

"If I had my dagger, no man would *dare* touch me without permission." She was of noble blood, of Druidic descent. And a warrior. The notion that she was now considered unable to defend herself twisted her stomach, caused bile to rise.

She didn't need a man to protect her. Not even her Gaul.

Especially not her Gaul. He was part of the *reason* she was no longer safe in her own homeland.

"I don't doubt you." His voice was grim. "I'm telling you how it is in the town. And . . ." He hesitated for a fleeting moment. "It's not only the Romans and auxiliaries I'm referring to."

He meant her people were following the invaders' culture and attitude. She clenched her fists, and realized her fingers were still entwined with his. She considered jerking free. And then expelled a long, measured breath instead.

She was fighting this battle with the wrong man. Enemy auxiliary he might be, but he had never treated her with disrespect. *Except for that one time.* She froze the recollection from her mind. *That was different.* Although she wasn't sure why, just that it was.

"My people"—she knew her voice cracked, knew he had heard it—"have lost their way." Because those they had looked to in times of need had abandoned them. First to the magical spiral, and then to the Isle of Mon. Could she blame them for turning their backs on their way of life, when all their leaders had vanished?

He didn't answer her. She hadn't expected him to. How could he, when it was his chosen way of life she scorned?

But as they neared the forests of Cymru, he gently rested his jaw against the top of her head, as if in silent sympathy.

They dismounted before entering the settlement. It reminded her of the town that had sprung up around the fortification erected near her own home village where Carys had met her Roman centurion.

Makeshift dwellings nestled between those of timber and stone; an untidy sprawl around the rigidly constructed enemy garrison that dominated the area.

There were no Roman-clad women here. Unlike Camulodunon,

her people had not blindly embraced the fashion to blend in. But even so, there were countless legionaries strolling through the bustling market, eyeing up the local girls, subliminally displaying the fact they were the conquerors in every arrogant glance and word.

"Stay close." The Gaul's arm tightened around her in clear protection. She couldn't decide whether she was touched or annoyed by his concern.

"I'm well trained in defense."

He didn't answer, but she didn't miss the swift glance he shot her way, and the annoyance sharpened. She knew he didn't believe her. And the irritating fact was, she couldn't blame him.

What else could he think when he'd come upon her when she'd been spread upon the ground, moments from being raped? The memory charred her pride. Although she'd had every intention of gutting the bastard slobbering over her, she knew her chances of survival had been nonexistent.

Until the Gaul had rescued her.

She was grateful. And that by itself was hard to accept, but harder still was the knowledge that, because of that first encounter, his view of her was forever tarnished.

"I'll find lodgings for you before I report in."

Lips compressed, she tugged one of her bracelets from her wrist and handed it to him. He looked at it as if he had never seen such jewelry before in his life.

Breath hissed between her teeth at his obtuseness. "Take it in payment." She shoved it against his chest but still he made no move to accept it. "For the lodgings."

"I don't want payment." He sounded as if she had deliberately insulted him.

Her own wounded pride eased a little at that. "I don't care what you want, Gaul. Take it and sell it and use the money to pay my expenses. I won't be in debt to anyone."

His eyes glinted. Perhaps it was a trick of the sunlight but she didn't think so. He may have trained his facial expression to show not a trace of his true feelings but he hadn't completely mastered shielding emotion from those incredible eyes.

Without a word he unhooked his arm from her waist, took the bracelet between thumb and forefinger as if it burned his flesh, and stuffed it into a pouch hanging from his belt. He didn't reclaim her waist and she slid him a sideways glance. He was staring directly ahead, a ferocious frown on his face, and looked as if he would rip the head off anyone who so much as dared to cross his path.

There wasn't much chance of that. People scuttled out of his way as if Arawn, lord of the Otherworld, stormed among them, and Morwyn smothered the irrational urge to giggle. It was hard to reconcile the obvious fear he evoked in others with the man she knew in private. In truth, she had trouble envisaging him killing anyone outside a battlefield, and yet still Maximus's words lingered in the back of her mind.

Her smile faded. She knew he was wrong, but why had he formed such a poor opinion of her Gaul? She burned to discover the truth, but knew she never would. Because that would involve asking him outright, and how could she do that without sounding as if she accused him of such crimes?

The lodgings were located in one of the stone buildings, and after entrusting the horse's care to a half-starved-looking boy, he accompanied her to her room. It looked very much like the rooms they had shared on the journey.

He stood in the doorway as she sauntered across the room and tested the mattress with the palm of one hand. "Will you be gone long?" She glanced over her shoulder. He was still scowling.

"I'll be back before sundown."

That would give her plenty of time to explore the settlement. "Then I'll eat when you return." And she wasn't simply referring to food either. The thought caused a glow to heat her lower belly. Gods, would she never have enough of this man?

He stepped toward her and her thoughts splintered as she stared at his raised hand.

"This is yours." Her dagger glinted across his outstretched palm. "I trust you won't cut my throat when I return this eve."

Silently she took her dagger and traced her thumb over the familiar pattern of jewels encrusted in the hilt. It hadn't occurred to her he would return it. He'd appeared quite attached to it, secured at his waist. She'd often caught him grazing his fingertips over the handle, as if the texture pleased.

"I won't cut your throat, Gaul." There was an oddly husky tone in her voice. She hoped he hadn't noticed but the chances of that were small. He seemed to notice everything she didn't want him to.

His fingers slid beneath her chin and she looked up at him. Irritation no longer carved his features and instead he looked the way she would always see him in her mind, whenever she recalled him in the years that stretched ahead.

Green eyes. She knew those eyes would forever haunt her. And his face, looking younger and less brutalized than when she'd first met him in the forest. Tough exterior but concealing so very much more than the rest of the world appeared to realize.

"Stay safe." His voice was rough but for one fleeting moment she saw vulnerability flash across his face, glitter in his eyes. So swift it might have been an illusion.

She knew what he really meant. He knew she intended to explore the settlement. That was why he'd returned her dagger. For protection. Her throat constricted, as if she had just received tragic news about a loved one, and something twisted deep inside like a serpent coiling, ready to strike.

"I will." Her words were barely audible but he offered her a faint smile in response before claiming her trembling lips in a tender, too-fleeting kiss.

And then he was gone.

It had been many moons since Morwyn had walked among so many of her own people. In Camulodunon she had felt as if she'd been transplanted to Rome itself. But here, despite the overwhelming presence of the fortification and the ever-present military, there was a sense of belonging. Of having returned home, despite never having been in this part of her country before.

She made her way back to the market, and caught furtive glances thrown her way. Eerie shivers raced along her spine as she caught some of the looks, only to have the curious hastily drop their eyes.

It wasn't the way people had stared before when her face had been newly injured. The bruising had faded to a dull yellow and she doubted it was noticeable from any distance. It was as if these people knew her from somewhere.

She had never been here before. And yet familiar faces teased her memory with every other step. As if she had somehow slipped through time and was once again walking through the village of her childhood.

An older woman suddenly stepped in front of her, and Morwyn pulled up short, staring at the careworn face, the untidy graying hair, the dull eyes, and again the sensation of *knowing* shivered through her.

"Mistress Morwyn?" The woman's voice was scarcely above a whisper, as if she didn't want anyone overhearing. "Is it truly you?"

"Deheune?" The name tumbled from her lips as recollection flooded her mind. "What are you doing here?" The woman was from her village; before the invasion she had taken in laundry and mended clothing for many of the Druids who had no time to attend to such mundane tasks.

Tears glistened in Deheune's eyes and she grasped Morwyn's hand, brushing a reverential kiss across her knuckles. "A lot of us left after that night the gods shook the earth and rained fury from the skies," she said. "We've been here for almost a full turn of the wheel now."

The night Aeron had called on the sacred Spiral of Annwyn

to annihilate all but his chosen few. The night the gods had risen against their High Druid and in retaliation for his betrayal had almost wiped out the populace of Cymru.

The night Morwyn's faith had begun to crumble.

She took a deep breath. "It won't be this way forever, Deheune."

Deheune gave a wistful smile, as if she knew otherwise. "As you say, mistress." She inclined her head as a mark of respect. Peasants did not openly disagree with members of their ruling elite. Then she looked back up, and eagerness had replaced the disbelief. "I'm so happy you're here, mistress."

Morwyn smiled uneasily and wished the woman would release her hand. "I'm glad you're safe. Did all your kin escape?"

"Yes. That's why I'm so happy to see you. My daughter gave birth to a son four moons ago—my first grandchild." Deheune fairly glowed with pride, and a chill shivered along Morwyn's spine as suspicion bloomed.

"May blessings be upon you." Her lips were stiff. It had been so long since she'd uttered such words. And even so, the words uttered were incomplete. The startled look Deheune shot her reminded her forcibly of *that*.

"I—" Deheune hesitated, as if Morwyn's stunted blessing had disorientated her. "Mistress, you're almost the first Druid any of us have seen since that night. We feared—we feared the Romans had slaughtered you all. All but our princess, but she was sacrificed to one of their officers to appease the foreign gods."

"I heard." Gods, what else could she say? That Carys had turned her back on her people and gone willingly with her Roman? How would that help Deheune and all the others struggling to survive?

And how could she blame Carys for leaving, when she and all the other Druids had abandoned their people also?

At least Carys had retained the courage to follow her convictions, to follow Cerridwen, however misguided Morwyn thought she was.

Finally Deheune released her hand. "You're an acolyte of the great goddess." Her voice was a whisper, almost lost against the noisy babble of the nearby market, the snort of horses, the panicked thud of Morwyn's heart. "Truly, you're the Morrigan's chosen one. I know you blessed our babes before that terrible night, mistress. Will you bless my grandson in the ways of our ancestors? Welcome him into the arms of the Morrigan?"

Nausea roiled in the pit of her stomach and she struggled not to let her horror show on her face. It was true; she had taken on the role of Druantia, their ancient queen, and blessed newborn babes after the invasion. She wasn't fully trained, but in all the ways that mattered she was. And she had passed on the Morrigan's blessing in the ways they had been passed on for generations without number.

But how could she bless an innocent babe now, when she no longer believed in the Morrigan or her selfish, destructive ways?

The woman before her chewed on her lip, anxiety clouding her tired eyes. Morwyn might not believe, but Deheune did. And maybe that was enough.

Chapter Twenty

Bren handed the dispatch over to the praefectus of his auxiliary unit, who would ensure it was delivered up the chain of command to the Legatus.

"How did you find the mood in Camulodunum?" The praefectus dragged his thumb over the seal of the dispatch and obviously satisfied it hadn't been tampered with glanced up at Bren.

"Subdued." His king's elderly advisor had trained him well in the art of opening sealed documents without leaving any noticeable trace. The information contained within this dispatch would boost Roman morale. He had to convey what he'd discovered to Caratacus, and soon, so they could plan debilitating strikes against the Legion before reinforcements arrived.

The praefectus made a sound of assent. "More civilized than this hellhole, I don't doubt."

Camulodunon had been raped and molded into the Roman ideal. That wasn't his idea of civilization. But the praefectus clearly expected an answer, and a favorable one at that. "A town worthy of Rome."

"A shame the barbarians in this western peninsula refuse to see that."

Bren didn't answer. He wasn't known for his conversational skills and yet still the praefectus attempted to draw him out every time they met. Sometimes he wondered if the Roman suspected his loyalty. But if that were so, he would never have been entrusted with delivering the dispatch.

"When this cursed Briton rebel is crushed beneath the Eagle, the people will finally see there's no point in fighting the inevitable." The praefectus gave Bren a calculating look. Bren returned the look, unflinching. "The Legatus wants a man on the ground. Your name was mentioned. I want you to spend time in the town, incognito. Listen to the gossip. Find out what you can about Caratacus. There must be people here feeding him information, and that goes both ways. I want to know what that bastard's up to."

Only years of brutally subduing his emotions and the rigid training he'd received under the Legion prevented Bren from reacting. This Roman was asking him to spy on his own people. Did he really think anyone would talk in front of him, knowing he was attached to the enemy?

But then, the Romans didn't assign much credit to the peasant population. The praefectus likely thought if Bren dressed as a Celt of Cymru, he'd be taken as one. The concept that the natives in their far-flung provinces possessed as much loyalty to their own as did the Romans—more, if what he'd learned about their blood-soaked Senate was true—was inconceivable.

To Romans foreigners were inferior, in both blood and intellect. Since Bren's duties hadn't taken him in direct conflict with the locals, the praefectus—and Legatus—obviously believed the populace hadn't noticed him.

"You want me to live in the town?" His voice was level but perhaps not as neutral as he'd imagined as the other man flicked an autocratic hand in a dismissive gesture.

"It's unpalatable. I know. But if your cover was exposed, your skills would ensure the likelihood of escaping unscathed."

Meaning his reputation for dispatching those who crossed him was a definite benefit as far as the praefectus was concerned.

The initial distaste of such a task faded, as possibilities filtered through his mind.

"Would this assignment be confined to the town or should I attempt to search for information farther afield?"

"If you need to follow up your suspicions, then you have permission to leave the immediate vicinity without obtaining leave of absence." The praefectus offered a chilly smile. "Within reason, naturally."

He could hardly believe it. The praefectus had just handed him carte blanche to come and go from the town as he pleased. Instead of waiting until his next official leave, he could ride from the town on the morrow to find Caratacus.

"I doubt I'll have reason to leave the town." He maintained eye contact. "I merely wished to clarify my position if such a circumstance arose."

"Obtain lodging." The praefectus flicked a glance over him. "And lose the chain mail. Report in at the end of the week. If you haven't made any progress by then, we'll have to abandon it— you'll be needed in the ranks again."

He only needed a week. During that time he could visit with his king and pass on conflicting and disturbing *information* direct to the Roman officers. Unlike other occasions when he'd needed to ensure the rumors couldn't be traced back to him, this time he didn't need to cover his tracks.

It was risky. But he'd lived with risk for too long to let that deter him. They hadn't linked him to the acts of sabotage plaguing the garrison or as the source of demoralizing morale among the ranks. And should suspicion ever be cast his way, he planned on being far from here. Standing by the side of his king.

It was done. In the dingy one-roomed dwelling Deheune had taken her, Morwyn handed the squalling babe back to his beaming mother and a small whisper of heat flickered through her barren soul.

May the blessings of the Morrigan be upon you.

When she'd started the ceremony, trepidation had crawled through her belly, as if her actions were sacrilege and prayers blasphemous. But the words had fallen from her lips, feeling as right and natural as if she uttered them every day. The mother and her kin surrounded her, their faces transfixed as she prepared a makeshift concoction from her limited supply of herbs and potions, before invoking the ancient rituals of the great goddess.

"Thank you, mistress." The mother, a girl who looked several years younger than Carys, had tears glittering in her eyes. "I was so afraid the Morrigan would never welcome him. But it doesn't matter now, does it? About his father, I mean."

A ripple of barely contained fury stirred among the others in the room, but the girl didn't appear to notice. She was once again gazing at her child with near-reverential awe.

"No." Morwyn's voice was strong, assured. No one would dare doubt her word. "The Morrigan has accepted him. Our heritage is his."

Her heart hammered against her ribs as she spoke for the goddess, as if she had every right to do so. But she couldn't let these people see her doubt. For them, her faith had to appear strong and shining and eternal. They believed she was still the Morrigan's chosen one, a Druid dedicated to the gods and all they represented. What right did she have to shatter those beliefs? When she had nothing of value to offer in their stead but a scorched sense of desolation?

Several times since the invasion, before she had fled to the Isle of Mon, she had assured distraught girls that as long as they brought their child up to honor the great goddess, the heritage of the father meant nothing.

Why should it, when the father neither knew nor cared that his brutal actions had sired a babe?

But back then, she had believed in the Morrigan with all her heart and soul. Had loved her unconditionally and without reserve. Had believed, unequivocally, in her benevolence and justice.

She had never before had to fake her faith.

Yet underneath her disdain, the need to believe flourished. And even though she couldn't embrace her goddess, couldn't forgive how the Morrigan had demanded they flee from Cymru on that night of devastation, she couldn't deny the comfort these people drew from their deity's name.

It was a small sacrifice. To pretend nothing had changed when everything had if it made such a difference to so many. She gathered her things, tried to smother the odd tug deep in the pit of her belly.

She didn't need this. She hadn't missed it. This bestowing from the goddess was no longer her calling.

"Mistress." Deheune hurried up to her and then paused, anxiety flashing across her face. She held out a small bundle. "It's not much, but I pray it's acceptable to the goddess."

Heat burned Morwyn's cheeks. She clamped her lips together against the words that tumbled on her tongue. By the look of things, these people could scarcely manage to feed and clothe themselves. She didn't want to take their meager offering from their mouths. But to refuse, no matter how delicately she worded it, would only cause grave offense.

"I thank you on behalf of the Morrigan." She took the bundle, felt like a thief. In the past, these naming rituals were a great and wonderful celebration; a cause for lavish sacrifice and feasting. Several babes would be blessed at the one ritual, the cost spread among countless kin and enjoyed in the sacred oak groves of their ancestors.

Not hidden inside a drafty shack, away from disapproving enemy eyes.

A dull ache gripped her heart. Just because she had discovered their gods were nothing but weak, malleable cowards, she realized she didn't want their names and ways to be lost, crushed underfoot by the equally despicable Roman deities.

But that wasn't going to happen. When the battle was won, when the invaders were driven from their lands, order would be restored. And in that order, their gods would once again reign supreme.

She just wasn't sure that when that happened, she could stomach taking her rightful place with her fellow Druids.

"I'll pass the word, mistress." Deheune's whisper was conspiratorial. Morwyn stared at her, uncomprehending. "To the others," she added. "There have been a great many births since the night of devastation. Your arrival's like . . . It's like a miracle, mistress."

Her mouth dried as panic kicked in her gut. How could she bear to repeat this ancient ritual, mouth the holy words, invoke the spirit of the great goddess *when she didn't believe?*

Sweat prickled her skin, her palms clammy. She couldn't do it. And not just because of her personal feelings. She was leaving, to join Caratacus. To fight for these people's freedom. Surely that was more important than staying and blessing innocent babes?

Deheune gazed at her, at first with wide-eyed trust and then with growing apprehension, as if she guessed Morwyn's thoughts. The notion horrified.

"Don't be distressed." Deheune dared to lay the tips of her fingers on Morwyn's wrist before hastily snatching her hand back as if she couldn't believe her audacity. "Only some have embraced Rome. Most of us long for the old ways. We know whom to trust, mistress. Your presence among us would never be betrayed to the enemy."

Because if the enemy captured a Druid, even a lapsed Druid, they'd crucify her without a moment's hesitation as a warning and reminder of their cursed Emperor's edict.

As they would Carys, if they discovered her true identity in Camulodunon.

Chills scuttled over her arms. That hadn't occurred to her at the time. Morwyn had scarcely thought twice about Carys's confidences. But if the Romans found out she was not only a Druid but also passing on her knowledge, pregnant or not, crucifixion would be the least of her tortures.

She stared into Deheune's anxious eyes, and realization dawned.

Carys might not intend to take up weapons and fight the enemy in hand-to-hand combat. But, in her own way, she was fighting them all the same.

How could Morwyn refuse to bless these people's babes? It would give them renewed hope and strengthen their faith to keep strong under the enemy's thumb. She could still find her way to the Briton king. She would just leave a few days later than she'd first intended—that was all.

A smoky vision of her Gaul drifted across her mind and she smothered a sigh. Yes, it meant she could also enjoy a few more days of his company, but that wasn't the reason she was staying.

It wasn't.

The thought thudded in her skull. *Liar.*

"We'd only share the knowledge of your presence with those we trust." Deheune edged a little closer. "There's one other Druid in hiding here. One of the Elders, a chosen one of Belatucadros. Those who've kept his presence secret these last five moons would never betray you, mistress."

Light was fading when Morwyn finally returned to their lodgings. Her head throbbed and heart hammered and blood thundered through her veins, yet despair dampened her excitement at the knowledge she could share nothing of what she had done or discovered with her Gaul.

In the morn she was returning to Deheune's home, where she'd be escorted to the Druid Elder, the chosen one of the god of war and destruction. It was his calling, the woman had explained without even a trace of resentment, that prevented him from participating in any of the Morrigan's rituals. Even though, as Morwyn well knew, he would be more than capable of undertaking such ceremonies.

The Gaul was leaning against the stone wall of the lodgings, arms crossed, looking formidable and deadly. And obviously waiting for her.

A sharp pain stabbed through her heart, as if he had plunged a dagger into her breast. Her breath stumbled, and for a moment the notion fluttered across her mind as to how different this would all be, if only he hadn't pledged his loyalty to the Romans.

But he had. And she was forever pledged to rid her land of the invaders. The pain dulled, curled into a hard knot, and she dragged in a deep breath in an attempt to dislodge the constriction blocking her throat.

Somehow, despite everything, she'd begun to like her Gaul. As she drew level with him, his harsh features relaxed and the faintest smile touched his lips, as if he hadn't been certain she intended to return.

Like him? Who was she trying to fool? She more than liked him, no matter how many times she reminded herself of the abduction or the way he'd chained her.

She cared for him. And it could lead to nothing but despair.

"You didn't lose your way." It wasn't a question, more a statement of fact. He threaded her fingers through his, as if he didn't care who saw them, and tugged her against his side.

"Of course not." When had she started to care for him? She'd tried so hard to keep her distance. But she should have known back in Camulodunon. When she'd declined Carys's offer to remain.

"Been shopping?" He glanced at the bundle she still grasped in her other hand. She'd almost forgotten about it. "There was no need. Food's included in the price of lodgings."

She didn't know precisely what was in the bundle, except it felt like an assortment of root vegetables. A rich sacrifice, but an odd mixture of choice if she had truly bartered for their meal that eve.

"I didn't realize." She glanced at a tiny beggar crouched by the side of the dwelling. "Here." She held out the bundle and after a moment of clear astonishment the ragged creature darted out and snatched it from her hand. Dark hair matted, skin embedded with grime, it was impossible to tell whether it was a girl or a boy.

With a silent sigh Morwyn turned away from the sight of the beggar tearing open the bundle. There was nothing she could do. Beggars appeared to proliferate under the mighty Roman occupation.

Once inside their room, the Gaul opened one of his pouches attached to his belt, turned her hand over and tipped a pile of coins onto her palm. "Your change from the sale of your bracelet."

Impressed, she stowed the coins in one of her own leather pouches. "You must have remarkable bartering skills."

"I don't get cheated, if that's what you mean."

"I can believe it." She rose onto her toes and brushed a kiss across his lips. Why not enjoy his touch while she could? She wanted to make as many memories with him as possible. Memories she could savor for the rest of her life.

"Tempting." He pulled back, a grin illuminating his face. She sucked in a shocked breath, tried to rearrange her thought but couldn't.

He was definitely grinning. And it transfigured his face even more fundamentally than his elusive smiles. Mesmerized, she stared, uncaring of the passage of time or how hunger growled in the pit of her stomach.

If only she could capture this look, seal it for eternity, so every smallest detail would remain fresh in her mind no matter how many seasons might pass.

"More than tempting, if you continue to look at me with such adoration in your eyes." His tone implied he was flirting in the most outrageous manner. Her Gaul, flirting, when only days ago she had wondered if he even knew the meaning of the word.

"It's tragically obvious *your* eyes require a thorough cleansing." Except she had the worrying notion he had seen more in her look than she intended. She accompanied her remark with a haughty toss of her head, in hopes of distracting his attention.

"Maybe."

Gods, and still he flirted. Fascinated, she could only continue to stare at him as if she had never seen him before. And it was almost as if she hadn't. He seemed . . . different. She couldn't place it. And then something odd about his appearance occurred to her.

"You're not wearing your chain mail or helmet." He always wore his armor, unless they were readying for bed. It was as if their absence lifted a great weight from his shoulders, and not a physical weight but spiritual.

"And that's why," he said, sliding his arm around her waist and escorting her to the door, "I have the strength to resist your charms in favor of eating first. Because I can spend the night with you."

Confused, she smiled up at him. Of course he was spending the night with her. Where else would he sleep?

They entered a room that was dark, stuffy and filled with a tantalizing aroma of simmering food. A swarthy man took one look at her Gaul and lumbered over to them, jerking his head to indicate they should follow. He then proceeded to grasp the hair of two youths sitting at a corner table and toss them across the floor.

"Here," he said, wiping the spills on the table with the sleeve of his tunic.

They sat opposite each other. "Wine?" The Gaul took a pottery amphora from a serving girl and picked up a goblet in readiness.

"This eve you offer me wine?" She raised her eyebrows. "Every other time you gave me water." Not that she minded. Had she wanted wine after that second night, she would have taken some whether he'd offered or not.

"You're welcome to have water. I thought you might prefer wine for a change since we're unlikely to be watched."

"Watched?" Involuntarily she glanced around the crowded room, where Celts ate with relish and drank local ale and Roman wine with abandon. There didn't appear to be any Romans. Unless they dressed as locals when off duty.

"Rome," the Gaul said, "doesn't approve of women enjoying wine."

"Rome," she said, "doesn't approve of *women*."

He laughed, and didn't try to smother it. She forgot about her wine and smiled back, entranced by his humor. "You're not of that same mind, then?"

"No." He took a swallow of the dark golden liquid. "Taken in moderation, why not?"

She leaned over the table, careful not to touch the sticky surface. "Is it an edict from their gods?"

"I doubt it." The faintest trace of derision threaded his words, although the smile still hovered on his lips.

There was so much she wanted to know about him. So much she knew she never would. But perhaps he wasn't entrenched in Roman culture. Perhaps she might be able to tell him a little of herself, after all.

"Do you worship their gods?"

He hesitated for the merest moment, not as if he didn't trust her with his answer but as if he'd never before been asked such a question.

"No."

Her heart thudded against her ribs in sudden excitement. "Our gods?" Her voice was scarcely above a whisper. Even if her faith had diminished, it would still be a bond between them. She didn't even bother analyzing why she wanted to find a bond between them.

"Do you believe in them, Morwyn?" His voice was low, his eyes mesmeric. Her breath caught in her throat, amplified her heartbeat.

"I don't know." It was a breathy whisper, and in that moment she truly didn't know. Only knew she wanted, more than anything, to believe in *him*.

He smiled again, but this time it was tarnished with bitterness. "All gods are the same." He finished his wine, poured another. "They speak through priests and oracles, or"—his gaze lanced through her—"Druids." The word dripped with venom.

It was as if he'd physically punched her in the face, and she only just prevented herself from reeling back in shocked reaction. His face was no longer twisted with revulsion, as it had when he'd spat *Druids* at her, but the image was burned into her brain.

She licked her lips, longed for water to moisten her dry mouth.

"You don't care for Druids?" She might be battling a personal crisis, but whatever she did with her life, nothing would change the blood in her veins, her Druidic ancestry or the destiny she had once been expected to fulfill.

"I feel nothing for them." He tapped the stem of his goblet as if recalling distant events. "Except contempt."

Chapter Twenty-one

⮞⋰⟡⋱⮜

Morwyn couldn't trust herself to speak. She picked up her goblet and gulped down the strong wine. It scorched her throat, but not as much as the Gaul's words scorched her heart.

Of course, she hadn't intended telling him she was a Druid. To admit such to one who worked for the enemy was tantamount to a death sentence. But the possibility of ever confiding in him, however remote that had been, crumbled to dust.

But she was leaving soon. Why did it matter?

The answer glinted out of reach, insubstantial. She didn't *know* why it mattered so much. Only that it did.

She sucked in a deep breath. He was staring at her, as if wondering why she was so silent. The notion flickered that perhaps she should confront his comment. After all, surely most of the populace still retained ample respect for the Druids? Or did they? She'd been sequestered on a sacred Isle. How could she truly know what the general population thought of Druids anymore?

She couldn't rouse his suspicions. Didn't *want* to rouse his suspicions—was there a difference?

Sweat slicked the back of her neck, the palms of her hands. She had the sick sensation there was a vast chasm of difference.

"It's fortunate"—her voice sounded cool, even slightly bored, although she hadn't the first idea how she managed such a feat— "the paranoia of the Roman Emperor drove all Druids into hiding."

She tensed her muscles, waiting for his response. No doubt he would now condemn all Druids as cowards, for abandoning their people in their time of need. Why else would he feel such contempt?

"Maybe not all." He paused while a serving wench deposited two bowls of steaming stew onto the table. "While in Camulo-dunon I heard rumors that the wife of the tribune there was a runaway Druid."

Her stomach churned, and hunger melded into horror. How safe could Carys be if such rumors were rife? What if her Gaul told his superiors of the suspicions surrounding the wife of one of their patrician officers? Did Maximus possess the power and connec-tions necessary to protect their princess from persecution?

The Gaul shot her a probing glance, as if her tangled thoughts showed clearly on her face. She struggled to maintain her composure but panic thudded through her blood, hammered against her skull.

She had to alleviate his suspicion.

"A Druid?" She injected as much skepticism in her tone as she could. And hoped he couldn't hear the ragged beat of her heart that punched through each word. "That doesn't seem likely." She feigned interest in the stew, but her appetite had fled. "Surely a filthy Roman officer would have a Druid's head on a spike before he'd welcome her into his bed."

"I imagine that would depend entirely on how desirable he found her."

Gods, she was going to vomit. Carys's life could depend on whether she managed to steer the Gaul's interest away from the likelihood of a Roman officer taking a Druid as his wife.

"A Druid," she said, fixing him with what she hoped was an expression that conveyed both exasperation and boredom, "would rather kill herself than submit to the enemy." The next words choked, but she forced them out. "Or she'd find a way to run and hide. Druids are good at hiding from danger."

He gave a grim laugh, as if he had personal experience of such things. "True. And no Roman patrician would want to damage his chances of rising through the ranks by taking such a wife." He speared a sliver of meat with his knife and regarded it, in much the same way she could imagine he regarded a severed limb of an enemy in battle. Dispassionately. "Rumor or not, it provided for great gossip in the bathhouse. He should have known by taking a foreigner he was asking for such trouble."

Had the danger passed? Did he still think the tribune, who could be none other than Maximus, had married a Druid or merely an ordinary Celt?

"I pity the woman." Morwyn's voice was lofty and she stirred her stew as if it fascinated her. "I only hope her love proves true. She must have given up everything in order to be with him."

"Perhaps she wasn't given the choice." His white, even teeth pulled the meat from the tip of the knife. "Perhaps, in truth, she's nothing more than his official concubine."

Affront slashed through her on Carys's behalf, at the mere suggestion her princess could be relegated to such a lowly status. But anything was better than adding even a hint of credence to the notion Maximus had taken a Druid as his wife.

For a moment she tumbled back in time, to that night when Carys left to be with her Roman. Morwyn had begged her to reconsider. Had told her the enemy would crucify her if they discovered her true calling.

Maximus had said they weren't complete barbarians. That they could honor a foreign princess. And after having seen them together, Morwyn knew he did honor Carys, loved her truly and would do all in his power to protect her.

But his Emperor hated Druids, feared the influence they had wielded for generations. Wanted to wipe even the memory of their existence from the face of the earth. How could one man, no matter how honorable, stand against the bigoted might of Rome?

Let her Gaul think Carys was little more than a common slave. It could help save her skin.

She had to divert his attention. But her mind thudded with only one thought, and before she could stop herself, the words spilled from her lips.

"Why do you hate Druids so?" She knew it wasn't personal. He hadn't the first idea of what she was. Yet still his contempt ate into her. "What did they do to you?"

For a moment she didn't think he was going to answer. He continued to chew the meat, took a second mouthful, and only after taking a swing of wine did he finally look at her.

"I don't hate them." His voice was level. "I despise them. There's a difference, Morwyn. Hate requires too much energy."

Heat crawled over her skin, prickling her flesh, and an odd despair trickled through her stomach as if he had told her she was the one he despised.

Would he, if he knew?

"Then why do you despise them?"

He regarded her in silence, as if contemplating whether or not she deserved an answer. The moment stretched, interminably. He wasn't going to respond. Didn't think her worthy of confiding even that much of his inner self to her.

And then he spoke. "Do you believe they're never wrong?"

Instantly the image of Aeron flashed across her mind. Aeron; impossibly beautiful with his long golden hair, strange silver eyes and the aura of mystical power that had always surrounded him.

A shudder flicked over her neck, her arms, along her spine and the backs of her legs. Once, she'd loved him. Would have done anything for him. And when her eyes had opened, when she'd seen the evil polluting his blackened soul, she had been the means for his destruction.

"No." Her voice choked on the word. Once, she'd believed it inconceivable for Druids to be in the wrong. They were conduits for the gods. And the gods were supposed to be infallible. "They can be wrong." *So horrifically wrong.* "They're only mortal, despite their blood."

Was it her imagination or did her Gaul's hard features soften by the minutest degree? As if he hadn't been sure of her response and her words gave him some measure of relief?

"Mortal." He appeared to savor the word. "And vindictive." His lips twisted into a parody of the smile she had come to cherish. "My contempt is personal, Morwyn. It doesn't stem from the bloody quagmire of battle." He paused as if reconsidering his words. "Although it certainly led me there."

"Personal?" Did she truly wish to know? Unease shivered through her mind, as if a premonition of disaster hovered on the near horizon. But how could she not want to know, when he was so close to confiding something of his past?

"You'll find it hard to believe, I know." He shot her a strangely defensive glance, although she had the strangest conviction that only she could see that trace of vulnerability in his look. And it pierced through her heart, as tangible as the blade of a Druid's sacrificial dagger. "But a trace of noble blood taints my veins."

Of course it did. She had always suspected he was more than a common auxiliary. Wild suppositions whipped through her brain. Perhaps the Romans held his noble mother and sisters captive, and in exchange for their safety her Gaul had to fight in the loathed Legions?

That wouldn't make him a traitor. And of course there were insurmountable reasons as to why he'd been unable to rescue his womenfolk. Perhaps the Druids forbade it. Perhaps they were in cahoots with the Romans. And that was why her Gaul despised them so.

Her grip tightened on her knife, and she silently willed him to continue.

"And as such"—bitterness iced his words—"my choice of bride was condemned."

For a moment she continued staring at him, wondering at his choice of words. What did he mean? What bride? What did that have to do with being blackmailed by the enemy?

The raucous background din faded, replaced by a dull buzzing that filled her ears and echoed inside her skull. "Your bride?" He was telling her *about his wife*?

It hadn't even occurred to her he was married. At first because he was nothing but her enemy and such things were of no account. But later, when he became more to her than merely the bastard Gaul, it should have crossed her mind. Yet still it hadn't.

"I knew her as a child. We grew up together. She was the daughter of one of our slaves." His gaze pinned Morwyn to her seat. Not that she was capable of moving. Even her tongue felt paralyzed. "A slave herself." And again bitterness tinged his words.

Her face blazed. Thank the gods for the dim lighting so he couldn't see. It was no great revelation, not truly, to know he was married. Doubtless he'd left her back in Gaul while he followed the Legions. And like so many barbarians he thought nothing of taking other women whenever the urge took him.

As he had taken her. And even that she could understand because it was the way of the world, even if it wasn't her world. But what she couldn't understand was the depth of tortured anguish glinting in his eyes, thundering behind his words.

He was not merely married. He clearly adored his wife.

It shouldn't hurt, but it did. And she had a terrifying notion as to why.

Because she cared for him.

"A slave." Her lips were stiff, her tongue swollen, and the words rolled from her as heavy as rocks. She didn't care if the bitch was a Gallic princess. The only thought that pulsed through her mind was the knowledge her Gaul loved the foreign whore.

"The Druids forbade our union." He twisted the stem of the goblet between thumb and forefinger. "Despite the fact that by then I'd secured her freedom."

Morwyn drained her wine, and the liquid scalded her still empty stomach. Her Gaul, despite his claim, must possess more than a mere drop of noble blood. Of course the Druids would forbid such a match. When it came to the nobility, they liked to keep the bloodlines pure. At least, that had been her experience in the past, and why should it be so different in Gaul?

"Naturally, you defied them." She couldn't pretend a lightness she didn't feel, and the words sounded harsh, as if she condemned him as had his Druids.

She did condemn him. But not for the same reasons.

"Naturally." His tone was dry and his eyes bored into her as if he suddenly noticed her discomposure. She gritted her teeth, regulated her breath. No matter how she felt, she wouldn't let him see that his revelations touched her. In another day or so she would leave him forever. His marital status did not matter.

"Morwyn." He reached across the table and trailed one finger along the line of her jaw. It took considerable willpower not to jerk back from his touch. "I didn't think *you'd* be so disapproving." To her disbelief there was a trace of censure in his tone as if her reaction somehow disappointed him in a fundamental way.

"Why do you care for my approval or not?" The words were out before she could prevent them. He would have to be dead not to realize she was wounded by his confidence. The knowledge scraped along her nerve endings and she straightened, severing their connection. "I fail to see why you think I should be interested in the—the daily habits of your wife."

He pulled back to his side of the table, his face hardening into the impenetrable mask she'd not seen for days. "You're right. It's nothing to you."

A sense of injustice bubbled deep in her gut, curdling the wine, spiraling through her blood. How dared he take offense? Was she a cheap whore who offered a man relief not only with sex but a false sympathy for him to pour out his sins in hopes of being forgiven?

She stabbed a piece of meat onto her knife with deadly precision. "I only wonder, since you're so besotted, that you didn't bring her with you. It's not as if lodgings aren't plentiful." She tore the meat from her knife. It tasted of ashes.

The silence screamed between them. She refused to look at him and concentrated on her lukewarm stew. The thought of eating it turned her stomach. But not as much as the thought of sharing the Gaul's bed this night when he would doubtless, once again, be thinking of his wife as he took *her*.

She knew she could refuse him. Perhaps she would. And her heart remained heavy within her breast.

"You misunderstand." His voice was emotionless. He may have been discussing the weather or the quality of their meal. "My wife died six years ago."

The grisly meat lodged in her throat and she choked. Tears prickled her eyes and she grabbed the amphora and took a long swallow straight from the source.

Gods. She flicked him a glance over the amphora and saw he was staring at her dispassionately. As if their growing closeness over the last few days had never occurred.

Shame burned through her at the cruel thoughts she'd leveled against his wife. It was one thing to curse the living. Quite another to curse those who were continuing their journeys.

She swallowed around the scraped flesh of her throat. Druids were not taught to apologize to outsiders when in the wrong. Because Druids were so very rarely in the wrong.

But then, she'd turned her back on her Druidry. And this was the result.

She risked another glance. He was no longer looking at her but instead finishing his stew as if nothing untoward had passed between them. Her sweaty fingers ached around the knife and she placed it on the table before surreptitiously wiping her hands on the lap of her gown.

"I regret your loss." She stared at her plate, unable to look at him in case he dismissed her condolence as false. "I thought . . . I had the impression she was waiting for you back in Gaul."

He didn't answer. Finally she could no longer bear the silence and looked up. He was regarding her but his expression was unreadable. Even his eyes appeared emotionless.

It was intolerable that she was in the position of having to defend herself before him. Why did she feel as if she were on trial?

In a vague, insubstantial crevice of her mind she wondered why she felt the overpowering need to explain herself. What did it matter if he'd misunderstood her flash of anger?

Wasn't it better for him to assume his choice of wife disgusted her rather than the unpalatable truth that she had been *jealous*?

Yes. And her upbringing had impressed upon her the importance of choosing wisely when it came to marriage and the creation of children. To fall in love with a slave was unfortunate. To marry her inconceivable. But despite the years of indoctrination it hadn't been, and wasn't, condemnation that pounded through her heart at his revelation.

"No." His voice was still even. "She no longer waits for me. The Druids took care of that."

Her fingers dug into her thighs as horrifying scenarios flashed through her mind. Druids weren't violent by nature—Aeron had been a shocking anomaly—but retribution when their laws were violated was harsh and unforgiving.

"What did they do?" Her whisper was scarcely audible. Before the invasion, had one of their nobles so blatantly disregarded the laws on matrimony, he would have been punished if he'd refused to recant. Exile was always a popular choice. But they would never have killed the woman. Not unless there was more to this than her Gaul was telling.

"It's more a question of what they didn't do." He took the amphora and shared the remainder of the wine between their goblets. "When her life hung in the balance they chose to heal me instead of saving her. And for that I will never forgive them."

Chapter Twenty-two

Bren caught the look of horror that flashed across Morwyn's face and downed half the goblet in one swallow. What the fuck was he doing, telling her about his personal life?

He'd buried that life and lost his last sliver of self-respect three years ago when he'd taken on Dunmacos's identity. And he hadn't spoken of Eryn for even longer.

But something about this night had loosened his tongue. He'd wanted to confide, to ease the poison in his soul. His unexpected freedom from the Legion, and the rush of relief and pleasure that had filled his chest when Morwyn returned to the lodgings, had obviously addled his brain. Corrupted his well-honed sense of survival.

She'd been repelled. As had the majority of his kin. What else had he expected? Morwyn might attempt to pass herself off as a trader. And she may well have spent years as a slave of a Roman. But he was convinced she possessed the blood of nobility.

And that blood had rejected the idea that love wasn't foul simply because it crossed between one class and another.

If she knew his true lineage, she'd be more revolted than ever by his perceived transgression. At least he'd had the presence of mind to dilute his heritage. Perhaps she'd be more forgiving, thinking he possessed only a drop of noble blood.

What did he care for her good opinion? The question pounded against his temples, demanding an answer. She was nothing to him but a good fuck. A warm body in the heat of the night. A woman who, despite the circumstances of their initial encounter, never deferred to him or cowed in his presence.

Morwyn. The first person, male or female, he'd been able to fully relax with in years. He didn't know how or why, only that somehow she'd peeled back the icy armor protecting the core of his wounded psyche and slid inside. Illuminating his darkness with her quick tongue and the incandescent beauty of her radiant smile.

A dull pain twisted through his chest. She had stayed with him so far because it suited her to go to Camulodunon, to visit her Roman friend. She had remained with him because he'd given her safe passage back to Cymru.

He couldn't fathom, now that he considered it, why she'd returned to the lodgings this night. She could have escaped, somehow, back to her village. She wasn't like Eryn, who would never have attempted such a dangerous journey by herself.

If Morwyn wanted to leave, she would have. But she'd returned. And that was why he'd just spilled his stinking guts to her.

Had he expected sympathy? Understanding? He deserved neither. Would receive neither. And couldn't comprehend why the knowledge seared the remnants of his shriveled soul.

"They didn't kill her?" Morwyn's voice vibrated with revulsion but her eyes were locked with his and it wasn't disgust he saw glittering in those enigmatic dark depths. It looked like fear.

His gaze sharpened, and now he saw the way she leaned across the table toward him, her body taut, her face drawn. As if, far from condemning him, she was waiting for absolution.

"No." But he was distracted, trying to comprehend her strange reaction. There was no reason why Morwyn should empathize. He was seeing emotion where there was none.

Yet still she gazed at him with that incomprehensible illusion of fear and anticipation.

"Then . . ." She hesitated, clearly confused. "You despise them because they couldn't save her life?"

She appeared strangely preoccupied with details, when he expected slighting words over his choice of wife. In truth he'd hoped her years in slavery, no matter how pampered she'd been, had broadened her mind.

He'd been wrong. She'd looked furious. But now his conviction wavered. *Had* she been disgusted by his confidence? Or had he misunderstood her initial reaction?

Had she, instead, been trying to hide her shock at his vitriolic outpouring against the Druids? As a member of the chieftain class, she would have been brought up to respect those cursed conduits of the gods.

"No," he said and again was distracted by the woman sitting opposite him, when until now the only woman who had ever distracted his mind had been Eryn. "They didn't try." And then the horror of that eve slashed through him, crippling with its brutality, and his chest constricted. "They let her bleed to death. She was unworthy of their sacred skills."

Morwyn blanched, as if he'd just physically assaulted her. As if she took the Druids' callousness personally.

"Did she perish in childbirth?" Her tone was so filled with anxiety it took a heartbeat for her actual words to penetrate.

Childbirth? How had she reached that conclusion? For a moment he was blinded by her stupidity, and then reason punched through the ancient, simmering rage. He sucked in a deep breath. Why had he thought it a good idea to try to share a sliver of his past with Morwyn? His past was foul. He was beyond redemption.

He didn't want to discuss it anymore. Because every word he uttered could only condemn himself further in her eyes.

She reached across the grimy table and curled her hand around his fist. Her touch was light yet firm. Completely unexpected.

"Tell me." Her voice was soft, compelling. "How did your wife die, Gaul?"

Gaul. How would it feel to hear his true name on her lips? He didn't want to contemplate it, because it would never happen. He'd always be her Gaul and, gods, that was fine because anything was better than hearing her call him *Dunmacos*.

"We were attacked at night." He'd been returning from a gathering of tribes in Gaul, where he'd represented his father. After three years of marriage his kin had finally, with varying degrees of reluctance, accepted his choice of wife, and once again he was involved in the political machinations of retaining his family's remorseless grip on the power they retained beneath the Roman Empire.

For no other reason than to prolong their time together away from the mantle of disapproval that still lingered in their home village, he'd decided to stay overnight in a hamlet. Nestled on the slopes of an inconspicuous valley, total population scarcely twelve, the danger of attack hadn't even crossed his mind. Neither did it cross the minds of the two warriors who'd accompanied them on the journey, as they offered no protest when he told them to continue onward.

Morwyn's fingers tightened around his, as if in silent sympathy. She wouldn't offer such solace if she could see into the evil pit of his soul.

"They burned the hamlet to the ground. Murdered the men, raped the women and children and took whatever they didn't kill as slaves." Bren should have died that night, along with Eryn. But by the malevolence of the gods and the cursed ministrations of the Druids, he'd survived.

Morwyn didn't speak. But she didn't look away either. He threaded his fingers through hers, rested his jaw against their joined hands.

"Someone escaped. Roused the local rulers." His kin. And

they'd sent a contingent of warriors and two of the most highly skilled Druids.

It had been too late. Drifting between this world and the next, he'd fought the Druids, his hoarse voice pleading with them to attend Eryn. To save his beloved.

But they'd ignored him. And used their powers to harness his maddened spirit, to wrench it back into his corporeal body, to anchor him once more on the mortal plane.

He was the one they had been sent to save. And by the time they finally deemed him capable of being moved, there was no one left in that ravaged hamlet who could benefit from their formidable skills.

"Is it possible . . ." She hesitated, as if unsure whether to continue. "Perhaps your wife was beyond their help before they arrived."

Smashed to a bloodied pulp, unable to move and scarcely able to draw breath into his damaged lungs, he'd still heard Eryn's every terrified cry as the attackers had brutalized her. When he'd finally pushed his broken body onto his side to try to protect her, one of them launched a spear in his direction. And the world turned scarlet.

Later, the Druids had proclaimed that the gods had guided the weapon, sparing his life, and he'd believed them. How else could he have survived such blood loss unless the gods wanted to keep him alive for their further vindictive pleasure?

He rubbed her knuckles across his roughened jaw. Focused on her dark eyes, so full of compassion. He could almost allow himself to believe she felt something more than lust for him.

"Perhaps she was." It was the first time he'd ever acknowledged the possibility aloud, even though the thought had tortured him incessantly over the years. "But they had no intention of even trying. They ignored her as if she were nothing but a piece of bloodied meat."

Morwyn didn't answer right away. Her other hand cradled his face, a tender gesture devoid of sexual overtones. As if all she wished to give was comfort.

She whispered words in a language he didn't know. Yet eerie shivers snaked along his spine, as if somewhere deep inside his subconscious he recognized the foreign incantation. But before he could grasp their significance she trailed her fingers through his hair and the sensation splintered.

And then she spoke. "It wasn't your fault."

Back in their room Bren watched Morwyn light two lamps and place them beside the bed. The ache in his heart was still there. Would always be there as a constant reminder of how he'd failed Eryn. But somehow, since sharing that small, vital segment of his past with Morwyn, the pain no longer crippled every breath he took.

Unease slithered deep in his gut. He didn't deserve even that modicum of peace. He searched his mind for Eryn's face, focused on the fragile memory and heard once again her agonized cries as he'd struggled against oblivion.

But the familiar guilt-soaked pain didn't rip through his chest and tear open his heart. Instead, the hazy image of Eryn smiled at him, a tender smile, as if she forgave him for being unable to save her that night.

The smile he saw so often during his tangled nightmares. Her unequivocal forgiveness, a shining star piercing his blood-drenched existence. The forgiveness he'd refused to acknowledge for so many torturous years.

He couldn't allow her to forgive him. Because he could never forgive himself.

"Gaul." Morwyn's voice dragged him back to the present. She was standing in front of him, tall and proud, her dark braid snaking over her shoulder to her waist. Her gaze caught his and didn't waver. "Within these four walls . . . do you trust me?"

He trusted her enough to tell her something he'd not told another soul in six years. He'd trusted her not to poison him in

Camulodunon, or thrust her dagger through his heart when they
arrived back in Cymru.

Did he trust her?

"As much as you trust me."

A small smile quirked the corners of her lips, but vanished
in an instant. With a stab of surprise he realized she wasn't as
confident as she appeared. He wrapped his hand around her braid
and tugged gently, tracing the knuckles of his other hand along
her jaw.

"I trust you more than perhaps I should." Again she smiled;
again he caught the flicker of uncertainty behind her words. "I fear
it crept upon me unawares."

How easy it would be to tell her the truth. Morwyn was strong,
brave. She'd know the necessity for silence. For stealth. She could
even assist in his cover, provide alibis for when he needed to meet
with Caratacus.

The vision glowed bright in his mind for one glorious moment
before turning to ash.

He would never put her in such danger. The life he'd chosen was
a solitary one, and the fewer people who knew of his true identity,
the safer they all were. Besides, he'd promised to escort her back to
her home village. He wondered why she hadn't reminded him. He
wouldn't offer. Perhaps she'd decide to stay in the town.

For a while.

"Within these four walls," he said, "I trust you with my life."

She cradled his face in a tender gesture, as if she were holding
something infinitely precious. He savored the sensation, relished
the thought, even as cold reality seeped through his consciousness.

Morwyn had no such finer feelings for him. And even if she did,
should she discover the depths to which he'd sunk, the atrocities
he'd committed, her affection would wither and pollute her soul.

Another reason why he could never allow her to discover who
he truly was.

"I don't want your life." Her voice was soft and her fingertips grazed his throat, hovered as if fascinated over his pulse. "I only want to look at you. As you have looked at me."

Instinctively he tensed. "No." It was harsh. Nonnegotiable. The thought of her recoiling from the hideous sight of his body caused his guts to clench in denial.

She rested the palms of her hands against his shoulders, and her heat seeped through the material of his tunic and branded his flesh.

"Please." Her voice was a breathy whisper. "Just this once. Just for this night. Let me see you as you are."

"That's the one thing you never want to see, Morwyn."

She gave an oddly vulnerable smile that caused a strange pain deep in his chest. "I've seen the scars of battle before, Gaul. For a warrior, you're astonishingly vain about preserving the illusion of your beauty."

A short laugh huffed from his mouth. Unexpected. He didn't mean to laugh. Except when he was with Morwyn he couldn't seem to help himself.

"I have no such vanity with regard to my beauty." What an extraordinary choice of words she'd used. "But these aren't battle scars. They're—" The words choked his throat. Because they were his scars of shame. Of degradation. The scars that reminded him every moment of every day that *he had survived*.

Something flickered in her eyes, as if she knew what he could never say. As if she had known from the moment she'd made her request how much capitulation would cost him.

Silently he pulled back from her and removed his belt. As he undressed, Morwyn didn't break eye contact and didn't offer to help. She simply looked at him, and as he ripped his undertunic from his body and tossed it across the floor he glared at her, daring her not to flinch or shudder or turn away in disgust.

Still her gaze meshed with his as she stepped toward him and grazed the tips of her fingers over his shoulders and along his biceps. Her warm breath dusted his chest, the evocative scent from her hair teased his senses, and despite his shame, desire speared his groin.

Finally she looked at him. Her breath stumbled and again he tensed. Waiting for her rejection. Expecting it.

Her lips brushed across the ragged scar where the spear had penetrated, its deadly trajectory only narrowly missing both heart and lung. His hands fisted by his sides, blunt fingernails gouging his palms. No woman but Eryn had ever touched him so. But with Eryn, the only scars he'd possessed were honorable.

Gentle fingers, as light as the whisper of a feather, explored the deep gashes carved into his chest. Reminders of the antiquated spiked club one of the attackers had slammed into him before he even comprehended their presence.

Her lips followed, tender and erotic, searing his skin with a flick of her tongue and tantalizing graze of her teeth. Hot breath breezed against his abdomen as she soothed every grotesquely twisted ridge of healed flesh and muscle, her kisses igniting the embers glowing through his blood.

Jagged breath hissed between his clenched teeth and, hypnotized, he watched her slither down his body until she kneeled before him, hands splayed across his arse. Her dark hair, still braided, teased his inner thigh as her tongue traced a leisurely path around his navel.

And lower.

He speared his fingers into her hair, gripped her skull. She looked up at him, and in the glow from the lanterns he saw her smile.

"Do you want me to stop now?" Her voice was uneven, throaty, and stoked the flames licking inside his skin.

He didn't want her to stop but warning pounded in the back of his mind, a throbbing counterpoint to the lust thundering through his blood. For the last three years he'd controlled his sexual encounters with the same degree with which he controlled his military persona.

With detached efficiency.

Except from the moment he'd met her, Morwyn had managed to shake his world sideways, caused him to question the essentiality of remaining silent, and nothing about their frenzied couplings was remotely detached.

His head jerked in denial, overriding his brain, and again she smiled. Pure decadence in the face of salvation. He screwed his eyes shut, fingers still tangled in her hair, and her hand trailed over his hips, between his thighs, and cradled his aching balls.

Her other hand slid around his shaft and he dragged open his heavy eyelids and fixed his gaze on her. The tip of her tongue peeked between her lips and then she leaned into him, breath scorching his sensitized flesh, mouth opening, sucking him inside. Slow, deliberate, but inexorable, her lips stretching around him, her tongue flattening beneath him, her teeth scraping against him as she took him deeper than he'd ever been before.

An agonized groan filled the room, echoed in his ears, but he hardly cared. Pulses hammering, he stared, mesmerized by the sight of Morwyn on her knees between his spread legs, his cock buried inside her wet mouth.

Fingernails scraped his sac, trailed along the insides of his thigh, probed between his arse cheeks. Her fingers were everywhere, exploring and teasing, gentle, then demanding. Driving need and desire and blinding wild lust thundering through his arteries, boiling in his gut, pounding the length of his rock-hard erection.

"Gods, Morwyn." His voice rasped; fingers dug into her scalp. He locked the muscles of his thighs, tried to prevent the inevitable, but as if anticipating his strangled thoughts, she increased the suction around his cock, clamped one hand over his backside.

He thrust into her mouth, hard and violent, unable to prevent the primal need to possess and conquer. She didn't pull back, even though such escape was futile, but met his thrusts, savored them, swallowing his length farther into her welcoming throat.

Harsh pants rent the air and he couldn't take his eyes from her. A sliver of sanity wanted to pull her from him, toss her across the bed and plunge into her, feel her come around him as he pumped himself into her. But even as the thought formed she slid a finger between his buttocks, probed the sensitive flesh, and reason splintered into infinity.

Nothing existed but Morwyn and this moment and the primeval urge for completion. Silky tendrils of her hair spilled over his fingers, and while one hand played with his arse her other captured his balls, caressing and tweaking and cupping his weight.

Too much. Need flooded, pumped through his shaft, hammered into her mouth. Hot and brutal and demanding, every thrust jerking her head back, and he could feel her glorious suction, a cocoon of sheer sensation; the mind-blowing ecstasy as she swallowed and milked him and swallowed again.

The sweetest oblivion beckoned. And he fell.

Chapter Twenty-three

In the silent moments before dawn, Morwyn stirred in her lover's arms. It was the first time she'd thought of him as such, and yet it felt so right. As if, in her heart, she had always called him so.

Her head on his shoulder, his arm cradling her in a possessive embrace, she traced his innumerable scars with gentle fingers. They disfigured, but she didn't find them unsightly. In truth, she had seen worse, although rarely had the victim survived. The only reason her insides clenched with horror when he had first undressed was because of the agony such injuries would have caused him.

She knew it wasn't their physical presence that tortured his soul. It was his entrenched belief that he was responsible for his wife's death. The scars were merely a visible outlet for his misguided convictions.

If only there were a potion she could concoct to ease his mind. But that wasn't her specialty. Gawain, Druid of truth and judgment, was trained to sooth such intricacies of the mind. Gawain, whom she would never see again.

A ragged sigh slipped free. Regret for Gawain's untimely death, regret for her Gaul's shattered peace of mind. And regret for herself, at the knowledge there was nothing she could do to change any of it.

"Why the sigh?" Her Gaul's husky whisper drifted across her cheek and she instinctively melded closer to his naked body, as if by so doing she could somehow alleviate his sorrow.

"Just recalling the past." She pressed her lips against his shoulder, savoring the flavor of sweat and sex and man. But not just any man. Her man.

For now.

She thrust the harsh reminder aside. Her Gaul was here with her now and she wouldn't spoil the moment by thinking of the future.

"A man you loved?" His breath caressed the top of her head; his fingers stroked the heated skin of her arm.

Silence lingered. Did he really want to know? Or was it merely an idle question?

She didn't have to respond. But something tugged in the pit of her belly, a strange compulsion to share something of herself with him. The way he had with her.

A bond, of sorts.

"There was a man." Her fingers played with the hair on her Gaul's chest as the first glimpse of dawn illuminated his outline next to her. "I loved him for years . . . blindly."

He continued to caress her arm. But remained silent.

A jagged sigh escaped. She'd not spoken of Aeron since that night. At least, she hadn't spoken of her shattered feelings for him. He had murdered their queen, destroyed her faith and left a legacy of hatred and incomprehension among her fellow Druids.

None of them could mention Aeron's name without cursing him to eternal isolation. She'd had to mend her battered heart alone, unable to grieve for the loss of a man who had never existed outside her own mind.

"But in the end he betrayed me. All of us."

Still he didn't speak, but he rubbed his jaw across the top of her head as if in silent sympathy. As he had once before.

Warmth spiraled from her breast to her womb, but it wasn't fueled by the need for sex. It was a strange sensation. As if his silence said more than words ever could.

She frowned, idly teasing his erect nipple with one finger. How odd, yet how fitting, that her Gaul could comfort her without the need of flowery speeches.

"He didn't return my love." She waited for the once-familiar stab of pain to accompany her confession, but her heart remained steady. Untouched. Had the last remnant of Aeron's poison finally leaked from her soul?

The realization she was at last free of his hypnotic grip sent shivers of strange delight through her mind. Pressing even closer to her Gaul, she hesitated for scarcely a heartbeat.

He had confided in her. She would confide in him.

Lifting her head, she whispered into his ear. "He was a Druid."

Her Gaul didn't physically recoil. But his entire body stilled beneath her fingers, as if his muscles and bone and blood repelled her words. A chill shivered through her. Had she made a terrible mistake by telling him? Would he now leap to the conclusion that she, also, was a Druid?

The chill invaded her mind as a barely registered memory surfaced. When she had tried to comfort him earlier, she'd unthinkingly whispered the ancient Druidic incantation of healing. Without appropriate rituals and sacrifice it was meaningless, yet still the words had slid free. Because her need to offer a modicum of comfort to this man had overcome her sense of self-preservation.

Had he noticed her slip into the tongue of the ancients? Would he betray her to his Roman officers?

She pushed up onto her elbow and gazed down at him. The light was muted but she could see the outline of his face, the gleam of his eyes. There was no reason for him to come to such a conclusion. And even if he did, he wouldn't hand her over to the enemy.

Her enemy. The reminder dripped like poison across her mind, but she ignored it. Because somehow she knew. He would *not* betray her trust.

"You loved a Druid." His tone was devoid of emotion, as if it meant nothing to him. Perhaps it didn't. She trailed her fingers across his jaw, fascinated by the rough texture of his night-grown beard.

"It was long ago." And here, sharing her bed with the Gaul, it did seem long ago that she'd loved Aeron. Another lifetime. "Before the Romans invaded Cymru."

He didn't answer and she continued to caress his face, tracing his temples, his cheekbones, his mouth, as if her fingertips were committing every plane and angle to memory. Meshed against his chest, she felt his heart rate increase, his breathing become ragged, and he speared his fingers through her tangled hair, pulling her toward him.

Openmouthed, she claimed his kiss, and closed her mind to the whispers that reminded her how ephemeral such pleasures could be.

After breaking their fast the Gaul hauled her into a bone-tingling hug before setting off to do . . . whatever it was he intended to do for the day. Unable to wipe the satisfied smile from her face, Morwyn watched him stride down the dirt path. Unlike Camulodunon, this settlement didn't groan beneath the weight of numerous Roman-constructed roads.

With a sigh of contentment she turned in the other direction. It was too early to go to Deheune's and meet with the hidden Elder. Perhaps, to distract her mind, she'd mend the gown her Gaul had torn from her the other night.

The contentment segued into nervous excitement at the thought of meeting with another of her kind. But another part quavered. Suppose he saw into her innermost core, saw how she scorned the Morrigan and all their gods? Suppose he cursed her for her blasphemy?

A furtive movement in the dingy alley next to the lodgings caught her eye. She frowned, and discerned a tiny shape crouching in the shadows.

"Come here." She accompanied her words with a quick flick of her hand. With evident caution the tiny beggar from last night edged into the light. Morwyn half stepped forward, then paused. She could almost feel the lice crawling over the child's hair and skin and had no desire to pick up any bloodsucking creatures if she could avoid it.

Pity sliced through her breast, sharp and acidic. Pity that a child had to live such a life, and pity that so little could be done about it. "Do you want something to eat?"

The child chewed its lip, as if unsure whether to take the question at face value.

Of course it did. She raised her finger to indicate the child should remain where it was and went back inside and haggled with the innkeeper for some leftover stew from the previous eve. Then she watched the child devour the entire bowlful, scarcely taking time to draw breath.

She returned the bowl, and the child still waited for Morwyn, eyes wide and dark and unblinking as if it were a puppy.

Suddenly at a loss as to what she should do next, Morwyn stared at the child. She didn't know why she had fed it, except she hadn't been able to ignore the pitiful creature. But what would happen on the morrow? Or the day after that? What would happen when Morwyn was no longer here to feed the child?

But she was here now. And she was still too early for the Elder. She might as well spend her time usefully. "Can you lead me to the river?" There had to be a river locally, and while she had no doubt she'd be able to find it, she might as well allow this child to show her the way.

And without a word, it did.

By the time they found a secluded spot at the river, Morwyn had decided the child was female. She pointed to the ground by the riverbank and waited until the girl sat.

"What's your name?" Morwyn pulled her medicine bag from

her shoulder and began to hunt through it for the ingredients she required. Frowning, she ran her fingers over her dwindling supply of willow bark. She'd have to replenish, and soon. It was a vital component of the contraceptive tea she drank throughout the day. She quickly checked another pouch, shaking the berries onto her palm. Not many, but they would have to do. They could be collected only when the berries turned black and the leaves fell from the trees, and that wouldn't happen for another three moons.

She retied the pouch, found what she was looking for and glanced up, to see the child watching her avidly. "Name?" Morwyn prompted.

"Gwyn."

"I'm Morwyn. Where's your mother?"

Gwyn pushed greasy hair back from her face. "Dead." A tremor belied her apparent calm. "Babe got stuck. I couldn't . . . pull it out."

Morwyn's fingers stilled on her preparations as a troubling scenario whispered through her mind. "Were you alone?"

The girl gave one brief nod.

It was inconceivable that a woman could go into childbirth with only a small child in attendance, and yet so much had changed since the invasion. Kin were splintered across the land and the familial support system she had grown up with and taken for granted could no longer be counted upon.

"Don't you have any living kin here?"

The scrawny shoulders shrugged. "Don't know."

"What of your father?" And if Morwyn got hold of him, she would soon knock some sense of responsibility into him. Allowing his daughter to roam the streets where anything could happen.

"Don't know." Gwyn wiggled her bare toes in the grass. "Never seen him."

"What about the babe's father?" Even if the man wasn't Gwyn's blood father, how could he allow her to degenerate into such an appalling state?

Gwyn began to dig a hole in the earth with the heel of her foot.

"Ma never knew who the father was." She shot Morwyn a furtive glance. "She said they were all the same to her."

"I see." The child was alone, in occupied and hostile territory. She smothered her inclination to gather the girl to her breast for comfort because what comfort would she derive from a stranger?

Besides, the child was riddled with lice.

"You," she said, deciding the best way to help was with action and not sympathy, "need to clean up."

Gwyn didn't move. "Why?"

Morwyn watched a louse crawl languidly across the child's forehead and resisted the urge to scratch her own head. "Because you're filthy."

Gwyn shrugged as if such an insult didn't worry her. "Stops men wanting to fuck me."

Again acidic pain slashed through Morwyn's heart. The child looked scarcely eight summers old. "No man will dare touch you while you're under my protection."

Gods! What had she just said? How had she given her protection to this pitiful creature when she didn't plan on staying for more than a few days—a moon at most?

But how could she *not* protect her, when it was obvious no one else would?

Gwyn blinked and began to scratch her neck, where red weals marked the passage of countless fleas. "All right, then." She didn't appear overwhelmed by Morwyn's declaration. But she proved adept at obeying her instructions, and as the sun climbed in the heavens Morwyn pulled out the small blanket she carried in her bag. It wasn't entirely clean but would do for her purposes. As Gwyn knelt by the river, her naked body scrubbed red raw and grease-smeared hair hanging over her face as she combed out the lice, Morwyn deftly turned the blanket into a serviceable gown.

It wasn't much, but better than the rags she'd told Gwyn to throw into the bushes.

"Let me look at you." She studied Gwyn's appearance. The

child's hair, now rinsed, fell to her shoulders and was no longer crawling alive. Morwyn would ensure the child treated her hair again in the morn, explain how the cycle could not afford to be broken. It was, after all, a basic hygiene necessity.

She handed Gwyn the gown and repacked her bag. If she didn't hurry, she'd be late for the Elder.

Deheune greeted her with the same deference she'd extended the previous day, and was happy for Gwyn to stay.

"She can help tend the babe," Deheune said, smiling at Gwyn, who now wore Morwyn's scarlet ribbon in her tightly braided black hair. Then she turned back to Morwyn. "If you're ready, mistress?"

Morwyn hesitated at the door and glanced back at Gwyn. She was sitting on the hard-packed earthen floor tickling the babe's tummy and wiggling his toes and, save for her evident undernourishment, looked nothing like the pathetic creature hiding in the alley that morn.

Unsure why she had the oddest reluctance at leaving the child behind, Morwyn sucked in a deep breath, checked her favorite green ribbon was perfectly tied at the end of her braid, and followed Deheune out of the dwelling.

The older woman led her through a confusing warren of back alleys, and finally came to a halt outside another small shack. She gave a strange combination of knocks on the door, as if it were a secret code, and instantly the door jerked open.

Another woman, who looked vaguely familiar, bobbed her head at Morwyn.

"Mistress. It's good to see you again."

"And you." Morwyn couldn't recall her name, doubted if they had even spoken in the past. But even so, this woman knew her because of her status. Her calling.

"The Elder awaits you." The woman led Morwyn through the tiny room. The back half had been partitioned, to give privacy, and without another word the woman turned and left the shack with Deheune, leaving Morwyn alone.

Hands suddenly sweaty, she wiped them on her gown and approached the gap that served as a door between the end of the partition and the outside wall. Now that she was here she didn't know what she was supposed to say to him. Would he interrogate her about that night? It seemed likely. All the Druids who'd turned up on Mon had been morbidly fascinated by the events of that night, apparently uncaring that for those who had lived through the horror, the last thing they wanted to do was relive those blood-soaked moments.

"Hurry up, child." The voice was strong, autocratic. "Stop dithering."

She gripped her wavering courage and stepped into the Druid's presence.

He sat on a bed in the corner, amber eyes blazing at her from a wizened face, his wasted body twisted by the ravages of aged disease. The breath lodged in her throat, power hummed through her mind, and without conscious thought she fell to her knees, head bent.

He was not merely an Elder. He possessed royal blood. She could feel it, smell it. His aura of power and otherworldliness clung in the air as tangible as the scent from newly turned earth.

He was as worthy of her reverence as Druantia, her queen and beloved matriarch; the Chosen One and blood descendant of the Morrigan herself.

"Rise, child." There was the faintest hint of approval in that voice, a voice that was so shockingly at odds with his appearance. His intense gaze never left her face as she rose from the ground. "Not yet fully trained but the great goddess has already marked you as her own. What's your name?"

Blood scalded her cheeks. Before the invasion she'd had a special affinity with the Morrigan, their great goddess. But the Morrigan had never specifically marked Morwyn as her own. And after the way she'd debased the goddess's gifts, the Morrigan never would.

She hoped the Elder hadn't read her discomfort in her expression. She would never wish to dishonor such a wise one with her personal doubts. Even if his wisdom wasn't as faultless as he believed.

"Morwyn, my king." He wasn't, of course, really *her* king. But his rank was unmistakable, and since she didn't know his formal name it was only courteous to address him as such.

He appeared satisfied by her response. "Why did the Morrigan lead you to me?"

She hesitated, unwilling to admit the Morrigan had led her nowhere and she wouldn't follow her even if the goddess demanded it. There were ways around the truth without having to outright lie. "I traveled from the sacred Isle of Mon," she began. "To gather . . . information."

His eyes bored into her, fierce and proud, containing all the power of his rank that his body could no longer employ. She had the overwhelming urge to squirm, to break eye contact, but instead she remained frozen in place, accepting his scrutiny.

"And what"—his voice was low but power still thrummed through every word—"information have you discovered, Morwyn?"

Prickles skittered over her arms and her jagged pulses hammered, igniting her blood with streaks of alarm. Somehow he knew of her liaison. Knew of her betrayal.

But she hadn't betrayed her people.

Mouth dry, she pressed her hands against her thighs so he wouldn't see how they shook. "I discovered my princess is content and happy."

Confusion flashed across his face, as if her words were completely unexpected. "Another Druid of royal blood resides in this cursed place?" He reached out and clasped bony fingers around the sacred hazel rod propped against the bed. "She conceals herself from me." He didn't sound impressed by the feat, as if such action were a mortal insult.

"My king, she resides in Camulodunon."

Silence crackled in the air. He stared at her and again she forcibly prevented herself from squirming. He made her feel like a small child, caught out in some misdemeanor.

"You left the sacred Isle in order to travel to Camulodunon?" He leaned forward, using his hazel rod to support his weight, and Morwyn shifted, unease snaking through her. Had she said something untoward?

"That wasn't my intention. I—I wanted to discover the whereabouts of the Briton king, Caratacus."

His eyes continued to blaze into her and her brain heated with sharp stabs of pain, as if he probed, unasked, to discover hidden secrets in her mind. Instinctively she smothered the image of her Gaul, swirling layer upon layer of disconnected shreds of memory across her consciousness. The Elder's eyes narrowed as if he knew precisely what she was doing.

"Why would the Morrigan allow you safe passage to Camulodunon?" It was a question, but not intended for her. She remained silent, heart thudding against her ribs with trepidation. It would be better if he assumed she'd gone there by the Morrigan's decree. He'd never understand why she'd accompanied an auxiliary of the Roman Legion without cutting his throat at the first opportunity.

Finally his grip relaxed around his hazel rod and he sank back against the wall. "You'll understand her reasons when the time comes." He spoke with authority as if in answer to her question. Except she didn't have a question because the Morrigan had nothing to do with it. But, to alleviate any suspicion he might harbor, she inclined her head as a mark of respect.

He regarded her in silence for a few moments. "You want to find Caratacus?"

Relief spun through her at the realization that he hadn't discovered her deepest secrets and branded her a traitor or blasphemer. "Yes. And then I can return to Mon and the other Druids will follow."

Was that a flicker of contempt in his eyes? She stiffened with affront, the memory torturing her of how she and her fellow Druids had been manipulated by Aeron into hiding from the invaders instead of confronting them from the outset.

"My fellow Druids," she said, her jaw angled with pride, "will leave Mon and join with the rebels. Caratacus will be grateful for the vast amount of knowledge and expertise we bring with us."

The Elder's lips twitched as if her words amused him. Had she mistaken that contempt in his eyes? Or had he misunderstood her original statement?

"Caratacus," he said, his tone dry, "has Druids enough to advise him already."

"Druids from Britain." The words were out before she could prevent them, before it occurred to her that this Elder himself might be a Briton. Silently she cursed her wayward tongue. "I mean no disrespect. But if Caratacus hides in our forests and mountains, the Druids of Cymru will be invaluable to him."

"Our Druids," the Elder said, "*are* invaluable to him."

Only then did the significance of the Elder's words penetrate. He was speaking as if he had intimate knowledge of Caratacus's inner circle. How else would he know the Briton surrounded himself by Druids? And Druids of Cymru at that?

"My king." Her whisper was barely audible. "Do you know where I may find him?"

The Elder's fingers caressed his hazel rod, as if considering her question. "On the night of devastation, when your High Priest spewed his wrath across the land, not all the power was contained within Cerridwen's Cauldron."

Morwyn remained silent. She hadn't borne witness to that phenomenon, but had pieced together the remaining events of that night from the fragmented stories other Druids had brought to the Isle of Mon. Somehow, with her wise goddess Cerridwen's blessing, Carys had defeated Aeron's intended plans.

"Splinters of the sacred bluestones used in his"—the Elder paused for a moment, as if searching for the right word—"extraordinary spiral of deflection he conjured to conceal you all from the enemy came into my possession."

Comprehension flooded, banishing the air from her lungs, and she swayed as vertigo cascaded through her mind.

"You've harnessed the source of Annwyn?" Panic spiked through her heart as she recalled Aeron's insane face that night, as he'd told them of his twisted designs. Of how he had used their gods for his own ends, while secretly tapping the Universal Life Force in a bid to destroy their deities and rule supreme.

For a fleeting moment she saw envy, greed and covetousness gleam in the Elder's strange amber eyes, and terror slithered through Morwyn's soul. Was this the reason he had deigned to see her this day? Because he thought she possessed the knowledge their High Priest had abused so utterly?

The Elder smiled. It wasn't particularly friendly, as if he could read her mind as easily as her facial expressions and found her fears pitiable.

"Alas, the knowledge to harness the Source died with your High Priest. While I could, doubtless, replicate his spiral under normal circumstances, these conditions are scarcely . . . conducive."

Thank the gods for that. She might not think much of her gods anymore but even they were immeasurably preferable to a mortal grasping such power within his hands.

"But." His fingers once again gripped his hazel rod. "The splinters of bluestone hummed with otherworldly energy. Enough for me to create a small enclave hidden deep in the forests, its location indiscernible unless one knows precisely where to look." He leaned forward, the wild glitter in his eyes verging on madness. "And that, child, is where Caratacus and his followers hide, protected by ancient Druid magic."

Chapter Twenty-four

As Morwyn made her way back to Deheune's shack, her brain thudded with the information the Elder had imparted. She now had detailed instructions on how to find Caratacus, and the Elder assumed she intended to leave immediately.

She hadn't corrected him. But of course she couldn't leave right away. She had babes to bless. Gwyn to settle safely somewhere. *And her Gaul.*

But whenever she tried to work out what, exactly, she hoped to accomplish by staying any longer in the settlement with regard to her Gaul, her mind shivered to a halt. As if she knew, deep inside, there was nothing she could do even if she refused to face that fact directly.

She let out an exasperated breath. She would stay another moon. Two at most. There was much she could do for her people here, who had been so cruelly neglected by their Druids for so long. After all, it wasn't as if Caratacus would be moving from his magical retreat anytime soon. It would be madness to abandon the haven the Druids had woven around the rebels. And unlike

Aeron, Caratacus used the advantage of concealment as a base from which to orchestrate attacks on the Legion.

Deheune was at the door of her home. "Mistress." She bowed her head. "We await you."

Morwyn smothered her unease over the ultimate fate of her Gaul. It was hard to reconcile that the victory of Caratacus, which of course she desired more than anything else, would result in the defeat of her lover.

There had to be another way. Something she hadn't yet realized. A compromise.

The words hovered in her mind, buzzing like discordant wasps. How could such a compromise ever come to be, when success for one necessitated the sacrifice of the other?

The small dwelling was stifling, overstuffed with anxious parents and uncaring babes. She glanced around, searching for Gwyn. The child had vanished.

Fear knifed through her, sudden and illogical. "Where's Gwyn?" she demanded of Deheune, who smiled vaguely as if she couldn't understand Morwyn's manner.

"She left, as soon as I returned. Was she meant to stay?"

Was she? Of course not. But for some reason Morwyn couldn't fathom, the desertion gnawed into her guts. Because she'd expected—no, she'd *wanted*—Gwyn to wait for her.

It didn't make sense. She tried to wipe it from her mind. But a whisper of a thought trickled through her brain. Perhaps the child would return later, when hunger clawed her stomach.

Mentally drained after projecting the illusion she was communing with the great goddess for eight separate blessings, Morwyn finally returned to the lodgings. She'd order a tub, luxuriate in a bath. Or perhaps she'd wait until her Gaul returned and give him another decadent show.

The smile hovered on her lips, not remotely concerned by her desire for a bath above washing in the local river. There was a lot to be said for the privacy of a tub in a room with her lover.

Then she noticed a familiar shadow crouched in the doorway of the lodgings. "Gwyn?" She didn't even try to analyze the relief that streaked through her chest at the sight. It eased her mind to know the child was safe, and not in danger of being brutalized. "Where did you go?"

Gwyn stood up, clutching a grass-woven bag. "Got something for you." She jiggled her bag. Intrigued, Morwyn ushered her inside, her hand between Gwyn's skinny shoulder blades, and directed her to her room.

"What did you get?" She closed the door and sat on the end of the bed. Gwyn tipped her bag upside down and tree bark scattered over the rough covering.

Morwyn stared, baffled. "Willow bark?"

"Yes." Gwyn scrambled on the other end of the bed and hugged her knees. She looked very pleased with herself.

Morwyn picked up a piece and examined it. "Why?"

"Because you were running out. I saw. You were frowning and poking at it. So I thought I'd get some for you."

Speechless, Morwyn stared at the child. Gwyn stared back, a malnourished, uneducated beggar—who had, without any prompting or instruction, collected willow bark because Morwyn's supplies were running low.

Gwyn's bare feet, already black again with filth, drummed on the bedcover. "I tried finding the berries," she said, as if Morwyn's silence was beginning to agitate. "But they were the wrong color."

Morwyn sucked in a deep breath. Perhaps Gwyn wasn't as ignorant as she assumed. Perhaps, before she'd been forced onto the streets, Gwyn had been taught of such things.

"Do you know why I need the willow bark and berries?"

Gwyn shrugged. "No."

Morwyn fingered the bark and an unexpected yearning to explain, to instruct, bloomed deep inside. As a Druid almost fully trained, part of her duties had been to impart knowledge to the children of noble blood, those who hadn't yet undertaken the rituals to determine whether or not they possessed the gifts to become acolytes. She'd always loved doing so. Seeing the children's avid faces as they learned of the ancient ways had always thrilled her.

Gwyn wasn't of the privileged class. There was little chance she possessed the elusive glimmer of perception the gods required of an acolyte. But then, teaching a girl of how the moon influenced her body, of how she could control her fertility and other such feminine wisdom, wasn't sacrosanct to Druids and nobles. Gwyn was old enough to learn of such things.

Morwyn opened her medicine bag and, as she showed various samples from her numerous pouches, explained the intricacies of the female cycle to an enthralled Gwyn.

As the sun dipped in the sky Morwyn took Gwyn to the market. If she was going to teach the child before she left to find Caratacus, then she would have her properly clothed. A fierce haggler, she procured a length of good-quality wool to be made into a tunic and leather for Gwyn's feet. The child hugged her treasures in one arm, and stuffed various exotic foods Morwyn tossed her as if she were starving. Smiling at the girl's delight, she bargained for a cheap necklace and bracelet of red and black beads and fastened them around Gwyn's throat and wrist.

Gwyn twirled on the dusty ground, her free arm outstretched, admiring how the beads glittered, and her spinning became more erratic by the moment. Laughing, Morwyn watched her, indulging in the simple pleasure of a child at play, not realizing until now how much she'd missed the children she'd left behind on Mon.

A mangy dog, clasping a bloodied bone in its mouth, streaked through the marketplace. Morwyn stepped aside but the dog careered into Gwyn, sending her sprawling over its emaciated body, and crashing into the legs of a Roman auxiliary.

The dog escaped, still clutching its ill-gotten gains, and Morwyn rushed to retrieve her charge. The auxiliary beat her to it.

"No bones broken?" He flashed a smile at Gwyn, who appeared more distressed that her wool was now dusty than the possibility of broken bones. The auxiliary straightened and transferred his smile to Morwyn. "I think she'll live."

She brushed the grit from Gwyn's knees and impulsively dropped a kiss onto her cheek. "I believe she will." She looked up at the auxiliary and before she could stop herself she smiled back.

How odd. Before she'd met her Gaul, she would sooner spit in the eye of a Roman auxiliary than honor him with a smile. No matter how blue his eyes or appealing his demeanor. But what did a smile cost? He had been gentle with Gwyn when another would have kicked her from his path, cursed at her carelessness.

"My name is Gervas." He inclined his head in greeting. "May I have the honor of knowing yours?"

Morwyn laughed and shook her head. His flirting skills were admirable, even for one of the enemy. Except he didn't strike her as one of the enemy. As if Romans and all their cohorts should be humorless, brutal thugs.

The thought sobered, but only momentarily. The warm bubble of excitement, at the knowledge she would soon see her Gaul again, smothered any negative feeling that attempted to penetrate her brain.

"Morwyn."

"A beautiful name. For a beautiful woman."

"You have very pretty manners." She gave Gwyn a handful of brown, wrinkly fruits to stop her from fidgeting. "For one not of Cymru."

"Even in Gaul we can appreciate quality."

"From Gaul?" His grasp of her language was excellent but now that she considered it, his accent was very similar to *her* Gaul's. "Then perhaps you aren't all primitive barbarians after all."

He laughed, a deep rumbling sound, as if he took not the slightest offense to her remark. "Morwyn, can I entice you and your daughter to share this eve's meal with me?"

She glanced at Gwyn, who was engrossed in the sticky fruits, and decided not to correct his assumption. "Thank you, but I must decline." She hesitated for only the briefest of heartbeats. "I'm involved with another."

He gave an exaggerated sigh. "Of course you are. Forgive me for intruding. It was too much to hope you might be free."

Gods, but he possessed a silver tongue. Once, she might have been tempted by his outrageous flirtation. But now she would gladly forsake such empty compliments for a single, slow smile from her Gaul.

"I assure you, I'm not enslaved." She knew that wasn't what he had meant, but the assumption she belonged to a man rankled. At least, it should have. Yet somehow it didn't. As if, obscurely, she *wanted* to belong.

"I've no doubt," Gervas said. "Your lover is entirely enslaved by *you*."

An unintentional laugh escaped. Truly, his tongue was gifted. But still she wasn't tempted. "Beware, Gervas. My lover is also an auxiliary in the Roman Legion. *And* a Gaul."

He grinned. "Then my last hope is crushed underfoot. Even I would hesitate to offend a fellow Gaul."

"You're wise. Dunmacos isn't one to cross with reckless abandon."

She'd said the words in jest, but Gervas stared at her as if she'd just announced she'd been with the Emperor of Rome himself.

"Dunmacos?" There was no more teasing laughter in his tone. He sounded utterly devoid of emotion.

"You know him?" But it was obvious Gervas knew of her Gaul. And clearly his impression wasn't glowing.

Affront stabbed through her gut. What was the matter with other men that they always thought the worst of him? No doubt Gervas had heard the same false rumors as Maximus, and had also jumped to ludicrous conclusions. She doubted the two men had even met.

"Yes, I know him." Gervas sounded reserved, his attitude no longer one of friendliness. He hadn't moved, yet his retreat was palpable. "Dunmacos is my cousin."

She forgot about ushering Gwyn in the direction of their lodgings and stared at Gervas, shock prickling along her spine. "His cousin?" Her Gaul had not mentioned such a thing. But then, why would he? She had told him nothing of her kin either.

"Have you been with him long?" Was it her imagination or did his glance flick with scarcely concealed condemnation to the bruises now fading on the left side of her face?

She tilted her jaw. "Long enough." Gods, it was obvious from his attitude he believed his cousin had inflicted the injuries upon her. Irritation bubbled. Gervas clearly didn't know her Gaul at all. "Indeed," she added in the tone she'd used when addressing recalcitrant children before the invasion, "he was the one who extricated me from those intent on pulverizing my face."

"My cousin, the hero." Gervas sounded faintly disbelieving. "I don't recall him being so considerate when we were young."

From the corner of her eye she caught sight of a familiar figure striding through the emptying marketplace. Instantly her irritation with Gervas melted away. She didn't care what he thought of his cousin. It made no difference to her.

"Then perhaps you'd better reacquaint yourself with him." She flashed Gervas a mocking smile. "My lover approaches."

Chapter Twenty-five

Negotiating his way through the marketplace on the way back to the lodgings, Bren saw the unmistakable figure of Morwyn by a fruit stall. She glanced his way at the same moment and her smile illuminated her face as if his approach pleased her.

Heat closed like a fist in his chest, hard and solid, constricting his lungs, but not wholly uncomfortable. Mostly it was renewed relief that, once again, she hadn't decided to leave.

That time would come. He knew it in his gut because there could be no other way, but for now he'd take whatever she offered. And hope she never discovered the true depths to which he'd sunk.

Only when he was almost by her side did he become aware of the man she was with. The Roman auxiliary who regarded him with a face devoid of expression and fiercely intelligent eyes.

A sense of danger speared through his brain and streaked along his spine. Bren didn't know who the man was or what he was doing with Morwyn. All he knew was every survival instinct he possessed vibrated with primal warning.

"It appears," Morwyn said, and in his peripheral vision he saw she had one hand clasped lightly over the shoulder of a small child, "you harbor as much love for your cousin as he does for you."

Cousin. He'd never seen the man before in his life. His heart thudded against his ribs and the fundamental imperative to attack flooded his blood. Poised to thrust his dagger through the man's throat if his enemy's fingers so much as twitched.

The man didn't move a muscle. They might have been the only two left in the market, so intense was their focus on each other. Except they weren't alone. Morwyn stood between them. And he couldn't risk her safety by launching the first move.

"Dunmacos." The man's lips barely moved. His eyes never left Bren's. "It's been a long time."

Every muscle rigid with tension, Bren remained silent. No matter how long it had been since the cousins had met, he couldn't believe this man would mistake him for Dunmacos. For whatever purpose, this Gaul had decided not to immediately denounce his cover. Likely the man wanted to corner him alone before gutting him.

He'd never get the chance.

"Gervas," Morwyn said, as if she was perfectly at ease with the other man. As if she was comfortable calling him by name. *At least he now knew the Gaul's name.* "Perhaps we can share that meal, after all? The four of us together."

Two things pierced his brain. One, Morwyn had just invited his deadliest enemy to share a meal with them. And two, the Gaul had obviously asked her to eat with him before Bren had arrived.

For one thundering moment he wasn't sure which fact infuriated him the most.

Another, inconsequential fact hammered through his pounding temples. *Four?* He shot a glance at the child, who was staring up at him with big brown eyes. Fearless.

Where the fuck had the child come from? He looked back at Gervas, who appeared to be waiting for his response to Morwyn's suggestion.

He couldn't afford to refuse. Couldn't let Gervas return to the garrison and report that Bren was an imposter.

"Why not?" Bren sounded as enthusiastic as he felt, and the words fell into the heavy silence like boulders.

"Good." Morwyn took the free hand of the child, slid her arm through Bren's and effectively erected a barrier between him and Gervas. She then proceeded to lead the way to a nearby tavern and procure them a table, and somehow he found himself sitting next to the child, opposite Morwyn, who had managed to seat Gervas in the corner by the wall.

As military tactics went he couldn't have planned his position better. But he hadn't planned it and Morwyn wasn't a tactician. He shot her a glance, but she appeared serene as she instructed the child to sit up straight and stop picking her nose. She certainly didn't give the impression that she'd arranged their seating with anything other than sheer coincidence.

"So, cousin." Gervas offered a chilly smile. "I've followed your progress over the last ten years. Impressive."

"You have me at a disadvantage. I've not followed your progress at all."

Morwyn glanced at Bren as if something in his tone alerted her there was more than simple family dislike in the atmosphere. He didn't return her glance. Couldn't afford to take his eyes from Gervas.

"That," Gervas said, "doesn't surprise me."

A serving wench deposited an amphora of ale on the table. It could stay there. Bren wasn't clouding his mind when his life was on the line.

"And you've never served together before?" Morwyn transferred her glance to Gervas, who favored her with a fleeting smile. Something rancid knotted deep in Bren's gut and he fisted his hands to prevent them from curling around Gervas's throat and squeezing the life from him.

"Never," Gervas confirmed.

"Then you both must have a great deal to say to each other."

Neither man spoke. If Morwyn noticed the animosity simmering in the air, she chose to ignore it. But why did she choose to ignore it? She didn't normally shy away from confrontation. Or was that only with him? Did she not feel the need to probe and demand answers from Gervas?

"I'd much rather," Gervas said at last, "spend my time talking to you, Morwyn."

Heat flared through Bren, scorching his mind. The bastard was flirting with her. *Under his nose.* And Morwyn didn't put him in his place with a sharp retort.

Instead she gave a soft laugh. As if she found the Gaul's words amusing.

"I fear I must disappoint you," she said, dark eyes flashing as if she enjoyed the interaction. Bren's chest seethed against iron bands intent on crushing his lungs. "This eve is for you and your cousin to reconnect. I'm only here to stop you killing each other."

Momentarily distracted from his rigid self-control, Bren glowered at her. Her choice of words were unfortunate since the only thing he and Gervas appeared to have in common *was* the desire to murder each other.

"I applaud you on your choice of Morwyn." Gervas was now looking directly at Bren. Challenging. "I find it hard to believe you deserve her."

He didn't deserve her. Never would. But that had nothing to do with Gervas.

Their food arrived. More stew. Was that all they served in this settlement? Beside him the child dived into her bowl, as if she was famished, and a flicker of memory stirred. Did he know this child? How could he know her?

"Gwyn." Morwyn lifted her knife and speared a piece of meat. Without any further instruction the girl picked up her own knife and followed Morwyn's lead. He glanced up, to find Gervas studying him through narrowed eyes.

"I find myself curious as to what's happened to you since last we met, cousin."

Bren deliberately ate some stew, while his brain plowed through old information he'd amassed years ago. He could recall no cousin of Dunmacos called Gervas. He thought he and the small band of warriors he'd once led had covered all their tracks three years ago. He should have known that was impossible.

"Nothing that hasn't happened to a thousand other auxiliaries attached to the Legions."

Gervas swirled his knife in his stew and Bren tensed, readying himself for a sudden flick of the other man's wrist. But Gervas didn't appear to be preparing for attack. He appeared to want answers first.

"Word reached me only recently of the massacre you endured three years ago." Gervas paused with his knife play and their gazes clashed. "I regret your loss."

Despite his focus on Gervas, Bren was aware of how Morwyn's head jerked toward him, as if the words held meaning for her. But they didn't. He had said nothing to her of that blood-soaked night and never would. He ignored her in favor of maintaining eye contact with the Gaul.

But said nothing.

"It must be hard," Gervas said, "being the only survivor. Knowing how many of your kin lost their lives that night."

Beneath the table, Bren unsheathed his dagger. From the awkward angle, he couldn't make a kill, but he could maim. So long as the child remained still by his side.

"Although at least, so I heard, you took out a great many of the enemy before incinerating your village."

Morwyn's knife clattered onto the table, distracting him. She stared at him, but her expression was unreadable; as if she herself scarcely knew how she was feeling.

This was why he could never confide in anyone. Even the few words of his past he'd admitted to her were now coming back to haunt him. But that didn't trouble him. What concerned him was the possibility she'd say something to dispute Gervas's recollection of the facts; that by doing so could put her life in danger.

He'd told her of his own loss. But Gervas was speaking of Dunmacos's.

His fingers tightened on his dagger and again he focused on Gervas. In the few moments Bren had been looking at Morwyn, the other man could have slung his own dagger through Bren's throat. Shit, he couldn't afford to be distracted. But Morwyn distracted him simply by sitting opposite him. Simply by *being*.

"The enemy perished." Let Gervas make what he wished of that. It was the truth. That night Dunmacos had died. But so, in every way that mattered, had Bren.

"Yes." For a long moment Gervas held his gaze. Then he finally speared a lump of meat onto the end of his knife and examined it. "They did."

The excruciating meal dragged on. Bren ate but only through force of habit. He tasted nothing and drank nothing, and listened to the banter between Morwyn and Gervas with growing irritation.

The irritation was irrational. He knew it but couldn't prevent it. When all his senses should be on full alert for attack, the greater part of his mind was eaten up by the fact Morwyn enjoyed the other man's company.

The child—Gwyn—tugged on his sleeve and he turned to her, banishing his frown only with difficulty. "Yes?" Was she wearing one of Morwyn's silk ribbons?

"I need to piss."

He stared at her. He'd not had much interaction with children since the night he'd lost Eryn, and virtually none since he'd become Dunmacos. The thought of escorting her to the latrines didn't fill him with enthusiasm.

Morwyn tapped her finger on the table. "Do you need to relieve yourself, Gwyn?"

Gwyn sucked on her upper lip for a moment as if processing Morwyn's question. "Yes."

Morwyn stood, and he rose to allow Gwyn access. Bren spared only a fleeting moment to watch them cross the crowded room before returning his attention to Gervas.

The other man's eyes locked with his. "So Dunmacos died three years ago." It wasn't a question.

"We'll take this outside." His voice was as low as Gervas's.

Gervas picked up his tankard, took a long swallow, and then regarded him over the rim.

"Dunmacos was distant blood kin. He was also the biggest bastard I've come across."

"He fought with courage." It was a lie. Bren had gutted him while Dunmacos staggered in a drunken stupor, and then forced his stinking entrails down his convulsing throat. Some things were better left unsaid.

Gervas circled the rim of his tankard with one finger. "Your reasons for taking on his identity don't concern me. Had you truly been Dunmacos, I would have already cut your throat." His smile chilled the air. "I've been relishing such retribution all week."

Bren needed a drink. He refused to succumb. Instead he sucked in a long breath, attempting to straighten his mangled thoughts. "You're not after my blood?"

Gervas shrugged. His eyes were cold. "I'd rather have taken his but it appears I'm too late. Was it personal?"

The question was unexpected. Bren tensed, his senses alert. "Personal?"

"His home village was razed." Gervas's voice was barely audible. "That wasn't a brawl that got out of hand."

Blood pounded against Bren's temple and he clenched his jaw in an effort to stem the useless rage that polluted his soul. *Personal?* The memory of Eryn's terrified whimpers shredded the fabric of his existence.

"It was." The words charred his throat.

Gervas's finger stilled on the tankard. "For me, also."

From the corner of his eye he caught sight of Morwyn and the child returning. He had one last question to ask.

"Did he murder her too?"

Finally Gervas dropped his gaze and stared into his ale. "No. After he finished with her, she took her own life."

Morwyn couldn't put her finger on it but something had changed between her Gaul and Gervas while they'd been alone. Antagonism still clogged the air but it no longer vibrated with the glinting edge of murder. It was as if, beneath mutual distrust, a bond had been forged.

Yet still an unformed suspicion clouded the outer reaches of her consciousness. It was too ephemeral to grasp but teased her with a hidden knowledge. Something important she needed to know that concerned the two men who eyed each other with such controlled restraint.

Something intrinsically entwined with that night her Gaul's wife had died. The night Gervas had mentioned. The discrepancy of when such atrocity had occurred.

As if by unspoken command, the two men stood and readied to leave. Dusk had not yet settled and they made their way back to the lodgings in silence. It appeared Gervas had lost his appetite for flirtatious conversation, and in truth all she wanted was to wrap her arms around her Gaul. Just to know that . . . she could.

"I go this way." Gervas was no longer by her side and she turned, along with her Gaul, to stare at him. He was looking at his cousin. "Do we understand each other?"

After a heartbeat of silence, her Gaul responded. "Yes."

Gervas raised his arm, and after another agonizing moment her Gaul grasped his hand, their forearms straining against each other, entwined fists clenched to the darkening sky. An odd shiver of apprehension scuttled along her spine, although she couldn't tell why. Wasn't this what she had wanted? For them to bury their differences and look to the future?

"Morwyn." Gervas inclined his head in her direction. "May the gods walk with you."

"And with you." The response was automatic, and as she watched him stride away the uneasy sense of apprehension slithered deep into her gut.

The three of them returned to their lodgings, and surprisingly her Gaul didn't mention the presence of Gwyn. She turned to him, to explain, but he was already turning to her, his hand grazing the curve of her shoulder.

"Morwyn, there's something I need to tell Gervas. Wait inside for me."

Without giving her time to respond he brushed a brief kiss across her lips and marched back the way they had come.

The apprehension gushed into her bloodstream, poisonous ribbons of dark mistrust, and she shoved Gwyn inside the lodgings, hurried her to their room.

"Stay here," she ordered. "Do you understand me, Gwyn? You'll be safe in here. I won't be long."

Without waiting for an answer she rushed back outside, but her Gaul had already vanished. She unsheathed her dagger, drew comfort from its familiar feel and weight, and ran to the corner of the road.

In the gathering twilight she saw him up ahead, before he turned down another road and disappeared from view.

Heart pounding, she raced after him, dagger poised should any unwary attacker attempt their luck on a lone woman. She didn't know why she followed him. Didn't know why every nerve she possessed screamed at her to reach him before he found Gervas.

All she knew was something horrific hung heavy in the atmosphere. A premonition of impending disaster scraped along her senses, pumping acrid fear through her veins.

They had clasped hands. A show of outward trust, at least. But there was something beyond the complexities of cultural tradition that colored their actions. She couldn't explain it—knew only that it existed.

And it was deadly.

Panting more with fear than exertion, she flattened herself against the wall before cautiously looking around the corner. If Gervas killed her Gaul—*not that he would, why was she even thinking that?*—she'd carve out his heart. Sever his windpipe. Wrench out his flirtatious tongue.

Terror slammed into her chest, crushed the breath from her lungs, paralyzed the panicked thoughts colliding through her mind. Less than a stone's throw from where she stood, her Gaul had Gervas thrust up against the wall, his dagger poised with deadly precision against the other man's throat.

Chapter Twenty-six

Morwyn sat on the bed, arms wrapped around her knees. In the muted light of the single lamp, she gazed, unseeing, at the huddled figure of Gwyn on the pallet in the corner of the room.

She hardly recalled returning to the lodgings after seeing her Gaul murder Gervas. Even now, when dawn threatened on the eastern horizon, she could scarcely believe she'd witnessed such.

A whisper in the back of her mind reminded her that she hadn't seen the fatal thrust. She'd backed away, unable to watch, unable to think. But what other outcome could there be? Her Gaul was a warrior. There could be only one conclusion to that sordid scene.

Was she mistaken? Perhaps she'd stumbled onto nothing more than a drunken brawl. Perhaps her Gaul hadn't followed Gervas with the sole intention of killing him.

Yet neither man had been drunk. And no matter how she tried to delude herself, she'd seen the icy determination in her Gaul's eyes.

It hadn't been a hotheaded fight. He had planned the attack. And, as if in confirmation, her Gaul had not returned to her all night.

A shiver rattled through her bones, although it was far from cold. *Had he deserted her?*

It was madness to dwell on such a thing. If she had any sense, she'd even now be rousing Gwyn, gathering their possessions and making haste to Caratacus. Except she couldn't creep away like a criminal. As if she had something to hide or was cowed by his actions. Because she had done nothing wrong, had nothing to hide from him—apart from her heritage—and gods knew she wasn't afraid of him.

Not even now. Not even when she'd seen what he was capable of doing in cold blood.

Her forehead dropped to her knees and she squeezed her eyes shut. Had Maximus spoken the truth about her Gaul? Was he truly the heartless barbarian the Roman had portrayed? And what of that night he had spoken of—why had he told her it had occurred six years ago when Gervas declared it three?

She should leave it. Leave him. It didn't matter what the truth was because it made no difference. Sooner or later they were destined to part. Except she didn't want to leave him when her mind was so confused over his actions.

She didn't want to leave him at all.

The thought blazed through her brain, condemning her. But still she refused to condemn him. There was a reason why he'd acted as he had. She wouldn't make her decision until she'd heard his side. Despite the evidence of her own eyes, she could be wrong. It was possible.

Druids had been wrong before.

With a ragged sigh she pushed herself from the bed and checked that Gwyn was still asleep, before stealthily slipping from the room with the lantern in one hand and her dagger in the other. As she approached the latrines, apprehension trickled along her spine and her grip on her dagger tightened.

The door was ajar. The stale stench of ale and vomit assaulted her senses and she gagged, protecting her mouth and nose with the back of her wrist. In the flickering glow from her lamp she saw her

Gaul sprawled against the far wall, amphorae broken on the floor beside him.

A pain so deep it stilled her breath shuddered through her heart. A pain that didn't diminish as she approached her lover but increased, engulfing not just her heart but her entire chest, her lungs. Even her stomach. As if the agony wrenching through her needed to escape its point of origin or else risk utter destruction.

She sheathed her dagger, crouched in front of him and placed the lamp on the floor. His head fell back against the wall and he stared at her, his eyes glazed through ale or grief or . . . She couldn't fathom.

Silence spun between them. Finally she curled her fingers around his hand, tightening her grip when he made to pull away. And then, suddenly, his fingers crushed hers as if she were his life-line to sanity and he never intended to let her escape.

Foolish thoughts, without base in reality. *She* was the one who no longer wanted to escape. Why did she continue to delude herself with half-truths and fabrications? She had no intention of leaving him for Caratacus. Not yet. Not until the Legion was in imminent danger of collapsing and she had no other choice but to join the rebels in the final onslaught.

The darkest corner of her soul prayed such a moment would never arrive. *Traitor* whispered through her heart but it was faint, insubstantial. Because all she could feel, in this moment, was her Gaul's pain. And it crucified.

"Why?" His voice was raw with ale and retching but not slurred. No matter how much he'd drunk this night in order to forget his actions, it had affected only his body, not his mind.

She didn't pretend to misunderstand. "I missed you." Her voice was soft but it rasped through the rancid air and he recoiled, as if she had physically punched his face. She flattened her free hand against his chest. Against his heart. "I thought you'd left me."

His lips twisted into a mockery of a smile. "I should." But his hand covered hers, pressing her more securely against his heart. Belying his words.

For a moment she lost herself in the beauty of his eyes. Eyes that, unguarded, showed shadows of secrets so horrific that madness glinted. But they were still the most mesmeric eyes she had ever seen.

Perhaps he had ensnared her by some ancient magic of his forefathers. But she knew the truth. Whatever it was she felt for him originated from her own heart.

"If you left me"—she leaned closer to whisper, in case a malevolent god lingered and overheard her treacherous confession—"I'd hunt you down, Gaul. I wouldn't let you escape me so easily."

His calloused palm clenched, crushing her fingers against his chest. "You should leave, Morwyn. Find traders from your village and go home with them."

"And yet I choose to stay." The words echoed around the room, her confession, her betrayal. She should go to Caratacus, but she intended to stay. She should kill her enemy, but she would sooner kill herself.

There was no chance of a life together, and yet she'd do everything in her power to find a way.

"If you knew . . ." His voice cracked and he closed his eyes as if he could no longer bear to look at her. Silence vibrated with words unsaid.

She swallowed around the constriction in her throat. "I do know."

His lids lifted as if weighted down with the sins of his ancestors. But he didn't speak. Just stared at her as if she didn't know what she was talking about.

A ragged breath tore through her lungs. "I followed you. I saw. And—still I remain by your side."

This time the silence thudded in her ears, dangerous and deadly, and still her Gaul remained mute, staring at her as if he now thought she had lost her mind. But within a heartbeat she watched comprehension wash over his features as the realization of her words finally hit him and wary disbelief mutated into shocked unbelief.

"You saw." But it wasn't a question, at least not for her. It was as if he needed confirmation that he'd not misunderstood. "You *heard*." He sounded torn between horror and raw desperation. As if her confession shook the foundations of his soul.

Heard what? No words had been spoken between them. At least, not at the end when she had stumbled upon them. "You don't have to tell me why you killed him." Except she wanted him to explain why he'd murdered his blood kin. But she wanted him to tell her without her asking. And somehow she knew he never would. "Do you still trust me enough not to poison you?"

He looked at her as if she had just said something incomprehensible. As if her open acknowledgment of Gervas's death had paralyzed what remained of his wits. Slowly his fingers slid from her hand and encircled her wrist. His thumb grazed her pulse, and despite his ravaged state she had to battle the urge to wrap her arms around his neck, draw him into her embrace. *Comfort him.*

For slaughtering his cousin.

"Yes."

That was all. A single word that said so much. She had the insane desire to weep.

"Then wait here. I'll build up the fire in the kitchen and boil water. I'll make you a tea to soothe your stomach and astringent wash to cleanse your mouth."

She began to stand and he slowly relinquished his grasp on her, as if reluctant to allow her to leave. And then his grip tightened on her hand and his head lifted from the wall. Green eyes flayed her with the depth of their despair and his jaw tensed, as if he battled against the want to confide and the need for covertness.

Want won. *"I didn't kill him."*

Later, in bed, Morwyn stroked the short black hair of her Gaul as he slept against her breast. A constant pain bathed her heart, a pain born of the bitter knowledge that she had fallen in love with a man sworn to destroy not only the freedom of her people, but her Druidic heritage.

She pressed her lips against his brow and cradled his head in an oddly protective gesture. He wasn't of Cymru. He wasn't even a Briton. He was from Gaul, and the Gauls had been conquered by the Romans four generations ago. Her Gaul wasn't a traitor because he had joined their Legion. He was just carving out a career. How could she condemn him for that?

As far as he was concerned, the Romans were a segment of his people. If Caratacus didn't drive the invaders from Cymru and Britain, would they, in time, become assimilated to the Roman way?

Her heart twisted at such a foul vision. She didn't want the old ways to be trampled underfoot, to be forgotten in the hazy streams of memory. Just because she had issues with her gods didn't mean she wanted them replaced by the heathen idols of Rome.

Aeron had betrayed his people by lying to them, by pretending one thing while planning another. But her Gaul had never pretended to be on her side. He'd never pretended to be anything other than what he was. A Roman auxiliary from Gaul.

A shiver slithered over her arms. Was she truly contemplating turning her back on everything she had ever known? Considering the possibility of forsaking her duty to fight for freedom—*because she had fallen in love?*

Her breath hissed between her teeth. Why was she continuing to lie to herself? There was nothing left to consider. She would stay with her Gaul. Face the consequences of her severed loyalty.

And not think about the inevitable battle that was sure to occur between Caratacus and the Legion.

She was back in the Morrigan's sacred grove on the Isle of Mon. But she didn't want to be here. Not again. Would she forever be haunted by these nightmares? Desperately she tried to awaken, sinking to the grass and digging her fingers into the pungent earth. She would not be ruled by her fear.

A breeze drifted across her face. She frowned at her hands, pulled them from the ground and stared at them in confusion. *What was she doing?* Scattered memories fluttered through her mind, a sense of urgency, of denial, but she couldn't grasp the essentials. Couldn't recall why she had sunk to her knees. Why she had the fading need to flee . . . somewhere.

The sunlight bathed the grove, growing brighter, blinding. Squinting, she looked up and panic slithered through her soul. The Morrigan stood in the center of the grove, a warrior maiden in all her youthful, terrifying beauty, her face turned upward to the perfect blue of the sky.

The great goddess extended her arm, and her sacred raven appeared from the forest to settle on her wrist. Storm clouds streaked across the sky, obliterating the sun, casting ominous shadows across the land. Morwyn shivered, tried to rise to flee, but couldn't move her paralyzed limbs.

This wasn't what she had witnessed before. The thought tumbled through her mind, almost making sense if only she could grasp its true meaning. Mesmerized, she could only stare at the goddess as terror and awe wrestled for supremacy within her breast. She'd turned from the Morrigan. Refused to honor her. But now the goddess had summoned her to her presence, and all the wonderful and fearful stories she'd ever been told of the goddess's deeds flooded her mind.

Raw power, as elemental as the earth herself, surrounded the Morrigan and throbbed in the air like a living entity. Morwyn sank farther to the ground, trying to make herself invisible to the goddess's wrath. For so many moons she'd deluded herself that the goddess was weak. Insignificant. Easily manipulated by the twisted will of Aeron.

Only now did she face the truth. Only now, when the great goddess slowly turned and looked at her, eyes blazing with rage and vengeance, could Morwyn finally confront her most guarded of secrets.

She was the weak one. *She* was insignificant and too easily manipulated by Aeron, their High Priest, the man she had trusted with her life and faith. And she had projected all her self-loathing and disgust onto the Morrigan. Because the Morrigan hadn't peeled the scales from her eyes. Had allowed her to blindly follow Aeron without sending a sign or warning.

The raven soared into the darkening sky, circled three times before returning to his goddess. A single black tail feather floated to the ground by Morwyn's clenched fingers, and iced fear froze her veins.

The Morrigan *had* sent her a sign. She recalled it as vividly as the moment it had happened. Sitting with Carys two days before the Sacred Spiral destroyed their cromlech, a raven's feather had crossed their path.

She hadn't understood its significance. Had thought it predicted war and death, and it had, but it had also meant so very much more.

Devastation. Betrayal. Why hadn't she meditated? Learned the true meaning behind the message? Would it have made any difference to the outcome of that night? *What else could she have done?*

The Morrigan spread her fingers, her palm directed at the ground between them. Instantly a raging river bubbled to the surface, bisecting the grove, and Morwyn scrambled back before the water sucked her under.

Goddess. The soundless plea she'd used until the exodus to Mon slipped easily through her panicked mind. She didn't know how or why but this river was familiar. The mountains, rising in the distance behind the Morrigan, were familiar.

Eerie shivers raced along her arms. Had she been here before? *Or was it a vision of what was to come?*

And then she was beside her goddess, walking on the mountain next to the stone ramparts that afforded them protection from the enemy below. War cries split the air but they were distant, unconnected from her. Warriors fought, bodies fell, but it was as if she watched it all from behind a veil, untouched and isolated from the reality of the events unfolding.

The Morrigan halted in the midst of the carnage. Fury and betrayal vibrated from her, and Morwyn stumbled as the mountain shuddered in response. She knew why her goddess was angry. Because Morwyn had betrayed her, not only by discarding her but by taking a lover from their enemy.

Heart hammering against her ribs, she took a stealthy step backward. Deep in the most hidden corners of her heart she'd always known of the Morrigan's strength. No matter how hard she'd tried, Morwyn had never quite managed to obliterate her ingrained reverence for her deities. They had been a part of her heritage since life first erupted from the womb of the earth.

She would face it now. Her gods had been deceived. Her gods had roared in vengeance. But they were still as powerful as they had ever been, as powerful as they would ever remain.

The Gaul had been her revenge on the Morrigan. She had intended to use him for her own pleasure and then leave him, dead or alive—such detail hadn't been important.

But things had changed. *She* had changed. She wouldn't desert her Gaul. Not for her people. Not for the Morrigan.

Not for anything.

The blasphemy of her thoughts thundered through her skull and she tripped on loose rocks as the goddess cast a disdainful glance her way. On her knees, palms bleeding from the fall, she watched, transfixed, as two figures materialized a stone's throw from her.

Gawain. Talking to another man. Embracing him. *Turning his back*.

"No." She heaved herself up, arms outstretched. She had seen this before, lived through this before, and, goddess show mercy, she couldn't stomach to see it again. *"Gawain."*

He didn't hear her. Perhaps he couldn't. The faceless warrior drew his dagger and it glinted in the ferocious gleam that emanated from the Morrigan, before he plunged the deadly blade into Gawain's back.

And in that moment she recalled the countless other times she'd been forced to watch his murder, unable to move, unable to help, but this time she clenched her teeth, unsheathed her dagger and fought through the paralyzing fear that gripped her limbs.

She would avenge his death. It was the reason the Morrigan had brought her here, because this time she wasn't dreaming. This time the events were real.

The warrior turned, his dagger dripping scarlet. Her heart slammed against her breast, disbelief collided through her brain and her own dagger slipped between suddenly lifeless fingers.

Gawain's murderer was *her Gaul*.

Chapter Twenty-seven

Her eyelids jerked open but for a moment she could see nothing, feel nothing, except for the horrified staccato of her heart, the erratic gasp of her breath. The sense of overwhelming dread seeping through every nerve and blood vessel she possessed.

Her Gaul. But there had to be a mistake. She couldn't believe it. Wouldn't believe it.

"Are you all right?" The childish voice slashed through her turbulent denials and she blinked, trying to focus on reality. Gwyn sat cross-legged on the bed next to her, staring down at her with evident interest.

Morwyn drew in a shaky breath, lungs resistant, heart still jackknifing in protest. "Yes." She struggled to sit up, drew the cover around her naked body, not because of modesty but because she could not stop shivering. "Just a bad dream, that's all."

Gwyn appeared satisfied by the explanation and continued to fiddle with something on her lap. "I'm hungry," she said at last, a hopeful note threading her words.

Just a bad dream. Morwyn repeated the mantra, and tried

to believe it. It was impossible that of all the men in Cymru, she had fallen in love with the one who had murdered Gawain. She wouldn't jump to any more conclusions without irrefutable proof. After all, she had been wrong about him killing Gervas. "Yes, we'll—we'll eat soon." Distracted, she glanced around the room, although she already knew it was empty. "Where is the Gaul?"

Gwyn shrugged. "Don't know. He said he had some business to deal with and that I wasn't to leave the room or wake you up." She gave a little bounce on the straw mattress. "I didn't wake you up, did I?"

Morwyn shook her head. Did his business have to do with Gervas? He'd told her he hadn't killed the other Gaul, but had offered no further explanation for why he had followed Gervas or why he'd drawn his dagger. In her heart she knew her Gaul had intended to end Gervas's life last night. But why? And why had he changed his mind?

She hugged her knees with one arm and cradled her aching forehead with her other hand. It had just been a nightmare. Like all the other nightmares she'd suffered since moving to Mon. None of them had been visions from her goddess and neither had this one.

She no longer had visions. She would never again have visions. *She didn't want to suffer from visions.*

From the corner of her eye she saw Gwyn resume playing with whatever lay half-hidden in her lap. A flick of black gripped her attention and she snatched the feather from Gwyn's hand.

"Where did you get this?" The words were scarcely audible. She couldn't take her gaze from the perfectly formed raven's tail feather.

"I found it." Gwyn wriggled. "Well, the man gave it to me. He found it outside the door when he left. But that makes it mine really, doesn't it?"

Shivers crawled over her flesh, burrowed into her skin, chilled the marrow of her bones. The Morrigan, aware of Morwyn's lingering resistance to accept what she didn't want to acknowledge, had followed up her vision with irrefutable physical proof.

Her stomach cramped, lungs contracted and heart quivered in denial but she couldn't close her eyes against the truth. Not anymore.

She believed in her goddess. Believed in her visions. In Camulodunon Carys had known the truth of the nightmares, and deep inside *she* had always known too. It was the reason she had been so angry with her friend's insistence that the Morrigan was trying to tell her something. The reason she had left Mon with the intention of avenging Gawain's death.

And now she knew, as surely as the sun set in the west, that the gods possessed a twisted sense of righteous retribution as vindictive as anything Aeron might have imagined.

How the Morrigan must have laughed when Morwyn had taken her Gaul as her lover as an insult to the goddess. How it must have warmed her stony heart to know Morwyn had broken her moons of abstinence with the one man she had vowed to destroy.

Nausea heaved and she hunched over the side of the bed, and the foul stench of the depth of her betrayal seared the air. Fingers clawed into the mattress, sweat dripped into her eyes and still she retched, helpless in the grip of self-loathing.

While Gawain's body lay rotting, she had enjoyed fucking his murderer.

A small figure clambered to her side, pressed a cold, wet cloth to her cheek. Eyes still clamped shut, Morwyn took the cloth from Gwyn and covered her face. Wishing she could hide so effectively from the rest of the world. From her goddess.

But most of all from herself.

Moments passed. Silence heavy in the air around them. Finally she scrubbed the cloth up over her forehead and pushed back her lank hair.

She'd sworn an oath on the memory of her foremothers to find Gawain's killer and avenge his death. It wasn't her fault she hadn't known the Gaul was responsible. But now that she did, it would be an easy matter to dispatch him.

He trusted her. She could poison him while he ate this night.

Cut his throat while he slept by her side. And before anyone found him she and Gwyn would already be halfway to Caratacus's camp.

Except she couldn't do it. Even with the knowledge he might have murdered Gawain in cold blood, without provocation, purely because the other man was a Druid and her Gaul despised all Druids, she couldn't exact justice.

How clever she thought she'd been, taunting the goddess with her refusal to enjoy her gifts. Flaunting her unsuitable lover in her face. It was madness to imagine a mortal could ever mock a deity and win.

Aeron had tried and lost his life. Morwyn had tried and lost her heart, her self-respect and her integrity. She had nothing else left to lose. If she couldn't kill the Gaul, she owed it to Gawain to kill herself, as the failure she had become.

"Morwyn?" The anxious voice, the tentative touch on her bare shoulder dragged her back to the present. Gwyn was gazing at her, her brown eyes fearful.

Morwyn sucked in a ragged breath. She had forgotten about the child. This child who, through no fault of her own, had been forced to live like a dog in filth-strewn alleys.

She didn't deserve a reprieve from her fate, but how could she turn her back on Gwyn? Condemn her to a life of degradation and starvation?

This, then, was the reason the Morrigan had allowed their paths to cross. So that when Morwyn faced the enormity of her crime, faced the unpalatable truth that she'd rather break a sacred vow than harm her lover, she was unable to sacrifice herself instead.

The air seeped from her lungs in defeat. The great goddess wanted to keep her alive, to revel in her debasement. To punish her for daring defiance, for harboring the audacity to believe she could triumph.

"Today"—she attempted to offer the child a smile of reassurance, but the look on Gwyn's face suggested that, even in that small measure, she failed—"we're going to the forest, Gwyn. To find . . . our future."

Bren sucked in a deep breath and resisted the urge to slump against the stone wall as two senior centurions passed him with barely a civilized glance. He'd needed to prove his cover was still intact. If Gervas had gone back on his word and betrayed Bren to the praefectus, every Roman and auxiliary would be on full alert.

But Gervas had honored his pledge. Which was more than Bren had done.

Curse the gods, what was happening to him? He'd pledged fealty to his king long before he'd exchanged that tentative bond of trust with Gervas last night. The safety of Caratacus was paramount. He could do nothing, allow no one, to jeopardize that, and the very fact Gervas knew Bren wasn't who he said he was put that fundamental tenet in peril.

He'd followed the other Gaul with one intention in mind: to slit his throat. The acidic sting in his gut, the insidious sense of wrongness— they were personal feelings, based on the knowledge of what Gervas had suffered at the hands of Dunmacos. It had nothing to do with this war. Nothing to do with the brutality of survival.

Without that shared knowledge he could have dispatched Gervas without a moment's hesitation. Without a heartbeat of remorse.

He'd remained loyal to his king right up until his dagger was in his hand, its blade poised to end the other man's life. But then, incomprehensibly, Morwyn's face filled his mind, her eyes condemning, and he hadn't been able to go through with it.

Instead, in that tortured heartbeat when his fractured loyalties thundered in his brain, he and Gervas had reached a silent understanding. And when he'd staggered back, dagger useless in his hand, Gervas had pledged to continue that silence to the grave.

He'd failed his king. The guilt scorched him, poisoned his veins as he finally made his way back to the lodgings. But inextricably entwined with his guilt was the stark realization that if he had murdered Gervas in cold blood, he would somehow have betrayed Morwyn's trust in him.

He hadn't been able to face her. Hadn't been able to face himself. But even stinking drunk the fetid memories plagued him.

"Dunmacos." The hated name jerked him back to his reality. He stared without masking his distaste at the speaker. Trogus. His fists clenched as the urge to punch the bastard's teeth down his throat threatened to overcome his hard-won restraint.

Trogus strutted toward him. "Bitch didn't murder you, then?"

With effort, Bren relaxed his fists. "Watch your mouth." His words were low, even. Spiked with menace. He watched Trogus's smug expression waver as if suddenly not so sure of the wisdom of confrontation.

"Just a civil question, Dunmacos. Bi—The woman murdered my tribesman. It's not unreasonable to think she'd do the same to any other man who got within spitting distance."

Bren took one step forward and derived mild satisfaction from the way Trogus only barely stood his ground. "Touch her, or insult her by a single word," he said as if they were discussing that day's training schedule, "and I'll break your neck, Trogus."

Loathing flared in Trogus's eyes, instantly smothered. "I've no need of another man's whore."

The words still echoed in the air as the tip of Bren's dagger dug into Trogus's neck. The other man's eyes widened at the speed of Bren's reflexes, at how he'd been so swiftly disadvantaged.

"I could find many legitimate reasons for ending your filthy existence." Bren allowed a trickle of blood to stain Trogus's flesh. "You may rest assured the praefectus would accept my reasoning." He wiped the blade on the sleeve of Trogus's tunic. "I can be very persuasive when necessary."

Trogus stepped back. It appeared an involuntary movement. "Fuck you, Dunmacos. You never struck me as the type to defend the nonexistent honor of a fucking woman."

Bren sheathed his dagger and stared at the other man until Trogus, jaw clenched, finally stalked off. Gods, he couldn't wait for the day until he watched the last gurgling breath leave that piece of shit's body.

Wandering through the market, Bren questioned why he wasn't on the way to Caratacus, to pass on the information he'd gleaned from Camulodunon. There was no excuse. The praefectus had given him leave of absence. He wouldn't be missed from the Legion.

And yet here he still was. Looking at ribbons and trinkets and trying to decide what would most delight Morwyn.

Morwyn. The reason he was still in the settlement.

His vision glazed as he stared at the jewelry displayed on the stall. Peasants and legionaries jostled him as they negotiated their way through the crowded market, but the noise of the populace, the stink of unwashed bodies and slaughtered livestock faded to a muted blur.

Morwyn had witnessed his suspicious actions last night. Had she been anyone else, he would have killed her without compunction. Witnesses were dangerous, even if they knew nothing of value. And although he'd been in no state to do anything when she confessed, he could have killed her as she slept.

But he had allowed her to live.

There had never been any doubt in his mind he would allow her to live. Even if she had, as he had momentarily suspected, overheard Gervas make his pledge. How could he murder her, when she put such trust in him? When she returned to him voluntarily? When she looked at him, last night, not with revulsion but with compassion?

When she had cleaned him, medicated him and held him in her arms?

When she was the reason he had failed to eliminate Gervas?

He picked up a bracelet, similar to the one she had asked him to sell for her. Similar, but not the same. Hers was of much higher quality, the engraving on the gold more elaborate, the jewels more precious.

For the first time in three years doubt clouded his mind. He knew the double life he led couldn't last indefinitely. Sooner or later, when his masquerade was in danger of collapsing, he'd have to leave the Legion for good, take up arms by Caratacus's side. But never before had the idea of abandoning the Legion prematurely beckoned.

Until now. When the enticing notion of being able to take Morwyn with him to his king, of not having to lie by omission to her anymore, glinted in the black corners of his soul.

She had her kin waiting for her in her village. But when she discovered he wasn't her enemy, that they were on the same side, there was a chance she'd go with him. She hadn't turned her back on him when she thought he'd slaughtered his cousin. He still couldn't believe she hadn't left him to drown in his own vomit, yet she'd tended him as if he was worth something.

He couldn't remember the last time he'd felt as if he was worth something. Apart from his skills at deception and subterfuge and killing in the name of his king, what did he have to offer?

Nothing. But when he was with Morwyn she made him remember how he used to feel. Made him hope his sordid past wasn't an irredeemable barrier to a less-fraught future.

As long as he ensured she never discovered the truth of that night three years ago, was it possible to imagine they might have a chance together?

It was midafternoon when he returned to their lodgings. The odd notion occurred to him how satisfying it would be for them to have their own dwelling. In his own village that had long ago settled into a reluctant peace with the Romans, far from this turbulent bloodied province.

Nothing but a hollow dream. He would never return to Gaul while Caratacus fought for freedom in this land. As long as his king needed him, Bren would serve. He owed Caratacus that, and so much more.

He owed the Briton king his sanity.

As soon as he opened the door to their room, prickles of alarm skittered across the back of his neck. It wasn't the fact the room was empty. He'd half expected it to be so. Morwyn wasn't the type of woman to sit at home all day, and although she hadn't confided as to what she had done the previous day, he was content by the fact she returned.

But something was wrong. Instinctively his fingers curled around the hilt of his dagger as he stepped into the room. The sharp tang of an astringent cleanser assaulted his senses, but underlying he caught the unmistakable stink of vomit.

His fingers tightened their grip as he glanced swiftly around. The child's—Gwyn's—pallet was in the corner of the room. For some reason Morwyn had taken the girl under her wing. He hadn't yet had the chance to talk to her about it, but there was nothing to talk about. If adopting a daughter made Morwyn happy, that was all that mattered to him.

The bed was rumpled. The few possessions he'd left in the room remained. There was no sign of a scuffle, nothing to indicate that Morwyn might not stroll back into the room at any moment, and yet still his senses spiked with unknown trepidation.

And then his eyes acknowledged what his subconscious had grasped instantly. Morwyn's pack had vanished.

Bren found Trogus on the training field beyond the garrison, practicing archery. Sword drawn, he marched through the center of the campus, unheeding of the warning shouts or the spear that narrowly missed impaling his brain.

All he could see was Trogus. All he could hear was the enraged pounding of his blood against his temples. He thrust a young legionary from his path, ignored the glances cast his way. Concentrated on the oblivious back of his prey.

Trogus let fly his arrow, and Bren wrapped his arm around the man's throat, jerking him back, crushing his windpipe. Trogus choked, gripped Bren's forearm, but before he could regain his senses and go for his dagger, Bren flung him around and pinned him against one of the numerous training posts fixed in the ground.

The tip of his sword pierced the soft flesh at the base of Trogus's throat. One section of Bren's mind acknowledged that an unnatural silence had fallen across the campus. That every eye was upon them. That no one attempted to interfere.

The rest of his senses were focused on the auxiliary before him, who remained frozen against the post as if realizing one false move would be enough for Bren to end his misbegotten existence.

"Where is she?" His voice was raw and when Trogus continued to stare at him with wary incomprehension, Bren twisted the sword and drew savage satisfaction from the strangled gurgle Trogus emitted.

"Dunmacos." The praefectus of his unit was by his side. But not too close, as if not convinced of his own safety. "This is hardly the time or place for an inquisition. If you have evidence against this man, then—"

"*What have you done with her?*" The words were low but vibrated with an unnamed terror. A terror he couldn't face; wouldn't face because Morwyn had to still be alive.

Sly understanding gleamed in Trogus's eyes, but he still retained the wit not to move a muscle. "I haven't seen her since that day in the forest."

Bren bared his teeth in a feral snarl. "Tell me where she is, you fucking piece of shit. Or I'll carve it out of you."

Trogus shot a glance at the praefectus. "I've been here since last we spoke, Dunmacos. I've six dozen men as witnesses."

Lies. Bloodlust pounded through his veins, demanding satisfaction. But what a hollow, meaningless satisfaction to watch Trogus's putrid blood seep into the earth. It wouldn't bring Morwyn back.

"Dunmacos." The praefectus's voice was sharp. "He speaks the truth. Is this connected to the matter we discussed two days ago?"

The thud of his heart vibrated through his chest. The rush of his blood deafened his ears. Trogus's face blurred. The campus shrank. All he could see was a vile blackness gaping before him. Remorseless and grasping into infinity.

Morwyn hadn't been abducted. She had left him. Voluntarily.

With a rough jerk he withdrew his sword and the world crashed back into focus. Every auxiliary, legionary and centurion stared at him in open speculation. He could read their minds as easily as if they shouted the words from the watchtowers. Dunmacos, the man with ice in his veins, the one who never raised his voice but never had to, had finally cracked.

Over a woman.

"Fucked off, did she?" Trogus wiped the blood from his throat and flicked it with contempt to the ground between them. A sneer crawled across his features. "Woman was a bitch but at least she had some sense."

"Dunmacos." The praefectus grasped Bren's sword arm and dragged him around. Perhaps he, unlike Trogus, had seen how close Bren was to thrusting the length of his sword through Trogus's filthy mouth. "Get off the campus and cool your head. I don't want to have to throw you in gaol. Do you understand?"

Bren wrenched his arm free and marched with deliberation across the silent campus. No one dared utter a word or cross his path. Never before had a field stretched so interminably into the distance.

For a few deluded moments he'd imagined a future with Morwyn. Growing old with a woman who, although she didn't know all of his sordid secrets, knew enough of his wretched existence and was still not repelled.

A bitter laugh escaped, scraping his throat like acid. He should have known better. At the first opportunity she had run. Afraid he would turn on her the way he had turned on Gervas.

He left the garrison, blindly walked the dirt-packed streets of the settlement. It was better she'd gone. Now he didn't have to concern himself with her safety. He could concentrate on his duty instead of constantly being distracted by the image of Morwyn's face, the feel of her silken hair, the captivating sound of her laugh.

Somehow he arrived back at their lodgings. He went to their room and sat on the bed, forearms across thighs. Staring blankly at the rush-covered floor.

For three years duty had sustained him. Given him a purpose, a reason for having survived when Eryn had perished. But deep in his gut the familiar knot of rigidly contained resentment tightened, and for once he allowed the treacherous thoughts free reign.

This life crucified him. Even in the beginning when he'd still been riding high on the bloodlust of having slaughtered Dunmacos, the reality of the existence he'd assumed sickened him.

But he'd given his word to his king. And the knowledge of what he owed the Briton outweighed his own considerations.

It was no longer enough. For the first time since Eryn's death the constant nightmare of his failure to save her had receded. The immovable rock in his chest had crumbled. He'd recalled how it was to speak without thinking, to laugh without guilt. To dare dream of a future without killing.

Because of Morwyn.

And she had left him.

He pulled a pouch from his belt. Tugged it open and withdrew its precious contents. The elegantly engraved gold bracelet with its tasteful jewels glinted up at him. Mocking him. He hadn't sold it when she'd pressed it on him. He'd had some vague notion of returning it to her someday. But now, he never could.

His hand closed around it. It was all he had left to remind him of the woman who held his heart captive.

Chapter Twenty-eight

Dusk was gathering as Morwyn approached a familiar stretch of forest. Familiar, because she was close to where she and her fellow Druids had been ambushed. How long ago that seemed.

She pulled the stolen horse to a stop and took their bearings. Their escape had been frighteningly easy. But she wasn't surprised. Because now she was obeying the Morrigan's will.

No one had seen them when they'd left the lodgings. No one had stopped them when she'd untethered the food-laden horse on the outskirts of the settlement.

And no one had followed them. A lone woman and child. Easy pickings. But the forest was empty of Roman, Briton and Gaul. As if the Morrigan, rejoicing in her victory, cleared the path for her errant Druid.

As she had before, the conviction gripped her that she was close to Caratacus. But this time she knew better than to search. His hidden enclave could never be found by conventional methods. The Elder had explained how the entrance could be discovered, and so she allowed her mind to relax. A difficult endeavor when every nerve screamed in protest of the desertion of her Gaul.

Briefly she closed her eyes. She wouldn't think of him. *Couldn't* think of him, or she'd tumble into insanity. Her priority now was ensuring Gwyn's safety. And safety lay in the Briton's camp.

She urged the horse forward, followed unseen paths, unerring in the knowledge she was going the right way. Deeper into the forest where undergrowth tangled and twisted branches tore at her gown.

The horse balked, ears flattening against its skull. Morwyn dismounted, lifted Gwyn to the ground and gripped the leather reins in one hand and Gwyn's hand in her other.

They had arrived. She pulled the reluctant horse forward, to an unremarkable gap between two great oak trees. As they passed through, a faint sensation of vertigo assailed her, and she was catapulted back in time to the Sacred Spiral Aeron had created.

This feeling was similar. But so very much diluted.

She glanced over her shoulder. The forest looked exactly as it had before. But she knew that, if anyone stood beyond those two sacred oaks, they wouldn't see her or Gwyn or the horse. All they would see was dense, uninhabited forest.

"Are we there now?" Gwyn's voice was plaintive as she rubbed her eyes with her knuckles.

Morwyn straightened her spine, looked ahead. To the bleakness of her future. "Yes."

Within moments of passing through the oak tree entrance a small contingent of warriors appeared, one brandishing a blazing branch that momentarily dazzled her in the gathering gloom. Gwyn huddled against her waist, trembling in silent terror, and Morwyn had the sudden, horrifying conviction that the Elder had directed her into a trap for her sins.

"Explain your presence." The voice was young, feminine and edged with power. Morwyn squinted, trying to see the owner of the voice, the one who held the flaming torch, but it was impossible.

She angled her jaw proudly. If she was to be slaughtered, she wouldn't give them the satisfaction of showing her fear. Perhaps they would spare Gwyn. Or at least kill her swiftly.

"My name is Morwyn, acolyte of the great goddess, the Morrigan." Thank the goddess for at least not allowing her voice to crack with nerves. "I've been searching for the Briton king, Caratacus, to fight by his side for freedom for my people. I was told the way here by the Elder."

There was a fraught silence. Nobody moved. Then the shadowy figure clasping the torch broke free of the semicircle of warriors and approached.

Morwyn caught sight of the long honey-colored braid that snaked over the young woman's shoulder. Her gown was richly embroidered, her gleaming silver jewelry exquisite. But she didn't need to see those things to know this woman was a noble. It was evident in her manner. And more than that, it was obvious by the deference of the warriors that she was also a Druid. Or, at least, an acolyte of some standing.

They maintained eye contact. Finally the other woman held out her free hand, palm facing up. "Welcome, Morwyn, acolyte of the great goddess the Morrigan. I am Nimue, acolyte of the moon goddess Arianrhod."

Morwyn smothered the rush of relief. She could allow no show of weakness.

"I thank you." She relinquished the reins and placed her own palm upon Nimue's.

Formalities over, Nimue smiled down at Gwyn, who still clung to Morwyn's waist. "You and your"—she hesitated, as if she had been about to say *daughter* but was now unsure—"child must be weary after your journey. Come, I'll show you where you may rest."

The four warriors parted to let them through; then two followed as if they were personal guards for Nimue. Perhaps they were. Morwyn detected no subtle nuance in the air to indicate they possessed Druidic blood, and they didn't give the impression of nobility.

Or perhaps, despite Nimue's words of welcome, they didn't trust Morwyn and followed merely to ensure she had no ulterior motive in entering their magical enclave.

They weaved through the trees, the forest becoming thicker until even the dull glow of dusk vanished beyond the canopy above. Nimue held her torch aloft and for a moment Morwyn feared the dry forest would catch alight. But instantly the trees thinned and they emerged into a small glade where an earth-covered dolmen hunched amid eerie shadows.

Morwyn's heart jerked against her ribs. Although this cromlech had only one circle of massive bluestones surrounding the edge of the glade and the earth barely reached the capstone of the dolmen itself, it reminded her forcefully of the much larger sacred glade that Aeron had embraced as his own.

Nimue glanced at her, as if aware of her sudden wave of discomfort. "You'll be safe here," she said, clearly misinterpreting Morwyn's reticence. "This is the resting place for Druids only. The masses camp wherever they so desire in the surrounding forest."

Morwyn swallowed her fear. It was foolish to let memories rule her. "Are there many Druids here?" Any she *knew*?

"The Elder has directed many here over the last few moons. They hail from all over Cymru and several from Britain." Nimue hesitated, as if debating whether to continue. "But only a few remain. They're supervising the great mission for Caratacus."

Morwyn glanced around the glade. A single lantern hung from the capstone of the dolmen and others were placed on the stone altar, casting flickering light and bottomless shadows. A small fire, set within a ring of stones, burned to one side of the dolmen's entrance. At the far side of the glade she saw horses tethered.

Nimue followed her glance. "We can accommodate your horse if you wish, while you refresh yourselves."

Morwyn decided not to mention the horse was stolen. Instead

she gently disengaged Gwyn's clinging arms and stripped the packs from the horse before allowing one of the warriors to take the reins. Nimue gestured for them to sit by the fire, and within moments she had water warming in a pot over the flames.

As Morwyn sorted through the food packs and handed Gwyn strips of dried meat to chew on, she reflected on Nimue's careless comment.

The masses camp wherever they so desire.

She'd always known Caratacus's rebels comprised, for the most part, of the general populace. But on Mon she hadn't known his camp was protected. How, then, could those without Druidic blood enter?

"Nimue, the Elder explained I could find my way here by following the call to my blood. And that was true." She paused, searching for the right words. Nimue regarded her in silence. "But even if the masses do manage to find their way here by themselves, how do they enter without the blood of the gods in their veins?"

"It's not easy to find without a guide," Nimue said. "Usually new recruits are brought by those who already know of the sacred gateway. And, of course, that helps ensure no spy may enter."

Morwyn frowned. That wasn't quite what she had meant.

"But the spiral itself." Perhaps Nimue didn't refer to it as the spiral, but even so diluted in power, what else could it be? "How do those who possess not a drop of Druidic heritage pass through the barrier?"

For the first time Nimue looked confused, as if she truly didn't understand Morwyn's concern. "No one may pass through the *barrier*. Only through the sacred gateway between the great oaks."

Morwyn stared at her, as the other woman's words filtered through her brain. "So anyone at all can enter this enclave, providing they find their way to the sacred oaks?"

"Of course." Nimue glanced at Gwyn, who was both chewing her food and listening to the conversation with equal interest. "How else could the child enter? She's not of Druid stock."

Morwyn looked at Gwyn and a chill stole through her heart.

That consideration hadn't even crossed her mind. But why hadn't it? It would have been impossible for Gwyn to have entered the spiral of Aeron's construction. He had ensured only his Druids could survive such feat. And, when he so chose, his deadliest enemy.

"I see." And she did. Hadn't the Elder told her his power derived from splinters of the original bluestones Aeron had used? The Elder had not harnessed the Source of Annwyn. Of course the magic protecting this enclave wasn't as powerful as the one she was used to.

Nimue leaned toward her, a strangely intense expression on her face. "What do you see, Morwyn?" Her voice was low, but it was no idle question. "Why do you ask such things about our sacred enclave? *Who are you?*"

Goddess, would she never be able to leave that night in the past? She drew in a deep breath. She wasn't responsible for the devastation Aeron had caused that night. But still it didn't ease the guilt she always felt for having been taken in by his ice-cold charm.

"It was my High Druid who created the original Sacred Spiral." She tensed her muscles, waiting for the inevitable derision. She could only hope Nimue possessed the sense of justice to accept Aeron had confided in no one about his plans. That despite appearances, the rest of Druantia's clan of Druids had been innocent of attempted genocide.

Nimue's eyes widened and lips parted. But she didn't draw her dagger, didn't go for Morwyn's throat. Instead she leaned even farther toward her, until Morwyn could feel her erratic breath whisper across her face.

"He was *your* High Druid?"

Morwyn stiffened. Something was very wrong. Nimuc didn't sound angry or disgusted. She sounded reverential.

She had to be mistaken. Perhaps it was merely condolence Nimue expressed.

"He was, I fear, completely insane." She realized her fingers were twisting the wool of her gown and only with great effort did she manage to stop.

"Insane?" Nimue raised her eyebrows and once again straightened. "Oh. Perhaps he was insane, Morwyn. But that doesn't negate the truly glorious vision he had for the people of Cymru."

Nimue's words thundered through Morwyn's mind. Individually, they made perfect sense. Collectively, they were as insane as Aeron had been when he'd murdered their ancient queen.

"Aeron." The name thickened her tongue, caused nausea to roil in her stomach. "Was evil. Vindictive. He cared for no one but himself. It wasn't victory for the people of Cymru he wanted. Only personal glory."

With a sense of detached disbelief she watched a flicker of irritation mar Nimue's proud face. How had this happened? When had Aeron's egomaniacal actions mutated from attempted mass murderer to thwarted savior?

Was this to be his legacy after all? Continued reverence, life everlasting—the very thing he had always desired?

"I confess I'm sorely puzzled by the attitude of all of your clan," Nimue said, sounding more annoyed than puzzled. Morwyn clenched her fists, tried to regulate her breathing. *She couldn't allow Aeron to be worshipped as a martyr.* "Why you insist his genius was corrupted I fail to understand. He devised the perfect weapon to rid our land of Romans for good!"

Morwyn's breath escaped in a noisy hiss. "He—" she began, and then the full meaning of Nimue's comment pierced through her broiling anger like a strike of lightning.

"All my clan?" Excitement churned, obliterating the sour taste of Aeron from her senses. "Nimue, who else from—"

The words lodged in her throat as three elderly figures approached the fire, and she leaped to her feet, pulling Gwyn with her. Nimue, also standing, proceeded with the formal introductions, and after the Elders seated themselves and began to speak of loyalty and obligations and the imminent evacuation of the enclave, the moment to question Nimue vanished.

But there remained a burning need to know within Morwyn's breast.

The morn dawned. Bren lay on the bed he'd so recently shared with Morwyn and stared up at the discolored ceiling, a dull sense of inevitability heavy as a rock in his gut.

There was no escape from his fate. He was pledged to Caratacus until death. The interlude he'd enjoyed with Morwyn was just that. An interlude. It could never have led anywhere. Even if she hadn't deserted him.

He expelled a measured breath. He had information to convey to his king. Information he should have conveyed the previous day. Except he'd been distracted by a woman.

But no more. She had gone. And with her had vanished his last chance at grasping a shred of comfort in this life.

Slowly he opened his fist. Her bracelet had gouged his palm, but the indentation would soon fade. The cavern she'd carved into his heart never would.

Trogus scowled as the party of exploratores left the settlement shortly after dawn. Always the same fucking mission. To try to find where the heathen Briton king hid among the forests and mountains of this barbaric province.

They'd scoured the area a dozen times. Never found anything. But there was a subtle shift in mood among the officers, as if they were in possession of information that could change the balance of this battle. Except it wasn't a battle, because Caratacus was a fucking coward who lacked the balls to face his enemy on the field.

All he did was set lethal ambushes, use the local topography to his advantage, send out assassins on covert missions. It was almost as if he had advance knowledge of the Legion's plans.

Not that Trogus gave a shit about the Roman Legion, but such tactical maneuvers could easily impact his own safety. And he cared a great deal about *that*.

The sun had passed it zenith as he descended, some way ahead of the other four exploratores, the sparsely wooded hill into the verdant valley, and the edge of the same forest where Dunmacos had rescued the whore. Gods, what wouldn't he sacrifice for the savage pleasure of running his sword through the other man's guts? It even rivaled his need to seek vengeance against the woman for the death of his tribesman.

From the corner of his eye he caught sight of a lone horseman entering the forest. He stiffened, pulling his mount to a halt. The distance was significant but he'd know that bastard anywhere. It was as if the gods had heard him, and granted him a boon.

Twice he had drawn Trogus's blood over the Cambrian bitch. The third time, it would be Dunmacos's lifeblood, from Trogus's blade, pumping into the earth.

The vision, as potent as any of those when he'd fantasized fucking the whore, jerked his cock to attention, an unwelcome side effect and yet another reason to exact vengeance from the other auxiliary.

He turned to a fellow exploratore who had just drawn alongside. "I'm going to check out the forest beyond. Saw something suspicious."

"You want to change our detail?" He made as if to call the others, and Trogus flicked his hand dismissively,

"No. I'll check it out and get back to you. No need to make it official."

"Fuck up and you're on your own," the other man said by way of agreement, turning to follow the others who were making their way to the forest at a point some distance from where Dunmacos had entered. Trogus dug in his spurs and galloped after his nemeses.

He planned to ambush the other man. Yet despite the acidic desire to prolong Dunmacos's torture, he had no desire to be caught in the act of murdering one of his own. So, an arrow through the neck. A dagger across the throat. Heavy mutilation to the face and removal of chain mail to prevent identification.

And a hasty burial among the undergrowth to hide the body. With luck, scavengers would strip the flesh from the bones before it was ever discovered.

A flash of armor ahead. A glimpse of equine flank. He urged his horse forward using thigh and spur, bow in one hand, arrow in the other. Waiting for Dunmacos to sense his presence, to turn and fight, to see who it was who was ending his filthy existence.

Dunmacos continued onward, as if oblivious. Trogus's fingers stilled on his bow, disconcerted by his prey's behavior. Was it a trick? Even though Trogus kept in the shadows and concealment of trees, it was surely impossible for a scout of Dunmacos's experience to be unaware of his presence.

But still the other man continued onward, scarcely glancing left or right, his mount's passage unerring. As if Dunmacos knew exactly where he was going.

The thought crawled through Trogus's brain like a drunken slug. Nudging him with a clouded knowledge. And then the question formed.

Where *was* Dunmacos going?

Slowly Trogus lowered his bow, but still kept hold of his arrow. He knew Dunmacos had been given leave of absence—fuck knew why. Although rumors circulated the praefectus, far from bestowing unjustified leave had instead charged Dunmacos with a covert mission.

Perhaps, then, he was following up a lead. But the supposition sounded hollow. Because even if Dunmacos was tailing a suspect for the praefectus, how did he know *exactly where he was going*?

Farther into the forest. Branches scraped against his face, tugged at his legs. An eerie silence descended, as if a blanket had been cast across the small creatures that scuttled in the undergrowth, the birds that nested in the trees. The certainty slammed into him. This part of the forest was cursed.

A shudder inched along his spine but he couldn't throw the feeling aside. He wanted, more than anything—even more than claiming Dunmacos's life—to turn and flee this silent place. Before it swallowed him and his existence was forfeit.

Sweat trickled into his eyes; his fingers were slippery on his weapon. Curse this. He didn't care where Dunmacos headed. They had traveled deep enough. His body would remain undiscovered for days.

Stealthily he drew back his bow, prepared to let fly. But before he could, Dunmacos, quite literally, vanished.

Chapter Twenty-nine

The following morn, far from being invited to join military practice or meet Caratacus—something Morwyn had half expected as her right—one of the Elders from the previous night entrusted her with the care of half a dozen clearly peasant children who all looked younger than Gwyn.

Morwyn bit back her frustration, but only just. The Elder offered her a faint smile, as if she understood Morwyn's sharp intake of breath for what it truly was.

"They need to be kept occupied while we arrange for the final exodus," she said. "And while they are not of Druidic blood, they can all be taught of the Morrigan. You're the ideal teacher, Morwyn. You are, indeed, the answer to our prayers."

Morwyn inclined her head, but respect was the last emotion bubbling in her breast. The Morrigan had brought her here, in order to be a *childminder*? She was relegated to watching over the young, and not even noble young at that, while her contemporaries worked alongside the Briton king on his *great mission*?

Rigid with affront, she followed the Elder's directions to a nearby stream, where she could supervise the children's cleansing rituals. And there, instead of merely handing out her supplies, she sent them on search-and-find missions to discover the raw ingredients nearby. Secretly impressed by their willingness to learn, she taught them how to process their haul. Truly, it was remarkable how quick-witted they were, considering they possessed not a drop of noble blood.

As the sun climbed to its pinnacle, she considered her thought. In the past, she had only ever taught the children of other Druids or nobility. Peasant children didn't have the luxury of obtaining an education. As soon as they were old enough they were set to work, helping their parents, and that was the way it had always been.

Was it the way it would *always* be?

So much had changed. Morwyn was still a noble but she had no home. She was still a Druid but her clan was fragmented. These children, Gwyn included, had been born into poverty. Did that mean they should be denied the means to improve their minds, to learn to the best of their ability?

A shiver trickled along her spine, and oddly she recalled Carys telling her, with defiance, how she taught Branwen the secret Druid ways. How Morwyn had been shocked at the blatant blasphemy.

And how now, looking at the eager little faces before her, she could suddenly understand why Carys, although only half-trained, had succumbed to the urge to pass on her knowledge.

It was what they did. Teach the younger generation. Without that, they were nothing. Their ways would die.

The Romans would win.

Her breath escaped in a shocked gasp and she pressed her hand against her breast. Children, whether they were of Druid or peasant blood, were the future. How could she, how could any of them, withhold their knowledge from any of their people who wished to learn?

Glancing around, to ensure they were alone, she smothered the ember of guilt and began to tell them of the Creation.

Not the diluted version that peasants had told among themselves for generations. But the full story. The sacred heritage of the Druids.

━◆◦◉◦◆━

For a moment Trogus froze, bow raised, body taut, eyes frantically searching the section of forest where just a moment before Dunmacos had ridden.

Nothing. Heart jackknifing, he dug in his spurs, urged his horse forward, out from the concealment of trees.

Dunmacos didn't leap from an overhead branch or barrel into Trogus's side from a hidden trap. Trogus held his erratic breath, strained his ears, but could hear no distant snapping twigs of muffled progress. Could feel no vengeful eyes upon him. No gut-deep conviction of surveillance.

Cautiously he edged between two massive oaks, and vertigo slammed into him, almost unseating him, and he clutched the front of the saddle for balance, his weapon digging into his hands.

Gods, he was going to vomit. The trees spun, the earth undulated, and distant, disembodied voices swam in his mind.

"Caratacus has been expecting you, Bren."

"I was unavoidably detained."

Trogus grimaced, crouched over his saddle. He recognized that voice. It was Dunmacos.

Bren?

Caratacus had been *expecting him*?

Instinctively, Trogus hauled reins and retreated from the oak trees. Instantly his head cleared, stomach calmed. And his brain went into overload.

He'd discovered the hidden whereabouts of Caratacus. And Dunmacos—*Bren?*—had led him there.

Despite the danger that thudded all around, a disbelieving grin cracked his face. Dunmacos, favorite auxiliary of their praefectus, was nothing more than a fucking traitor. The one who had been selling secrets to the enemy. Putting his own countrymen's lives at risk.

The grin faded. He could return to the garrison, share his information. The Commander would send the elite of his Legion to wipe out the rebels. Crucify Dunmacos.

Trogus would rather deal with Dunmacos himself. Then inform his superiors.

For several moments he remained mounted, scanning the area. There was something unnatural, something that made his flesh crawl about the trees that concealed Caratacus's camp. Something that made him want to avert his eyes, turn away.

Then he focused on the gap between the two great oak trees. And the insidious feeling of repulsion faded.

Magic.

It could be nothing else. Somehow, Caratacus was using magic to conceal himself from his enemies.

Heart thudding, he urged his horse once more through the gap. Again the vertigo assailed him but he pushed on, gritting his teeth, and the sensation faded. He glanced around but the forest stretched in every direction, with nothing to indicate he was now within the perimeter of Caratacus's camp.

He had traveled scarcely the length of a full-grown oak before two blue-daubed barbarians confronted him, primitive spears pointing at his heart.

Trogus raised his hands, dropping his arrow to the ground but leaving his bow across his saddle. "I come in peace." His words appeared to have no visible effect. He took a deep breath. If he was wrong, he might take out one of them before dying. "At the request of my blood brother, Bren."

The barbarians didn't move a muscle, but neither did they launch their spears at him. His breathing grew a little easier. "I come to fight by Caratacus's side against the Roman bastards."

The barbarian on the left jerked his spear, a clear indication for Trogus to dismount. He did so, slinging his bow across his shoulder as he landed on the ground.

"You, follow me." The barbarian turned to his compatriot. "I'll send reinforcements back."

The other one nodded, but didn't look overly happy by the situation. Trogus smothered a sneer. They were woefully unprepared should an attack occur. Were the Romans in charge—or even the Gauls—this entrance would be crawling with guards. Not a mere two or three.

As soon as they were a safe distance from the entrance, Trogus dispatched the barbarian with insulting ease. And they called themselves warriors? How had such ill-prepared specimens managed to so rile the Legion?

He hauled the body into the undergrowth, gripped the reins of his horse, and went farther into Caratacus's lair.

As the children used reeds to blow leaves at one another, Gwyn appeared more interested in watching Morwyn prepare darts with berry poison. It was hard to reconcile the child's low birth with her aptitude to learn. She would make a more than satisfactory acolyte.

The ember of guilt didn't even stir. She'd take that as a sign the Morrigan didn't disapprove. Yet in a small, rebellious section of her mind she wondered—wouldn't she continue to teach Gwyn, whatever the opinion of her goddess?

An elderly peasant woman hobbled to the stream, to inform Morwyn the midday meal was ready. As they returned to the cromlech, Morwyn excused herself. She was in dire need to relieve herself.

She walked some distance from the cromlech and found a suitably concealed patch of earth behind some bushes. How odd that in such a short space of time she'd got used to the convenience of Roman latrines.

A jagged sigh escaped and no matter how she tried to skirt the thought, her Gaul intruded. Was he angry that she'd left him? Would he miss her at all? Or had she been so blinded by her own feelings that she'd imagined that tender look in his eyes?

Approaching footsteps and raised voices, taking no care for stealth, headed her way. Goddess, she hoped they didn't intend to march right through her privacy. It was one thing to share such necessities of life with friends, but she didn't relish being caught by strangers with her gown around her knees.

She hunched lower, willing them to hurry and pass so she could finish in peace. Now they were so close she could distinguish the words of their conversation.

"It's no good shouting at me, Bren." The man sounded exasperated, as if he had repeated that statement many times in the past. "We don't have the resources to man the entrance the way you'd like. Four warriors is the maximum we can spare."

"There were only three." The voice vibrated with fury. Morwyn choked on a breath and leaned forward, squinting through her prickly green-leafed shield.

She was mistaken. She'd been thinking about her Gaul, and her depraved mind had allowed her to hear his voice in place of the stranger's. Her Gaul couldn't be here, in Caratacus's enclave, because that would mean—

Chills streaked along her arms. Did it mean he had followed her? Had she led the enemy into the king's camp?

From her vantage point she could see only their legs. Even their feet were invisible, concealed by the tangled undergrowth. Goddess, let her be mistaken. *Her Gaul couldn't be here.*

Chapter Thirty

"Yes, so now our resources are more stretched than ever," the first man said.

"Why?" It was a demand, and it was most certainly her Gaul. Morwyn held her breath, as if he might be able to hear her, but she couldn't quell the thunderous staccato of her heart that echoed around the forest in horrified disbelief.

"No doubt the king will inform you." The voice grew fainter as they marched farther into the forest.

"No doubt." Even from a distance, her Gaul sounded grim.

She fell onto her knees, dug her fingers into the dried earth. Her Gaul—*Dunmacos*. She would call him Dunmacos because he *wasn't* her Gaul. He never had been her Gaul except inside the deepest recess of her heart. And no matter what the other man called him, no matter what lies Dunmacos had woven, *she* knew the truth.

And he was being taken directly to Caratacus.

She scrubbed her hands in the dirt, as if that might scrub the stain from her soul, but still the ache of betrayal consumed her. Staggering to her feet, she peered into the forest, caught a glimpse of the men ahead.

The other man knew him. Called him by name, even if it wasn't his true name. That meant she hadn't led him here. That meant he had been here before. Was trusted enough to be taken to Caratacus.

Nausea turned her stomach, caused her limbs to shiver. She'd thought she had nothing left to lose. She had been wrong.

Dunmacos was her enemy. *He had murdered Gawain.* But until now she'd never doubted his loyalty to his Roman masters.

It was, she now realized, something she'd clung to. His innate integrity.

Even that illusion was now torn from her. He possessed no integrity. No matter how much she hated the invaders or disliked the fact her Gaul had chosen a career as an auxiliary in their Legion, she'd drawn comfort from the knowledge he'd never lied to her. He hadn't pretended to be on her side. Hadn't tried to manipulate her by telling her what she wanted to hear.

He had pledged himself to the Roman Empire. She had grown to respect his choice even if she could never embrace it.

But it was a duplicitous facade. He had done nothing but lie to her from the moment they had met. He was a Gaul, pledged to Rome and betraying them to the Britons. He was nothing more than a traitor to his people.

Just like Aeron.

She kept to the shadows as she followed the two men deeper into the forest. She may not have struck the blow that killed Aeron, but she had been the means to his destruction.

Just as now she had the means of destroying . . . her Gaul.

The forest opened to a clearing, where half a dozen steep slopes cut into the surrounding tree line. As she darted from the cover of one tree to the next she saw a group of men, who pulled back from their leader as Dunmacos and his companion entered the dusty clearing.

"Bren," the man—Caratacus?—said, and Dunmacos fell to one knee in greeting. Morwyn shivered in distaste at his hypocrisy and slid cold fingers over the hilt of her dagger.

Caratacus jerked his head at his men, who instantly left the clearing. She pulled back into the shadows, held her breath, but none of them came close to her hiding place. Goddess, what lengths had Dunmacos gone to in the past, in order to have secured the king's trust that he would dismiss his warriors?

When she returned her attention to the Briton, Dunmacos was once again on his feet. She edged closer until she was at the perimeter of the clearing, until she was a child's stone's throw away from the two men.

". . . feared something had happened to detain you," Caratacus said.

"No." Her Gaul no longer looked deferential. In fact, he looked as if he was trying to hold on to his temper. "I thought you'd discarded your plans for outright combat."

Queasiness churned. Dunmacos had inveigled himself very close to the seat of power if he could suggest such things without being accused of treason.

"No, Bren. *You* want to discard our plans. Not I."

"Gods' sakes, Caratacus!" The words erupted from his mouth. "The Romans will fucking slaughter us. Our warriors don't have the discipline to meet them as equals on the killing fields."

She huddled against the trunk of the tree, the rough bark scraping her face. Why was he cautioning against open combat? Just because he was betraying Rome didn't mean he possessed any loyalty toward the Britons. Why would he care if Caratacus's followers were slaughtered?

Was he was trying to prevent needless bloodshed for the Legion?

Except if he was deceiving the Romans, that made even less sense. Whose side was he on?

For the first time anger flashed across Caratacus's features. "Our warriors are fearless. We're more than a match for the spineless Roman barbarians."

Dunmacos swung on his heel and marched directly toward Morwyn. As if he knew her hiding place. But then he whirled, paced back to the Briton. "Our tactics are working. They're sending the Legion of Ostorius Scapula from Camulodunon to boost morale. Continue as we have been and we will prevail."

"Another Legion?" Caratacus expelled a breath between gritted teeth. "All the more reason to change tactics, Bren. They won't be expecting it. We can wipe them out."

She had never heard of Ostorius Scapula, but it was clear Dunmacos had gleaned that information from the dispatch he'd opened that night in Camulodunon. Goddess, she was so confused. Was he betraying the Romans or Caratacus?

An unsavory answer slithered into her mind. *Both?*

"And nothing I say can change your mind?"

"It was already done the last time we spoke, Bren. The last of our Druids and warriors are leaving this enclave today. I was waiting only for your return."

Breath ragged, she stealthily retreated as a sickening realization clawed into her heart. Whatever the truth was, Caratacus believed Dunmacos was loyal to him. The Briton wouldn't believe the word of her, a stranger, above that of a man he obviously trusted.

But it wasn't that that sickened her. It was the knowledge she couldn't expose her Gaul as a traitor, even now. Not to the Briton king, not to the Roman Legion.

She had no love for the Romans. But something deep inside her soul withered at the evidence Dunmacos could so easily betray those to whom he'd given his pledge.

The tip of a blade pierced between her shoulder blades and she froze. She'd been so intent on watching her Gaul, so intent on her tumultuous thoughts, she'd given no heed to where she was going.

Would she be hauled before the king for eavesdropping, thrown at his feet in an ignoble heap?

In front of her Gaul?

"We meet again." The hoarse whisper was eerily familiar although she couldn't place it. She began to turn, and the blade jabbed against the top of her spine, paralyzing her in sudden terror. That voice. She recognized it, but from where?

A hand closed around her biceps and dragged her farther back into the forest and she stumbled on the tangled roots, unable to see where she was going. Then he jerked her around, flung her against the broad trunk of a tree. And she remembered.

"You?" The word gasped, disbelieving, and instinctively her fingers flew to the hilt of her dagger. He grinned, a slashing of lips and a flash of teeth, and waved his own dagger in front of her eyes, stilling her hand.

"I'm guessing," the Gaul barbarian said, "Dunmacos didn't bring you here himself."

She wasn't going to talk about Dunmacos, not to this piece of filth. "You're with Caratacus?" Was the entire auxiliary unit of the Legion working for the Briton king?

For a moment he didn't answer, merely traced the tip of his blade along the length of her nose, over her compressed lips and jaw, until he came to a halt at the base of her throat. She hoped he couldn't see how frantically her pulse raced. She didn't want to give him the satisfaction of knowing how badly he affected her.

"Caratacus charged me with finding the bastard who's been selling information to the Romans. You're lucky you escaped when you did. He was out for your blood yesterday."

She didn't believe him. And yet in a dark corner of her mind his words made obscene sense. How else would he know she'd escaped Dunmacos the previous day?

"I'm more inclined to believe you're the traitor, not him."

"Yes, that would make it very convenient, wouldn't it?" He trailed his dagger downward, as if it were an extension of his finger, tracing across the vulnerable swell of her breast. "But untrue. If you could see the slaughter his betrayal's cost us. Children. Babies. A quagmire of innocent blood. All because Dunmacos would sell his soul for extra coin in his pouch."

She forced a derisive laugh. "And you, a brutal would-be rapist, are the savior of Cymru?"

The tip of his dagger ripped through the top thread of her bodice. She refused to acknowledge his action. Maintained eye contact. Because at the first flicker of distraction, she would strike.

"Caratacus," he said, ripping through a second thread but not even glancing at his handiwork, "trusts me with his life. Why else do you think he sent me undercover in the Legion to spy on Dunmacos?"

Within moments of leaving his king, Bren froze as the unmistakable voice of Trogus's came from seemingly nowhere. Was he losing his mind? Was his fury over Caratacus's plans causing him to hear things?

There wasn't any way Trogus could have found his way into the hidden enclave. And then a chill scuttled along the back of his neck. He hadn't been as meticulously careful in concealing his tracks this day. Gods, was it possible that because of his black preoccupation, Trogus had been able to follow him?

Bren unsheathed his dagger, turned in the direction from where the voice had originated. Although whom Trogus was talking to he couldn't imagine. Far more likely the bastard would kill anyone he saw on sight.

And this was why they'd needed sufficient guards at the entrance. Gods, it drove him insane when—

"No one in their right senses would send a creature like you to spy on a warrior such as Dunmacos. He possesses more honor in one glance than you could hope to salvage in seven lifetimes."

For one amplified, echoing heartbeat that vibrated every bone in his body and rattled his brain against his skull, Bren knew he had tumbled into madness.

Morwyn couldn't be here. Captured by Trogus—*once again*—and forced to listen to the filthy lies that spewed from the other man's mouth.

And instead of pleading for her life, or agreeing with Trogus in hopes of lowering his guard, she was *defending Bren*?

The last revelation slammed him back to the present. She was at Trogus's mercy—there was no doubt in his mind of her predicament—and yet she *defended* him against Trogus?

"Bastard fooled you easy enough." Trogus sounded amused. Bren edged forward and now he could see how Trogus had Morwyn pinned against a tree, how his dagger traced insolently over her partially exposed breast. "Would you like me to tell you of his bloodlust as he slaughters your countrymen for the might of Rome?"

Bren sucked in a calming breath through his mouth, but his blood boiled in his veins at the knowledge it was his fault Trogus had found the enclave. His fault Morwyn was, yet again, in danger.

He angled into position, calculated the distance and drew his sword in his free hand on the slender possibility that his first assault wouldn't sufficiently disable Trogus.

Morwyn laughed, the sound sharp and eerie and wrong, and it momentarily threw Bren off balance. "How much longer do you intend to regale me with the bold deeds of Dunmacos? Can it be his exploits excite you? Is that the only way your putrid worm of a cock thickens?"

Curse the gods, what was she thinking? Did she want Trogus to plunge the dagger through her heart? Even from this distance Bren could see the mad gleam in the other man's eyes. Without waiting for further proof of Morwyn's inability to protect her self-interests, he sent the dagger flying and it impaled Trogus's cheek, hurling him to the ground.

Bren covered the short distance in an instant, intending to prize Morwyn from the tree and crush her in his arms to comfort her. But she was already on her knees by Trogus, who was trying desperately to tug Bren's dagger from his cheek, and she gripped his hair in one hand, forcing his head back so his throat was fully exposed.

"You fucking barbarian," she said clearly, before she spat in his face and opened his artery. Then she dropped his head, wiped her blade on the grass and looked up.

Chapter Thirty-one

Relief that she was safe, fury that she had antagonized a man who'd held her life in his hands, flooded his mind in a jumbled torrent. Faint bruising still marred her face, traces of blood streaked her nose, her mouth, her jaw and her throat, her hands were bloodied and engrained with dirt, and she was the bravest, most beautiful woman he had ever seen.

"Were you trying to get yourself killed?" His voice was harsh, and to stop himself from shaking sense into her he swiftly retrieved his dagger to occupy his free hand.

"I had no intention of being killed." Disdain dripped from every word, as if his concern was beneath her.

He straightened and glared at her for her foolish pride. "You mocked his masculinity and you think he wasn't *this* close to murdering you?"

"That's right." As she rose to her feet, as regal as a queen, her dark eyes flashed and breasts heaved, as if she was having trouble filling her lungs. Blood surged and his cock responded and he clenched the hilts of his sword and dagger until his knuckles ached.

"He was so insulted, his attention wavered." Her breath hissed between her teeth. "I had no need for you to rescue me, Gaul."

He glanced at the body of Trogus. Dark blood soaked the earth and pumped from his opened throat. "Would you rather I stood by and watch him maul you?"

"That," Morwyn said, thrusting the tip of her dagger to the prone body, "is what happens to those who *maul* me."

The stench of foul blood and the pungent aroma of clean earth thudded in the air, mingling with the scent of arousal and denial. He sheathed his sword, flexed his fingers and gripped his dagger as if he faced his deadliest enemy.

She continued to glare at him, as if the feeling was mutual, her dagger no longer pointing at Trogus.

"Did he bring you here?" When? How? Trogus would have disarmed Morwyn at the earliest opportunity. But how else had she entered the enclave?

Her lip curled in clear disgust. "I have no need for traitors or barbarians to bring me anywhere. You're not the only one with secrets, Gaul."

Her warm breath grazed his face. Had he moved toward her? Or had she stepped toward him? He couldn't remember, didn't care. Danger pounded with every thud of his heart, hot and heavy and, gods, it felt good, right. As if only with Morwyn his senses became fully alive.

Barely aware of his actions, he let his fingers trail along the proud angle of her jaw. Her skin was warm, silky. She didn't jerk away, but loathing filled her eyes as if his touch repelled.

Yet her breathing quickened and a blush heated her cheeks. It was clear she hated the way her body responded to his touch.

"Secrets?" He should step back. Allow them both space to think, to breathe. But Morwyn didn't move and neither did he, as if they were imprisoned within the deceptive beauty of amber.

"Oh, yes." The tip of her dagger pressed against his heart. He could feel it like a brand against his skin, even through the chain mail he wore against the praefectus's orders. "This Sacred Spiral that hides so much is a cursed legacy from my High Druid."

For a moment he didn't understand the significance of her words, why she sounded so bitter. And then fragments of reality intruded: the rumored source of this magical enclave, the holy martyr who had died while attempting to cleanse the land of the invaders.

"You were from his village?" No wonder she hated the Romans so.

She bared her teeth in a mockery of the smile he had thought never to see again.

"*His* village? He owned nothing. Not me, none of my compatriots." Her blade slid against his chest, as delicate as a lover's caress. "I'm a Druid, Gaul."

His fingers stilled against her face. A Druid. No shock ricocheted through his blood; no disgust hammered through his brain. He'd always known she was more than a trader, had guessed she possessed noble blood. It was as if, in a buried corner of his soul, he had always suspected the truth.

Her pride. Her fearlessness. The cut of her gown, the quality of her jewelry. And then he was catapulted back to that night when he'd told her of Eryn, when she had whispered strange words of comfort. Only now did he recall they were the same words the Druids, who had feverishly worked to save his life six years ago, had intoned over his broken body.

How had he, for even a moment, imagined she had been a slave?

Gods. The woman in the forum. Morwyn's lifelong friend. *The wife of the tribune.* No wonder that strange, haunted expression had flickered over her face when he'd told her of the rumors surrounding the tribune's wife. Had she imagined he intended to betray her friend's secret to his superiors?

"Yes." The word was a hiss. He realized her free hand gripped his forearm, as if she would drive his dagger through her heart. "One of the despised Druids. What do you think of *that*?" She sounded triumphant, despairing, as if she truly thought it made a difference to the way he felt.

"I don't care what you are." His fingers tangled in the curling tendrils that escaped her braid. "You're mine now." Because there was no going back. Not for him to the garrison or for Morwyn to her previous life. Now that she knew he wasn't her enemy, there was nothing to keep them apart.

Her blade slipped beneath the layers of iron rings and pierced his flesh. He gritted his teeth, laid the flat of his blade against the tempting swell of her exposed flesh. She didn't try to prevent him. Instead, her grip tightened around his arm, as if she wanted him to mar her skin, draw blood as she drew his.

It would never happen.

"I belong to no man." Yet even as she spoke she swayed toward him and he hastily altered the angle of his dagger so she didn't injure herself. "I'm not yours, and I never will be."

Her lips parted; her dark eyes invited. He scarcely comprehended her words as he lowered his head. "I don't recall offering you the choice, Morwyn."

Warm, spiced breath tantalized his lips as she struggled to maintain some vestige of control. "I don't fuck traitors." The words lanced his lust-drenched senses, scorched his brain.

"Traitor?" He pulled back, but only enough so he could scrutinize her face, to ensure she wasn't indulging in some warped jest.

She looked utterly serious. And utterly wretched. As if she believed she knew the truth.

"Morwyn." He softened his tone, cradled her face, attempted to remove his dagger from her breast. But she tightened her fingers around him, and since the last thing he wanted was a fight, he ceased resisting. "I'm not a traitor. These are my people. Not the Romans."

He half expected her to melt into his arms with joyful relief. But this was Morwyn. And Morwyn never did anything he expected. Even her expression of resigned misery didn't alter. As if his words didn't surprise her, but didn't sway her either.

"Bren." The voice echoed through the forest and he bit back a curse as Morwyn immediately pulled back. With the history they shared, Judoc was the last person he wanted to see while he was trying to convince Morwyn of his loyalty.

Judoc, blood kin on his mother's side, a close aide to Caratacus and the only one left alive who knew the full depths of depravity to which Bren had sunk on that night three years ago.

"Fuck it, Bren." Judoc glared at him. It was obvious he hadn't seen Morwyn, who had retreated into the shade. He kept her in his peripheral vision. She wouldn't escape him a second time. Not now, when he no longer needed to keep up the pretense of being Dunmacos.

"What?" Bren's impatience was clear in his voice and he tapped his dagger against his thigh in mounting irritation.

"Caratacus—" Judoc's glance fell upon Trogus's body and his stance instantly stiffened into warrior mode. He whipped out his dagger and advanced, his eyes never leaving the prone figure by Bren's feet.

It was obvious to a half-wit the bastard was dead. And Judoc was far from witless. Bren gritted his teeth. It was clear an explanation was required. Perhaps then Judoc would leave and let Bren finish convincing Morwyn to take a chance on him.

Judoc made an odd gagging sound, his eyes widened in stupefaction, and then he collapsed at Bren's feet, one hand clutching his neck.

For a moment Bren stared at the other man, his brain unable to process the evidence of his eyes. Then Morwyn grabbed Bren's arm and tugged him until he tore his gaze from Judoc and looked at her.

There was a wild look in her eyes and the blood and dirt that smeared her face gave her an exotically feral appearance. Her dagger was sheathed and in her free hand she held a slender reed.

"Move." Her voice was guttural, vibrated with terror. "Just go. What are you waiting for? He wouldn't have come alone."

He glanced once again at Judoc. The other man's hand had

fallen from his neck and now Bren saw the small, deadly dart protruding from the flesh.

"You poisoned him." He heard the words fall from his tongue, but could make no sense of them. Why had she poisoned Judoc? He crouched and pulled the dart free, allowing blood to trickle over the clammy skin.

She shoved him, hard. "What are you doing?" She glanced around, as if ensuring they were still alone. "You don't have much time. You have to go, now."

Slowly he pushed himself to his feet. "I'm not going anywhere. And neither are you until you explain why you just tried to kill Judoc."

She bared her teeth as if she hated him. "So he wouldn't kill you, you treacherous bastard."

The trees compressed, his vision darkened, and all he could see was Morwyn's pale face and accusing eyes. And all he could hear was a recurring echo of her furious words.

So he wouldn't kill you.

She had been prepared to kill his blood cousin—to save *him*.

The breath staggered from his lungs, leaving him light-headed as if he'd overindulged with the incenses used by the Druids during his coming-of-age ceremony so long ago.

"He wasn't going to kill me." *But she hadn't known that.* She had thought he was in danger and had acted—instinctively.

His guts clenched, agony twisted through with a rare, unimaginable ecstasy. Disbelief entwined with a fragile thread of hope.

And awe melded with incredulity that anyone, least of all Morwyn, had been prepared to kill one of their own in order to save his worthless skin.

"He saw the dead auxiliary. He drew his dagger. Of course he was going to kill you. He thought you'd just murdered their spy."

He needed to take her in his arms. Wanted to explain everything to her. But Judoc was dying. He once again crouched, felt his cousin's pulse. It was slow, sluggish, but did not appear to be fading any further.

"Trogus"—he jerked his head at the auxiliary—"was nothing. I've been Caratacus's eyes and ears in the Roman Legions for the last three years."

She didn't answer, but he saw her fingers tighten on the reed until her knuckles glowed white beneath the dirt. He lowered his head to Judoc, fastened his lips around the wound.

"Don't." Her voice sounded oddly dull. "The poison won't kill him. He'll awaken naturally soon enough."

He sat back, spared his cousin a brief glance. He'd not left Bren's side during the hunt for the murderers of Eryn. It was more than mere relief to know Morwyn, the woman who held his future in her hands, wouldn't be responsible for ending Judoc's life.

"I'm sorry I couldn't tell you the truth, Morwyn." He looked up at her. She hadn't moved, still stared at him as if she had never seen him before. "Knowing my true identity could have endangered you."

The tip of her tongue flicked over her lips. "And what is your true identity?"

There was nothing else he could do for Judoc and so he stood, his cousin lying between him and the woman he loved.

"Brennus, son of the Chieftain Brennus of the Rhine and"—he hesitated for a heartbeat—"the Princess Olwina of the Catuvel-launi tribe of old Camulodunon."

Her gaze flickered. He wondered if she recalled him telling her that he possessed a drop of noble blood. Even in that, he'd not told her the truth.

Now he would hold back nothing. *Except for one thing.*

"Caratacus is my mother's cousin. I swore him a blood fealty. It's the reason I followed Gervas that night." Morwyn had guessed his intention. Gods, she'd assumed he had murdered the Gaul, yet still she'd remained by his side. Guilt haunted him, as he knew it would forever haunt him, at the knowledge he had knowingly risked his king's safety by not killing a potential threat. And the reason why he had risked everything stood before him now, oblivious. He didn't expect Morwyn to forgive him for what he'd intended that night, but he hoped, someday, she'd at least understand.

"Yes." Her voice was hoarse. "I understand the bonds of blood."

Of course she did. *She was a Druid*. They were obsessed with preserving the purity of their bloodlines, the purity of the nobles they allegedly served. She might not like it, any more than he did, but she understood. And because of her heritage she considered there was nothing to forgive.

"I've never been your enemy, Morwyn."

She swallowed, and for a moment he thought she was going to step toward him, take his offered hand. Instead a shudder rippled over her and she straightened, as if coming to a decision. But she didn't speak, and silence stretched between them, a chasm he didn't know how to breach. As the deathly hush invaded his heart, the marrow of his bones, she finally responded.

"I know."

Breath hissed between his teeth. He hadn't realized he'd been holding it until that moment. Hadn't acknowledged just how uncertain he'd been that she would accept his word. Accept the reason why he hadn't told her the truth.

That she would be willing to let them start again.

He stepped over Judoc. With one dead auxiliary and one unconscious blood kin, the surroundings were hardly ideal. But what did that matter when he needed to reassure Morwyn her faith in him was justified? That her actions, while she still thought him her enemy, had touched him more profoundly than anything else he'd experienced?

"I understand why you left me." He stood before her, not touching, but drinking in the sight of her face, the fragrance of her hair. The reality of her presence. "But I would never have hurt you." He hesitated, unsure, and then knew she deserved to hear. "Not even if Caratacus himself ordered me to."

Her bottom lip trembled, just once, before she tensed her jaw and jerked her head in a gesture of acceptance. "I've never been afraid that you'd hurt me, Ga—Brennus."

Gods, to hear his true name from her lips. It was sweeter than he'd even imagined.

"And," she said, raising her hand in a warding gesture as he pulled himself up. Not yet. She needed to clear her mind before they touched. Because when they touched he'd need more than a fleeting kiss, and there would be no need for words to convey how much she meant to him. "Gervas had nothing to do with why I left you."

He'd been so sure that was the reason. Why else? What could possibly have persuaded her to leave, when her recent actions all pointed to the astonishing fact she cared about him?

"Then why did you leave?" He glanced at Trogus, but he no longer believed she had been abducted. Morwyn had left while the auxiliary had been surrounded by dozens of witnesses. She had gone of her own accord and he couldn't fathom why.

Her hand dropped to her side. She was close enough for him to feel her breath on his face but with every frantic beat of his heart he could feel her inexorable retreat.

"For something that happened before I even met you."

Ice clutched his gut. It was impossible she could know. Words tangled in his throat, guilt strangled his air supply and all he could do was stare at her in rising disbelief.

Again her bottom lip trembled and her eyes glittered as if tears shimmered in those dark, mysterious depths. "I want you to know that I don't hate you." Pain twisted through every word as if they tortured her as much as they did him. "I should. But I can't. All I can do is . . . walk away. And ask you to never approach me again."

Chapter Thirty-two

A part of Morwyn—a despicably large part of her—hoped the Gaul—*Brennus*—would charge after her as she left the blood-soaked scene. But he didn't. He didn't even ask her what she was talking about, demand she explain her accusation.

His guilt had glowed for one soul-destroying moment in his beautiful, unforgettable green eyes.

Biting hard into the soft flesh of her lip, she glared ahead as the trees shifted out of focus and the path became blurred. Yesterday morn, after waking from her vision, she had imagined it was impossible to feel any worse.

Again, she had been wrong.

Brennus, far from betraying his people, the Romans, had put his life at risk every moment he remained within the Legions. From the start his loyalty had been absolute to his king. *To his kin.*

A useless tear slid down her cheek and she dashed it away, gritting her teeth as she approached the cromlech.

In the beginning she'd called him a coward. Thought him a traitor. Despised him for his values and alleged allegiance.

His courage and convictions in his cause put her to shame.

More than anything she had ever wanted in her life before, she wanted to stand by his side. Offer him her love, her heart, her undying devotion.

The specter of Gawain vibrated between them. She couldn't desecrate the memory of Gawain by pledging her life to Brennus. And she couldn't condemn Brennus, the most honorable man she had ever met, for killing Gawain.

Brennus had had his reasons. Of that she had no doubt. And perhaps, one day, she'd discover those reasons. But for now it was all she could do to keep herself from sinking to the forest floor and allowing her shattered heart to consume her sanity.

They left the enclave that afternoon, the last of the Druids, the few remaining children, and a strong contingent of warriors to guard the king. Including Brennus.

As they traveled through the green valleys, skirted the peaceful hills and forded the sparkling rivers of her beloved homeland, she caught sight of him more often than her heart could bear. Sometimes she imagined he watched her, also, but she never caught his eye. Even in this he honored her wishes and kept his distance.

It crucified her to know that, deep inside, she'd hoped he would try to change her mind. That he would present her with an explanation so supremely justified for his actions it would somehow negate her blood pledge to her foremothers.

Allow her the luxury of cleaving unto him, without the crippling guilt that was eating her alive every moment of every day.

And night. The visions worsened. The first night of their journey the vision had descended instantly, plunging her into the battle without any preliminary.

This time Gawain had heard her frantic calls. Had turned to her. And as Brennus approached, dagger glinting, Gawain's features had melted, twisted, morphed into Caratacus.

And Brennus had stabbed his king in the back.

The second night, fearful of repeating her embarrassing performance during which an Elder had been summoned to quiet her feverish terrors, she took a sleeping potion.

And the nightmares flourished, in vivid hues of green and scarlet, the scents more pungent, the sounds of battle and death escalating. And this time Gawain murdered Caratacus.

Drenched in sweat, she jerked awake, shivering as icy chills rattled over her bones. The Morrigan was trying to show her something, but all she could see was the two men she trusted with her life betraying every fundamental principle she believed in.

Brennus would never betray his king. And Gawain—Gawain couldn't stab anyone in the back because he was already continuing his journey.

In the black of the night a tiny, vulnerable doubt flickered.

Gawain was dead. *Wasn't he?*

On the second day they arrived at Caratacus's destination. Steep mountains soared all around the valley, and as they forded the treacherous river and led their horses up the nonexistent pathways of the highest peak, a dread certainty coalesced in the pit of Morwyn's stomach.

This was the place she had seen in her dreams for so many moons. The bloodied killing fields where, no matter how many stirring speeches Caratacus gave his followers, carnage would ensue.

Rocks were strewn across many gentle access points. The ramparts she'd seen in her visions. And hidden farther up the mountain several tribes had laid claim to their own campsites, as if they'd been there some time, and children played mock battle with sticks and stones.

Druids dispensed wisdom, gave sacrifice to the gods, strategized with the king and tribal chieftains. On the third afternoon after leaving the enclave, as Morwyn watched a group of bluedaubed warriors practise their war cries, a cold sensation of finality washed through her.

No matter how just the fight or brave the cause, against the mighty Roman army her people would lose.

Her skin prickled with awareness and she turned, to see Brennus standing some distance off, watching her. Her heartbeat sped; her breathing stumbled. She should go. Ignore him. It would be easier that way.

But instead she picked her way across the rocky incline until they stood within touching distance. His warmth and vitality reached for her, ensnared her, battled against her conscience, and she remained rooted to the spot only by sheer force of her ingrained Druidic willpower.

And then he spoke. "You should go, Morwyn."

His rejection hurt. More than it should, but wasn't this what she had asked of him? To keep his distance? But why, then, had he sought out *her*?

She stepped back, unable to trust her voice, and instantly his hand gripped hers. Strong. Comforting. Memories flooded through her of entwined limbs and heated kisses, but overriding all else the memory of his tender touch before he had left her on the morn before Gervas had intruded into their delusory existence.

"I mean, leave this mountain." His voice was low, his focus on her absolute. "Before it's too late. Take Gwyn—gods, take as many of the children as you can—and get out of here, Morwyn. It's a death trap."

She knew it was. But still the Morrigan had led her here. For a purpose she could not yet fathom. "Is there no way we could claim victory?"

His grip on her hand became less brutal, as if he'd expected her to try to pull free or dispute his words. The gentle caress of his thumb across her knuckles threatened to shatter the fragile barrier she'd erected around her heart.

But still she allowed him to hold her hand. It might be the last time he ever would.

"No." It was just one word, and filled with fatalistic despair. And she knew it was the truth.

"I can't leave." Her voice was soft, but her resolve implacable. They couldn't win, but she couldn't leave because the time had not yet come to pass. She couldn't explain it to Brennus; couldn't explain it to herself. But when could any mortal truly explain the twisted, contradictory messages of the gods?

All she knew was when the Morrigan decreed the time was right, she would know.

"I've had enough of all this." He jerked his head at the warriors. "It's been my life. Kept me sane. But . . . now I've had enough." As if he couldn't help himself he tugged her closer. And, weak fool that she was, she allowed him to. "I dared to dream of a different life with you, Morwyn." Raw pain gave his whispered words an agonized edge. "Dared to imagine we could overcome my past. But you're right. I don't deserve a second chance. This is all I'm fit for."

"No." Before she could stop herself her free hand cradled his jaw, her thumb grazing the rough stubble that darkened his features. She couldn't be with him, but goddess, she wanted him to find some peace in his life. Some happiness. "You're worth so much more than this, Brennus. You have to survive this battle. You have to find that other life you crave."

A smile twisted his lips, a smile that wrapped itself around her heart and magnified her despair a thousandfold. A smile that told her more clearly than any clumsy words that, without her, such other life was nothing but a fragile dream.

Dimly she became aware of a cacophony of shouts, of sudden movement, of frenzied excitement. Sliding her hand from his face to his shoulder, she followed his glance and saw several Druids, chieftains and warriors ascending, doubtless on their way to Caratacus.

"And so it begins." Brennus sounded resigned. "And I can't persuade you, a Druid of honor and integrity, to remain out of the line of fire with the non-fighting women and children?"

"Can I persuade you to do so?"

His free hand clasped the length of her braid, allowed it to slide against the palm of his hand. Then he released her hand and stepped back and the chill of this final parting invaded her heart, her soul.

"Grant me one last favor." The incredible green of his eyes captivated her, as they had captivated her from the very first moment they'd met. "How did you find out?"

She swallowed against the rising constriction that threatened to choke her. "The Morrigan showed me." Her voice was husky, filled with tears as yet unshed. Treacherous words trembled on the tip of her tongue and she flung caution aside. Her Gaul, her Brennus, was more important to her than placating her goddess who for all her power was still vindictive. Still cruel. *"I wish she hadn't."*

From her vantage point, concealed behind a natural barrier of rock and bush, Morwyn crouched beside Nimue. Chieftains went from rank to rank, encouraging their warriors, and Caratacus appeared to be everywhere bolstering morale and appealing to his forefathers for victory.

In the valley, already fording the river, the Roman Legion advanced.

"It should be easy to defend our position." But even as she spoke Nimue frowned as if she hadn't imagined the army would be so vast. "We have the advantage of height. They will drop like flies before our missiles."

And at first it seemed as if they stood a chance. She and Nimue aimed their arrows true into the enemy ranks. Roman soldiers fell and a flicker of hope ignited deep in Morwyn's breast. Maybe they could defeat the might of the Eagle, after all.

But then, in sudden precise movement, they re-formed their ranks and raised their shields in such a manner as to protect the entire Legion. Arrows glanced off the makeshift roof, missiles had no impact and, impervious to attack, they began to systematically tear down the stone ramparts.

"Should we advance?" Morwyn wiped sweaty hair from her eyes and glanced at Nimue, who appeared transfixed as legionaries felled their woefully ill-equipped warriors with swords and javelins.

"No. It appears our warriors are retreating." Nimue stood. "Let me find out, Morwyn. I'll be back directly."

Morwyn remained in place and watched the pitched battle between half-naked tribesmen and fully armored Romans. Courage didn't come into it. They were being slaughtered because the enemy possessed strategies and equipment foreign to her people.

"Nimue."

The male voice came from behind and sounded strangely familiar although, distracted by the bloodshed, Morwyn couldn't quite place it. As Nimue changed direction and began to run up toward the source of the voice, Morwyn pushed herself to her feet so she could see the speaker.

The battle cries faded. Her heart gave a mighty thud against her ribs, then appeared to die. Her peripheral vision narrowed until all she could see was Nimue.

And Nimue was talking to Gawain.

Chapter Thirty-three

He was alive. The thought pounded against Morwyn's skull but she couldn't move, couldn't speak. As if hypnotized, she continued to stare at him, and as her vision blurred and the landscape undulated, shivers trickled along her spine.

Gawain turned his back on Nimue, but it was Caratacus's face who stared blindly at Morwyn. And as Nimue drew her dagger, her hair rippled and changed from honey to gold, and it was Carys who plunged the deadly blade into the displaced Briton king's back.

Jagged gasps tore from Morwyn's throat and her borrowed bow fell to her feet as, in slow motion, she watched Gawain and Nimue turn toward her. In the heartbeat before recognition hit Gawain, comprehension flooded, singeing her blood and causing nausea to roil.

The Morrigan had never told her Gawain was dead. She had shown her, over and over, betrayal by a trusted one. But Caratacus was the one who was betrayed, and only after she had met the king, after she could recognize his face, had her vision changed.

But why show her Carys?

The answer swam into her mind, in perfect clarity. *Royal blood.*

"Morwyn?" Gawain made as if to approach, but in that instant a strong arm wrapped around her shoulders, dragged her against a chain-mail-protected chest, and a bloodstained hand gripped her jaw, forcing her to look up.

"Are you trying to get yourself killed?" Her Gaul's green eyes blazed with fear and fury. For her. "You're a perfect target. Keep down and keep moving back up the mountain."

With that he crouched low, dragging her with him, protecting her back with his body, and unceremoniously shoved her up where Gawain and Nimue had retreated behind a stand of trees.

The power of her vision thrummed in her mind, danced through her blood. There was more she needed to learn, more she needed to understand concealed within the Morrigan's message. But she swept the thought aside and gripped Gawain's hand.

"You're alive."

"For now." He sounded grim. Then his features softened by the slightest degree. "I wish I could say it was good to see you, Morwyn. But, gods, you shouldn't be here."

Without even looking at him, she knew Brennus tensed behind her. She turned and wiped a trail of blood from his face. "I thought you'd murdered him." A bald statement that meant so much. That meant everything. A relieved laugh escaped but it sounded more like a gasp, a cry of pain.

"No." Brennus's voice was guarded as he thrust her bow into her hand.

"He's not the first to bear a grudge against Druids," Gawain said. "I've held one or two myself." He glanced back down the mountain. "A clash of male pride is scarcely of any import at this time, Morwyn. We drew blood but didn't break any bones."

"Much as I am loath to interrupt this touching reunion"—Nimue sounded irritated—"we do have the Roman Legion methodically slaughtering our people. Caratacus needs to change tactics."

Morwyn caught the swift glance that passed between the

two men. Condemnation from Brennus, defiance from Gawain. Another eerie certainty coalesced in her mind.

"You fought over this strategy." It wasn't a question. It was another facet of the vision that had plagued her. Gawain in the midst of battle, embracing it. And Brennus fighting for his king as he would always fight for his king, but knowing it was doomed to failure.

Neither man answered as they continued to half run, half scramble farther into the heart of the mountain. When Morwyn glanced over her shoulder, around Brennus's protective arm, she saw warriors and Druids alike retreating, as they were, to find strategic crevices and rock shelters behind which to launch a renewed attack upon the advancing enemy.

Raw panic punched through her gut as realization suddenly hit.

"They're going to find the children, Brennus."

He didn't answer. He didn't have to. The children and the women caring for them were in their direct path, and once the legionaries cut their way through the final warriors, the defenseless would be rounded up and taken as slaves.

"Bren." The hoarse shout came from ahead, from a blue-daubed warrior she recognized as Judoc, the one she'd poisoned with her blowdart. "We have to get Caratacus out. He can't be taken by the Romans."

Panting with exertion, fear and the high, mountainous air, Morwyn broke free of Brennus and skidded down a rocky incline to the grass- and flower-filled slope where the children camped among the chariots. Where was Gwyn? Had the little girl obeyed Morwyn's command to stay out of danger?

A familiar figure broke away from a group of children and raced toward her, arms outstretched. Morwyn scooped Gwyn into her arms, held her close, rejoicing in the thin little arms around her neck, the frantic beat of Gwyn's heart against her breast. Still holding her, she turned and saw Brennus and Gawain and several others arguing with his king. Clearly, he wasn't convinced flight was the only chance of survival.

As she drew closer, more warriors flooded over the ridge into the illusory safety of the camp. Brennus gripped Caratacus's arms.

"If you're captured, everything we've fought for has been for nothing. This doesn't have to be the end, but if you stay, it will be."

Caratacus tore himself free. "Where's the queen?"

"I'll find her and your daughter." Nimue unsheathed her dagger. "Where are you heading?"

"The land of the Brigantes," Judoc said. "We have allies there." He glanced at Caratacus. "Under your leadership, we can re-form the resistance."

Nimue nodded and ran back to where the battle raged, and a contingent formed around the king as they sought escape, after urging as many of the women as they could to take the children and flee into the surrounding hills and valleys.

"Shall I take her?" Brennus offered, and Morwyn handed Gwyn over and watched how tenderly he held her, shielding her from harm, without any dip in speed as they made their way to the horses.

Goddess, let them come through this. Let them have a chance of a life together. Let her give Brennus a child of his own.

The last thought caused her to trip over a hidden rock and she stumbled, winded. Shocked by the pure simplicity of her thought. How right it felt.

"Morwyn." He was by her side instantly, his face a mask of brutal ferocity. Yet worry gleamed in his magnificent eyes. Despite the fact they were fleeing for their lives, that the Romans would tear them apart if they captured them, a smile began to curve her lips.

And froze.

Above Brennus, in the pale blue of the sky, ravens soared, cawing their bloodlust at the battle below. She gasped, clutched her throat, mesmerized as the manifestation of the Morrigan screamed in victory and defeat, devastation and regeneration.

"What the fuck?" Brennus sounded unnerved, and only then did she realize she wasn't the only one staring at the sky, that all the Druids had stopped in their tracks.

"The great goddess is angry." The Druid, an older woman, reached supplicating hands to the sky. "We should stay and fight for our way of life. Not let the Romans crush it underfoot."

Morwyn gripped Brennus's outstretched hand and hauled herself up. Nobody moved. Everyone was staring at the Druid, or up at the circling ravens. And as she watched, one broke from the formation and soared toward the earth, its trajectory unerring.

Too late, Morwyn felt Brennus try to avert the inevitable. But he was impeded with Gwyn in one arm and Morwyn holding his free hand, and besides, there was nothing he could do. The Morrigan had come for her.

She heard the audible hiss of countless indrawn breaths as the raven sank its claws into her head, sliced her skull, before once again taking to the heavens. Warm blood dripped over her forehead and a black feather fluttered to the ground by her feet.

Even Brennus appeared shocked into silence. But his grip on her hand never wavered.

Finally, she understood. Everything she thought she had concluded by herself had come from the Morrigan. She had been following the goddess's will right from the start.

"There are more ways than one to fight the enemy."

"Morwyn," Gawain said. "What does the Morrigan tell you?"

She recalled her visions. In all their varied versions.

"We must never give up the fight." The war goddess would expect nothing less. How she must have raged against Aeron's binding magic. At the way her will had been subverted. She had wanted her Druids to retreat to the sacred Isle of Mon only in order to gather their strength. Before they once again took up arms against their enemy.

"Then—we must return?" the older Druid said, but she no longer sounded so certain.

"If we return, we'll die." In her visions, Gawain had represented her people, their culture, their way of life. And her people risked annihilation. "The Morrigan never surrenders. We have to find other ways to fight repression."

The way Carys had. Slowly Morwyn turned to look at her Gaul. Had the Morrigan sent him to her? To show her the way to Camulodunon, to open her eyes to other ways of surviving this occupation?

Had she sent Brennus to show her it *was* possible to love again?

"Then let us not delay any further." Caratacus's voice was strong and sure. He inclined his head at Morwyn in a show of respect, as if she were an Elder of great standing instead of an acolyte who had only recently returned to the fold of her goddess. "It will take several days to reach Cartimandua." Frowning, he glanced at the bedraggled group of women and children who had decided to follow them instead of choosing their own paths.

"Cartimandua?" Morwyn said as Brennus lifted Gwyn onto a horse.

"Queen of the Brigantes." He shot her an odd look, as if he couldn't understand why she was still with him. As if he hadn't yet registered the fact that Gawain alive made all the difference in the world.

The thought shivered through her mind, tugging on the edges of her consciousness. Something was wrong, something she couldn't quite place. But before she could grasp its significance, his words slammed through her like an icy river.

Royal blood. She gripped his fingers, willing him to believe her. "She's going to betray Caratacus. I don't know how—or even why—but she is. You have to warn him."

Before he could do any more than frown with incomprehension, the king rode up. Morwyn sucked in a breath, prepared to tell him herself, but Caratacus spoke first.

"Brennus." He reached down and grasped Brennus's forearm. "You've served me well these last three years. I have one last command and then your debt to me is paid in full."

Debt? What debt? Morwyn glanced at Brennus but his face was inscrutable.

Caratacus swept his hand at the group of terrified civilians. "I can't take them north with me. Even if they had horses, they'd slow us down. Ensure their safety, Bren. And then return to Gaul, to your kin, and forge the destiny that was always yours." He glanced at Morwyn before once again looking back at Bren. "As the great war goddess said—there are more ways than one to fight the enemy."

And then he was gone, and Morwyn leaped on the horse behind Gwyn and galloped after him, only to have Gawain wave her to a halt.

"I'm going with him," he said without preamble.

Holding Gwyn tight with one arm, she reached for him, grasped his hand. "Treachery awaits in the land of the Brigantes. You have to persuade Caratacus to change course."

"Morwyn, there's nowhere else." A tired finality threaded through his words. "The British tribes have all succumbed to Roman domination. Only in the far north do they still resist."

She tugged his hand to her lips, her heart aching for all that had been. All that could never be. "Gawain, watch your back. Come out of this alive. We need you."

"I don't know," he said. "Do our people really need us anymore?" Before she could answer he pulled free. "Be happy, Morwyn. That's all I ever wanted for you." And then he was gone.

Chapter Thirty-four

As night fell they camped deep in the forest, not risking fires to cook their food in case the Romans were still searching for fugitives. Judoc had also joined them, and they'd traveled a fair distance from the battlefield, all things considered.

Morwyn leaned back against a tree. The women and children gave the three of them a measure of privacy, as if in deference to their status, but instead of sitting next to her, Brennus sat opposite, forearm resting over his raised knee, other hand occupied with his dagger.

Perhaps he didn't wish Judoc to know of their relationship?

She smothered the pain that thought caused, but couldn't help the subsequent one. Was he ashamed of her, because of her Druidry? She knew he still cared. He couldn't hide the raw emotion in his eyes from her. But did he still *want* to care?

"What," Judoc said in a low voice, "are we supposed to do with them all?"

"Some can still return to their home villages." Brennus shrugged one shoulder and she caught him looking at her, until he realized she saw, and then he jerked his attention back to Judoc. Goddess, did he now hate the way he still desired her?

Did he still desire her? After they'd left the mountain he hadn't so much as touched her hand. In fact, he'd gone out of his way so they didn't touch even by accident.

"But not all. Some of their villages are destroyed." Judoc appeared supremely unaware of the tension vibrating in the air around him. Perhaps she would blow another dart in his neck, render him unconscious. Perhaps then Brennus would deign to talk to her, to tell her why he no longer sought her company.

"Some wish to return to the Roman settlements." Brennus sounded as if he had no opinion on that one way or the other. "Wherever they want to go, I'll ensure they reach their destination."

"Perhaps," she said, feeling she had been excluded from the conversation for long enough, "some would embrace the adventure of starting over, in Gaul." That was *his* final destination, after all. Would it be hers? Could she bear to leave behind her beloved Cymru, never again see her kin still ensconced on Mon?

But she had already left Cymru. Where could she go, if she stayed? Back to Mon, back to trying to persuade the other Druids they should leave the sacred Isle? And do what?

Caratacus's rebellion had failed. There was no rallying point any longer.

In the gathering gloom she caught Bren's furtive glance before he once again concentrated on stabbing the ground with the tip of his dagger. "If that's what they want."

The pain inside her breast magnified. Not once had he asked where *she* wanted to go. What *she* wanted to do. He accepted her presence as if it were an inevitable, yet ultimately uncomfortable, burden.

"What about Camulodunon?" She glared at him, knowing he couldn't see because it was too dark. "There are plenty of opportunities there." Such as begging, whoring, slavery, degradation—

"I always intended to take you there before I left, Morwyn." His voice was stiff, as if she had insulted his honor.

Her hands fisted on her lap. "If I wished to return to Camulodunon, *Gaul*, I could do so by myself. I certainly wouldn't wish to put *you* to any inconvenience."

Judoc made an odd sound, as if he attempted to suppress a laugh. She rounded on him. "Do you have something to say, Judoc?"

"No. I wouldn't presume." He still sounded as if he was amused. Goddess, she'd give him something to laugh about if he interrupted her again.

"I'm well aware you could return to Camulodunon on your own." Brennus still sounded insulted. How dared he be insulted? It wasn't *she* who had turned her back on *him*. "And I regret Gawain was unable to accompany you. But whatever your thoughts, I'll deliver you safely to your friend in the colonia."

He would *deliver* her? Like a fucking *dispatch*?

And then his other comment penetrated the fog of fury in her brain.

"Gawain?" She hoped she didn't sound as stupid to Brennus as she did herself. "Why would you regret such a thing?" She remembered Brennus had pulled alongside her as Gawain had left. He'd had a hard, shuttered look on his face as he'd watched the other man ride off and now that she thought about it, that look had barely diminished.

A shiver scuttled over her arms as the insistent, nagging uncertainty that had plagued her all day spilled from the abyss into her consciousness.

Brennus had not killed Gawain. That had never been the reason why he thought she left him. And yet Brennus assumed she knew something—something so devastating it would cause her to give up on their love.

But what?

"Because"—there was a hard, ugly edge to his voice—"I know you still love him."

She stared at his dark silhouette. If only there were light enough to see his face, his eyes. "Why would you draw that conclusion?" As far as she could recall, she had never even mentioned Gawain's name to him.

He shifted, as if the conversation irritated him. "You called out his name in the night. I hoped it wasn't the same man I'd fought for his beliefs. Then I hoped it wouldn't matter. I was wrong."

She hugged her knees and leaned forward as if that would help pierce the encroaching darkness. "In my visions, I saw Gawain murdered. That's why I called out his name." She could feel the truth shimmering between them, insubstantial and fragile. She had to find the right words, had to discover what Brennus thought she knew. "I don't love Gawain, Brennus. But he is the reason I left you."

She could scarcely see him, but she knew he tensed. Fleetingly she wished Judoc would have the decency to leave them alone, but obviously he possessed no such sense of honor. She blanked him from her mind, and concentrated solely on the man she loved but was so perilously close to losing. "On that final morn, the Morrigan showed me the face of Gawain's murderer. It was you, Brennus. I thought she was showing me you, my beloved, had killed the man whose death I'd vowed to avenge. That's why I left. Because I couldn't bring myself to kill you."

For a moment the silence of the forest was absolute, as if it held its breath, waiting for the final denouncement. And then, so suddenly she scarcely saw him move, he was kneeling before her, his hands on her knees, her legs pressed against his chain mail.

"Morwyn." There was an odd crack in his voice that tore her heart anew. "I thought the only reason you accompanied me this day was because Gawain turned his back on you."

She threaded her fingers through his. "No."

His head dropped and his lips moved over her fingers, gentle, reverential kisses that seared the core of her being. "Come with me to Gaul. Build our lives together."

Her head dropped also, their foreheads touching, breath mingling. Her heart implored her to agree, agree to anything and everything because it was all she wanted. To be with him, build a life together, share her knowledge of the old ways with all those willing to learn.

But she couldn't. Not until she knew the entire truth.

"Why did you think I left you? What did you think the Morrigan had shown me?"

"It doesn't matter." His heated words grazed her lips and his hands cradled her face. "Nothing else matters, Morwyn. Only this."

It would be so easy to agree. To push the questions to the back of her mind, allow them to rot into obscurity Except if she did, the past would forever haunt her; a decaying fog of suspicion and doubt.

It couldn't be connected to his wife. And yet somehow she knew that it was. Knew it was intrinsically connected to that night six years ago that he'd told her of. And the night three years ago—that he had not.

"Tell me what happened that night at Dunmacos's village."

His fingers bit into her flesh, molding the bones of her face, but she refused to flinch, refused to cry out. Refused to defend herself because she knew his reaction was purely instinctive, without malice.

"Nothing happened." His voice was guttural. His brutal grip lessened. "It doesn't matter anymore."

She threaded her fingers through his hair. She wished she could see him but there was a false sense of safety in this darkness. "What happened that was so horrific you thought I could leave you because of it?"

Air hissed between his teeth. "Leave it, Morwyn. I'll never speak of it again. Not to you, not to anyone."

She tightened her grip on his skull. "It's killing you, Gaul. From the inside out, it's eating you alive. And I won't let it. Do you hear me? *I won't let it*."

"She's right." The disembodied voice shocked her for a moment. She had forgotten Judoc's presence. There was no longer any trace of amusement in his voice. "You're consumed with guilt and you have no reason to be. What you did—"

"Shut the *fuck* up."

"Have you even told her of Eryn?"

"Yes." Morwyn wound her ankles around the backs of Brennus's thighs. He refused to surrender to her touch but she clung on regardless. If he left her now, physically or emotionally, she would lose him forever.

"It took more than a year before he regained strength enough to pick up a weapon," Judoc said.

"I swear," Brennus said, "I will tear out your tongue, Judoc." But he didn't pull from her embrace, nor cease caressing her face with his thumbs.

"Tell her of Caratacus's offer, Bren. If she's worthy enough to be your wife, she's worthy enough to hear the truth from you."

Silence echoed. Finally he sucked in a ragged breath.

"He offered me a contingent of his finest warriors to hunt down the man responsible for the death of Eryn." His fingers slid along her face, broke contact. "We hunted, and eventually we found our prey."

"Three years ago." Now it made sense. "And you burned his village, as he had burned that hamlet." It was just. Why did the memory haunt him so?

"We thought the village was long deserted. And it was. Only Dunmacos and his followers should have perished that night."

"But?" The whisper trembled between them. Because she knew what he was going to confess.

"But." The word fell from his tongue like iron. "The bastard had brought his young wife along."

She closed her eyes, tried not to let him feel the distress rippling through her body. She understood his code of honor. It was no different from hers. Justice demanded retribution. How could she condemn him for exacting such justice from his enemy's wife?

But, goddess. For him to have inflicted such heinous crimes turned her stomach. She tensed her muscles, smothered the urge to vomit. Refused to show him by the slightest sign how repugnant she found his confession.

Whatever sins he had committed that night, he'd suffered for them a thousandfold every night since.

Could she forgive him? She didn't know. But could she leave him for seeking such justice for his own wife?

No. Never. Because the man of that night wasn't the man Brennus was. Not in his soul. His mind had been turned with grief, his reason blinded with bloodlust. He was not, at heart, a rapist or murderer of the innocent. He was . . . her Gaul.

"I understand." Her voice was faint. She needed air. Space. She needed—

"I killed her, Morwyn. It was my fault."

The world was already black, but now the blackness entered her heart, filled her soul. A cold, clammy blackness that sank insidious fingers into her brain, numbing her senses. Killing her from the inside out.

"Fuck it, Bren." Judoc sounded furious. "You might want to be a martyr but I was there, remember? I was part of it."

"Yes." Brennus's voice was remote, as if he were no longer in the forest but reliving that blood-soaked night. "You were."

"So why don't you tell Morwyn the truth? Why don't you explain what our honorable men were doing while you and I systematically searched the huts for signs of life before setting them ablaze?"

"I was still the reason they were there, Judoc. The reason the last moments of her life were filled with pain and terror."

A thread of distant light flickered in the suffocating black. Blindly she reached for him, dug her nails into his biceps. "Caratacus's men raped her."

"They were animals." Disgust filled Judoc's voice. "They dragged her from her hut, bleeding and scarcely conscious. Threw her at Bren's feet. And urged him to brutalize her, the way Dunmacos had brutalized Eryn."

"But you didn't." The certainty glowed in her mind, destroying the earlier crippling suspicions. How had she imagined for even a fleeting moment her Gaul was capable of such despicable acts?

He believed in justice and fighting for his cause. But she knew he didn't relish violence, as some men did. Bizarrely she recalled the man in the latrines whom Brennus had punched. At the time she had seen no reason for his outburst. But now, knowing the man, knowing his protective instinct and tortured guilt at having been unable to save Eryn, she realized he had defended her honor.

His captive. A woman who believed him her enemy. And yet when the other man had called her a whore, Brennus had leaped to her defense.

"She begged me for mercy." His voice was devoid of emotion. Except, beneath that facade, she could hear the agony. "I took her in my arms but it was too late."

Chapter Thirty-five

"No one could have saved her." Judoc sounded weary. "You know that, Bren."

Brennus tore from Morwyn's embrace and she clawed wildly, but he'd retreated beyond her grasp. "I wasn't there," she said into the pitch of night. "But I've seen what a pack of men can do to a woman. How long had you been searching for Dunmacos? How many men had you lost to the cause?" Goddess, if only she could see his eyes. See if she was getting through to him. "If Dunmacos hadn't murdered your wife, you wouldn't have gone after him. If Dunmacos hadn't brought his own wife to that village, she would still be alive." She pushed herself to her knees, shuffled across the forest floor until she bumped into Brennus's outstretched legs. "You did show her mercy. You gave her comfort in the last moments of her life."

No breeze stirred the leaves. No nocturnal creature rustled among the undergrowth. Brennus was so still he might have been one of the stone statues in Camulodunon. Except she could feel the heat from his legs, hear his ragged breath, and then his battle-scarred hand grasped hers, as unerring as if he could see through the enveloping night.

"Caratacus pledged me his men on the understanding that if we wiped out Dunmacos and his closest followers and kin, I would take his place in the Legion. Shoulder his reputation for brutality. Use his military history as leverage." A shudder racked through him and Morwyn edged closer until she could wrap her arms around him, offering him whatever comfort her body could provide. "We'd already slaughtered his kin before we tracked him down. But none of us had heard mention of a cousin, Gervas. Or the fact Dunmacos had recently taken a bride."

"War is brutal." Her whisper barely made it past the constriction blocking her throat. Brennus had suffered at the hands of his enemies. But he suffered so much more at the mercy of his conscience.

She swallowed, gathered her courage. Her offer was small, but all she had. And if he rejected it, she would understand. Never confront him with her heritage again.

"Brennus." She hesitated, unsure whether she could continue, but he rubbed his jaw against the top of her head in a familiar, comforting gesture, and she sucked in a deep breath. "I want to return with you to your homeland. To Gaul. Take my place by your side."

His arm tightened around her waist, a painful grip edged with desperation. As if, until this moment, he hadn't been certain she would want any such thing.

"Be my wife, Morwyn." His voice cracked on her name. "Gods know I don't deserve you, but I can't help loving you. I'll defend you to my last dying breath."

"Oh." She threaded her fingers through his, glad he couldn't see the foolish tears trickling down her cheeks. "I don't need defending, Gaul. I'll just take your love. If you take mine."

"Always." His pledge muffled against her hair and she closed her eyes, willing herself to continue. To offer him a chance of spiritual peace.

If he could accept.

"I'm a chosen one of the Morrigan." How could there be any doubt in her mind of that now? "A Druid. I can't change that."

"I wouldn't want you to." A jagged sigh speared his body. "Morwyn, your Druidic heritage is a fundamental part of who you are. I can see now. Not all Druids are blinded by ancient prejudice."

"There's something . . . I wish to offer you." Goddess, she hoped he could not hear the tremble in her voice. "If it wouldn't offend you, when we reach Gaul, I want to perform the sacred ritual of Arawn. The ceremony for those of noble blood who are continuing their journey." She flicked the tip of her tongue over her lips. "For your wife, Eryn."

He gave a sharp indrawn breath. "You would do that—for Eryn?"

"You have royal blood. She was your wife. She deserves nothing less."

"Gods." The word tangled in her hair and his warrior hard body shook as emotion ripped through him.

Had she ever loved him as much as she loved him in this moment?

She blinked back the dampness stinging her eyes. "If it doesn't offend, I also wish to attend the restless spirit of the . . . other girl."

He didn't answer. But the jerk of his head in assent was answer enough.

With a shaky sigh she sank against him. She would call on her foremothers for guidance and strength. Invoke the ancient rituals, ease the troubled spirits of Eryn and the girl, not only because she was a Druid of the Morrigan and it was her sacred duty.

But because by so doing, she would soothe the wounded soul of her beloved Gaul.

Epilogue

Ten Months Later
Gaul

"By the goddess, Gaul, say something." Morwyn shook her head and then laughed before she once again returned her attention to the tiny scrap cradled in her arms.

He glanced at Gwyn, who sat on his hip with one arm hooked around his neck. She also appeared transfixed.

"I fear words fail me." Gingerly he sat beside Morwyn on the bed, once again gazing at the bundle she cradled so tenderly. *His son.*

"Because you're awed by my cleverness in birthing such a perfect babe."

"Yes."

Morwyn looked up at him, sweaty hair streaking her face, remnants of the severity of her labor etched around her eyes. Faint scars from Trogus's dagger traced her nose, and her forehead was forever marked with the claw of the sacred raven.

She was beautiful. Brave. And his.

"He is perfect," she whispered. "Because he's yours."

A year ago, he had nothing but a blood pledge to his king and bittersweet memories to keep him alive. Now he had everything. A wife whose strength of will would never cease to astound him, a daughter he adored and a newborn son.

Was this why the gods had kept him alive?

He tugged Gwyn's braid. "What do you think of your brother, princess?"

She reached out one tentative hand and he angled her over the babe, so she could trace her finger over his dark thatch of hair. "Soft." Her tone was reverential. She glanced up at Morwyn and her plump lower lip trembled. *"Safe."*

One arm around Gwyn, he slid his other around his wife and she melted against him. So deceptively soft and fragile a man could be forgiven for thinking she needed protecting.

But she was a warrior, a Druid of ancient stock. As willing and able as he to defend herself and their family against the enemy.

Yet she was and would forever be his vulnerability.

He'd have it no other way. She had dragged him back from the precipice, demanded that he open his eyes and his heart, and in return she had given him a new world.

Beloved.

Author's Note

During the first century AD, the languages used in Britain were Brythonic by the native tribal peoples and Latin by the Roman invaders. In both *Forbidden* and *Captive* I have used words not in common usage in the English language until the fifteen hundreds and later, on the reasoning these peoples had words of similar meaning in their own languages at that time.

Glossary of Major Gods and Goddesses

CELTIC GODS AND GODDESSES

Annwyn: the Otherworld; source of the Universal Life Force

Arawn: lord of the Otherworld

Belatucadros: god of war and destruction

Camulus: warrior god, important in pre-Roman times; equated with Mars

Cerridwen: goddess of wisdom

Gwydion: greatest of the enchanters; warrior magician

The Morrigan: triple aspect Great Goddess: maiden, mother, crone; goddess of war and rebirth

Taranis: god of thunder and lightning

ROMAN GODS AND GODDESSES

Charon: the Ferryman; takes the dead across the river Styx

Jupiter: king of the Roman gods; river, sky, lightning, thunder; symbol is the eagle

Mars: god of war, revenge, courage

Minerva: goddess of wisdom, learning, the arts

Venus: goddesss of love and beauty

Wings of Mors: god of death